1998

SARA'S SONG

Fern Michaels

Zebra Books
Kensington Publishing Corp.
http://www.zebrabooks.com

This Large Print Edition, prepared especially for Doubleday Direct, Inc., contains the complete unabridged text of the original Publisher's Edition

ZEBRA BOOKS are published by

Kensington Publishing Corp.
850 Third Avenue
New York, NY 10022

Copyright © 1998 by Fern Michaels

ISBN 1-56865-693-9

Printed in the United States of America

**This Large Print Book carries the
Seal of Approval of N.A.V.H.**

For the real Barbara McDermott

Nurse Nellie Pulaski was an old warhorse with forty years of experience, all of those forty years having been spent in the Emergency Room of Benton Memorial Hospital. She snapped and crackled in her starched uniform, her nurse's cap riding precariously on her gray corkscrew curls as she ruled the ER with an iron hand. The newer nurses, especially the younger ones, wore nylon uniforms and had long ago given up their starched caps. Some of them even wore sneakers, much to the disgust of Nurse Pulaski. She herself preferred the rubber-soled oxfords that were soundless and didn't make those little snicking sounds on the marble floor. Nobody died on Pulaski's shift. That was a given. Everyone at Benton Memorial, Los Angeles's finest private hospital, said the patients who were nearing the end waited for Pulaski to go off duty so they could go to their Maker in peace.

Nellie Pulaski was an in-your-face, gravel- and molasses-voiced, do-it-my-way-and-you'll-be-out-of-here-before-you-know-it nurse. She was loved, hated, and feared.

Dr. Sara Killian loved Nellie. She listened to her now, an amused smile on her face.

"Trust me, this is going to be a night to remember, Sara. It's a full moon. Every loony and his brother will be out tonight."

Sara grinned as she popped a diet drink. "It's a harvest moon, Nellie. Forget that full-moon stuff. I have to admit, though, it hasn't been this slow in months."

"That's because the whole town is at Dallas Lord's benefit concert. It should be breaking up soon. The concert I mean. Then there will be fender benders, fights, and all that stuff that goes with those awful concerts. We'll be jamming in here in another two hours. I've got my off-duty list right here in my pocket. I'm surprised you and your sister didn't go to the concert. My daughter is crazy about Dallas Lord and she's forty-three. She said he's better than Elvis on his best day."

Sara pretended horror. "Better than Elvis! I don't think so."

"I don't think so either. I did love the way he swiveled those hips of his. It's time for you to think about settling down, Sara," she said, changing the subject in mid-flight the way she always did. "All these nice dedicated doctors are just waiting for you to give them the time of day."

"I am not interested in dating or marrying a doctor. I don't do one-night stands, and that's all they're interested in right now. I started down that road twice, and it didn't work out. If and when I decide to get married, it will be to a plumber. I like my life just the way it is. Then there is the flip side to that coin. Maybe he just hasn't found me yet."

Nellie snorted. "How can any man find you? You work double shifts and sleep the rest of the time. You have to do your share. That means getting dressed up and looking around on your own. Makeup helps. So do fashionable hairstyles."

"Are you trying to tell me something, Nellie?"

"What's the point? You never listen. You need an image to go with that fancy Jaguar you drive. A ponytail and shiny nose aren't going to turn any man's head. Take right now. We're sitting here doing nothing. You could go into the lavatory, bounce up your hair a little, put on some makeup, and when the first patient comes in—and he will come in—he'll feel better because you look good. Give it a shot, Sara. You do have makeup in that black bag you lug around, don't you? Do it!"

"I will not. I am what I am." Sara's voice turned defensive. "There is nothing wrong with the way I look."

"That's bullshit, Sara. I think you're afraid of men. If you aren't afraid of men, then you're afraid of commitment. I think you need to get laid!"

"Nellie!"

"Don't Nellie me. You're thirty-nine years old. So what if you bombed out twice. Just because it didn't work doesn't mean all men are like those two . . . bums. It's time for you to start thinking about a life outside the hospital. I don't want you to turn out like me."

"Oh, Nellie, turning out like you would be wonderful. This hospital couldn't run without you. The best part is they know it. You're loved and respected, and there isn't a better nurse anywhere. You're probably the best nurse in the whole world. Patients get better because of you. You were meant to do what you do just the way I was meant to do what I do."

"That's my professional life. When I go home, I go home to a house with two cats and a dog that are just as old and cranky as I am. We eat in front of the television in our *comfies* and wait for the telephone to ring. Guess what, Sara, it doesn't ring. It doesn't ring because other people are busy with their families. My daughter lives in New York, and she never gets the time thing straight. I want you to find someone who will be the wind beneath your wings. I had that once, and I was a lot younger than you. It's a wonderful feeling. Now go fluff up your hair and put some makeup on. Dr. McGuire is going to stop by later with some catnip for me to save me a trip to his office. A vet is good, Sara. They make more money than some MDs. He has his own practice, his own house, a car like yours. Already you have something in common. He does things. He goes fly fishing, parasailing, and has a pilot's license. He knows how to cook and he irons his pillowcases. He cuts down a real tree at Christmas and throws a party that will blow your socks off. He's a good catch. I heard he was great in bed. People start those rumors all the time. Aren't you curious? Do it for me, Sara."

"All right, all right!" Sara's voice was suspicious when she said, "How do you know he's good in bed?"

Nellie smirked, "I know."

Fifteen minutes later, Sara returned to the ER, her hair curling loosely around her shoulders, her eyes sparkling behind subdued makeup, her brows more defined. Her lips were past the pink stage and glossy. Definitely kissable. "Are you satisfied, Nellie?"

"You clean up really nice. All you need now is one of those spandex dresses the younger nurses wear."

"And have my circulation cut off. No thank you. This is it."

"We can work on that later. You'll do. Ten-thirty. I say we trundle outside for a few quick puffs before all hell breaks loose. I have a bad feeling, Sara."

"Don't tell me that, Nellie. I hate it when you spook me like this. It's quiet. We have quiet nights sometimes. Don't look for trouble."

"We're so shorthanded. When you've been around as long as I have you recognize certain things. I'm hardly ever wrong. It's the way it is, Sara. Either I'm blessed, or I'm cursed. I wish I could quit smoking."

"I wish you could too, Nellie. Oh, oh, here comes a patient. It looks like appendix to me the way he's doubled over. Take him to #3. The father looks worse than the kid. Do your thing, Nellie."

A gurney appeared as Nellie whisked the father to Admitting before she raced back to #3, where Sara was pulling on a pair of latex gloves. "Dr. Joyce is on her way." A thermometer was in the boy's mouth as Nellie strapped on the blood-pressure cuff. "Show me where it hurts. Ah, how about here, here, and here? Shhh, don't be afraid. I'm Dr. Killian, and this is Nurse Nellie. Do you want to tell us your name?"

"Mickey. Mickey Logan. I want my mom. Dad said Dr. Joyce is coming. It hurts bad."

"I like that name. I think it's one of my favorite names. Because . . . I love Mickey Mouse. How old are you, Mickey? It's going to be okay. Your dad is right outside, and Dr. Joyce is on her way. So is your mom."

The little boy's face scrunched up. "I'm gonna be seven tomorrow. I never had a bellyache like this. Dad said it's bad gas."

"Definitely elevated, 102," Nellie said, shaking down the thermometer.

"We're going to take a little blood from your arm, Mickey. I promise it isn't really going to hurt. It will sting at first. If you hold my hand real tight, you won't even feel the sting."

"The white count is going to be off the chart. That appendix is boiling in there and no, I'm not psychic," Nellie whispered.

"Damn, where's his doctor?" Sara whispered as she smoothed back the little boy's hair. He was crying openly now instead of trying to be a brave boy the way his father had instructed. "I want my mom," he howled. "Give me some of that pink stuff. My mom always gives me pink stuff when I have a bellyache. Dr. Joyce calls me Sport."

"Do you think you can wait for the pink stuff until Dr. Joyce gets here? It's important that you don't eat or drink anything right now. You hold my hand and let's see who can squeeze the hardest. If I win, I have to sing the Mickey Mouse song, and if you win, then you have to sing it. Do you know all the words?"

"I forget them," he said, squeezing her hand as hard as he could. Sara exerted just the right amount of pressure. "You're doing fine, Sport. Look who's here."

The little boy opened his tear-filled eyes. "Who won?"

"I think you did. I guess I'm getting old," Sara smiled. "Long time no see, Joyce. Nellie, what's the count?"

Nellie handed the pediatrician the blood report which had just come back from the lab. The doctor's keen eyes registered the abnormalities. "Let's get him prepped and into OR before that rascal decides to burst. Will you talk to Mickey's father? I don't think we have much time."

"He's so little. He's scared, Joyce. When he's out of Recovery call me. I promised to sing to him. You wouldn't happen to know the words to the Mickey Mouse song, would you?"

"Every single one. Hold on, Sport, we're going for a ride. Thanks, Sara."

Sara nodded as she headed out to the waiting room.

"Mr. Logan, your pediatrician just arrived and has taken over. Mickey's on his way to surgery. Appendix is a pretty routine operation. You got him here in time. A little longer and his appendix would have ruptured. Mrs. Pulaski told me you signed all the necessary papers. Can I get you a cup of coffee?"

"No. One more cup today and you'll be peeling me off the ceiling. I'll wait here for my wife. She probably got held up in traffic. He's going to be okay, isn't he?"

"Yes. Do you happen to know the words to the Mickey Mouse song?"

"Are you kidding? I say them in my sleep."

"Then I have a job for you. Write them down and give them to the nurse to give to me. I promised Mickey I'd sing it for him when he gets out of Recovery."

"Sure. Sure, I'll be glad to."

"Try and relax. I know, easier said than done. We'll talk later, Mr. Logan."

"Thanks, Dr. Killian." Sara nodded as she walked back to the ER.

"Here comes another one. In a limo no less. Let's go, Nellie, duty calls."

"The last patient to arrive in a limo had an

impacted bowel. The one before that had the DTs. What's your guess on this one?"

"Drug abuse," Sara shot back.

Nellie pursed her lips. "You're probably right."

Sara had only a brief glimpse of the man exiting the back of the limo before the orderly with his gurney blocked her view. Blue denim and boots. She sighed. Drugs. She could hear him even with the door closed. "C'mon, c'mon, man. This is serious stuff here. Can't you see him clutching his chest? Never mind the damn straps. I'll hang on to him. I don't want to hear about rules. Go, go, go!"

The voice continued to rail as the orderlies rushed down the hall to the ER. "He wasn't drinking. He doesn't do drugs. He's never been sick a day in his life. There are no records, man. Check him out, man. C'mon, c'mon, where's the damn doctor? I don't know what kind of insurance he has. Here, will five thousand cover it?" A wad of money flew through the air. "Take care of him. I'll build a new wing, a whole annex. Take care of my friend! Don't let anyone in here but me. Do you hear me?"

Sara came out of the cubicle. "The whole

hospital can hear you. Go out to the waiting room and let us do our job. Right now we need a name. Pick up your money, sir."

"Sure, sure, whatever you say. It isn't serious, is it? Look. Money is no object here. Get him the best. I want the best."

Sara placed both her hands on the man's shoulders. Her gaze locked with his. She felt suddenly weak in the knees and didn't know why. "Look at me. I don't know if I'm the best there is or not, but right now I'm the best you've got. Now let me do what I've been trained to do. Just so you know, I'm the doctor."

"A woman doctor! Jeez. Billy Sweet. That's his name, Billy Sweet."

"Sit down and wait. I'll be back when there is something to report."

Dallas Lord stared at the woman in front of him, a frown building above his eyes. He felt strange, almost as if he were someplace else and observing what was going on through someone else's eyes. "Okay, okay, I'm going to sit down and wait. Please, don't let him die. Billy is my best friend. Suddenly he just grabbed his chest, sweat dripping down his face. I thought it was the lights and the sound. I'm going, I'm going. Just don't let him die."

"I'll do my best."

"We are famous tonight, Sara," Nellie said. "Tomorrow morning all of us, and that includes this hospital, will be on the cover of the *LA Times*. That was Dallas Lord, and Mr. Sweet is his lead guitarist. They look different in person. They look *normal*. I always thought celebrities looked . . . you know, kind of plastic, with tons of makeup. They look ordinary. Working the second shift in ER allows you to learn something new every day."

"People are people, Nellie. It's what's inside that counts. Mr. Lord is worried about his friend. Move it, Nellie. Stat!"

Dallas Lord returned to the waiting room, his own face dripping sweat. He folded his hands and prayed, something he hadn't done in a very long time.

An hour went by, then another.

"Hey, mister, is that bus out there yours? You gotta move it, buddy, there's been a nine-car pileup on the interstate, and they're coming in," the hospital guard said.

Dallas looked around the small waiting

room. He was the only occupant. Staring at his snakeskin boots, he muttered, "I don't have a bus."

"The limo, buddy. You gotta move it."

"Oh. Sure, sure, I'll move it."

He was back in the waiting room in ten minutes. He looked at the clock. What was taking so long? He said another prayer. Then he thought about Billy Sweet and their friendship. He'd met Billy in kindergarten at the age of five. They'd been best friends ever since. Inseparable friends. He was godfather of Billy's three children.

Thirty-three long years. It couldn't end like this. Not here in this sterile, antiseptic place. He should call Billy's wife Nancy, and tell her, but tell her what? There was no way Nancy and the kids could make it here to LA tonight. He could charter a plane for Billy's family. If he did it now, they could be here by morning. Chicago wasn't that far away.

Dallas stomped his way over to the row of telephone booths. Using his phone card he placed the call and spoke in a tortured whisper. "I don't know, Nancy. We were on the last set, and he just turned white, grabbed his chest, and collapsed. I rushed him here to the hospital. I thought it was indigestion.

He ate three chili dogs before we went on and guzzled a couple of root beers. I saw him pop some Tums a couple of times. It's been more than two hours. They don't tell you anything here. Hang up, I'm going to call and charter a plane for you. I'll call you back with the details. I did pray, Nancy. I'm still praying. Let me give you the number of this phone. You can call me from the plane. I'll get back to you when I have the flight information."

It was a full thirty minutes before Dallas contemplated his snakeskin boots for the second time. Three hours! Three hours meant Billy was still alive. He wondered if they were operating. How long did operations last? He banged his booted feet on the tile floor, his eyes filling just as the double glass doors swished open to admit gun-toting police, first-aid volunteers, paramedics, bloody patients on gurneys, and crying ambulatory patients. Outside, bedlam reigned as fans and members of the Canyon River Band arrived to see what had happened to Billy Sweet. Dallas tried to shrink into the hard plastic chair.

Down the hall and around the corner, Nellie Pulaski mopped at her perspiring brow.

"Told you it would hit the fan. We're finished here, Sara. Do you want me to speak to Mr. Lord?"

"I'll do it. Prep number two and give me an update on the interstate. Tell Dolores to call my sister to come in. She should be home by now. Does Harry the Hawk," Sara said, referring to the hospital administrator, "know who our famous patient is?"

"He does now. He's probably in the waiting room getting Mr. Lord's signature on the dotted line saying he agreed to build a wing or an annex."

"Only if Mr. Sweet lives. It doesn't look good, Nellie. When my sister comes in, have her sit in ICU to monitor him. I know it's against the rules, but have her do it anyway. I don't want anything coming back here to haunt us later on. Mr. Sweet gets one on one. The Hawk will agree."

"See, you're already thinking like one of *them*, and you aren't even a partner yet. That's what I mean about getting a life."

Sara nodded. It really was true. Nellie Pulaski could do three things at the same time. Four if you counted talking. With Nellie every minute, every second counted. She was shaving, cleansing, and bandaging an open wound as she rattled on to herself about the next patient awaiting her help.

"Mr. Lord."

"Is he all right? What is it? Did you operate?"

"Mr. Sweet has suffered a coronary. He's in ICU right now. A private-duty nurse is on the way to monitor him. Does he have family?"

"They're on the way. Is he going to make it?"

What incredible blue eyes. How sad his voice was. How lonely he looked. "I don't know, Mr. Lord. We're doing everything we can. You can go up to ICU now. I'll check with you later. As you can see, we're busy here, and we're shorthanded."

"Can I do anything?"

Taken aback, Sara stared at the man in front of her. "Thank you for saying that. If you were a surgeon, I'd snatch you right up. If you really want to help, I would appreciate your asking those people outside to quiet down. I'm assuming they're your fans or your people. I'm being paged. We can talk later, Mr. Lord."

Dallas brushed at his dripping brow. How

could someone as pretty, as gentle-sounding as that doctor, know what she was doing? Billy needed an experienced older *man* to treat him, someone who'd been around twenty or so years. He wanted brash and bluster, clean-shaven and confident eyes, not lipstick and *poufy* hair.

He'd been given an order and he had to obey it. Just the way he always obeyed his brother Adam's orders. When you obeyed orders, according to Adam, things worked. It was when you ignored those orders that things got shot to hell. There was no way he wanted to shoot down Billy's chances. He took a moment to compose himself. He needed to look confident. The barracudas out there would sense any little thing that didn't sit well with them. The tabloids already had their scoop. He wondered if helicopters were flying overhead.

"Mr. Lord, I'm Harry Heinrick, the hospital administrator. Dr. Killian has informed me of Mr. Sweet's condition. This is a fine hospital, Mr. Lord, and our staff will do everything humanly possible to treat your friend. Would you like me to go outside with you to make a statement? A vigil is fine, but it's getting rowdy out there, and we have our patients to think about. The police are cordoning off the parking lot. A few words from you will go a long way. The media is . . . I guess I don't have to tell you about the media, do I?"

"No."

"It was a wonderful thing you and your band did this evening. I wish more celebrities felt as you do."

"Billy's dad has Alzheimer's disease. Will this hospital get a share of the proceeds? Right now I can't think clearly or remember the list. It was Billy's idea to do this benefit. The band agreed."

"A small share. We're a private hospital, and our research is kept to a minimum."

Dallas waited for the sliding door to open. "Why is that?"

"We rely on donations and requests. When you're private, you have more say in the way things are done."

"I'll look into it. I'll be paying for Billy, so if you want money now . . ."

"That isn't necessary, Mr. Lord. Later will be fine. Let's just worry about Mr. Sweet's comfort right now. Good Lord, there must be a thousand people out here!" the administrator said, his voice full of awe. For the first time in his life the suave money man was at a loss for words.

Dallas held up his hands for silence. He drew a deep breath, his eyes searching the crowd for someone to home in on. He always did that when he was onstage singing. Sandi Sims. She looked like she was crying. He flapped his hands in the breeze to stop the questions. "Billy's had a heart attack. His family is en route and should be here in a few hours. I'd like to ask all of you to say a prayer. Mr. Heinrick, the hospital administrator, will give you a further update in the morning. Please, move back and keep the noise down. This is a hospital, and there are a lot of sick people here. I'll see you all later. Two prayers would be better than one."

Harry Heinrick moved closer to the yellow tape as Dallas sprinted across the parking lot to the Emergency Room door. Strobe flashes traced his route. He did his best to look annoyed and wondered if they were capturing his best side. He couldn't buy publicity like this. "I can give you five minutes."

Dallas stopped in the rest room on his way to the elevator. Who *was* this haggard-looking individual staring back at him in the harsh light? He cried because he didn't know what else to do. He knew his life was going to change. His life as he and Billy knew it would never be the same again. What would he do without Billy in his life? Who would he talk to in the wee hours of the morning? Who would he confide in? Share his memories with? Adam? Adam was his blood brother. Older by three years, Adam was the brain behind Dallas Lord and the Canyon River Band's success. Adam was the point man, their manager, their idea man, their investment banker, their attorney and broker. Adam had marketed them like a pro for the past fifteen years. They were a household name that even little old ladies in Punxsatawney, Pennsylvania knew. But Adam wasn't Billy Sweet. Adam was a suit with a Wall Street haircut and mono-grammed Brooks Brothers shirts.

Adam never went fishing with him the way Billy did. Adam never played baseball with him the way Billy did. Adam never shared a pizza and a beer with him, never shared a secret with him. Hell, Adam didn't even like their music. What was worse, he didn't bother to pretend he liked it.

Cold water rushed from the tap. Dallas

stuck his head under the faucet until he thought his eyeballs would freeze. A glob of paper towels wiped away the ice-cold water. He didn't feel one damn bit better.

Dallas combed his hair with his fingers, the springy curls going any which way. From his hip pocket he withdrew his Padres baseball cap and settled it firmly on his head. Billy had one just like it. Billy even wore his in concert. They were old, frayed, the stitching barely discernible. They'd gotten them the day Billy's dad took them to their first baseball game. Light-years ago. If something happened to Billy, who was going to take care of his dad? Nancy had her hands full with the three kids and her own parents. He made a mental note to look into the elder Mr. Sweet's care.

Dallas decided at that moment that he hated this hospital. It was too white, too hushed, too smelly. Was the smell a death smell? He didn't know anything about death. Everyone he knew was physical and vital, front and center, even old Adam. Death was something he never thought about. Billy thought about it, though, and worried about his elderly father. Nancy had told Dallas that.

He heard them whispering as he strode down the hall. They knew who he was, and they were speculating. About what he didn't know. Childishly, he crossed his fingers that none of the nursing staff would be crass enough to ask for his autograph.

An older nurse with cherub cheeks pointed to Billy's room and nodded. He walked up to the plate-glass window, clenched his teeth as he jammed his hands into his pockets. The person lying in the bed wasn't Billy Sweet. The Billy Sweet he knew needed a king-size bed because he was a sprawler. Billy Sweet was perpetual motion, playing music in his head even when he was sleeping.

When Dallas finally managed to open the door, his hand trembled. The machines were evil eyes glaring at him, defying him. If they worked, if they helped, he could live with them.

"If you're going to stay in here, Mr. Lord, you have to be sterile. There is a room at the end of the hall where you can change," the nurse said. "I'm Carly Killian."

Dallas accepted the folded garments. "Is . . . has . . . how is he?"

"There's been no change, Mr. Lord."

"Where's the doctor? She said she'd be up to talk to me."

"We're having a busy night, Mr. Lord. Dr. Killian's shift was over some time ago. However, if she said she'll talk to you, she will. No one at Benton actually works an eight-hour shift. We always go into overtime. The patients come first here. Time clocks aren't important when you compare them to a life."

Dallas nodded and backed out of the room. *I can handle this. I can do whatever has to be done. I know I can do this. I will do this.*

It was an hour before dawn when Sara Killian opened the door to Billy Sweet's room. She motioned for Dallas to leave. He stood outside the door and waited, his breath exploding from his mouth in soft little puffs of sound. He looked across the hall to the nurse's station. A tired-looking nurse smiled at him. He nodded. How could she smile? Was this just a job? Didn't they care? Suddenly he was holding a cup of coffee in his hand. "It will help you to stay awake," the smiling nurse said.

Dallas consumed the coffee in two swallows. He was handing the empty cup back to the nurse when Sara motioned him to follow her to the ICU lounge at the opposite end of the corridor.

"I wish it were yesterday," Dallas said, before Sara could say anything.

"Yesterday's gone, Mr. Lord. All we have is today because tomorrow isn't here yet. The truth is we never really see tomorrow. Perhaps you can write a song about that someday."

"He isn't going to make it, is he?"

"We don't know that. Miracles happen every day of the week. When do you expect his family?"

Dallas looked at his watch. "Another hour or so. Is there a specialist you can call in? Who's the best heart specialist in the country? I'll fly him here, pay him whatever he wants. Isn't there anything we can do?"

"Sit down, Mr. Lord." Sara reached for Dallas's hands. "I did call Dr. La Cross. We spoke at length about Mr. Sweet. He arrived about ten minutes ago and is on his way up here as we speak."

"That's a relief. It's not that I don't have any faith in you. A second opinion is always good. Billy got six opinions when the first doctor diagnosed his father with Alzheimers. It didn't change anything, though. This won't change anything either, right?"

Sara shrugged, aware that she was still holding Dallas's hand. She was about to remove it, when he said, "Do you operate?"

"Yes."

"What kind of doctor are you? Do you have a specialty?"

"I'm an internist." She smiled at his discomfort. "It's all right. I agree with you about the second opinions. One night a month I work the ER. Last night was my night. I wish there was something more I could do."

"I always thought Billy would live forever. Me too, for that matter. Something like this just never entered my mind. His wife and kids are going to be devastated."

"You'll have to be strong for them," Sara said. Reluctantly, she withdrew her hand from his. She couldn't help but wonder why she felt so reluctant to let go of this man's sweaty hands. Something was tugging at her heart, something she hadn't felt for a long time.

"How do you do it?"

"I do my best. When my best isn't enough, I surrender the patient to other hands. I learned that from Dr. La Cross. He was my mentor."

"You're making me feel like an ass, Doctor."

A smile tugged at the corners of Sara's mouth. "If I were in your place, I'd probably be doing and thinking the same things you are. I think he's here. Wait here, Mr. Lord."

"Call me Dallas."

"When Dr. La Cross completes his examination, he'll come out and talk to you. Get another cup of coffee and try to relax. Conjure up your happiest memory with Billy and hold on to that. Can you do that?"

"Sure. Sure, I can do that. Look, don't let him suffer, okay. Nancy will tell you the same thing when she gets here. Promise."

"We'll do our best."

Damn, why did she had to let him die, bitch?

Sara watched the funeral services for Billy Sweet on the eleven o'clock news in her bedroom on a small television screen. She felt her eyes mist over when she saw Dallas and seven other members of the band carrying the bronze casket from the church. How strange. A week ago she hadn't a clue as to who Billy Sweet was. A tear rolled down her cheek when she saw the three children hovering near their mother. She turned off the television set and the night-light.

Sleep eluded her; she tossed and turned. She got up and made a cup of tea. On the kitchen counter was a large brown package and a smaller one on top of it. Nellie Pulaski had thrust it in her hands as she was leaving the hospital. "It's Mr. Sweet's personal belongings. It would be nice of you to take them to Mr. Lord to give to his family." She'd accepted the package and was now sorry. She didn't even know where Dallas lived. Ha! Trust Nellie. The directions and the phone number were taped to the larger package.

Sara looked at the kitchen clock. Eleven-forty-five. Go in darkness and get it over with. Or, go in daylight and have the media follow her. Should she call first? Maybe she should just drive to the house and slip the packages through a gate. Rock stars and movie stars always lived behind gates and walls. She could pen a short note expressing her condolences and staple it to the brown package.

"I thought I heard you down here. Couldn't sleep, huh?" Carly said, setting the kettle back on the stove. "Some doctor you are. Don't you know tea, like coffee, will keep you awake?"

"Then why are you drinking it?"

"Because I'm just a nurse, and you're a doctor. You're supposed to have more brains. Did you watch the news?" Sara nodded. "So, are you going to take his stuff up to his house or what?"

"I've been sitting here thinking about it. Want to go along for the ride?"

"Nope. I have the morning shift. Tonight probably would be better than tomorrow in daylight. I'm glad we're close, Sara. Dallas talked to me a lot while we sat in the room together. He was close to Billy Sweet but not to his brother. That's strange, yet I understand it. I think he liked you, Sara. He said you were honest and compassionate. Traits he never gets to see in his business. Do you know what else he told me? He said he's been tactfully trying to break off a relationship with one of his backup singers. He doesn't want to hurt her feelings. He asked my advice."

Sara stared at her younger look-alike sister. Carly, the fixit kid. "Carly, tell me you didn't offer advice."

"I offered. You know me. I told him to tell

her straight out. This way she gets on with her life, and he gets on with his. Life is too short to be unhappy. I try to tell you that all the time, but do you listen to me? No, you do not."

"I'm not unhappy. I love my work. I love puttering around the house. I try to keep it the way Mom did. For us, Carly. I have a good life. If I meet the right man someday, good. If not, that's okay, too. I think I will take that stuff to Mr. Lord. Mandeville Canyon isn't that far."

"That whole thing with Billy Sweet bothers you, doesn't it?"

"Yeah, it does, and I don't know why. Maybe it's because Mr. Lord said he didn't think he could keep the band going without Billy. I don't think he was thinking clearly. It was his grief talking. If he gives it up, all those people who depend on him will be out of a job."

"And the music world will lose one of the greatest entertainers of all time," Carly said as she dumped sugar into her cup.

"Okay, I'm going to get dressed and drive up there," Sara said. "I'll see you in the morning. No, I won't. I'm off tomorrow. Who cooks dinner tomorrow?"

"The one who stays home. I'm in the mood for some stuffed pork chops. Sweet potatoes, snap peas, a crisp salad, and maybe some made-from-scratch dinner rolls."

"I know where you can get that—the Sunflower Grill," Sara shot over her shoulder.

Carly gulped at her tea. Tomorrow evening dinner would be just as she requested, right down to a linen tablecloth and matching napkins along with crystal glasses of Evian water. Sara was the best doctor in the world. The best cook in the world, the best sister in the world. Sara was simply the best.

Carly craned her neck for a better look at the note taped to the brown package. Dallas Lord's phone number. Hmmmnn. She reached behind her for the phone. Without hesitating, she dialed the number. "Yes, hello. This is Carly Killian. I'm a nurse at Benton Hospital. I just wanted to leave word that Dr. Sara Killian is on her way to Mr. Lord's house to drop off Mr. Sweet's belongings. It would be nice if someone would admit her through the gates. Please give the message to Mr. Lord. I think he wanted to speak to Dr. Killian personally. Thank you. Yes, I know it's late. Doctors work very long hours. No problem." Carly dusted her hands dramatically. "Matchmaking has always been my strong point," she said aloud.

Carly was rinsing out her cup when Sara entered the kitchen. "You look like you're going on a . . . hayride. It's a given that some cop is going to pull you over at this time of night in that racy Jag. Maybe you should fix yourself up a little. A little rouge, some earrings, some of that sinful perfume. You look like a farmer, Sara."

"Maybe you should mind your business, Carly. I'm dressed for comfort."

"Bib overalls! Ponytail! Nike Airs! Give me a break."

"I'll see you in the morning. Lock the door behind me and don't let any strangers in."

"Yes, Mother." It was standing routine each of them used when she went out and the other remained at home. It was also something their mother always said to them.

"Be careful. It's dark out there."

"I'll be careful. Go to sleep."

"If you see Mr. Lord, tell him I said hello. Get his autograph for me, okay?"

Sara slammed the door so hard the cups rattled on the drain board.

Chapter Two

The engine of the powerful Jaguar throbbed as it gobbled up the miles on the way to Mandeville Canyon and Dallas Lord's palatial estate. It occurred to Sara to wonder how Nellie Pulaski had gotten such precise directions.

Why was she doing this? Was it because of the strange feelings she'd experienced when she looked into Dallas Lord's eyes? Why was she doing this? There were at least fifty other people at the hospital who would have fought each other to deliver what was in her car. Nellie had to be behind this little venture in some way. When it came to matchmaking, Nellie was worse than her sister Carly. No, she contradicted herself. She was doing this because she wanted to do it. Dallas Lord touched something in her, something she'd thought was dead and buried. She'd *felt* something.

Sara lowered the window, taking great

gulps of air. Until tonight she hadn't thought about Eric Evans in a long time. Her first love. Her only love. She knew now that a first and only love didn't mean it was true love. She'd never told anyone, not even Carly, about Eric, though she wasn't sure why. He was an intern like herself when they first met. The attraction had been instantaneous and physical on her part. It had taken all of her willpower, physical as well as mental resources, to stay tuned to her profession. All she'd wanted in those early days of the relationship was to have Eric's arms around her. The precious snatched minutes here and there when they made wild, passionate love in utility closets, supply rooms, and the dark, steamy basement had left her weak and dizzy. It had all gone bad in the second year when she realized Eric was helping himself to the drugs in the drug lockup. Her heart breaking, she'd confronted him. He'd lied, but then she'd been prepared for the lie, so she set a trap for him with the Chief of Staff, and he'd been caught red-handed, his promising medical career crashing down around him. She'd begged him to go into a treatment center and he'd laughed at her, saying cruel things that made her crawl into herself with shame. He'd left the hospital without even saying good-bye. Word got out because things like that always got out, and Dr. Sara Killian became a pariah within the confines of the hospital. With the help of the kindly Chief of Staff, she'd obtained an appointment back home in California and tried to put it all behind her. To this day she had no idea where Eric Evans was, nor did she care. Her other two affairs didn't bear thinking about.

Was is possible that Dallas Lord reminded her of Eric Evans?

"This is stupid," Sara muttered to herself. She eased up on the gas pedal until the powerful car slowed, allowing the two cars behind her to pass, then executed a perfect U-turn in the middle of the road. She drove for a mile before she slowed again and made a second U-turn, heading up to the canyon. She always finished what she started.

The Jag slowed a second time as she approached the turnoff Nellie had marked on her direction list. She listened a moment to the soft night sounds all about her. A dog barked somewhere to the right of the iron gates. She loved dogs. A lump formed in her throat when she remembered old Elmer, who had lived to be eighteen. Someday she was going to get a dog. Someday she was going to do a lot of things. Oh yeah.

The slice of moon overhead shone down on the hood ornament of the Jaguar poised in mid-leap. The sudden urge to spit and snarl startled her. Gritting her teeth, she slid from the car, her back end exposed as she leaned over to lift out the two packages on the passenger seat. When she turned around, the world was suddenly dark, the silver wedge of moon sliding behind a dark cloud. She waited for her eyes to become accustomed to the darkness before she walked up to the massive iron gates. She was about to slide the packages between the metal spikes when a gentle voice said, "Stand back, Dr. Killian, so I can open the gates."

"Oh, Mr. Lord, that isn't necessary. I was going to slide the packages through the spokes. It's late. I didn't want to disturb you. I thought if I came by in the daylight there might be media here and . . . I didn't want . . . I have things to do tomorrow . . . I hope I didn't wake you." Damn, she was babbling like a schoolgirl. "Here," she said, thrusting the thick envelopes into Dallas Lord's hands.

"It was kind of you to bring these up. I could have sent someone for them. Nancy and the kids left earlier for Chicago. I'll send them on. Please, come in. Can I get you some coffee or maybe a glass of wine?"

"Thanks, but I'm fine. Are you all right, Mr. Lord?"

"No. I was sitting out by the pool thinking. There's no way I can sleep."

"I can give you a sleeping pill. My bag is in the car."

"I think I'm afraid to go to sleep. I don't want to dream because dreams turn into nightmares. Reality is the lesser of the two evils."

"Have you slept at all these past days?"

"Not really. Please, come in. How about some tea? I really would like to talk to you and thank you for everything you did for Billy."

"Well, all right, for a few minutes," Sara capitulated. *I'm doing this because he needs a friend, someone to talk to. For no other reason.* "I thought reporters would be hanging out here."

"They were. They'll be back before it gets

light. Don't be surprised to see your car on the news tomorrow. I can lend you one of our Jeeps to ride back to town if you're concerned about your privacy. They're merciless. There's this one guy who dogs me night and day. He actually earns a living getting pictures of me. No matter what I do, I can't shake him."

"This is a nice car," Dallas said, settling himself in the passenger side of the Jaguar for the ride up to the main house.

"I call it my bon-bon. The truth is I think I bought it because of the hood ornament."

"I do things like that. My brother is on my case all the time when I do things he considers frivolous. He's the money man. I'm the music man. I hate all that financial stuff. It's good, though. If Adam wasn't in charge, Billy's family could be wiped out. He's got . . . the kids have to go to college. Billy never wanted Nancy to work. He wanted her with the kids all the time since we were on the road so much. Stability where kids are concerned is important. I just found out today Adam had Billy take out an insurance policy when he found out his dad had Alzheimers. I never would have thought of that and neither would Billy."

"It's good to have someone you can count on. My sister and I are like that. I'm really glad we're close."

"Adam and I aren't close. Billy was more of a brother." Dallas's shoulders started to shake. "I don't know what to do without him. When I got back from the cemetery I just wandered around for hours. I don't think it has sunk in yet. Park in the garage. In the morning helicopters will be flying overhead."

"Mr. Lord, I won't be here in the morning."

"I thought you were going to call me Dallas and I was going to call you Sara. You might change your mind. If not, I'll simply open the garage door. Wanna sit by the pool and put your feet in the water? Billy and I used to do that all the time and drink root beer. That guy was so hooked on root beer. We even did a couple of endorsements so he could get the stuff free."

"Okay."

Sara garaged the car. She felt jittery when the door slammed downward. "Are you here alone?"

"The houseman left about a half hour ago. I'm alone. I told everyone I wanted some time to myself. Watch your step. Just follow the lighting. The pool's down below. Are you on call or anything? The reason I asked is, I took the phone off the hook."

"No, I'm not on call. Does your brother live with you?"

"Adam has his home base in New York. He has houses all over the country. His favorite is an old plantation house in South Carolina. If he ever retires, I think he'll live there. He rarely comes here. We talk on the phone, that's it. If he does come here to the coast, he stays in one of the guest cottages. He never stays more than a day or so. I tried to get close to him, but we have nothing in common. He's in Hong Kong right now. I called and left a message about Billy. He didn't return my call."

"Perhaps he didn't get the message. Hotels are . . . notorious for mixing things up."

"Take off your shoes. The pool's heated. Want a root beer?"

"I'd love a root beer."

"Two root beers coming up. I put this refrigerator in the cabana just for Billy. The only thing in it is root beer. We started out with 2,500 cases of the stuff. We have 2,111 left. Adam had a fit when we made the commercial. It was the first time I did anything without his okay. We made a truckload of money from those commercials, too."

Sara swigged from the bottle. "I like this. Lots of fizz. I bet I can burp louder than you can." *God, did I just say that?*

Dallas smacked the palms of his hands on the tile. "Billy always used to say that. He could do a number that sounded like a bull-frog." Sara laughed.

"What are you going to do now? Do you have plans? If you'd rather not talk about it or if you think it's none of my business, it's okay."

"All I've been doing is thinking. Adam has us scheduled for a Pacific Rim tour. We just wound down from our European tour. The benefit was our last show. The PR tour starts in January. This is downtime. Time for the guys to be with their families. We're all in a funk right now. No one wanted to talk about a replacement for Billy. If we decide to continue, it has to be done. Right now I don't even know if I want to do this anymore. The guys feel the same way. It won't be the same. We were our own family. Thanks to Adam, we could all retire tomorrow. It's not the money."

"It's too soon to make heavy decisions like that. You have to allow yourself time to grieve and then you ask yourself what Billy would want you to do. There's a healing time you have to go through. It's another way of saying you take it one day at a time."

"I don't think I properly thanked you for all you did. The entire hospital staff bent over backward for me, and I know it. I told Mr. Heinrick I'd donate the money for a new wing to your hospital as long as he calls it the Billy Sweet wing. He said he would. That alone should bring Adam home on the run. He hates what he calls my philanthropic gestures. He says I don't think things through. What's to think through? If you want to give, you give. There's no right or wrong time. Do you agree or disagree, Sara?"

"I'm really not the person to ask. I earn a paycheck every week and live on a budget. My charitable bequests are minimal. I think I agree with you, though."

"You're a nice person, Dr. Sara Killian. Your sister's a nice person, too. Do you like music, Sara?"

"I love music. Carly and I sing in the church choir. Your music pretty much gives me a headache. I like ballads. You know, sweet, slow, gentle music that tears at your insides. Your music doesn't make me feel romantic."

"No kidding," Dallas said, his face full of awe.

"Did I offend you?"

"No. Did you ever go to a rock concert?"

"No. My sister goes all the time. She's hooked. I loved Elvis Presley. I guess that kind of dates me, huh?"

"Not at all. Elvis was Billy's and my idol. In the beginning we tried to pattern ourselves after Elvis, but it didn't work. It's the way it should be. One Elvis. One Dallas. It's the lights, the sound, the crowds. It gets in your blood. Music is my life."

Sara smiled. "See, you just answered your own earlier question. You can't give it up because it's your life and in your blood. You know what they say about stopping to smell the roses."

"How'd you get to be so smart?"

"I don't know about the smart part. I think it's more common sense. It's getting late. I should be leaving, and you should be going to bed."

"Don't go. Would you like some break-

fast? I can make scrambled eggs and bacon. Coffee or root beer. We could watch
the sun come up. I haven't had a one-on-
one conversation with anyone for a long
time. Are you seeing anyone?"

"No. Are you?"

"I was. It didn't work for me. Your sister
gave me some advice. I tried it out the day
before the funeral and it wasn't . . . a good
thing. My answer is no." Sara laughed at the
intensity in his voice.

"Do you think you'll ever get married and
settle down?" Sara asked curiously. She
didn't realize she was holding her breath until Dallas responded.

"Sure. It's all I think about. I love kids. I
keep hoping the right person walks into my
life, and that I'm smart enough to know she's
the right person. Do you really want to know
what I want?" Not bothering to wait for her
reply, he said, "I want a house full of kids
and animals and a goat outside. I always
wanted a goat. I want my house to smell
good, you know, like something's cooking
that will taste wonderful. I want dogs and
cats running after the kids and a wife who
will roll her eyes and hug me so tight I get
tears in my eyes. Billy had that. Adam . . .

Adam says I'm a sex symbol to millions of fans and my popularity will go downhill if I get married. Believe it or not, I'm a stay-at-home guy. I don't get off on all of that wild stuff. Don't believe my promo stuff. Adam puts that stuff out by the bushel. We go with the flow if you know what I mean."

"Are you saying all that stuff they print is *lies?*"

Dallas threw back his head and laughed. "Absolutely. The truth is the guys and I are so boring, we could put you to sleep. Take Chico for instance. He's got Latin good looks and a love 'em and leave 'em profile. The guy's married with three beautiful little girls. He adores his wife, he plants tomatoes and bell peppers and builds model airplanes. He mows his own lawn and car pools when he's home. We're normal people. The fans don't want normal people, so we pretend."

"I don't think I like your brother," Sara blurted.

"Adam is okay. Everyone gets what they want. The fans are happy. The guys are happy. Adam's happy."

"Are you happy, Dallas?"

"As long as I have my music, I'm happy.

Would you like to see my sound studio? Did you agree to breakfast or not?" He reached for her hand. Sara allowed it to be taken because it felt right.

"Yes to both. This is an enormous house. Do you entertain a lot?"

"Never! It has fourteen rooms. The grounds are about four acres, maybe a little more. I have two guest cottages and a five-car garage." He stopped in mid-stride. "It's not a home yet. It's still a house. It doesn't have all that stuff mothers and wives put around to make it look real. What's your house look like?"

"Why don't you come and see it. I have a lot of junk and green plants. Lots of books and magazines. I could give you my overflow. I've been thinking about getting an animal, but I'm not home that much. Carly's never home either, so it wouldn't be fair to the animal. The house was left to Carly and me by our parents. We kept everything the way it was because we grew up with the furnishings and we're comfortable with things. This is pretty sad," Sara said, looking around Dallas's living room. He was still holding her hand. It still felt good, and it felt right. Did he move closer, or did she? She started to feel warm all over.

"I bet you're going to hate my kitchen."

A moment later, Sara gasped. "You're right. It looks like an institution kitchen."

"Billy said the same thing. His kitchen in Chicago is all yellow and green. Real sunny. Does that mean you can't picture yourself eating scrambled eggs in here?"

"Why don't we just have another root beer?"

"Sounds good. Would you like to see my projection room and the sound studio? We record here quite often. It's a little more lived-in than the rest of the house." Dallas reached for her hand again and squeezed it slightly. Sara's neck grew warm and stayed that way. She found herself looking up at him, aware suddenly of his height and the breadth of him. She was aware for the first time of how muscular he was, how loose-jointed as he walked along, pointing out the names of his equipment. He was still wearing his baseball cap. She wondered why. What would he look like in a suit, shirt, and tie? She tried to imagine him ringing her doorbell for a date. She stumbled over a cable. Dallas caught her before she could fall, drawing her close to him.

Sara felt her heart take on an extra beat or was it Dallas's heartbeat she was hearing and feeling? Suddenly her tongue felt three sizes too big for her mouth, and the lump forming in her throat had to be as big as a lemon. Her eyes locked with his. He was going to kiss her. She closed her eyes and swayed dizzily as she waited for his lips. And then nothing.

"Good God, are you okay? That was my fault. I should have moved the cable. I knew it was there, but I walked over it. Are you sure you're okay? You look . . . strange. Say something, Sara."

"I thought you were going to kiss me." *I said it, but I don't believe I said it. They need to lock me up somewhere.* She was flustered now, unable to meet his gaze. To her inexperienced eye he looked frazzled. If Nellie Pulaski was here, she'd have the right spin on things in seconds.

"I thought about it. I wanted to. I'm not real good at stuff like this. *You're a doctor!*" He made it sound like she was God's chosen messenger.

"I can tell." There was a definite edge to

her voice. Nellie was right—she needed to get out and about more. She needed to know how the game was played these days. She'd never really dated Eric Evans. She'd just sneaked around with him. One of these days she was going to give that whole scene some serious thought. "I think I'd like that root beer now."

"Out by the pool?"

"Sure."

"If I called you and asked you out, would you go?"

"A date?"

"Yeah. I bring flowers, and you get dressed up."

"Will people follow us and try to rip your clothes off?" *Oh yessss.* She was begining to think Nellie was right. She did need to get laid.

"Probably. What will the hospital think if your picture's plastered all over the paper?"

"I have no idea." She felt herself cringe when she imagined bold, stark headlines. Rocker Dallas Lord partying with Benton's senior staff doctor. She should have been a dermatologist or a podiatrist. Nobody cared what they did.

"I guess it isn't such a good idea. Unless . . ."

"Yes?" God, was that breathless voice
hers? *Sara Killian, you are a party waiting
to happen.*

"Unless I arrange things here. I can have
our dinner catered and I can order the latest
movie. I have a wide screen in my projection
room. And, I have a popcorn machine as well
as a soda fountain. If you bring your bathing
suit, we can take a late night swim. We could
carry that one step farther if you throw in a
nightie for a slumber party. How about tonight? Should I kiss you now to show you
what you're in for or should I wait?"

"Procrastination doesn't work for me."

"Ahhh."

It was the kind of tremulous kiss that,
given the right circumstances, could lead to
other things and both Sara and Dallas knew
it. Sara broke away first, her face hot and
tingly. "I have this mental picture of you
strutting around the stage blasting out a
song while millions of people shout your
name and young girls throw their panties on
the stage. I don't know if I can handle that."

"I have this mental picture of you cutting
open someone's chest cavity while blood

and gore spill out. I don't know if I can handle that."

Sara started to laugh. "I don't do heart surgery. What time is dinner?"

"After dark unless you want tabloid pictures. Do you want to leave your car and take one of my Jeeps? Personally, I think it's a good idea. There's an automatic gate opener on the visor so you can scoot right in. I changed the code on the gate earlier this evening. No one can get in here but me." Sara thought his voice was defensive-sounding when he said, "I'm not being paranoid here. I just want to be left in peace for now. Yes or no on the Jeep?"

"Yes."

"I'll ride with you down to the gate. I'm glad you came, Sara, and I'm looking forward to dinner. Want a root beer for the road?"

Sara shook her head as she climbed behind the wheel. "Will you try and get some sleep now?"

The cell phone in Dallas's back pocket buzzed. He yanked it out of his pocket, flipping the lid and antenna. "The only people who have this number are Nancy and Adam," he said. "Dallas here."

Sara tried not to listen as Dallas's voice went flat. She expertly backed the Jeep out of the garage. She shifted gears as she headed back the way she'd come.

"How do you think I feel? It was pretty goddamn shitty of you not to show up for the funeral, Adam. You could have chartered a plane. You know what you can do with that tour, don't you? The boys and I talked about it, and we're not sure we want to do it. Put it on hold. I don't care that it's all set up. Listen to me, Adam, I don't care. Now, what part of that don't you understand? No, I won't feel differently tomorrow or the day after. Don't rush home now, it's after the fact. I want you to know right up front I'm not going to forget this. Nancy and the kids aren't going to forget it either. The media will have a field day."

Sara slid to a stop at the gate. She waited for Dallas to finish his conversation. He hopped out of the Jeep, his voice rising when he said, "Ask me if I care, Adam. By the way, I just agreed to build a wing at Benton Memorial Hospital. Take care of it. I don't have to ask your permission. It's a done deed. I have to go now. What the hell do you think got into me? My best friend in the whole world was buried a few hours ago.

My own brother was a no-show. Go to hell, Adam."

"Sorry about that, Sara. Sometimes Adam is a real pain in the butt. Every time I look at him I see dollar signs in his eyeballs." The huge gates swung open. "Drive carefully. Listen, if anything comes up, call me." He scribbled the cell-phone number on the corner of a Chinese menu lying on the floor. "Hurry, the gate only stays open for thirty-five seconds."

Sara waved as she shot through the gate.

On the drive home, Sara mentally cataloged her wardrobe. Something not too dressy. Definitely feminine. Maybe a trip to the hairdresser. A manicure wasn't out of the question. A new bottle of perfume would be nice. She absolutely had to buy some new underwear. Something lacy, that fine cobwebby stuff Carly wore all the time. She could take a short nap and hit Rodeo Drive by noon.

Should she keep it a secret or should she tell Carly? For now it might be better to keep quiet. Carly would chatter incessantly. God, she'd probably have Dallas's music piped through the house. She'd tell everyone at the hospital. Sara snorted in disgust. How was she going to explain the Jeep? If she told a lie, she'd have to tell more lies. A long sigh escaped her lips as she pulled the Jeep alongside Carly's Jeep.

Carly was waiting by the back door, tea-cup in hand. "I want to hear *everything*. Don't leave a thing out. Where's your car? Guess you didn't just slide the stuff through his fence, huh? What's he *really* like? How is he? Did he ask you out?"

Sara told her.

"Are you excited? You don't look excited. What are you going to wear? You're going shopping, right? Don't worry, I won't tell any-one. The brother sounds . . . awful. I bet he's one of those control freaks. All that stuff is lies! I love reading all that junk in the su-permarket tabloids, and now you tell me none of it is true. You actually drove his Jeep here. I bet one of those rags would pay you a hundred thousand for your story and a picture of you sitting in his Jeep."

"Everything is going to change now. This is probably a mistake. Maybe I was too hasty, you know, caught up in the moment. If it gets out, what will the hospital think?"

"It's none of their business, Sara. Your private life is no one's business but yours. And mine," she said flippantly. "People do talk, though. Dallas is trying to protect you, even I can see that. He lives with the media and knows how the game works. Play the game, Sara. It's time you had some fun and romance in your life. Now, listen to me, I'm going to tell you where to shop. The best store for sexy lingerie is . . . not that you're buying it for that reason. You're going to get it just to make yourself feel good. It's a tiny shop called Sassy. They keep the stuff in boxes and not on models. Get an outfit that's bright and colorful. A French manicure is a must. Go to Lisa and Company and get some sunglitz in your hair. A trim, too. Get those eyebrows more defined. You're a mess, Sara." Carly's voice was so cheerful-sounding Sara couldn't take offense.

"It's just dinner, Carly, not an assignation."

"You don't know that."

"You said he was still involved with someone. He said . . . what he said was it wasn't good. He meant he followed your advice, and it didn't turn out right. That could mean anything. If she didn't take it well, that means she . . . might still be on the fringes. It makes me uncomfortable."

"You'll get over it! A dinner date with Dallas Lord! Woweeee! Stop looking at me like that, Sara. I swear I won't tell anyone. I wonder what the brother is like. They never show pictures of him when they do those stories. Eagle-eyed, chiseled jaw, lean and mean. Let's make a bet, Sara."

"Don't be silly. Dallas said he's the reason for his success."

"Maybe his financial success. His music is his own. No one can claim success for that except Dallas and his band. *Rolling Stone* magazine said Dallas Lord has more money than Michael Jackson. That's a lot of money, Sara. I hate to say this, but he's more famous than Elvis and Michael Jackson put together." Carly clapped her hands in glee. "And my big sister, the doctor, has a date with him! Absolutely mind-boggling."

"I'm going to bed. His money doesn't interest me. He was like this gentle, wounded bird. He's worried he won't fly again. Yes, he's grieving for Billy Sweet, but it's more than that. They were a support system for one another. He's not sure if he can or if he wants to continue without his friend, and he's going through a very real trauma right now. I don't know what time I'll be home tonight, so don't wait up for me."

Carly grinned as she waved her index finger in Sara's face. "Take notes!"

Sara slid between the sheets as she rolled over on her side. She was asleep within minutes, dreaming not of Dallas Lord but Eric Evans.

"You tricked me, Eric. You stole my key to the drug cabinet. I cannot, I will not cover for you. You need help, Eric."

"What are you talking about? All I wanted was my guitar. You're the one who put it in the drug cabinet. Adam said he could get me a real good price for it. He doesn't like you, Sara. That's why you're so upset. Admit it. He has the combination to the gate, too. He isn't going to like it when he sees you. It's your turn now, Sara. You'll see how it feels when your world is ripped out from under you."

"You were abusing drugs, Eric. You were stealing from the drug cabinet using my key on my floor. That's why you don't have a life anymore. Did you ever love me, or was that all a lie, too?"

"Of course it was a lie. It was all a lie. Sneaking around was the only thing that was exciting. How do you think you're going to feel when Adam finds out you're trying to

steal Dallas out from under him? Dallas Lord and the Canyon River Band is Adam's livelihood. He's going to blame you, blame you, blame youuuuu."

Sara rolled over, and then sat up. She brushed at her hair as she stared at the bedside clock—12:10. She leaned back into her nest of pillows. She rarely dreamed of Eric Evans these days. Eric belonged to the past. Sara tried to burrow into the bed. Maybe she should just return the Jeep, take back her car, and go on with her life. Maybe the dream was an omen of some kind. *Make up your mind, Sara. Being blind to something was what caused the problems with Eric. Open your eyes and look at this situation. Right now Dallas Lord is just someone you met who is a nice person. If you let it go further, you will eventually have to deal with the brother. Is that what you want? Can you handle that?*

Sara swung her legs over the side of the bed, Nellie Pulaski's words ringing in her ears. "For God's sake, it's just a dinner. It's not even a real date." She continued talking to herself as she stared at her reflection in the bathroom mirror, which was starting to fog up from the steamy shower. The clothes she'd slept in came off in a rush. She hadn't slept in her clothes since her intern days. Another omen?

"Oh, Sara, you look . . . wonderful. Actually, you look downright gorgeous."

"Am I overdone? Is it too much? Is the dress too . . . you know, flashy?"

"Not at all. You look perfect. Gold is definitely your color. It brings out the gold flecks in your eyes." Carly's eyes were clinical as well as critical when she scrutinized Sara's new haircut, manicure, and sniffed her new perfume. She nodded approvingly. "Don't mess yourself up when you get in that crummy Jeep. Oh, jeez, the wind's going to do a number on your hair. Wear a scarf till you get there."

"Any other instructions?"

"Do you have a condom in your purse? You're a doctor, Sara. These days women have to take responsibility for themselves. You can't depend on the guy. You went to the same lecture I did."

"Carly, I am not going to bed with Dallas Lord. I'm going to dinner. I would never go to bed with someone I just met. The answer is no, I do not have a condom in my purse."

Carly's voice was breezy, devilish. "That's okay. I put one in for you. It's in that little zipper compartment. Just in case. You always have to be prepared, Sara."

"This is wrong. I'm the big sister. You are the little sister. I should be telling you things like this, not the other way around."

"Only by thirteen months. I bloomed early, Sara."

Sara looked around for her keys.

"You left the key in the Jeep. Have a good time. I won't wait up. I might even stay at Hank's place tonight. I'll see you tomorrow. Sara, loosen up and enjoy the man's company. Be open to whatever is in store for you. Sometimes you are just so tight-assed I want to kick you."

"You're sure I look okay?"

"You're so ugly I can't stand it. Go already!"

"All right. I'm gone."

"Remember now, take notes."

The smile stayed on Sara's lips all the way to Dallas Lord's palatial estate.

Chapter Three

Dallas looked around the cluttered kitchen. How was it possible to use every pot, every pan, every utensil, plus every dish, to make spaghetti? He'd done just that, and he would have used more had more been in the cabinets. All in his desire to impress Dr. Sara Killian. Maybe Adam was right and he really was some kind of misfit. "Shit!"

His eyes wild, Dallas reached for the cell phone on the counter when it buzzed to life. Thinking it was Sara Killian, he forced cheerfulness into his voice that he was far from feeling.

"Sweetie, it's Sandi. I'm out by the gates, and they aren't working. Will you buzz me in?"

"I changed the code, Sandi. Look, we went through this. You said you understood. It was what it was. I've moved on. You need to do the same thing." He eyed the clock on the wall and then the spaghetti splatters on his white tee shirt. He needed to change and pick some flowers from the greenhouse for the table.

Sandi Sims's voice was a coy whine. "Oh, Dallas, honey, that's just your grief talking. We were so good together. We made music together. Surely you haven't forgotten all those wonderful nights."

Dallas wondered what wonderful nights she was referring to. Sandi had come to an audition when one of his backup singers made the choice to go back to school to finish her degree. It was short notice, and she'd been the best of the lot, appearance-wise. Voicewise she left something to be desired, but the high-tech equipment made it work. He regretted the six-week relationship. He knew it was a mistake. Billy had said it was a mistake. Even old Adam had voiced an opinion saying business and pleasure didn't work. If it hadn't been for Adam's comments, he probably wouldn't have let it get off the ground. Billy said Sandi was like chewing gum. Everywhere he stepped, there she was. Feathering her nest was the way Billy put it. He offered up his favorite phrase a second time "Oh shit!"

"Dallas, honey, open the gates. I have an

exquisite bottle of wine and some wonderful cheese and crackers. We can sit out under the stars and talk. The guys are all worried about you. I'm worried too, honey. You shouldn't be alone at a time like this. That's what friends are for. Open the gates, Dallas."

"Right now the best thing you can do for me is to leave me alone. I'd like to do my grieving in private. Don't make me say things I'll regret. It's over, Sandi. I'll have Adam get in touch with you when I decide what I'm going to do. Your paychecks will be in the mail."

"Why are you being so ugly to me, Dallas? If you don't want me to come in, at least come down to the gate and talk to me. Please, Dallas."

Dallas eyed the clock. Sara would be arriving any minute. "Shit, shit, shit!" The spaghetti bubbled, splattering the huge white stove. He still had the salad to cut up. "I have to go now, Sandi. Please don't call again." He broke the connection. Now he was going to have to get a new number.

He was whirlwind as he chopped and pared the vegetables. He turned down the stove and took the stairs three at a time. He was in and out of the shower in three minutes, dressed in five. He used up two more minutes running his electric razor over his face and neck. Two seconds to splash on cologne and another two seconds running the brush through his tight springy curls. Done!

Back in his kitchen, Dallas looked at his polka-dotted room. He didn't dare go near the stove. What he needed was a goddamn raincoat. Spaghetti, his favorite food, was supposed to be easy to make according to the cookbook on the counter. You just put everything in a pot and watched it cook. Instead of the sauce cooking down, the mess had seemed to *expand* at an alarming rate of speed. He'd switched pots four times so far. He didn't have a clean pot for the pasta. That meant he had to wash one and risk splattering his clean shirt. The raincoat idea was looking better and better. The urge to give it a try was so strong, Dallas burst into laughter as he headed for the mudroom and one of the yellow slickers hanging on the peg near the door. He put it on, buckled it, sniffing appreciatively at the garlic- and basil-scented kitchen.

The only pot for the pasta was the one the

sauce was cooking in. Dump it out and let it finish cooking in the microwave. Oh, yeah. He carried the bubbling mess to the sink and poured. He flinched when the sauce splattered on the pristine organdy curtain above the sink. The white cabinets became one long smear of red. The sauce dripped down the yellow slicker onto the shoelaces of his new Nikes. "Oh, shit!"

The electronic pad next to the door came to life. "The main gate is now opening. A vehicle is driving through. There are ten seconds left and counting. The main gate is now closing. No other vehicles have entered." Dalla pressed the End button to cut off the transmission. The cell phone rang again. Answer it or not? It might be Nancy, Billy's wife. He clicked the on talk switch to hear Sandi's angry voice. "I thought you said you wanted to be alone, Dallas. Who was that? It was your Jeep. I recognized the license plate. Why did you lie to me?"

"Because I didn't want to hurt your feelings. I told you, Sandi, it's over. Please don't call me. Furthermore, it's none of your business who comes to my house. Let's leave it at that, or you'll be looking for another job. I hate pushy people, especially pushy women. As I said earlier, it's what it is. I never made you any promises. In fact I was very careful not to lead you on. There's no point in prolonging this conversation. Adam will be in touch when it's time. Just so you know, there's every possibility I might break up the band and retire. Now, please, leave me alone." For the second time Dallas broke the connection. He looked around, his eyes full of panic. Where to stash the phone? The moment he saw the headlights arc on the kitchen window he opened the freezer to stuff the cell phone down among the ice cubes. He thought he heard it ring. Maybe it was the ice cubes settling. He wondered if it would plug up the ice chute. Not that he cared. A stuffed ice chute was preferable to listening to Sandi Sims.

Fright, unlike anything he'd ever experienced onstage, washed through him when he heard the sound of Sara's heels on the concrete apron. God, she was coming to the kitchen door. He felt his feet take root on the tile floor. He was muttering his favorite expression when the screen door opened.

"I thought you'd come to the side door or the front door," he managed to croak.

Sara's eyes took in the raincoat, the red-

and-white stove, the polka-dotted organdy curtains. Tongue in cheek, Sara said, "I can go back out and walk around to your front door. I think I understand everything but the raincoat."

"It's a long story. I really do know how to cook. Sort of. For some reason this . . . got away from me. I think what happened was I used this really big can of tomato paste and I had to keep adding water because the sauce was like glue. I kept switching pots till I ran out of them. I think I ruined the microwave a few minutes ago. The reason I know this is because the sauce is oozing out under the door. I was going to have dinner catered, but decided to do it myself because I hate it when people *hover*. I love spaghetti."

He could cook. And sing. And he was going out of his way for her. Sara felt a definite head rush.

"I wanted to impress you," he said.

"Oh. Why?" *He wanted to impress me. Oh God.*

"I don't know. I like you. You aren't like all those other women I meet. You're normal. You're the kind of person my brother associates with. I guess I wanted you to like me."

"I do like you. I wouldn't be here if I didn't

like you, Dallas. Is it safe for me to come in, or should I wait outside?"

Dallas loved the smile in her voice. "I'm going to salvage this dinner if it kills me. My housekeeper has some stuff in the closet in the mudroom. It's not glamorous or anything. That dress you're wearing is much too pretty to ruin. You know how sauce splatters. I could get you a matching slicker, complete with hat if you want."

His and hers. His suggestion. Hmmm. "Okay."

"Okay? Are you kidding?"

"Nope. I'm game. I have to tell you, though, I don't clean up. You're going to need those Disaster Master people. Your housekeeper might quit if she sees this mess. It smells heavenly, though. Spaghetti is one of my favorite foods. I love basil and garlic."

Dallas preened, his chest puffing out. "Get your raincoat while I try to salvage this mess. Dinner will be ready as soon as I cook the spaghetti. Be careful you don't slip on the floor."

Sara laughed. "Where are the hip boots?"

"In the garage with my fishing gear. Do you like to fish, Sara?"

"My dad used to take Carly and me when we were little. I haven't gone in years. We used to go in a canoe. My mother cheered us from the dock."

"Would you like to go fishing with me?"

Sara didn't hesitate. "Yes I would."

"Do you rollerblade?"

"I never tried it. Carly loves it and says it's wonderful exercise. I like to hike."

"You're kidding! I love to hike. Someday I want to do that survival thing. You know, climb the real mountains with ropes and pulleys and all that stuff. You ride the rapids, live in tents, eat off the land. I just never have the time. I also don't like doing things alone. I'm the only unmarried guy in the band. When is your next vacation?"

"The entire month of December. My contract is up at the hospital, and it will take that long to negotiate a new one. I'm not sure I want to stay at Benton Memorial. I've been thinking about going into private practice."

"What's stopping you?"

Sara buckled the yellow slicker. "Money. I'm still paying off student loans, and I don't know if I want to go further into debt. It's very expensive to become a doctor, even worse if you have a specialty. Malpractice insurance is prohibitive. The water's bubbling. Can I set the table?"

"Sure. We're eating in my fancy dining room unless you want to eat out here in this mess."

"I don't mind. I'm a kitchen person. Carly and I have this wonderful breakfast nook with a wraparound window. It overlooks a small garden. We have bird feeders and a few squirrels. I love to sit there on Sunday mornings with my coffee and the paper. Just tell me where the dishes are."

Dallas pointed to the cabinet to Sara's left. He watched as she set the table, folding the napkins, placing them just so, arranging the silverware. "Root beer, right?" He nooded. "Glasses or do we swig from the bottle?"

"I'm for whatever saves on dishwashing."

Sara's voice was full of awe. "Me too. Carly and I use those plastic throwaway dishes. The shiny ones. Everything's throwaway. Even though we have a dishwasher, you have to rinse off everything, load it up, put in the soap, clean up. That takes time.

"Laundry takes time, housecleaning takes time. Mowing the lawn takes even more time. Then you have to go to the dry cleaners, the supermarket, the gas station, the auto-body shop, the drugstore. Some days I can't get everything done. You're the lucky one, you have people do all that stuff for you."

"I never thought about it like that. Sometimes I'd like to do those things. Adam keeps me on a tight schedule and an even tighter leash. I really understand the time thing. Well, time is standing still right now for both of us. I love this mess. Just look at it. If I tried, I couldn't have done this. And all because I wanted to impress you. Tell me I impressed you."

Sara's face was solemn when she said, "You did. You are. I will always remember eating spaghetti with Dallas Lord wearing a yellow slicker. I hope you have lots of garlic butter." Maybe her purchases at Sassy's weren't a mistake after all. She blinked when she remembered the price. Did men really pay attention to women's underwear, or was that a myth?

"I made my own garlic butter. Sit down, Doctor, and I will serve you the best spaghetti you ever ate."

"What's that noise?"

"What noise?"

"The noise coming from the freezer."

"It's probably the cell phone. I would have thought the wires were frozen by now."

"I see."

Dallas propped his elbows on the table. "No, you don't, but that's okay. I had a short-term . . . thing with one of the singers in the band. Didn't I tell you about that yesterday? It wasn't going to go anywhere. I knew it. I thought she did, too."

Dallas's announcement demanded she make some kind of comeback. Sara rolled her spaghetti on the fork, using the table-spoon to wrap it smoothly. Suddenly she felt uneasy, afraid for some reason.

"How about you, Sara? Is there anyone in your life?"

"No. I'm not sure I want anyone. When things don't work out it hurts too much. I had that twice, actually three times. I don't think I could handle it again."

"I never experienced that kind of feeling. What went wrong? If it's none of my business, tell me."

"It wasn't meant to be. I guess I loved too much, and they didn't love enough. Now when I look back I don't think it was love at all. They were party people. My idea of a party is four people for a barbecue in the backyard. I'm a home-and-hearth kind of person. I don't know how you do it. Entertainers like you are so . . . visible, so front and center. You have to be *on* all the time."

"I don't know anything else. It's all I've ever done. I've never gone to a four-person barbecue or sat in front of a fireplace with a girl. I guess you think that makes me some kind of jerk. Maybe I am." At his devastated look, Sara wanted to reach out and touch him.

"It's a question of priorities. Your lifestyle doesn't make you a jerk. You're a jerk when you do stupid things. I don't think you do stupid things. This is very good spaghetti. Do you ever see your old friends for get-togethers?"

Dallas shook his head. "The guys in the band are my friends. Billy was my only real friend from childhood. Adam and I aren't close. I've accepted the fact that we're never going to bond. It's what it is."

Sara leaned across the table. He looked so . . . *needy* in the candlelight. "I'm just surprised that you aren't married. I think your phone is ringing again."

"Let it ring. Marriage isn't for everyone. Do you want to get married?" It was Dallas's turn to lean across the table.

"I suppose if I met the right person. I like the idea of going to bed with someone and waking with him next to me, of sitting across the breakfast table with that person. It's hard to be alone. I view marriage as sharing. You can have every advantage in life, mega-wealth, everything money can buy, and if you don't have someone to share it with, what's the point to it all? My mother always said if something is meant to be, it will be and nothing you can say or do will change things. Is your brother married?"

"No. He's always on the road. The sad truth is, I know very little about my brother. I had a nightmare once where I was in a hospital and in the dream I needed a kidney donor. The doctor asked Adam if he'd donate one of his. Adam's response was he had to *think* about it. If it were the other way around, I wouldn't have to think about it."

Sara didn't mean to ask the question, but the words rolled off her lips. "Does your brother like you? Wait, don't answer that. I had no right to ask such a question. It's none of my business."

"It's a reasonable question. I don't know. In his own way I'm sure he has feelings for me. Adam's a cold, clinical, analytical person. Billy said Adam's assessment of me was that I didn't have enough sense to come in out of the rain. That smarted for a long time. I try not to think about it. Adam has some very good qualities. The Canyon River Band wouldn't be what it is without Adam. He's a bottom-line person."

Sara sucked up a long strand of spaghetti, the sauce splattering on the yellow slicker. "I can do that," Dallas said.

"Yeah," Sara tested, "but can you do it without splashing your raincoat? You're right, this the best spaghetti I ever ate."

"There, what'd you think of that?" Dallas demanded as he sucked up not one but two strands of spaghetti.

"I think you got lucky is what I think. Can you do that grass thing between your fingers or skip rocks on a pond?"

"Nah. We were city boys. We can do those things when we go fishing. You have to pack a picnic basket with fried chicken, hard-boiled eggs, cheese, and all that stuff. They always do that in the movies."

Sara dabbed at her lips. "Did you ever go on a picnic, Dallas?"

"If I did, I don't remember."

"That's so sad. Maybe it isn't so sad. The only reason my dad taught Carly and me those things was because he wanted a son and got two daughters instead. He never seemed proud of our accomplishments. He yanked us both out of the Powder Puff League when we failed to hit home runs. I heard him tell my mother we embarrassed him. Sometimes I think it might have been better not to have done those things. We just never measured up. Feelings like that stay with you forever."

"Now, that's sad. I'm taking time off. You're going to be off the month of December. We can do some of those things together if you want. We can start off as friends and if anything develops, fine, if it doesn't, we'll still be friends. I think my problem is I was never a kid. In the early days I had to hustle. There was never enough money. Comic books and music, that was my life. Billy's too. I probably would have ended up in a gang if it wasn't for Adam."

"What about Christmas?"

Dallas looked blank. "What about it?"

"Don't you *do* Christmas?"

"I think you need to explain what you mean by the words, do Christmas."

"You know, cut down a tree, get out the heirloom ornaments, decorate the house with balsam, buy poinsettias for the whole house, hang a wreath on the front door, invite friends over, go caroling, buy presents and wrap them to put under the tree, cook a wonderful Christmas dinner to share with all your friends. Then when the day winds down you build a fire and talk about all the wonderful things that are going to happen in the new year. That's what I call doing Christmas."

"That's what families do. I've been on the road every Christmas for as long as I can remember. The hotels always have a tree in the lobby. It's just another day. I give the guys checks for themselves and their families. We don't do that present thing. Adam's never around. What you just said, is that what you and your sister do?"

"For the most part. We do it Christmas Eve, though. Both of us usually work Christmas Day since we're single and it gives the married women time to be with their families. It's a good feeling. I told you, I'm a home-and-hearth person. This year Carly is going to Austria with her ski group, and I'll be off. It will be the first time in my life that I'll be alone for Christmas. I'm not looking forward to it."

"I'm going to be alone, too. That means both of us will be alone. If you have no objections, maybe we could *do* the Christmas thing together. If you get a better offer . . ."

"You might get a better offer. It's something for both of us to think about. Maybe we should tackle Thanksgiving first. That's just a few weeks away."

"Do you *do* that, too?"

Sara laughed. "Oh yeah. We could give it a shot. I make a pretty good pumpkin pecan pie. There's a downside to Thanksgiving, and every year it proves to be a bigger and bigger challenge. What to do with the leftover turkey. I have seventeen tried and true recipes. That translates into seventeen days of turkey. Eighteen if you count Thanksgiving. Your place or mine?" Sara said boldly.

"We'll be safer here. I don't want your privacy invaded. Once the press sniffs you out, your life will never be the same. Then we have a date for Thanksgiving?"

"We have a date. I'll bring everything.

Some things like the stuffing, have to be prepared the night before, but not put into the
bird. I like to do the pies the night before,
too. I have a problem with this kitchen,
though."

"It'll be cleaned by then. I'll call those people you suggested tomorrow."

"That's not what I mean. This is so . . .
sterile-looking. I have sterile all day at the
hospital. You need color, plants, *stuff*. I
could turn this kitchen into a room you'd
want to hang out in all the time. If you're a
kitchen person, that is. Are you a cozy person, Dallas?"

A flustered look appeared on Dallas's
face. "If I'm not, I could be. What makes for
a cozy person?" He leaned across the table,
his eyes intent.

Sara moved back slightly in her chair but
allowed Dallas to take her hand. "It probably
means different things to different people.
To me it means plain, simple, comfortable.
You know, basics. I personally do not re-
quire a lot of what my mother called trap-
pings. I'm not ostentatious. I'm what you see
is what you get. That's not to say I don't like
a little glitz and glamour once in a while. To
me it isn't real. Maybe it's because I'm a

doctor, and I've seen so much pain, suffering, and hardship. Your world seems so unreal to me."

Dallas laughed. "Your world sounds like a fairy tale to me. I bet if both of us tried, we could find a common middle ground. You have my permission to do whatever you want with my kitchen. What do you want to throw out?"

"Nothing. That's not what I meant. I'll add to it. What's your favorite color?"

"Red. Red's a cheerful color. I like blue. You know, the color of the sky on a bright summer day. You have golden eyes. They're beautiful. Did anyone ever tell you that?"

"A time or two. What should we do with the dishes? Your sink is . . ."

"Let's just throw everything away. We'll get new stuff."

"Really?"

"Really."

"But that's wasteful. We do have our raincoats on. I suppose we could clean up the worst of it."

"Plan B would be good."

"Which is?" Sara laughed at the look on Dallas's face as he glanced around.

"The Disaster Master people. Let them do the whole thing. Now would be a good time to shed our rain gear and sit outdoors if you like. It's a warm evening. I do have some new movies if you'd rather watch them. I'd like to get to know you better, Sara."

"Then outside it is. No more root beer, though."

"I have some really good wine. Fragile stemmed glasses. I bought them when Billy and Nancy had their first baby. We were on the road and wanted to make a toast."

"I like fragile stemmed glasses." Drinking wine from fragile stemmed glasses with Dallas Lord. This was tabloid fodder at its best. "Your phone's ringing again. Maybe you should answer it. It could be important."

"No. In your world you have to answer the phone because it could be a matter of life and death. In my world it just means someone wants something. Humor me."

"Okay."

"Are you always so agreeable?"

Sara answered honestly. "For the most part. Did you know it only takes nineteen muscles to smile and twenty-one to frown? Why be disagreeable when you can be agreeable?"

Dallas reached for the wine bottle and the corkscrew. "You can carry the glasses."

Settled on matching chairs at poolside, Sara said, "Tell me about Dallas Lord."

Dallas was quiet for so long, Sara nudged him. "I . . . don't like talking about myself because sometimes I say something personal, and it finds a home in the tabloids. They pay top dollar for dirt on me and the guys. I guess I'm trying to ask you if we talk about ourselves, will you talk to reporters?"

"I'm a doctor, Dallas. I cannot nor would I ever divulge a confidence. You aren't my patient, but I live by my oath every day of my life. For me to repeat anything you say to me would be betrayal. That word is not in my vocabulary."

They talked like old friends then. They were so intent on sharing confidences they didn't hear the soft rustling on the other side of the fence. Nor did they see long, slender fingers tear at the branches of the overgrown privet hedges that hid the ugly cyclone fence and the young woman who spied on them with hate-filled eyes.

It was well past the witching hour when Sara set her glass on the small table at her side. "I have to leave now, Dallas. Five-thirty will be here before I know it."

"You haven't even left, and I think I miss you already. Moonlight becomes you, Sara."

Sara felt flustered. Damn, why was it she was so cool, calm, and professional, not to mention unflappable in her profession, and in her private life she was a mess? "It's been a long time since anyone said something that nice to me. Thank you for the compliment."

"Will you come back tomorrow evening?"

"Is that an invitaion?"

"Yes it is. This time I'll order in. Take the Jeep, Sara. The sharks don't know about you yet, and I'd like to keep it that way. If you don't mind."

"I don't mind. The truth is, riding up here in that thing made me feel like I was seventeen. The Jag is kind of stodgy if you know what I mean."

"I'll ride with you to the gate." Sara nodded as she climbed behind the wheel. At the gate Dallas pressed the button to open the gates. He leaned over and kissed her full on the lips. "I wanted to do that all night," he blurted.

Thirty seconds was all she had to get through the gate. "Guess what?" she shouted over her shoulder. "I did too." Dallas's booming laughter stayed with her until silvery moonlight slid behind its protective night cover. The velvety darkness prevented her from seeing a black BMW that picked her up halfway down the canyon. It stayed with her until she parked the Jeep inside the garage, the driver straining to see the house numbers outlined under the yellow glow of the porch light.

Sara tiptoed up the stairs, careful not to step on the fourth step from the bottom. She continued to tiptoe down the hall to her room.

"Hold it right there, Doctor. I want to see those notes. No, I did not wait up. I was asleep but heard you drive into the garage. It's okay that you woke me. Hank and I had a fight, and that's why I came home. Come on, sit here on the side of the bed and tell me everything. Don't leave out the good parts either."

"Why did you and Hank fight?"

"He said he wasn't going on the ski trip. The ski trip was his idea. I got mad, and then he got mad. We paid our money, and half of it is nonrefundable. I'm going with or without him. I told him so, and he didn't like it. Now, tell me your stuff."

Sara flopped back onto the bed. "It was a nice evening. Actually it was kind of funny. Dallas cooked, and we had to eat in raincoats. He absolutely destroyed the kitchen. You never get spaghetti sauce off white walls. He put his cell phone in the ice maker so he didn't have to take calls from an old . . . I guess she was a girlfriend. She's one of the backup singers in the band. We talked for a long time. I like him. I really do. He's nothing like what they write about. He's a sweet and gentle and caring person. He didn't have much of a childhood. I think he has bad dreams. He said nice things to me all evening. He makes good spaghetti, too."

"That's it! There must be more. There has to be more. I want there to be more, Sara. Did he kiss you? Did he try to get you to stay over? I tell you everything."

"He kissed me as I was leaving. He asked me to come back this evening. I said I would. He said sweet things. We shared a bottle of wine. That's it. Listen, Carly, you can't tell anyone the things I tell you. He's so paranoid about the tabloids writing stuff about him. I want your word. Don't even tell Hank."

"I promise. Did you want more? Tell the truth. Would you have stayed if he asked you?"

"No. We're friends getting to know one another. Later on it might be a different story. I'm going to cook Thanksgiving dinner for us at his house. We sort of made plans for Christmas. With you going away, I thought it would be okay. He doesn't seem to know what a family holiday is all about because he was always on the road entertaining during the holidays. Can you imagine?"

"I'm trying to, Sara. If you're telling me the truth and there isn't any *good* stuff, then I'm going to say good night."

"Good night, Carly."

"Sara, do you really like him? You know, *really* like him?"

"Yes, I really like him. I think I'm going to like him more in the days to come. Sleep tight. Call Hank in the morning and make up with him, or he'll be calling me all day at the hospital to plead his case."

"Okay. I'm glad you had such a good time, Sara."

"Me too."

Chapter Four

Heads turned, but then heads always turned when Adam Lord walked into a room. His loose-limbed stride seemed to say, I'm here. Men said he had a presence. Women said it was his striking looks and the Armani clothes he wore to perfection that caused them to take a second look. The truth was, very few people knew Adam Lord's name. When a commanding person like Adam walked into a restaurant and was given the best table in the house one understood implicitly that someone of importance was in their midst.

Oblivious to the admiring glances and fawning waiters, Adam slid into the booth he'd requested at the far end of the restaurant. Almost immediately a scotch on the rocks was placed in front of him. He drank rapidly, at the same time raising his index finger to signal for a second drink. With his right hand he was busily punching out numbers on his cell phone. A frown crossed his features when he was informed the number he was dialing was no longer in service. He made three more calls in rapid succession demanding the new number for his brother. Once he raised his voice an octave, an implied threat in his tone. It produced the desired results. A second later he punched out the new numbers. His fingers drummed on the tabletop as he waited for Dallas's voice to come over the wire.

"Dallas, it's Adam. It would be nice if just once you let me in on what you're doing. How much trouble is it to call and give me your new number? I'm not even going to ask why you have a new number."

"Where *did* you get this number, Adam? Never mind. You're the man who can do anything, anytime, anyplace. I put the phone in the freezer and the wires froze. I'm on R & R, but then you know that. That means no business, so what do you want, Adam?"

"I wanted to tell you I was sorry I couldn't make it back for Billy's funeral. I sent flowers and a fruit basket. I had some masses said at St. Steven's. I also sent Nancy a letter. I'm truly sorry, Dallas. I know what Billy's friendship meant to you."

Dallas's voice was bitter. "Sure you're sorry. Tell the truth, Adam. You're worried about what Billy's death will do to the band. You don't give a hoot about Billy. He was a guitar to you, not a person."

"For God's sake, Dallas, that's not true. I knew Billy just as long as you did. He was your best friend, but he was my friend, too."

"Is this where you go into that tired old song about we'd all be nothing if it wasn't for you? We know that. The reason we know that, Adam, is because you jam it down our throats on a weekly basis. It's starting to get real old. I don't want to talk about this."

"You need to grow up, Dallas, and take responsibility. An almost forty-year-old rock star who doesn't have his shit in one sock is pretty pathetic. No, I do not, nor have I ever jammed anything down your throat, Dallas. Where in the hell is this coming from? Are you by any chance referring to all the papers you and the guys have to sign? You have to do that, Dallas, in order to have pension funds, health insurance, mortgages, car payments, the different foundations, and everything else you and the band have. I have no control over state and federal taxes, but you still have to sign papers. If I didn't stay on top of you guys and keep you to a schedule, you'd be playing in Burger King parking lots. Life simply is not one tune after another."

"I'm getting real tired of hearing this, Adam. Can't you leave me alone for a while? I need time to think. I need to figure out how I'm going to go on without Billy. I don't want to talk about tours, business, or health insurance. I might even be getting married one of these days."

"Sandi Sims is a twit. You'll be divorced in three months. Think things through before you go off half-cocked."

"Stay out of my personal life, Adam. I can screw it up on my own without any help from you. I know you have other complaints, so let's get them out of the way."

"Dallas, give me one good reason why you bought three BMWs and gave them away to three punks."

"First of all, they weren't punks. They were college kids who helped us when the tour bus broke down. They chauffeured us around, fed us, made sure the bus got fixed, and shook our hands. They did it for five goddamn days. Hell, they even did our laundry. That means they ironed our shirts. They bought root beer for Billy. It was my way of saying thank you. They honest to God didn't want to accept the cars. I had to write notes to their parents explaining the gift. I'd do it again, too."

Adam sighed as he rubbed at his eyes. He hadn't slept in thirty-six hours. "Tell me now what it is you plan to do for Billy's father. I know you're going to do something, so let's get the wheels in motion. There's no need to do anything, but if you feel it's something you want to do, I certainly won't stop you. I just want you to know that it has been taken care of. Billy had a two-million-dollar life-insurance policy payable to his father. I'm the trustee of the estate. We set it up that way in case anything happened to Billy. I'm sick and tired of your surprises, Dallas."

"Then quit, Adam. I don't know what I'm going to do about Billy's dad. I will do something, though. I don't want to do this anymore. I'm tired. I'm tired to my soul, Adam. I'm telling you now I don't want to do the next tour. Cancel it."

"When are you going to grow up and deal with reality, Dallas? We committed. That means we—as in you and I—gave our professional word. The guys signed on, too. *You* signed for it. You don't just cancel a tour because suddenly you feel tired. I don't feel like having my ass sued off. If you check with the guys, I'm certain they'll tell you the same thing. What about the band? What are they supposed to do? You have a payroll. Money has been paid out. This isn't some Mickey Mouse operation, Dallas. People will lose their jobs if you cancel. Are you going to go on prime-time television and tell your fans you're sorry but you're *tired?* No one is irreplaceable, Dallas. There's someone out there almost as good as Billy. Maybe even better. It will be an adjustment. Life goes on. It has to go on. It's all we have. It's called dealing with life."

"Get a life already, Adam, and stop running mine."

Adam clenched his teeth. "I don't run your life, Dallas. I run the business side of your life. If I didn't, you'd be in some honky-tonk singing for your supper."

"You don't know that any more than I know that. Are you going to tell me I'm slow-witted now? It's what you think, isn't it?"

Adam groaned. "I'm not going to tell you any such thing. You're wrong. I do know what would happen if I wasn't around. The root-beer commercial is proof. Sometimes I wonder how the hell you find your way back home. Most times you don't have enough sense to come in out of the rain. You're almost forty years old and all you do is sing and float through life. Excuse me, you write music, too. Dump the twit and get back on track. I don't like talking to you like this, Dallas. I don't want either one of us to say things we'll regret."

"Fuck you, Adam. I'm sorry you ever gave me that harmonica. That's what started all of this. Don't ever make the mistake of sticking your nose into my private life again. If you do, you're on the street. Don't call me, I'll call you. Then again, maybe I won't."

Adam squeezed his eyes shut as he pressed the End button and returned his cell phone to his briefcase. He was so tired he could barely keep his eyes open. His shoulders started to slump. He had this same conversation with Dallas on a monthly basis. Maybe it was time to pack it in and sit in the sunshine. This time, though, there was something different in his brother's voice. It must be the twit. Tramp was more like it. He wished then the way he wished every day of his life that Dallas would find and fall in love with a nice, normal girl who would love him the way he deserved to be loved and not for who he was or what he could provide in the way of material things. He tried to shrug off the feelings, but it wasn't working. This time he was strung tighter than Dallas's guitar strings. *I don't want to do this anymore either,* he admitted to himself. *I haven't wanted to do it for the past three years, but I kept at it because of Dallas and the guys. Maybe this time, Dallas means business and really is going to pack it in. Maybe. Maybe a lot of things.*

A small black notebook, properly embossed, materialized in his hand. He didn't remember withdrawing it from the inside pocket of his jacket. He scribbled furiously. A full investigative report of Sandi Sims was definitely in order. He should have done it months ago.

"Mr. Lord?"

"Yes. Mr. Soung? Please, sit down." The man's handshake was bone-crushing. Adam nodded approvingly. "What will you have to drink?"

"Tea will be fine. We are in agreement then on the terms, Mr. Lord?"

"We are in agreement, Mr. Soung. I finalized everything with your people yesterday in Hong Kong. Signing the agreement makes it a done deal. The Asian tour will begin in Hong Kong on the fifth day of January." Dallas's words ringing in his ears, he added, "Barring any unforeseen events that we'll deal with at that time."

Soung nodded, his opaque eyes scanning the two contracts in front of him, one in English and one in Chinese. He signed his name with a flourish. Adam did the same. "Our binder check in the amount of $10,000,000," he said, handing Adam a yellow check. "You must sign the release form." Adam signed his name a second time. The check went into his briefcase.

"We have your assurances, then, that Mr. Sweet's demise will change nothing. We wish to extend our condolences to you and Mr. Sweet's family."

"Thank you. You have my assurance the fans will be satisfied. No one, Mr. Soung, is indispensable."

"I have read much about the closeness your brother shared with Mr. Sweet. He is grieving, yes?"

"Yes, he is grieving. One must grieve first

in order to progress with whatever life has in store for us."

"Ah, yes. Old Chinese proverb, no? We will make a toast, Mr. Lord, to our mutual success. Shall we drink to life and whatever is in store for . . . all of us?"

A chill ran up Adam's arms. The tour damn well better come off as scheduled. He nodded, his expression as inscrutable as that of the man sitting across from him.

"Will you be staying in New York, Mr. Lord?" Soung asked.

"I'll be leaving for Los Angeles tomorrow morning. You have my number should you wish to reach me. For any reason."

"I understand the pine nut chicken is very good. My secretary tells me they put a mystery spice in the sauce."

Adam forced a smile. "I love a good mystery." He hated small talk. All he wanted to do was go back to his hotel and think about Dallas's ominous words and the intricately worded contract he'd just signed for Dallas Lord and the Canyon River Band. He needed a shower and sixteen straight hours of sleep.

* * *

Adam rolled over, cracked one eyelid. It was dark, the glowing numerals of the bedside clock straight up. Midnight. Should he go back to sleep or get up? If he went back to sleep, he would dream the same terrible, horrifying dream that had plagued him for years. Getting by on a few hours' sleep for the past week, jet lag, Billy Sweet's demise, and his worry about Dallas demanded he close his eyes to seek the rest his body needed.

His sleep was restless, fitful, the way it always was before the dream started. He knew he should get up, but his weary body slipped over the edge.

"Get out of the tree, Dallas. Tell him to get out of the tree, Billy. Uncle Charlie said we shouldn't climb the tree. Tell him to come down."

"He ain't gonna listen to me, Adam. He likes to sit up there and look at the sun through the leaves. You're his brother. You climb up and git him."

"I'm climbing up to get you, Dallas. Uncle Charlie is going to give us both a good strapping. You're going to fall, and Uncle Charlie won't take you to the hospital. Come

on, Dallas. If you come down, I'll give you a present. A really good present."

"I don't want no present. Go away, and Uncle Charlie won't know I'm up here. Want an apple? You want an apple, Billy?"

Ten-year-old Adam stared up at his seven-year-old brother. "Don't go any higher, Dallas. It's almost suppertime, Dallas. Uncle Charlie will be home from work real soon."

"I don't want any supper. I'll eat an apple."

"Them apples ain't ripe yet," Billy called from the base of the tree.

"There's a real red one right over there. I just have to crawl out and reach for it. Do you want one, Adam? Do you, Billy?"

"I gotta go home, Dallas. I'll see you tomorrow."

"I'm going too," Adam shouted. "Stay up there forever. See if I care."

Dallas snaked his way out to the skinny limb that held the red apple. He reached for it just as the limb snapped. His squeal of fright brought his brother and friend on the run.

"Oh jeez, oh jeez. Hey, Dallas, wake up. Look how white his face is, Adam. We have to do something."

Adam leaned down and pressed his ear to his brother's chest the way he'd seen actors do in the movies.

"His heart's beating."

"I gotta go home," Billy Sweet said. "You said his heart is beating, so that means he ain't gonna die."

"Some friend you are, Billy Sweet."

"You shoulda climbed up and brung him down. You're his brother, so you're supposed to take care of him. Pour some water over him. I gotta go, Adam."

"Then go. If Dallas dies, I won't even tell you. You don't even care if he dies. I'm gonna remember this, Billy Sweet. You see if I don't."

Adam hunkered down next to his brother. Should he call his aunt Millie or not? She wasn't much good for anything if she spent the afternoon drinking wine. By the time his uncle Charlie came home he'd be liquored up, too. "Wake up, Dallas. I don't want you to die. If you die, I won't have anyone left. Soon as I'm old enough, we're lighting out of here. I'll get some kind of job and take care of you. Wake up, Dallas. I'll get you that present I promised. I swear I will." A tear *splashed down on his brother's face. Adam wiped at it with his finger.*

When darkness settled he heard his brother moan. "You okay, Dallas? Can you move your arms and legs and stuff?"

"Yeah, why?"

"You fell out of the tree."

"How come it's dark?"

"Cause it's night, that's why."

"My head feels funny. You look funny."

"Maybe you should lay still for a while." Adam's heart pounded in his chest. "What do you mean when you say your head feels funny and I look funny?"

"I can't see good. You have a whole bunch of eyes. Am I gonna die, Adam?"

"Nah. You just whacked your head good. As long as your heart beats, that means you're okay. You scared me, Dallas. Why didn't you listen to me? You were lucky this time. You swear to me right now, right this minute, that you will always listen to me. That means forever and ever. If you swear, then I swear I will always take care of you. I won't forget about the present either."

"I never got any presents, did I, Adam?"

"This is going to be the first one. It's going to be the best." His heart still thundering in

his chest, Adam said, "Do I still look like I have a bunch of eyes?"

"Yeah."

"Maybe I should take you to the doctor's, Dallas. I could pull you in the wagon. We don't have any money to pay, though."

"Maybe if I take a nap for a little bit, your eyes will go away. Will you stay here with me?"

"Sure. I'm your brother. That shit-ass Billy hightailed it home. What kind of friend is that?"

"Stay here with me, Adam. I'm going to sleep now."

"Okay, Dallas. I won't move."

It was almost light when Dallas finally woke. He pinched Adam, who jerked to wakefulness. "Whasamatter?" he asked groggily.

"I woke up. My back hurts, and I have to pee."

"Wait a minute. How many eyes do I have?"

"Two. Boy, that's a stupid question."

"That's good. That means you're okay."

"Thanks for staying with me, Adam."

"I'm your brother, Dallas. We have to look out for each other."

Adam rolled over, his legs fighting with the coverlet. His head pounded, and he was drenched with sweat. The dream was so real, so vivid, it was as though it had happened yesterday instead of thirty-one years ago.

His head in his hands, Adam fought the sobs that tore at his throat. "I should have taken him to the doctor's. Why didn't I? Because I was ten years old and stupid, that's why."

Dallas had never been the same after his fall. Even Billy noticed the change, but he kept his thoughts to himself. The teachers at school said Dallas had a learning disability, but they didn't say that until Dallas was in the seventh grade. Charlie and Millie just shrugged. That was when Adam learned to wheel and deal, so Dallas could get through school. Even with all the deals he cut with other kids to do Dallas's homework, whisper answers to him on verbal quizzes, and switch test papers, Dallas managed to graduate from high school last in his class. The only thing Dallas excelled in was music. As one music instructor put it, Dallas had the beat.

Adam never begrudged the hard life or his

responsibilities to Dallas, even when he went to college and worked a full-time job. Academics came easy to him, and Dallas did his best to carry his own weight by singing and playing his harmonica in bars and sleazy supper clubs with Billy Sweet taking up the slack when it was time for midterms and final exams. By the time Adam graduated from law school, he was so far in debt he didn't know where to turn. It was Dallas's idea to start up the Canyon River Band with a new sound he said would rock the music world. When Dallas asked him to manage the band and put his career on hold, he'd agreed; within two years Dallas Lord and the Canyon River Band had taken off like the proverbial rocket to land at the coveted number one spot on the charts. The rest was history.

Damn, he was wide-awake now. He reached out for the phone. Twenty-four-hour room service was something he was used to. He ordered a large pot of coffee and two sticky buns.

When the coffee arrived he gulped at it, his eyes on the television, the volume turned low so the sound wouldn't carry to the guest in the next room. He thought about his own life. How much longer could he manage the conglomerate that was the result of Dallas and the band? More to the point, did he even want to continue? He was sick of slick promoters trying to put one over on him, sick of the travel, sick of the hotels and living out of a suitcase. Where were his roots, his stability? He was almost forty-two years old. He should be married with a house, kids, and a couple of dogs. Hell, he didn't even have a girlfriend.

Maybe it was time to take Dallas seriously and cut him loose. They could go out while they were still on top. Neither he nor Dallas would have to worry about money for the rest of their lives. With his expert management they could live luxurious lives. Most of the band, those members who had turned their investments over to him, were in the same financial situation. Several of the guys had taken over their own portfolios. It had been a slap in the face at the time, but he had agreed. He neither knew nor cared how well their investments performed.

What he did care about was Billy Sweet's family. Billy hadn't cared about things like financial security and health insurance. Adam had practically had to hog-tie him to go for the physical for the five-million-dollar life-insurance policy for his family. If Nancy invested wisely, the money would take care of her and the girls for the rest of their lives. Thank God he'd had the foresight to insist on a second policy when he found out about Billy's dad. Mr. Sweet would never want for anything. He lived in his own little cottage in an upscale retirement community with round-the-clock attendants. That would continue until the day Mr. Sweet joined his son.

Did he have regrets about giving up his life for Dallas? Once in a while, when Dallas went off on him the way he had last night.

Adam thought about the ten-million-dollar check in his briefcase. Was Dallas blowing smoke? Was he pushing his buttons out of frustration and grief? Was he afraid he couldn't carry on without Billy? Did Dallas have secret fears about his own abilities that he didn't care to share with his older brother?

Adam's head dropped into his hands when he remembered Dallas coming to him one day and asking why he couldn't function efficiently in the outside world. He'd point-blank asked him if he was retarded. Instead of answering his brother, he'd thrown the question back to him. "Do you think you're retarded?" Dallas had just stared at him and walked away. What the hell did retarded mean anyway? How could somebody with Dallas's gift be retarded? How could he write songs, record them, and then perform them on a live stage for millions of people if there was something wrong with his mind? And if there was—and he didn't believe that for one minute—then it was because of falling out of that tree. It was Adam's fault for not taking him to a doctor. Son of a bitch!

Maybe he should take a step backward and give Dallas the freedom he wanted. Instead of going to Los Angeles, he could change his ticket and go to South Carolina. He could call ahead and have someone come in to get the fifteen-room house on Battery ready. He could spend the next two months doing whatever he wanted to do. He could sleep, read, watch stupid shows on television, putter in the walled garden, prepare for the holidays, throw a party. Hell, he might even get a Christmas tree, a real one that would smell up the whole house. He'd go to Harris Teeter and stock his pantry and refrigerator the way normal people did. He'd go to the post office, the bank, eat lunch out, stroll through the marketplace. Things he had promised himself he'd do when he bought and renovated the historical house. Ha! He hadn't been in the house in two years.

He'd spent over a million dollars renovating the house and the walled gardens with the hope that someday he'd move there and settle down. Maybe this was the someday he'd been waiting for.

But how was he going to cut Dallas out of his life? By his own choice, he could never do it. If Dallas took matters into his own hands, there was nothing he could do but stand in the wings and be ready to pick up the pieces if he fell. If it meant calling it quits, then that's the way it would be.

Sweat beaded on Adam's brow. What would happen to Dallas if he broke up the band and married Sandi Sims? How long would it take her to realize he didn't have both paddles in the water? Would she go to the tabloids? Of course she would, and she'd get seven figures for her story. Dallas would be devastated and withdraw further from the real world. He was already on the edge because of Billy's death.

"I hate this business. I fucking hate it!"

Adam hissed through his clenched teeth. Damage control. One always had to be prepared and be one step ahead of the ghouls. He needed a plan. A headache started to hammer behind his eyes. He closed his eyes tight to stop them from burning. Maybe he should try for sleep again. "Oh, no!" he muttered. If he went to sleep again with this headache, his other nightmare would take over. There was no way he was going to deal with a set of parents who had left him and his brother on the steps of the police station and never come back for them. He bolted for the shower, his personal demons thrashing at his heels.

At eight-fifteen, Adam was airborne. He'd taken care of business as soon as it grew light. A cleaning service would have his house on the Charleston Battery aired and cleaned by noon. From his upstairs bedroom, he could see Fort Sumter off in the distance. He tried to look forward to getting there, but his thoughts continued to drift to the ominous things Dallas had said. The investigative team of Moody & Moody had been hired to do a comprehensive background check on one Sandi Sims. The

$10,000,000 check had been deposited on his way to the airport via the night deposit slot. As far as he was concerned he was a free agent until January 2 or until his brother Dallas severed the tie that bound them together.

Adam stopped for lunch at Magnolias, ordering a third cup of coffee until he was certain the cleaning crew would be finished with his house. With no taxi in sight he opted to walk to the Battery, asking the hostess if she would hold his bags, he would pick them up later. A folded bill was pressed into her hand.

Adam sucked in his breath when he walked up the steps of his house. He looked around. It would have been so wonderful to grow up in a house like this, with a loving family. Now, nearly forty-two years old, he finally had a house, but no family of his own. He let himself in. The fresh scent of citrus assailed his nostrils. Everything sparkled. The heart of pine floor gleamed beneath the Persian rugs. He'd furnished the house himself, buying a piece here and there and having it shipped from every part of the world. Nothing matched, but he didn't care. The house looked as if someone actually lived in it. It was nothing like the sterile, institutional house Dallas lived in, and for that Adam was grateful.

The kitchen was his favorite room. It, too, had been restored to its original beauty. The old oak rocker that was big enough for two people sat next to the rebuilt cavernous fireplace. The old Charlestonian brick had been taken out, brick by brick, scraped clean and reused. It matched the brick floor to perfection. Double-hung windows over the stainless-steel sink overlooked his garden and the three-hundred-year-old angel oak that sat in the middle, its branches shading the entire garden like a giant umbrella. All he had to do was open his kitchen door, walk down two steps, and he would be in another world. The garden was the main reason he'd bought the place.

Adam's eyes fell on the note hanging from the refrigerator door. He plucked it off.

Dear Mr. Lord,
We followed your instructions to the letter. Our bill is in your mailbox. We raked and blew out all the dead debris in the garden and cleaned the benches and chairs. We did not disturb your dog and

the pups. We did, however, feed them
and left some extra food. The bill for the
dog food is stapled to our invoice. You
have a lovely home. Thank you for calling Merry Maids Cleaning Service.

Sincerely,

Allison Meyers

Dog? Pups? Adam raced to the garden.
He dropped to his haunches to stare at the
animal who was eyeing him with suspicion.
When he spoke, his voice was soft and gentle. "It's going to get cold out here tonight. I
can get you a nice warm blanket and make
a fire if you want to come inside. These little
guys look like they might like that. I'm harm-
less, I want you to know that. I'm not even
going to ask how you got in here. You can
stay, though. I'll be glad for the company. I
always wanted a dog. Six pups, huh? I'm the
guy that can buy the dog food if you want to
stay." He held out his hand for the dog to
sniff. "I'm going to leave the kitchen door
open, and then I'm going to build a fire. You
come in when you're ready."

Inside the house, Adam took the polished
steps two at a time. The linen closet held
the finest linens, the warmest comforters,

That is so stupid—will be useless shortly,

the fluffiest towels money could buy. He whipped out a thousand-dollar goosedown comforter and a pile of soft yellow towels. He took the steps at a gallop, missing the last three completely as he ran back to the kitchen. He doubled the comforter in front of the fireplace and added the towels to make a perfect nest for his new houseguest.

Within minutes he had a fire blazing. His eye on the door, he picked up the phone to call Harris Teeter. "Listen, I need some groceries, and I can't get out. Whatever you charge for delivery is okay with me as long as you bring the stuff right away. I want five pounds of chicken livers and gizzards, some baby food. Yeah, yeah, mix and match sounds good. What's pablum? Okay, throw some of that in. Dog cookies. Milk, coffee, eggs, bacon, orange juice. Thirty minutes. Great." Adam rattled off his address just as the dog approached the open doorway.

Adam sat down on the rocker. "Come on in. Real food is on the way. You can bring the kids in when you're ready. That's your bed," he said, motioning to the folded comforter. The dog, a spaniel of some sort, eyed him warily. She advanced slowly, sniffing and looking around. She pawed at the comforter, sniffing the towels, one eye on Adam. He continued to rock, his voice low and gentle when he talked to her. Satisfied, the spaniel turned and went back to the garden. She returned six times, carrying each pup by the scruff of the neck, settling them one by one on the fluffy yellow towels on top of the comforter. Adam thought he heard her sigh when she settled herself next to her offspring.

Should he close the door or not? Maybe he'd leave it open a little so she could go in and out. On the other hand, leaving it open might cause a draft. He knew diddly-squat about dogs or puppies, but if he had to take a guess, he'd say the pups were newborn. Drafts were not good. He continued to talk as he got up from the chair to cross the kitchen floor to close the door. He later swore the dog sighed again when she realized she was indoors and wouldn't be put out in the cold, damp garden with her new pups.

Ten minutes later the groceries arrived. Adam made coffee while the chicken livers were frying. The spaniel's soulful eyes followed his every move. When the livers cooled, Adam scooped them onto a dish mixed with a scrambled egg. He set the dish down next to the comforter. When the spaniel made no move to go to the food, Adam sat down on the floor and hand-fed her. She took the food daintily, a small bit at a time. He held out a dish of water, watching as she drank.

Adam added another log to the fire and poured himself a cup of coffee. He wasn't going anywhere. He had a family to take care of. All he had to do was call the restaurant to ask them to bring his bags over. "Just put the bags on the steps. I'll leave twenty bucks for your efforts in an envelope."

Twenty-five minutes later his bags were inside, and he was back on the rocking chair, coffee in hand, the television on the counter tuned to the early-evening news. The dog and her pups slept contentedly. Adam wished there was someone he could call to tell about the past hours. He wondered what Dallas would say.

Adam dozed in the rocking chair. For the first time in years he felt contented, at peace with himself. He slipped into a deep, peaceful, dreamless sleep.

Chapter Five

"Sara, are you going back to the canyon this evening?"

"Yes. Why do you ask?"

"I guess I'm kind of wondering why you never invite Dallas to come here or why the two of you don't, you know, do the town. I understand the publicity thing, but there are ways to get around that. What *do* you do up there? You've been seeing him for almost a month now. Nothing's happened, according to you. You say you're just friends. Is there something you aren't telling me? We've always shared everything. I'm starting to worry about you. You have this pensive look in your eyes all the time. Nellie mentioned it to me today. Are you starting to fall in love with Dallas Lord? Some of the edge should be off his grief by now. If my opinion counts for anything, I think he's starting to depend on you. That can't be good. For either one of you."

"You always did have an active imagination, Carly. We're just friends. If you led the kind of life Dallas has been living all these years, you would want some private time, too. We watch movies, take walks, listen to music, and we talk. He's torn right now. He doesn't know if he should cancel the tour and break up the band. Part of him wants to do it, and part of him doesn't. He also has to find a replacement for Billy Sweet. He views that as some kind of betrayal on his part and told me he had a terrible row with his brother. The way Dallas talks about him he must be the most hateful person walking the earth. He said Adam let him down. He didn't elaborate beyond that. The other thing is, he doesn't want my privacy invaded. Yours would be, too. I'm surprised no one has found out about me. What else do you want to know?"

"Are you serious about him, Sara?"

"I don't know. I like him tremendously but . . ."

"But what?"

Sara took so long to respond that Carly had to prod her. "I don't know. Sometimes he seems so . . . he's somewhere else even though he's talking to me. I'm embarrassed and even ashamed to say this, but sometimes I don't think he's . . . literate. I find myself testing him in little ways. I try to be clever and sometimes he picks up on it. It's unsettling. He says things like, oh, you're playing Adam's game. I do like him. A lot. Sometimes I see myself in him. He seems to need me. For now. There are days when I think I need him. He's so sweet. He's kind and gentle. He doesn't put the moves on me. He's always complimentary. He tries very hard to please me."

"And you haven't been to bed with him?"

"No. He's kissed me, though. The world more or less exploded if that's your next question."

"And?"

"That's it. He tells me he trusts me. He places great store in trust. It might have something to do with my being a doctor. He trusts Adam, but he doesn't like him. I can't figure that out."

"Does anyone call or visit?"

"No. And to my knowledge he doesn't call anyone."

"What does he do all day when you aren't there?"

"He says he writes songs."

"Why would he do that if he's going to break up the band?"

"I don't know, Carly."

"Maybe this isn't a healthy relationship."

"He needs me at this time. Yes, he depends on me, but I think it's a temporary dependency. I look forward to spending time with him. He lost his best and only friend. He's devastated."

"Aha! Thirty-eight-year-old men are not supposed to need anyone. Boy, this guy is nothing like they portray him in those supermarket rags if what you say is true. What would happen if you didn't go up there every night?"

Sara shrugged. "He'd probably watch a movie by himself. Is that so terrible?"

"I think you're getting involved in something you aren't going to be able to deal with later. I know you, Sara, you commit and you trench in. He doesn't sound to me like he's wrapped too tight."

"That's a terrible thing to say. People react differently to grief. Look, I can wean myself away from him if I want to. Believe it or not, I enjoy his company. He can make me laugh, and I can make him laugh. I'm getting pretty sick of root beer, though. He guzzles it by the gallon. Don't worry about me and tell Nellie to stop worrying, too."

"Oh, Sara, I forgot to tell you. You can't go to Dallas's this evening. Nellie fixed things up with that vet. He's stopping by this evening to take you out for coffee. I don't know how I could have forgotten to tell you that."

"She did *what?*"

"You heard me the first time, and the doorbell is ringing. Guess it's him."

The panic on her sister's face made Carly laugh.

"Get rid of him, Carly."

"Oh, no. Nellie said you said it was okay."

"That was a month ago. He was a no-show. I waited for two hours."

"Nellie said she told you this morning and you said, 'uh-huh.' You better open the door, Sara. I'll call Dallas and tell him you're running late, or should I cancel you for this evening?"

"Cancel me," Sara barked as she yanked at the heavy front door.

Standing in front of her was one of the handsomest men she'd ever seen in her life.

"Dr. Killian, I'm Steven McGuire. I think we have a coffee date."

"Yes, Please, come in. Just let me get a sweater."

"Listen, if this is a bad time, we can do it some other time. You have the look that says, oh, God, I forgot."

Straining to hear Carly's voice in the kitchen, Sara's tone was more brisk than she intended. "Why would you say something like that?"

"Body language. The look in your eye. You're overdressed for a coffeehouse."

"You certainly know how to make a girl feel at ease," Sara snapped.

"This *is* a bad time. My mother always told me to be wary of women who snap at a guy on the first date. I'll call you." He was out of the door and walking down the walkway to his car before Sara could think of a suitable retort.

"Guess you're going to have to stay home tonight," Carly said, her voice sly. "Dallas said okay, and he hopes you have a good time."

"You told him the truth! For God's sake, why?"

"You didn't tell me to lie. He didn't sound like he cared one way or another. I'd go for the bird in the hand. He's almost to his car.

If you hurry, you can catch him. He's a hunk. A guy that good-looking should not be on the loose."

"Stevennnn. Wait!"

Carly watched from the window as Sara tried to explain the misunderstanding. Her eyes intent, she ran the conversation she'd had with Dallas Lord over in her mind. He'd sounded puzzled and vague. The conversation had been short, but in her opinion he'd become distraught when she mentioned the name Dr. McGuire. She'd been careful to stress the word "friend" and doctor in regard to Steven McGuire, and she didn't know why. Something wasn't right where her sister was concerned, and she couldn't pinpoint that either. When Sara climbed into Steven McGuire's Saab, Carly sat down on the sofa and thought back to the time Dallas Lord had spent at Billy Sweet's bedside. It wasn't anything he said, and it wasn't the way he'd looked. It was what he *did*. He'd hummed the whole time he was in the ICU. Humming to the sounds of the machinery Billy Sweet was hooked up to. He'd even tapped his foot. Once he'd demanded to know if the sound of the respirator *ever* changed. When she said no, he stopped humming and tapping his foot. How strange that she should be thinking about that now. She shrugged. She looked at her watch. Fifteen minutes to get ready for her date with Hank. Dallas Lord was her sister's business, not hers.

"Are you sure you don't mind waiting, Steven? I only have two patients I want to check on."

"Not at all. You were a real sport going to the clinic with me to check on Bessie. How could I do less? A patient is a patient even if yours is two-legged and mine is four-legged. I hope yours is resting as comfortably as my sheperd."

"Mrs. Osborne is old, and she's frightened. Having your gall bladder taken out at the age of seventy-six is traumatic. She's got herself convinced some state agency is going to slap her in a nursing home. Nellie and I try to spend as much time with her as we can to reassure her it isn't going to happen. Being old and alone is very frightening."

"Why do you think I put all that junk in Bessie's cage? She'd old, too. She cuddles with her teddy bear and blanket. I think she has a few good years left. I hope the same applies to your Mrs. Osborne. Take your time. I'll balance my checkbook while I wait."

She looks like a precocious squirrel, Sara thought when she entered Sadie Osborne's room. "You're supposed to be sleeping, Mrs. Osborne. It's almost midnight. What's wrong? Please, I can't understand what you're saying if you keep crying. Tell me what happened."

"Dr. Granger came in a while ago, and he said they're sending me to one of those centers tomorrow."

"That's not true, Mrs. Osborne. Dr. Granger is mistaken. You're going home tomorrow, and Social Services is sending someone to help out four hours a day. Nellie and I arranged it all. One of our volunteers is going to drive you home in the morning when I discharge you."

"He said they're taking me at nine o'clock. He showed me the paperwork. One of the nurses packed my bag. I want to go home. My animals miss me. I know they miss me because I miss them. My neighbor is taking care of them, but it is such an imposition."

"I'll straighten everything out. Is everything else okay? Let's take your blood pressure and temperature first, though. You've been walking around with the walker, haven't you? No dizzy spells or rapid heartbeat?"

"No."

"Tell me something, Mrs. Osborne. I know it's late, but if I discharge you now, would you object to my taking you home?"

"God love a saint. I would not object at all."

"I'll be back in a few minutes."

Sara tore down the hall to the doctor's lounge where Dr. Granger was sipping coffee and leafing through *Playboy* magazine. She ripped the magazine out of his hands and tossed it across the room. "How dare you upset Mrs. Osborne," she almost shouted. "You had no right, Granger, to say one word to my patient. If you ever do it again, I'll drag you before the board. Mrs. Osborne is not going to a rehab center. She's going home. In fact, Granger, she's going home tonight, and I'm taking her. She's frail and she's scared. You with your thoughtless know-it-all attitude could have brought on a heart attack. I smell liquor on your breath, too. Push me one more time, Granger, and it's all over."

"Get off it, Sara. Who the hell do you think you are? First of all, I was following orders. Addison McKinley, you do know who he is, don't you? He signs our paychecks in case you forgot. McKinley told me to inform her of his decision. I was following orders."

"Mrs. Osborne is my patient. I decide where she goes and when she goes. Not you and not Addison McKinley. How dare you attempt to take her dignity away. How dare you, Granger! Mess with me one more time and I'll . . ."

"You'll what?" Granger sneered.

"I'll personally kick your ass all the way to the Santa Monica Freeway. Me. By myself. Alone. With no help. On top of that, I'll take out a full-page ad in the *LA Times* telling the entire city what a crapola doctor you are. I think it's safe to say every nurse and staff member in this hospital will donate to the cost of the ad."

The senior doctor tried to bluster. "Jesus, you get your panties in a wad real easy. For God's sake, she's just an old lady who has lived her life. Inside of a month she'll be back here, and you know it. She belongs in the center where people can watch over her."

"Read my lips, Granger. I didn't save that woman's life so you could screw it up. She belongs at home with her things and her animals and not in some rehab center where she'll be a Social Security number and nothing more. Don't for one minute think I don't know you have a vested interest in that rehab center. What's your percentage, twenty-five, thirty percent? I'm beginning to think I might make a good whistle-blower. Now, get the hell out of my way before I do something *you'll* regret."

Seething with fury, Sara stopped at the nurse's station long enough to write Sadie Osborne's discharge and to call Nellie. "I'm going to take her home, Nellie. I don't want a snafu tomorrow morning. The poor thing is so rattled she's been crying all evening. I would appreciate it if you could meet me at her house. I did ream him out, Nellie. I'll probably get fired in the morning. Of course Addison has a percentage. Not Harry, though. It's a dollar thing, Nellie. No, I am not sorry. I'd do it again. We should be there in about forty-five minutes. Yes, Nellie, he's very nice. Exceptionally nice. No, there were no sparks. I think he'll make a very good friend. I'll see you later."

Sadie Osborne was decked out in her fuzzy robe, raincoat and yellow boots when Sara entered her room. Her small satchel was next to her walker. "I'm ready, Dr. Killian."

"Then let's get this show on the road. Hop in this wheelchair. It's the rule as you well know. I'll bring the walker."

"They can't make me go tomorrow, can they?"

"Never. Listen to me, Mrs. Osborne. I'm going to tell you something I shouldn't. It's just between you and me for now. If at some later time you feel the need to mention what I'm about to tell you, it will be all right. But, not now. Lately, I just don't seem to care about a lot of things around here. The LifeQuest Rehab Center where they want to send you is owned by a group of doctors, two of whom practice here at Benton. It's to their advantage to send patients there. For you to go home won't put money in their pockets. If anyone from this hospital other than Nellie or I contact you, stand your ground. You are fine, Mrs. Osborne. Your arthritis is not life-threatening. You came through your surgery very nicely, and you rebounded better than I anticipated. You do not need to go into rehab. I told you this so you know your rights. As I said, it won't be wise for you to mention anything we discussed. For now."

"Dearie, my lips are zipped. I knew there was something weird about that doctor. He couldn't look me in the eye when he was telling me about the center. I knew it. I just knew it. Should I get a new bolt on my door?"

Sara had a bad moment then. Maybe she shouldn't have said what she did. She smiled then at the light of battle in the old lady's eyes. "I don't think that will be necessary, Mrs. Osborne."

Outside in the night air, Sadie Osborne threw her hands up in the air. "I feel like I've been sprung from jail. Do you have any idea of how good it feels to be going home? I know, Dr. Killian, that there isn't a sweeter word in the whole language than the word home."

"I think you're probably right. Ms. Osborne, this is Steven . . ."

"I know who he is. He takes care of my animals. We've never met socially, though. Dr. Killian sprung me from that . . . that squirrel house. What do you think of that, Steven?"

"Ah . . . is that what you did?" he said addressing Sara.

"I suppose you could say that. I discharged her tonight instead of tomorrow morning. She has no desire or interest in going to the LifeQuest center. Do you think you could lift her into the backseat while I return the wheelchair?"

"Sure."

An hour later Sara entered her house through the garage, tossing her purse and house keys on the kitchen counter. The clock said it was ten minutes past two. She could call Dallas if she wanted to. She could even take a run up to his estate. If she wanted to. She decided she didn't want to.

Sara reached for an apple and bit into it, juice running down her chin as she made her way to her bedroom. What she should do was sit down and think about Steven McGuire. He was everything Nellie said he was—charming, handsome, warm, considerate, and he hated root beer. They'd spent an enjoyable evening talking about four-legged versus two-legged patients. She liked his sense of humor. What she liked even more was the way he spoke about his family and his brothers and sisters. Obviously they were a close-knit family. What she liked most about him was the way he'd pitched in to help with Sadie Osborne without asking a lot of pointed questions. She'd allowed him to kiss her good night but it had been one of those brotherly kisses that friends give each other from time to time. Steven McGuire would be a friend, nothing more.

Sara finished the apple, wrapping the core in tissue before she tossed it in the wastepaper basket. Rummaging in her sewing box for a cigarette, she lit up. She'd given up both sewing and smoking long ago. A doctor who smoked did not instill confidence in his or her patients. She stared at the Surgeon General's warning on the side of the package. Defiantly, she puffed on the cigarette. She wasn't sure why. Dallas smoked. He said all the guys in the band smoked and so did his Adam. Not that that meant anything.

Tomorrow was her last day of work, providing she didn't get fired. The day after tomorrow was Thanksgiving. The following week was her first week of vacation, at which point she became a free agent. Last year she'd worked while she was in contract negotiations. She'd made up her mind that she wasn't going to do the same thing this year. This year she was going to wait it out, since she'd demanded a hefty salary increase. What would she do with her time? Steven McGuire said he could use her on a voluntary basis three afternoons a week. She'd halfway agreed.

Sara looked down at her hand holding the portable phone. She dialed Dallas's private number. It rang six times before it was picked up. "Hi, Dallas, it's Sara. I called to apologize and to say good night. It's a beautiful evening, isn't it?"

"How was your date?"

"It wasn't a date, Dallas. We just went out for coffee. You'd like Steven. What did you do all evening?"

"Nothing much. I watched some videos of the band. I had dinner. I talked to Nancy and the kids. Are you coming up tomorrow?"

"After work. It's my last day. Are you going to order the groceries, or shall I bring them with me?"

"I'll order them. Everything will be ready

when you get here. Why don't you plan on staying through the weekend. Bring your stuff with you. I was thinking, Sara, would you like to take a trip somewhere? How about New York? I'm sure I can come up with a suitable disguise so we aren't bothered. Think about it."

"I'll think about it. I've got to be up early so I'll say good night. Oh, Dallas, have you been starting up my car?"

"Yes. I drive it up and down the driveway. I like that Jaguar hood ornament."

Sara laughed. "I think I bought the car because of the jaguar. They don't put them on the hoods anymore because people break them off and steal them. Good night, Dallas."

Dallas Lord was waiting at the gates when a dark blue sedan swept through the moment he pressed the release button. He walked around to the side of the car and climbed in. "Mr. Heinrick, I'm glad you could come up on such short notice. We can sit out by the pool and have some coffee and Danish."

"Is something wrong, Mr. Lord? Did you

change your mind?" Benton's hospital administrator asked anxiously.

"Not at all. I'm interested in doing even more for your hospital. However there is a condition. Just park anywhere. I made the coffee myself."

Harry Heinrick sat down in the chair Dallas pointed out to him. He accepted a cup of coffee, his hands trembling slightly.

"I'd like to build you a super-duper cardiac wing or whatever you call it. The latest equipment, as high-tech as you can get. I can set the wheels in motion tomorrow if you like."

"I like the idea very much. You said there was a condition."

"Yes, a condition. I don't want your hospital to renew Dr. Killian's contract. That's my condition."

"Good Lord, are you saying she did . . . what are you saying?"

"I'm saying I don't want you to renew her contract. No, Dr. Killian didn't do anything wrong. Can you keep a secret?"

Harry Heinrick preened. "Of course. All of us at Benton pride ourselves on our integrity."

"I'm going to ask Dr. Killian to marry me. I travel with the band. She wouldn't be able to go with me if she was under contract with your hospital. I'm more than willing to set her up in her own private practice where she can consult or whatever it is doctors do so that they can take time off. I don't want you to tell her you aren't renewing her contract right away. Maybe after Christmas. I'll let you know when you can tell her. Are you interested in my offer?"

"I'm interested, but what about Dr. Killian? She's a fine doctor. Does she know about . . . any of this?"

"Nothing. I don't want her to know anything either. Are you one of those people who has to think about things for a long time or can you give me your answer today? This is Sara's last day, as you probably know."

"I think I might want to think about this for a day or so. This is a very serious thing you're asking me to do."

"How about if I throw in a pediatric wing?"

"We're talking about a lot of money here, Mr. Lord."

"Yes, it is a lot of money. I *have* a lot of money. It's barely a drop in the bucket when you compare what I'm willing to give you as opposed to the salary increase Sara's asking for. Are you still having a problem with my request?"

Sweat beaded on Heinrick's brow. "No. It's nine-thirty. I can have an answer for you by eleven. Is that good enough?"

"I'll wait for your call. Don't be late. Did you like the coffee?"

"Very much. How do I get out?"

"I have the remote here. See the monitor attached to the cabana? When you reach the gate I'll open it for you. Thanks for hearing me out."

Heinrick walked on jittery legs to his car. The things people did for love. It was hard for him to picture Sara Killian with this rock star, but Dr. Killian's love life was no concern of his. Benton Hospital was what counted. The stunt Sara Killian pulled with her patient wouldn't make matters any tougher. He knew he would have an affirmative answer for Dallas Lord before eleven o'clock. The private owners of Benton Hospital were not fools, and neither was he. It occured to him once on the drive back to the hospital to wonder if Dallas Lord was a fool. Well, that wasn't his business either. Signatures on dotted lines, money changing hands, that was his business. With this little coup he definitely had job security till the end of his days. He'd see to that. An addendum to his present contract to that effect would not be out of order. Not at all.

When the phone rang promptly at eleven o'clock, Dallas picked it up on the second ring. "Fine. That's fine. I'll call my manager now and have some contracts drawn up. He'll want to set up a meeting with you. I'll be in touch, Mr. Heinrick."

Dallas dialed six different numbers before he reached Adam in Charleston. "It's Dallas, Adam. I want to talk to you."

"I'm on vacation, Dallas. I don't feel like discussing business."

"Rise to the occasion. This is important. I want you to take care of something. I want you to do it now. You're my employee in case you forgot."

"That's tough, Dallas. I'm busy. I can take a page out of your book and get a new number so you can't reach me. Try this one on for size. I'm sick of taking your orders and hustling for your cockamamie whims. I've been sitting here thinking, Dallas. I'm going to resign. I'll put it in writing and fax it to you and then send a hard copy via FedEx. Now that it's out of the way, we should hang up before one of us says something he'll regret later on."

"Just a minute, Adam. You're my brother, you can't quit. Who's going to take care of all that shit you have us involved in? No. I refuse to accept your resignation. I'll get a lawyer and hold you to the contract. So there, Adam."

Adam snorted. "Did you forget that I'm a lawyer, and I'm the one who drew up my contract? There's a clause in there that allows me to resign at any time I see fit. Hire someone. Spin your wheels, and he'll tell you what I just told you. It's nice of you to finally acknowledge the fact that we're brothers. The last time you mentioned it was when you were eight years old."

"Are you ticked off because I got a new phone number?"

"No, Dallas. I've had enough. This whole thing wore real thin the past couple of years, but I gritted my teeth and held on for you. I don't intend to do that any longer. The tour is set up. I banked the signature money. It's your responsibility from here on out. Notify the band. One word of advice, watch whoever you hire like a hawk or he'll rob you blind. When it comes to money, Dallas, you aren't the smartest person in the world."

"Just like that you're quitting. When were you going to tell us?"

"The day after Thanksgiving. That gives you forty days to get ready."

"If you're quitting, then we're quitting, too."

"It doesn't work that way, Dallas," Adam sighed. "You and the band are the performers. I was just your manager. I'll be sending you everything you need by express mail. Once it leaves my hands I am no longer responsible. If you choose to do one of your hideout scenes, refusing to talk to anyone and not accepting the materials I'm sending, you are still liable. I scheduled the upcoming tour in good faith, and you all agreed. Do you understand what I just said, Dallas?"

"I'm not stupid, Adam. Why are you doing this? Just tell me why. Is it because of Billy?"

Adam sucked in his breath. "I guess because it's time. In a way it has something to do with Billy. I want a life. I finally realized I don't want to end up like you. I have seven houseguests who made me open my eyes. I've been your slave since the day you fell out of that damn tree. I took care of you. I protected you. I made sure everything ran smoothly for you. You never lacked for a thing. I made sure of that because I am your brother, and as such I assumed responsibility for you. Why don't we just say good-bye now. Have a nice Thanksgiving and a wonderful Christmas. This will be my first holiday season at a home of my own in thirty-five years. I refuse to allow you to ruin it for me. I have someone to share the season with this year, and I intend to enjoy every minute of it. Hell, I might even send out Christmas cards. Handwritten. I wish for you, little brother, what I wish for myself, the best."

"Wait a damn minute, Adam, and don't you dare hang up on me. I didn't get to tell you why I called. I want to do more for Benton Memorial Hospital. I promised them two new wings."

"That was very generous of you, Dallas. You certainly have the money to fund it. You know I don't approve of such costly gestures unless they're planned and well thought-out. When you act in haste the way you usually do, things go awry. You will need someone to monitor the whole process. Good Luck. Call me sometime." He had to hang up, and he had to do it now. A second later the connection was broken.

Dallas stared at the silent phone in his hand before he broke into tears. Rage, unlike anything he'd ever experienced, rivered through him. He punched his brother's number into the cell phone a second time. The phone in Charleston rang thirty times before he threw the cell phone against the wall.

In Charleston, Adam Lord's fist shot in the air. "Do you have any idea how good I feel right now? I feel like someone just took a thousand-pound load off my shoulders." The spaniel stared at her new master with wet adoring eyes, her tail swishing happily. "We need a name for you and all these little guys. God, I don't even know if your offspring are boys or girls." He bent over to stroke the dog's silky head. She licked at Adam's outstretched hand. "You trust me, don't you?" Sure you do, I can see it in your eyes. My own brother doesn't trust me. One time he asked me if I would donate a kidney to him if he was dying. The thought of Dallas dying was so horrible I couldn't think beyond the statement. He hung up on me. Oh, well, one of these days I'm going to figure out where I went wrong where Dallas is concerned, but right now I need to go to the store to get our Thanksgiving dinner. Then I'm going to the hardware store to get a padlock for the gate. I don't want you wandering off. I can't be sure of this, but I think you made your way in here and hid when the meter reader came this month. It doesn't matter one way or the other. You're mine now, and I accept full responsibility for you and your pups. I might stop at Super Pets and get you guys some gear. When I get back we're going to find a suitable name for you."

Adam didn't give his brother or his phone call a second thought. It felt wonderful simply to walk out of the house and know there would be no demands on his time now or in the days to come. He could read comic books for the rest of his life if he wanted to. Or, he might open his own law office in town. If he wanted to he could buy a four-wheel drive, load up the dogs, and take a trip around the country.

Damn, for the first time in his life, his world was looking sweet. He crossed his fingers, the way he had when he was a kid hoping that things would turn out the same way for Dallas.

*   *   *

His rage spent, Dallas looked around at the glass littering the pool deck. He vaguely remembered smashing the root-beer bottles. When the headache hammering inside his head let up, things would be clearer. He should clean up the mess before Sara arrived. He looked at his watch. Her arrival was hours away.

The headache took on a drumbeat of its own as he stomped his way to the room Adam had set up as an office. At the most he'd only entered the room five times in the last fifteen years. He looked around. The desk was mahogany and shiny. A blotter, a leather holder containing pens and pencils sat alongside a beige telephone. It was a manly office. It even smelled manly. Burgundy leather chairs with little brass nailheads, shiny tables with glossy plants, brown-striped draperies, matching carpet that caressed his ankles. Subdued lighting. He opened one of the mahogany cabinets to see a large-screen television, a VCR, a wall safe that was empty. His *real* safe was under the floor in his closet. A copy machine, a fax machine, and recessed file cabinets completed the room. This was an Adam office, not a Dallas office.

"We'll just see about that!" Dallas was a whirlwind of motion as he slammed doors and drawers until he had the yellow pages of the phone book in hand. Impatient, he dialed the information operator, rattled off an excuse that he'd lost his reading glasses, and needed several numbers. He painstakingly wrote them down, thanking the young voice profusely. He made a call, announced himself, and gave his address. "I want it done today. Work through the night. Of course I realize it's going to cost extra. Write this down. Any idiot can paint and hang wallpaper. The room is twelve by twelve. You can take the desk, the chairs, the tables, and the carpet and drapes. Then bring a goddamn sewing machine and make the drapes while you're here. You're supposed to be the decorator. If you don't want the job, just say so. Fine, fine, that sounds fair. There's no one here to bother you or get in your way. Just give me a yes or no. Bring everything you need in one load, because I'm not opening and closing the gates every time you think you forgot something. An hour and a half is good. Yeah, yeah, autographs for all your employees and kids. Okay, pictures, too. Okay, ninety minutes.

Don't be late. I hate it when people don't live up to their word."

Dallas broke the connection to make his second call. "Just send everything for a Thanksgiving dinner. Yes, a fresh turkey. Thank you."

His immediate chores taken care of, Dallas walked over to the wall unit and opened it. The double row of file cabinets were filled to overflowing. He yanked and tugged, until he had the contents on the floor. Seven trips later, Dallas looked at the mess on his bed. The pounding inside his head threatened his stomach when he looked at the stack of files on his king-size bed. For the first time in his life he felt total fear sweep through him.

Adam had told him to take care of his own business. He yanked at one of the folders, the contents spilling onto the floor. The highlighted sticker on the flap said PROPERTIES. Plot maps, contracts, tax bills, insurance bills, utility bills, caretaker and maintenance bills all neatly stapled and filed in separate smaller folders. He read highlighted notes; PAY, DO NOT PAY, PROBLEMS, ERRORS, TAX FILE, UPDATE, FILE QUARTERLY. USE ACCOUNT # 6667432. REFER TO LINKED ACCOUNTS # 8767651 AND # 2287903.

He blinked, the headache threatening to rock his head off his shoulders. His eyes wild, Dallas looked at the other folders that were attached to the one in his hand. He flipped through them, his hands trembling. They all had the same kind of highlighted notes.

He realized he wasn't capable of reading the folders, much less handling them. The hard realization forced him to do his best to stack the folders neatly into piles. When he was finished he sat down at the foot of the bed and hugged his knees, rocking back and forth, humming quietly.

A single tear dropped to his cheek. He made no move to wipe it away. He wished he was a little boy again. When he was little, he didn't know there was something wrong with him. He wished he'd never gone to school because that's when his problems started. The kids called him a dumbbell, a retard, and stupid. Even when Adam came to his defense and beat them up they didn't stop. He tried to remember how many nights in his young life he had cried himself to sleep. He wished now that he could remember how many prayers he'd said asking God to change His mind and make him like everyone else. How many nights had he locked himself in the bathroom trying to fathom his homework? Hundreds? Thousands?

Dallas swiped at the tears on his cheeks. He choked back a sob when he recalled the day Billy Sweet, at the age of fourteen, told him he couldn't spend too much time with him anymore because he had a girlfriend. "Cissie says I shouldn't hang out with you so much because I'm starting to act stupid like you. She said you belong in one of those special schools where they work on your brain to see what went wrong." He choked back another sob. How could a best friend say something so mean and deadly? Adam had found him that day in the garage with his head buried in an old greasy blanket howling his head off. His eyes murderous, Adam said he would take care of Billy Sweet. Two weeks later when Cissie dumped Billy for the co-captain of the basketball team he came over to the garage to ask if they could be friends again. Billy didn't say he was sorry until Adam beat him black-and-blue.

Adam never, ever said Dallas was re-tarded. He'd always explained his difficulties by saying some people were quicker than other people, and it didn't mean anything.

He'd go on to say some people were more coordinated than other people. He even said Einstein was only good at one thing, and he wasn't dumb. The last thing Adam had said about that particular episode was that he had to start believing in himself and stop listening to all the assholes like Billy who didn't know what the hell they were talking about.

All these years he had been so mean and nasty to his brother when all Adam had ever done was protect him and look out for him. "I was jealous. I hated him for being so smart when I was so dumb." Admit something else, Dallas, a niggling voice nagged. "You blamed him because you fell out of the tree. You believed that bullshit Billy fed you about being normal before you fell and cracked your head. All these years you blamed your brother, and it wasn't his fault. It was your own fault. Adam told you not to climb the tree. Adam told you to come down."

"It wasn't the fall from the damn tree. I was like that before, but no one noticed but me and my mother. Maybe that's why my mother gave me and Adam away."

Dallas slammed his fist into the bedding. The stacks of files teetered and fell off the bed, papers spewing everywhere. Dallas stared at them helplessly. How was he to figure out which papers went into which folder? He started to sob then, his whole body shaking with his unhappiness. "I wish I could run away and never come back. I wish . . . I wish . . . I was someone else." He said the prayer again, the same prayer he'd said thousands of times when he was little, "Please God, make me like everyone else. Please."

Dallas sat quietly, the same prayer tumbling off his lips until the gate buzzer announced a guest. Locking his door behind him, Dallas walked out to the pool deck to open the gate. Fifteen minutes later the fixings for his Thanksgiving dinner were in the refrigerator. Thirty minutes later a large white van appeared at the gate. He opened the gate a second time but failed to see the small sports car directly behind the van.

Dallas gasped when he saw her climb from her car.

"Sandi!"

"Hi, sweetie."

Chapter Six

Dallas frowned as he stared at the long white van and the small sports car behind it. He led the decorators into the house, looking over his shoulder, the frown still on his face. "This is the room. Rip everything out, the drapes, the carpeting, the furniture. The built-in cabinets stay. Just redo the woodwork. I want this room to be electric. I want you to hang my gold and platinum records on this wall. They're all in boxes in the closet. On this wall I want my autographed pictures. I want to be shocked every time I walk into this room. Give me color, give me electricity. I want my eyeballs to stand at attention when I walk into this office. Can you give me what I want by tomorrow morning?"

"We can do it, Mr. Lord."

"Then go to it." Dallas smacked his hands in satisfaction. Money could buy anything.

On the walk down the hall and through the kitchen Dallas wondered what he would do with the room once it was finished. If he wasn't capable of understanding the business end of the files and folders, why did he need an office? He stopped to look back down the hall. This must be what Adam meant when he said he didn't think things through and plan ahead.

"Yoo-hoo, Dallas honey. Where are you? What are you redecorating? This kitchen could use a little work. It's been a while, Dallas, and I'm in the mood for some Dallas Lord music. Let's go into the studio and do what we do best—sing. Just like old times, okay? I'm really looking forward to the tour. How about you?" It was all said in a breathless rush.

Dallas's head throbbed. Maybe Sandi was right and some music would soothe his soul. "I have to decide about Billy's replacement before I think about the tour. There seems to be some problems with the tour schedule at the moment. What's wrong with my kitchen? I'm redoing my office." This, too, was said in the same breathless rush.

"Have those decorators make a pit stop here. It's just blah, Dallas. I don't know, maybe some colored dishes or a hanging plant. Kitchens like this belong in orphanages or places like that. You should have a carpet on the floor by the sink. So, what's new?"

Dallas looked at the floor by the sink and made a mental note to order a carpet. "I might be getting married. The tour might get delayed. I'm decorating. What's new with you?" He wondered if he cared or if he was asking to be polite. He had to get rid of her. Quick.

"I'm having trouble meeting my bills. I haven't been with the band long enough to enjoy all the benefits your brother set up for the members. I was hoping you might ask Adam to give me an advance. Christmas is coming and everything kind of snowballed if you know what I mean. Who's the lucky girl? I wish it was me. I fell real hard for you, Dallas."

"Her name is Sara. Adam doesn't like advances. He says it screws up his book work. How much do you need?"

Everyone in the band knew Dallas had no money sense. From time to time they would rib him good-naturedly. He could always be counted on for a loan and from all she'd heard, he never asked to be paid back. Most of the time he forgot who and how much he'd loaned. Sandi crossed her fingers when she said, "Twenty-five thousand." When Dallas didn't blink, she said, "On second thought, I want to get something really nice for my parents for Christmas. Make that fifty-thousand. Can you spare that, sweetie? Will Adam chew you out if you write me a check?"

Dallas stared at his backup singer. He had no idea what her salary was. Adam handled the payroll. But, she'd said the magic words as far as his brother was concerned. "My checkbook is in the studio. Are you sure it's enough? What are you going to get your parents?"

"I was thinking about a cruise. You know, one of those land-to-water things. For say three months. They live part of the year in Wisconsin, and you know how cold it is there in January and February. You can't count on March either."

With absolutely no idea of what a cruise cost, Dallas pretended to think. "I think I should give you an even hundred thousand. I'll tell Adam the next time I talk to him. A hundred should cover everything. It will give your parents a very nice memory."

"Oh, Dallas, this is so wonderful of you.

I'm going to put your name on the card, too. My parents are going to be thrilled out of their minds."

"That's nice, Sandi. Do you want to hear the song I'm writing for Sara?"

"Oh, yes. Did you finish it, or are you still working on it?"

"I'm still working on it. It's in my head. I think it's the best thing I've done so far. On second thought I think I'll wait until I finish it. I might jinx myself."

"When do you think you'll finish it?"

Dallas shrugged. "Next week. I'm trying to do one for Billy, too, but it isn't going well. I need more time on it. Each time I start to work on it I get choked up."

"What kind of wedding are you planning, Dallas? You said we were going to get married. You even asked me to set the date and now you're marrying someone else."

"A simple one. Secret. Sara's a doctor. She saves lives. You said you didn't want to marry me." Why the hell was he even bothering to talk to this girl? Because Adam had always told him not to hurt people's feelings and to be polite.

Sandi's voice was sly when she said, "She must not be a very good doctor. If she was really good, she would have saved Billy's life. Is she better than me, Dallas, because she's a doctor? You must have been really serious when you asked me to marry you too. You broke my heart. You said ugly things to me. I would never hurt your feelings that way, Dallas. Never, ever." Her tone was so vehement, Dallas reared backward.

Dallas bit down on his lower lip as he scribbled a check.

"Is Sara prettier than I am, Dallas?" The check disappeared like magic.

"Sara's plain and normal. She doesn't wear all that makeup you wear. You really have to be smart to be a doctor."

"If she's so smart, then why did Billy die? Just answer me that, Dallas Lord."

"Because it was his time to die. Sara said the best doctors in the world couldn't have saved him."

Sandi snorted. "I'd say that, too, if my patient up and died on me. Sometimes you are not in touch with the real world, Dallas."

Dallas stared at the young woman across from him. She was prettier than Sara in a glamorous way, and she was in good physical shape because she worked out daily. Sara was a little thick in the middle and admitted to being seven pounds overweight. Sandi he knew weighed in at 110. Her shellacked good looks were an asset to the band, and he knew it. She was good in bed, too.

Sandi sat down on the floor. "You know what, Dallas, I'm sorry I didn't agree to marry you when you asked me. You spooked me when you said you wanted a whole houseful of kids. I'm only twenty-four. I don't want to have children until I'm in my thirties. I'll be a better mother then because I'll have done all the things I want to do by then. I do things the way my mother did them. That's how you learn." Sandi wondered if God would strike her dead at some point for all her lies. "How old is Dr. Sara? I bet she's almost *forty*. That's too old to have children. My mother said women shouldn't have children after thirty-five. Things go wrong. Sometimes kids are born deformed or *retarded*. I don't know that for a pure fact, Dallas. I'm only going by what my mother said. Mothers don't ever lie. That's a given."

Dallas's face turned an ugly red. "Then we'll adopt kids. Sara knows all about stuff like that."

Sandi stretched her long body out on the floor, her palms supporting her as she proceeded to do body lifts. Her voice was hushed when she said, "It won't be the same thing, Dallas. Adopted children won't be your flesh and blood. They won't have any features of you and your wife. Or your brother's features. The Lord name won't continue. Unless your brother fathers a child. This is really sad, Dallas. You should think about this a little more before you make such a big decision. *Forty* is really old. Women start to go through the change of life around that time. My mother told me that, too. They get those ugly red, hot flashes, and they *sweat.* Big-time. They have to take *drugs.* I know how you feel about drugs, Dallas. She could make a *mistake* in the operating room. Then the family files a lawsuit and they come after you. When Adam hired me he gave me this lecture. You know the one about clean living and any hint of scandal puts us on the street. That little speech is burned into my brain. Does Dr. Sara have a sense of humor, Dallas?"

"Of course she does. She makes me laugh and I make her laugh."

"That's really nice. Laughter is important."

Sandi's voice turned sly again when she said, "Does she love your music? Does she get off on it? Does she *really* open up people and touch their organs? All that blood. Marrying someone like that, to me, would be like marrying a *mortician.* Let's make some popcorn and watch *Dirty Dancing.* Or we could go into your room and . . . you know. I've really missed you, Dallas. I haven't been with anyone since we . . . since you said you didn't want to see me anymore."

Dallas looked down to find his hand in Sandi's tight grasp. He wasn't engaged to Sara. Then he thought about the files and folders on top of his bed. That thought led to other thoughts and what Adam would think about this situation. He wouldn't approve. His brother had morals and ethics. "I'd rather go for a walk."

On her feet, Sandi reached for Dallas's hand. He allowed it to be taken and didn't know why.

"Do you miss Billy, Sandi?"

"Sure. I didn't know him all that well. He was always polite and all that. The guys all have families and didn't want to mess with me and the other girls. We didn't try to mess with them either. We respected their families. That's one of the things we liked about being with you and the Canyon River Band. Your brother did a real bang-up job putting everything together and making sure it stayed that way. They call him the Great White in the industry. It doesn't get any better than that. I wish I had a brother like yours. Is Billy's family okay? I sent flowers, and one of the girls said Billy was a Catholic, so I sent some mass cards. It was okay to do that, wasn't it?" She squeezed his hand tighter. Dallas squeezed back. "Boy, this is really like old times. Didn't you miss me even a little bit?"

Dallas thought about the question. "Not really. I miss Billy. I should go to the cemetery, but all those reporters will be there. Do you go?"

"Every day," Sandi lied. "I take flowers. I knew you wouldn't be able to go, so I did it for you. I don't take elaborate bunches of flowers because I can't afford it. I just pick up some daisies or some colorful blossoms at the supermarket. Billy knows my heart's in the right place and that I'm just your stand-in. You don't mind, do you, Dallas?"

"Jeez, why would I mind?" He swung her hand as they walked along.

"Tell me about the song you're writing for the doctor. Are you sure she deserves a song by Dallas Lord?"

"Sure I'm sure. It's about friendship and loyalty. How people care for one another. I'm calling it 'Sara's Song.' "

"Hum a few bars, Dallas, and I'll give you my honest opinion." He obliged. He grinned when Sandi clapped her hands. "I like it, Dallas. Try it now using my name and see how it sounds." Dallas obliged. Sandi's voice was playful when she said, "I think I like it with my name better. Do it again and get the beat. See what I mean. Oh, well, it's your song so you can do whatever you want. I do think, though, you should play it for the guys and get their opinion. What are you doing for Thanksgiving? Would you like to come to dinner at my parents' house? They come here in the winter."

"I can't. Sara's coming up and we're going to make dinner."

"That's nice. I just worry about you being alone. Do you know what I'm going to do, Dallas? I just got this great idea. I'm going to call Nancy and invite her to my mother's. I know she doesn't have any family, and this is going to be rough for her. It's a really good idea, don't you think, Dallas?"

"It's a great idea."

"Sara isn't part of our family the way Nancy is. You need to give some thought to what it will mean if the guys don't accept her. After all, Billy died in her care." Sandi looked at her watch. "It's getting late. I think I'm going to leave now, Dallas. If Nancy is agreeable to coming here, should I charter a plane or what? It's your decision, Dallas. Do you have to call Adam for something like this? I can make all the arrangements, you just have to pay for it. If I could afford it, you know I'd do it."

"I don't need Adam's okay to do anything. Go ahead and call Nancy and take care of the arrangements if she wants to come. Then call me back and let me know the method of payment."

"I can't call you back, Dallas. Don't you remember, you got angry with me and got a new number? All I wanted to do that day was try and comfort you in your grief. I was grieving, too, Dallas. I loved Billy, too. It's okay, I forgive you. It's easy for me to forgive you because I still love you."

"Call me on the house phone. I plugged

them all back in. Those cell phones are a pain in the neck. I have a lot of decisions to make, Sandi. Adam's forcing me to take over more of the responsibilities of the band. I'll think about everything you said."

"Do you want me to send up my friend? He's tops, Dallas. He's been a fan for twenty years. He's clean so Adam would approve of that. He just needs an advance for some new threads, a class styling job on his hair, and some new wheels. He's got the same kind of wonderful personality Billy had. He's got red hair and three zillion freckles. How about Monday afternoon? I'll bring him up, and we can audition him. Trust me, Dallas, this is a good thing."

"Okay, but call first."

Sandi stood on her toes. She kissed him lightly on the tip of his nose. "Do you still love me, just a little?"

Dallas felt so uncomfortable he backed up. "We've been all through this, Sandi. I'm in love with Sara. Whatever was between us is over and done with."

"Keep working on that song and try my name when you get stuck. Record it, Dallas, and then play it back. You'll see what I'm talking about. Promise."

"I'll think about it."

"See you, sweetie."

Dallas stood in the driveway watching the small blue car until it was out of sight. Somehow Sandi had wiped away his horrendous headache. He would not think about the mess in his bedroom. He absolutely would not think about anything but the song he was writing.

Sara stepped from the elevator, her eyes searching for Nellie Pulaski. When she spotted her she smiled. "I have this strange feeling, Nellie, that I won't be back. You know me and my intuition. Have you heard anything?"

"Plenty," the older nurse blustered. "I know everything that goes on in this hospital. Most of the time I know it before the muckety-mucks know it. And if what I heard is true, I'm outta here."

Sara's heart took on an extra beat. "That sounds pretty ominous, Nellie. Do you care to share, or is it gossip that shouldn't be repeated?"

"There was some kind of meeting in Heinrick's office around ten-thirty. I got it straight from Tessie, Heinrick's secretary. The board voted against renewing your contract. She said they talked, using words like 'downsizing,' 'cost efficiency,' and 'limited donations.' Salary raises are out of the question. Just for the record, Tisdale and Granger got raises when their contracts were renewed. That goes for everyone, not just you. Tessie actually heard Harry say that. I have an appointment with Heinrick when I go off duty. I'm going to ask him point-blank if it's true. If it is, I'm giving my notice."

Sara felt like she'd been kicked in the stomach. "I guess they have to do what they have to do. I'm sure Mrs. Osborne played a part in this somewhere. I'm not sorry for what I did, and I'd do it again in a heartbeat. Please, Nellie, don't quit because of me. This hospital needs you. I better go back and get the plants in my office." Her eyes filled with tears. "Did they say anything specific about my work? 'Downsizing' and 'cost efficiency' are the only words Harry knows. They were supposed to counter and we'd negotiate. Are you sure Tessie got it straight? I'm a damn good doctor, Nellie."

The old nurse's face was grim. "Not just damn good. You are the best. Tessie said she's sure and she repeated the conversation word for word. She said Heinrick looked *elated*. I meant it, Sara, I'm leaving. Steven McGuire offered me a job. It's part-time. I think I'm going to take him up on his offer. I'm of retirement age anyway. Working with animals opposed to people has its perks. The animals don't complain. All they do is love you for taking care of them and making them well. I don't want you to panic now. Listen to me, Sara, you can get a job anywhere. And you'll probably make more than what you asked for in your new contract. My advice would be to send out your résumés to every hospital in town. Take the month off just the way you planned. Start the new year right. By the fifteenth of January the offers will be rolling in."

Sara blew her nose. "I haven't even walked out of here. They certainly made the decision quickly. Everything happens for a reason I suppose. Why is it, Nellie, when you care, when you give 110 percent, they kick you in the gut. If I was a lousy doctor like some people around here whose names I won't mention, I might be able to understand it. Do you think it's that good-old-boy thing?"

"It's this whole place. Mostly it's the money-hungry owners."

"Nellie, tell me the truth, do you think Billy Sweet's death or Sadie Osborne have anything to do with this?"

"I don't know, Sara. I truly don't know. I go off duty in ten minutes. Wait for me in the parking lot, and we'll go for coffee."

"I was supposed to go up to Dallas's house this evening. Now I don't feel like it. Sure, I'll meet you in the lot. You can have my plants, Nellie. Monty's café?"

"Sounds good. You can go ahead, and I'll meet you there. I don't want to see any more tears either. These people aren't worth your little finger."

Sara did her best to smile for Nellie's benefit.

Nellie Pulaski yanked at her starched uniform before she settled her cap more firmly on her springy curls. She then stomped her way to Harry Heinrick's office. She knocked as she opened the door. "Harry!" she called. Being of an age with the administrator and years of familiarity allowed for personal names in private. On the floor she was always careful to address the administrator as Mr. Heinrick.

"What is it, Nellie? I'm pretty busy right now."

"I quit."

"What?"

"You heard me. I quit. How dare you not renew Sara Killian's contract. How dare you, Harry!"

"Where did you hear that?"

"You know I know everything that goes on in this hospital. You also know that I know you know, so don't pretend with me. Sara is one of the best things this hospital has going for it and you know it. Why didn't you fire Granger? Twice this week he came in here with liquor on his breath. I smelled it on him, Harry. He's a drunk. You renewed his contract last month. Tisdale dispenses medication on the golf course and treats patients on his cell phone. He hasn't been in here in a month, and you renewed his contract two months ago. With hefty raises for both of them. Sara has been doing their jobs, and all the nurses cover for them. I'm going to file a report with the AMA and everyone else I can think of. What do you think of that, Harry?"

"Do you think I don't know all of that, Nellie? What you have to realize is I can't control the board." His stomach started to churn. If there was one thing Benton Memorial needed, it was Nellie Pulaski. He wished he had a dozen curmudgeons like Nellie. "This job is the end of the line for me. I'm close to retirement age. What's more, Nellie, I need this job because I, like you, make a difference around here. I live with that the way you do. The end sometimes does justify the means."

"I guess that means you sacrificed Sara for the betterment of Benton. In your mind, Harry. You are a . . . *wuss,* Harry Heinrick. You're afraid of your own shadow. Did you hear me, I quit?"

"You quit three times a week, Nellie. Benton Memorial is your life just the way it's my life and everyone's life who works here."

"*Was* my life, Harry. I'm quitting because of what you're doing to Sara. I want to make sure you understand that. I am not giving notice either. When I walk out of here it's for the last time. Carly Killian will be the next one to go. You better shore up your personnel files. I can see the malpractice suits flying all over the place. You're turning green, Harry. God help the lot of you. Good-bye, *Mister* Heinrick. Have a nice Thanksgiving.

I'm sure you'll find *something* to give thanks for."

"Nellie, wait. You better than anyone should know things aren't always black or white. There are reasons for everything, extenuating circumstances . . . things I'm not at liberty to discuss. What about the patients? You can't just walk out of here."

"Watch me, Harry. I already have a new job. Yes, I'm leaving you. However, I am not leaving you without ER coverage. Therein lies the difference. That's what I call professionalism. What you just did to Sara was not professional. Couldn't you at least have waited until she was gone? See you around, Harry."

Nellie looked up and down the hushed, pristine white corridor. Would she miss this place? Maybe. Then again, maybe not. What she'd just done felt right and good. She hoped she had the courage to follow through on her threats about Granger and Tisdale. She squared her pudgy shoulders. Already they felt lighter now that she knew she didn't have to pull double shifts so that she could keep her eyes on the two young doctors who, in her opinion, weren't fit to practice medicine. In a pique of something she couldn't define, she opened Harry's office door and bellowed, "Make sure you send my gold watch by overnight mail!" She slammed the door so hard the knob came loose under her hand. For spite she gave the door a good kick before she marched her way out of the hospital to the parking lot.

Nellie Pulaski took one last, long look at the hospital she'd worked in for so many years. "Life goes on," she muttered. "You get a cat, you plant some rosebushes, and you learn more ways to cook hamburger. My reward will be that I sleep at night and the knowledge that I stood by a damn fine doctor."

Monty's Café was the home of every white-collar professional within a seven-mile radius. It was one of the last bastions for smokers, and it was jammed to capacity twenty-four hours a day. The costly, intricate ventilation system allowed smokers and nonsmokers to eat and smoke in peaceful coexistence. It was Nellie Pulaski's favorite eatery.

She spotted Sara sitting at her favorite table. She waved the hostess aside, muttering, "I'm sorry I ever told your boss to serve

Starbucks coffee. I'm even sorrier he listened to me. You can't hear yourself think in here."

"Bad day, huh, Nellie?" The young hostess grinned.

"Six of one and a half dozen of the other. I quit today. I am officially retired from Benton Memorial as of," Nellie looked at her watch, "fourteen minutes ago. Don't broadcast the news, honey."

Nellie weaved her way across the room to where Sara was sitting and lowered her bulky figure gingerly into the comfortable captain's chair. She immediately fired up a cigarette and proceeded to blow three perfect smoke rings in succession. "Congratulate me, Sara. I told Harry what he could do with his job. I also told him to send me my gold watch by overnight mail. I didn't even give notice. What do you think of that?"

"If you did it for yourself, okay. If you did it for me, then you were wrong. I've been sitting here wailing to myself. I don't understand. Are you sure you told me everything?"

"Absolutely. Don't you dare start to question your profession or your abilities. You are not at fault here. Both of us gave quality care. I stayed because I knew I made a difference. I think you stayed for the same reasons."

"God, Nellie, when I think of all the years of study, my specialty training, my student loans . . . That's most of my life. I gave up everything to be a doctor and that . . . that money jockey tells me I'm not worth it. Sure I can send out résumés by the dozen but how do I explain the fact that a second-rate private hospital didn't renew my contract. I can't even give them a reason why other than money. Should I go further in debt and strike out on my own? I feel like an old sweater that's starting to unravel. My parents sacrificed everything for Carly's and my educations and it still wasn't enough. I've been sitting here thinking about going to some third-world country for a couple of years to wipe out my loans. You can do that you know. I have two mortgages on the house, my car is on time payments. We had to buy new kitchen appliances, and they're on time, too. There's no money left at the end of the month. There should be, but there isn't. I know I'm worth more than I'm paid. It was stupid of me to buy that expensive car. Every time I get behind the wheel I think about the $710 a month payment. It's obscene the way that car guzzles gas. Neither Carly nor I have much in the way of savings. I'm really going to need the unemployment insurance. Nellie, I'm going to be forty. I should have a family of my own and be comfortable in my profession. I need to know, Nellie, where did I go wrong? I bought into that myth that doctors make megabucks. That's got to be the biggest joke of the year. The malpractice insurance alone can wipe you out."

"You didn't go wrong. Let's drink this delicious coffee and talk about other things. I'd really like to know what's going on with you and Mr. Dallas Lord, popular rock star. Is it serious? What do you have planned for Thanksgiving?"

"I was planning on going up to Dallas's house this evening. We were going to do a big Thanksgiving dinner. Carly's going to Hank's house. I really don't feel like going now. All I want to do is go home, crawl into a corner, and suck my thumb."

"Then do it. Stop worrying about other people. When are you going to learn to do what you want to do? I'm sure that retinue of people Mr. Lord surrounds himself with will come up with a dinner."

"That's just it, Nellie. There is no retinue. He gave the gardener, the pool man, and the housekeeper time off. He wanted to be alone. The band members are scattered all over the country with the exception of one of his singers, who hangs around by the gate. He's counting on me. He's so lost and lonely. Right now I feel exactly the same way he does. I can relate to him in so many ways. After today, more so than ever."

Nellie snorted as she held her coffee cup aloft for a refill. "What happened today was not your fault. We all go through periods like this. It takes guts to go forward. If you pamper and coddle him of course he's going to latch on to you. You're his crutch. The hard edge should be off his grief by now. The man has a brother, Sara."

"I don't even want to get into that, Nellie. I think I got myself in a little too deep. At first I was flattered, and it was fun. Now it's a strain and an effort. I think it's me. I like Dallas tremendously and I think I'm falling in love with him. He kisses me but he hasn't sexually hit on me. I find that . . . weird. He has this, for want of a better phrase, old-world respect for me. Sometimes I like it, and other times I don't."

"You could come to my house for Thanksgiving dinner. I bought a twelve-pound bird. I'm going to do my pies tonight. I have to tell you, though, I invited Steven McGuire, and he's coming. I'll fix up a dinner and take it over to Sadie Osborne. Usually Steven goes home to his family in Indiana, but he has some surgery scheduled for the day after Thanksgiving. He's doing two hip replacements on two shepherds from the same litter. Isn't that amazing? What did you think of him?"

"He was very nice. I think we could be friends. It's getting late, Nellie, I should be going. I appreciate your loyalty. I'm going to worry about you, though."

"Baloney. I'm applying for Social Security. My pension is sufficient. My little town house is paid for. I'm going to be just fine. Working with Steven a few hours a day is just perfect. Don't forget, I can always do private duty. You worry about what you're going to do. Just don't make hasty decisions. I want your promise, Sara."

"I promise, Nellie. At least I'll be able to go on that diet and go back on my exercise routine to take off the ten pounds I put on since last year. That was going to be my New Year's resolution. Now I won't have to wait to start it. You should think about starting a program to give up smoking."

"It's something to think about. This was my treat, Sara. Are you sure you're all right?"

"No, Nellie, I'm not all right. I need to do some hard thinking. I wish I was a schoolteacher. My mother wanted me to go into the education field. It was my dad who wanted me to be a doctor. He wanted Carly to be an architect. She didn't buckle under the way I did. I actually allowed my father to convince me I wanted to be a doctor. For a long time I had myself convinced I wanted to be a doctor all my life. I did it for my father, not for me. I'll call you over the weekend. Thanks for the dinner invitation. Don't eat too much. Say hello to Steven for me."

"Make sure you call me, Sara."

"I will. Thanks for everything, Nellie. Without you at Benton, I would have quit after two weeks. Enjoy your retirement."

* * *

It was close to seven o'clock when Sara set the contents of her hospital locker on top of the clothes dryer in the garage. She took a moment to study the Jeep Wrangler she'd just parked. She hated it. She wanted her Jaguar back.

Sara kicked off her shoes at the top of the garage steps before she pressed the numbers that would deactivate her security alarm. The kitchen phone and Carly's personal phone rang at the same moment. She made no move to answer either one. Instead she sat down and stretched her legs out in front of her. She eyed her medical bag on the kitchen table. She wished again that she was a schoolteacher with nothing to do but make up lesson plans. Both phones continued to ring. Obviously the person doing the calling knew the answering machines for both phones switched on after the fifth ring at which point the caller broke the connection and redialed. With Sara's zero social life it had to be Dallas Lord doing the calling.

Never one to run from her responsibilities, Sara picked up the phone to call the house in Mandeville Canyon. Dallas picked up the phone on the first ring. His voice sounded worried and concerned to her ear.

"Dallas, I'm afraid I'm going to dissapoint you. I won't be coming up to the house this evening. Right now I'm feeling sorry for myself and I wouldn't be good company. I hope you have a nice Thanksgiving. I think I'll just spend mine sleeping."

"You sound funny, Sara. What's wrong? Did something happen?"

"Yes, something's wrong, and yes, something happened. I found out today the hospital isn't going to renew my contract. I can't be without a job. I have a mountain of bills, so that means I have to start to scramble for another job. This is not a good time of the year to be out of work."

"I thought you said you had a whole month and that the contract had to be negotiated. How did you find out?"

"That's not important. Besides, I can't betray a confidence. Nellie quit in protest. You met Nellie at the hospital when you brought Billy in. She's the one I talk about all the time. It's not fair, and it's not right. I might just go to a lawyer and find out if I've been discriminated against because I'm a woman."

Dallas's voice became anxious sounding. "What will that get you but a big legal bill? How can you hope to fight and win against a big hospital?"

"With what I know and with what I can prove, a lot. Nellie and my sister are behind me. When I get done airing all Benton's dirty laundry, private donations will be just a memory. Don't mind me, Dallas, I'm upset. I'm going to take a hot bath and go to bed. Have a nice Thanksgiving. I'm really sorry, Dallas, but I know you understand. I'll try to get up there in the next couple of days to get my car. I really don't like your Jeep."

Sara took the phone off the hook and laid the receiver on the kitchen counter. The total silence was wonderful. She did the same thing with Carly's phone in her room.

Ninety minutes later she was sound asleep.

Chapter Seven

Dallas hung up the phone, his thoughts whirling. *Think things out, make a plan, and then follow through.* Adam's words. Adam's advice. Both of which he constantly ignored. If Sara ever found out what he did, she'd hate him. Right now she probably didn't like him very much, or she would have come up to the house to talk about her disappointment. She wanted her car back. That alone had to mean something. Benton's dirty laundry. What did that mean? Would Harry Heinrick be forced to tell Sara's lawyer about the deal he'd made if he reneged?

Dallas felt a headache coming on. If he didn't pay attention to it, he'd have a full-blown migraine before long. Maybe it was time for some music; music always made things better. Even though he wanted to call Adam, he wouldn't. He needed to do something before he lost control of everything. Where was he going to sleep tonight? Even though the decorators were on the first floor, the sounds would carry upstairs. Then there was the mess on his bed. Of course he had six other bedrooms to choose from. Sara wanted her car back. What the hell was he supposed to do with all the food in the refrigerator? Adam would have the answer to everything in less than five seconds. He, on the other hand, needed *hours* just to think about the problem, never mind solving it.

Dallas looked around the state-of-the-art sound studio that ran the entire length of his house. He'd seen professional studios that weren't half as well equipped as this one. He flicked dials, turned switches and knobs. Sound blasted his eardrums. When he and the Canyon River Band recorded an album, the whole canyon rocked with their sound. He turned the knobs, switches, and dials to the Off position. For the first time in his life, music wasn't his answer. He needed to talk to Billy, only Billy was dead. He could never talk to Billy again. The only other person who seemed to understand him and offer encouragement was Sara, and he'd screwed that up just the way he screwed everything up. According to Adam. He wondered if Adam *ever* did anything wrong.

Disgusted with himself, Dallas tore out of the kitchen and then out to the garage. Good, Sara's keys were still in the ignition. Two keys. One for the car and one for the house. He backed the Jag out of the garage, barreled down the driveway just as the gate opened wide. No hangers-on, no fans, no paparazzi anywhere. The thought was disconcerting as he tore down the canyon roads at ninety miles an hour. Did that mean he was losing his appeal or did it mean they were respecting his right to grieve?

Dallas rode around for an hour as he tried to remember the landmarks Sara had spoken of. It was after one in the morning when the headlights of the Jag arced on the front of the house. He closed the car door quietly. Just as quietly, he opened the garage door. He stared at the alarm panel. Only the green light glowed. The system wasn't armed, which meant he could enter the house through the kitchen.

The kitchen was warm and cozy, the night-light shedding just enough light for him to find his way. Small indoor sensor lights in the wall sockets lighted his way the moment he stepped in front of them. At the top of the steps he leaned over the balcony to stare down into the family room. Sara and her sister probably played in that very room. Maybe checkers, maybe Monopoly. Family pictures were everywhere. The fireplace was fieldstone and rose all the way to the ceiling. Bright red Christmas stockings probably hung there on Christmas Eve. His eyes started to burn with unshed tears when he remembered the year Adam had found a red mesh bag from a sack of oranges and made him a stocking filled with licorice sticks, Jujubes, and a brand-new comic book. Because he didn't have anything for his brother and because he was stupid, he'd thrown the homemade stocking at Adam and run out of the mean, ugly, barren house but not before he'd seen his brother's shoulders slump or the tears in his eyes. There was no way he could ever make that right.

Dallas tapped lightly on the only closed door on the second floor, calling Sara's name as he did so.

Sara woke instantly. "Dallas, is that you?"

"Yeah, it's me. I brought your car back. I let myself in with your house key. Is it okay for me to come in?"

"You're here so I guess it's okay. Let me get my robe. Is anything wrong, Dallas? I didn't mean for you to bring my car back to-night."

"I know. I wanted to see you. You sounded so unhappy. Let's go down to your kitchen and have some coffee. I want to talk to you about something. Show me the corner where you put your Christmas tree. It's Thanksgiving."

Sara tied the belt of her old flannel robe so tightly she gasped. What was happening here? Goose bumps dotted her arms.

"In the corner across from the fireplace. My mother always piled the extra presents that didn't fit under the tree on top of the piano. It was always very . . . festive around here during the holiday season."

"I like this house," Dallas said as he trailed her to the kitchen. "They're redeco-rating my office, and they make a lot of noise. That's why I came down this evening. Plus I knew you wanted your car."

Sara measured coffee into the percolator. "I didn't know decorators worked at night."

"*Through* the night. I told them I wanted the office finished by morning. You have to pay extra for that. Sometimes it's good to have a lot of money. Listen, Sara, I want to help you. I can set you up in practice, and you don't even have to pay me back. I remember everything you said about all the bills you owe. Right now, right this very second, I can write you a check to cover everything. Your student loans, your car, the mortgages, and all those appliances you bought. Then, when you're the richest most important doctor in the country, you can pay me back. If you want to. If you don't, that's okay, too."

"Dallas, I can't take money from you. I can't borrow another cent. I can collect unemployment for a little while. I'll find a job. Doctors collect unemployment all the time," Sara lied as she crossed her fingers. "Carly helps out. We'll be able to make the mortgage payments. The worst-case scenario is I might lose the car. So, I'll get a bicycle."

"Are you saying no?" Dallas's eyes were wide with shock.

"I'm saying no. I would never, ever, abuse our friendship by borrowing money. That's the best way in the world to lose a friend."

"Will you marry me?"

The coffee Sara was pouring into the cup splashed out onto the counter. She yelped as some of the scalding coffee dripped on her big toe.

"Will you? If you do, that means half of everything I have will be yours and you can do what you want. I don't believe in prenuptial agreements. Marriage is forever. Adam doesn't agree, but I don't care."

"Dallas, sit down. Listen to me. I like you a lot. I enjoyed the time we've spent together, but I don't know if either one of us is ready for any kind of serious commitment. We've only known each other for a little over a month."

"I guess that means you aren't sure if you love me. I'm not sure either. What I do know for sure is I've never felt about anyone the way I feel about you. So, you see, it's okay. If we get married, we won't have to pretend with each other. Will you think about it? Think about all the good we can do together."

"Dallas, I . . ."

"Sara, I could build you the biggest, the best hospital in the country. Maybe in the world. You'd be the boss. The tour in January will make me a lot of money. New albums are on the schedule. I've got new songs ready to go. In a way the money is unlimited. It really is. It would make me very happy to know my music helps people who need your help. Kids with heart problems, old people with heart problems. You could take care of them and not even charge them. What's the name of that wrinkled old lady in India who works with all those poor, sick people?"

"Mother Teresa?" Sara said in a strangled voice.

"Yeah, her. You could do good stuff like she does. You might end up being more famous than me. I've made up my mind I'm going to cut back on my tour schedule. That means I'll be home for supper. We can just cut records. The band will love it. The guys' wives will love it even more. Please, Sara, say yes. We could even live here if you want or we could get a house just like this some place else. I'll have to keep the house in the canyon because of the recording studio. Say something, Sara."

Sara cleared her throat. "Is there something you aren't telling me? Did something happen? What made you ask me to marry you? There must be millions of young women in this world who would marry you and love you for who you are. I'm almost as old as you are, Dallas. It's not my intention to have children this late in my life. I've made that choice, and I intend to live by it. Don't you want children?"

"Sandi Sims asked me the same question. I said yes because I thought I did. Later when I thought about it I realized I probably wouldn't make a good father. So, my answer to the question is no, not particularly. I don't want to pass on my bad genes or whatever it is kids get from their parents. I'm not the . . . the brightest person. I'm good with music. That's all I'm good at. I can't read well. I don't understand things when I do read them. I'm . . . slow."

At Sara's stricken look, Dallas said, "My brain just can't handle . . . you know, normal stuff. Stuff that's easy for you and Adam. I can't get a handle on it. One time Billy got mad at me and called me dim-witted. He used to call me a lot of names. I always forgave him because he was my only friend. I don't think I ever truly forgave him, though, in my heart. That's the same as retarded. I didn't speak to him for a whole month. He said he was sorry and didn't mean it, but he did mean it, and I never forgave him for that lie. At the cemetery I did, but then it was too late. I'm just . . . retarded."

Sara gasped. "Where did you get an idea like that, Dallas?"

"From my brother and from Billy. I told you, the only thing I'm any good at is music."

"Oh, Dallas, that doesn't mean you're retarded. You might have some sort of a learning disability, that's all. Millions of people have learning disabilities. There's no shame in that. Look what you've done, look what you've accomplished. Were you ever tested in school?"

"All the time. Nobody ever told me how I did. Adam made sure I got through school. Adam's the smart one. Charlie and Millie didn't care how we did in school. They never asked to see my report card. Adam always asked."

Tears pricked Sara's eyes. "I have an idea. Let's take our coffee into the family room and light a fire. You trust me, don't you, Dallas?"

"Sure."

"I mean *really* trust me. We'll curl up by the fire, and I want you to talk to me like I was Billy. I want you to tell me everything about your life." Something stirred in Sara then, something maternal and something else. She wanted him to reach out to her and she wanted to cuddle in his arms. What was happening to her?

She lit the fire, and they settled in front of it with their mugs of coffee.

"What if you don't want to marry me after I tell you all the things about me and Adam?" Dallas asked.

"I asked you if you trusted me. You said yes. Your answers won't affect my decision."

"Will you promise me that you won't be angry with Adam after we talk? It's okay for me to get mad at him because he's my brother. I don't like it when someone else gets mad at him. I'm going to Las Vegas on the tenth of December. We're doing a charity benefit for aging musicians. It's a sold-out performance. I'd like us to get married when I get back. That's a really nice fire, Sara. Too bad you don't have some weenies and marshmallows."

"Oh, but I do. You sit right there, and I'll get them. While I toast the weenies and marshmallows you can talk. Dallas, would you mind if I recorded our conversation? I give you my word no one but me will ever hear the tape. I often record with a patient.

Mostly it's so I don't make a mistake. If you want, I'll swear on Billy Sweet."

"Sure, okay. I'm like that, too, Sara. I never break a promise, and when I give my word or shake hands it's good as gold. See, we have more in common than you think."

It the kitchen, Sara leaned against the refrigerator. She needed to think, but her brain was a beehive. She returned to the living room with the skewers, the marshmallows, the weenies, and rolls. She felt numb. From the top of her head to the tip of her bare toes. In some way she knew this was a turning point in her life.

"I'm going to cook as soon as the fire's hot. You just talk. Say anything you feel like saying. I'd like it if you'd start with your earliest childhood memories. One last thing, Dallas. I will not judge you." Dallas nodded.

It was full light when Sara shut off the tape recorder. She slid the bundle of tapes into an envelope. The recorder went back into the cabinet where she kept her CDs.

"I don't think I ever ate four hot dogs in my life," Sara said. "My New Year's resolution is to exercise and lose ten pounds."

"Why don't you go to one of those fat farms?"

"Because those fat farms cost a fortune. Are you saying I'm *fat?*"

"Are you going to marry me? Maybe you aren't fat *yet.* A little chubby. Well, what's your answer?"

"Dallas, I need a little time to think. It has nothing to do with the tapes and our talk here this morning. I've been so unlucky in my relationships, I don't want to jump into anything. The fact that neither one of us is certain if we're in love bothers me."

"Get over it."

"Just like that, get over it."

"Don't think about it. As long as you *like* me and I *like* you, we'll do fine."

"You've just given me the biggest headache of my life, Dallas Lord."

Dallas hooted with laughter. "That's because you know you need to lose ten pounds. We'll get married after you lose it. That gives you two weeks. Guess what else, Sara Killian. I'm going to have a surprise for you very soon. I want you to think of it in terms of a wedding gift."

And so Dr. Sara Killian agreed to marry Dallas Lord for all the wrong reasons. She further agreed to a private no-frills ceremony at Dallas's Mandeville Canyon estate. There

would be one guest on the list: Nellie Pulaski. Big Al Cherensky, the Canyon River
Band's drummer and the father of nine, was
to be the best man and Carly, Sara's sister,
the maid of honor.

"Let's go up to my house and cook our
dinner," Dallas said when she agreed. "I'm
anxious to see how my new office came out.
I'm really sorry about your job, Sara." His
face brightened, "Now you don't have to
worry about it. We can start to make all
kinds of plans in my new office. Do you want
to follow me in your own car or ride with me?
How would you like a chauffeur and a Rolls-
Royce?"

"I don't think so, Dallas. I like to drive. I
like doing things for myself. I don't think I
could ever get used to having a housekeeper fussing around my house."

"You get used to it. It gives you time to do
the important things. You always have clean
clothes, the floor is clean, there's food in the
cabinets and refrigerator. I had some bad
ones in the beginning. They used to steal
my stuff until Adam cracked the whip. Now
anyone who works for me has to be bonded
and fingerprinted. Security is the big prob-

lem. Adam said the payroll is outrageous. Sandi is bringing a friend up on Monday to audition for Billy's spot."

Sara nodded. Dallas spoke so fast, his thoughts changing at the speed of light. "Let me get dressed, and we'll go to your house. I'll follow you. We can get the turkey ready to go in the oven. Dinner should be ready around five. Is that okay with you?"

"Sure. Whatever you want, Sara. Do you mind if I use your phone while you're getting ready?"

"Go ahead."

Dallas waited until he heard Sara close her bedroom door on the second floor. Did hospital administrators work on Thanksgiving? He dialed and asked for Harry Heinrick. He waited a moment, then announced himself, his body shaking with anger. His voice a venomous hiss, he said, "You gave me your word that Sara wouldn't find out until I was ready for you to announce it. Sara already knows. The whole hospital knows. Sara was upset. She's still upset. What the hell kind of deal are you trying to pull on me? I don't want to hear excuses. I have a good mind to back out. I'm going to think about all of this until Monday. I'll call you and give you my decision. I don't like doing business with people who go back on their word."

Dallas hung up the phone. Would Adam have done it any differently? Hell, yes, he would have. He would have told Heinrick to fuck off, the deal was dead in the water. Adam wouldn't have said he would think about it till Monday. *Shit, I can't do anything right.* He had three days to think about it and to decide if he wanted to act like Adam or act like Dallas Lord.

"I'm ready, Dallas."

"Me too. Are you happy, Sara?"

Sara stared at Dallas's anxious face. He had such beautiful dark eyes and the most winsome smile she'd ever seen in her life. In his crisp khakis, pristine white shirt, whose cuffs were rolled to the middle of his arms, and his loafers, he looked nothing like the famous rock star that he was. "I think I am, Dallas. If happy isn't the right word, then contented will do. How about you?"

"I'm happy. I haven't been this happy in a long time. I haven't thought about Billy since I got to your house. I guess that means I'm making progress."

"I'd say so. I'll follow you."

Dallas was like a child when he hopped from the Jeep. He could barely contain himself until Sara climbed from her car. He reached for her hand. Together they ran to the house. "I can't wait to see the office."

The six decorators were sitting in the kitchen drinking coffee. "I hope you don't mind, Mr. Lord." Andrew Morrison, the owner of the decorating firm, motioned to the coffee cups on the table. "We finished about an hour ago. We didn't want to leave until you got back. If there's anything you don't like, we can change it now. We have everything in the van."

"Help yourself." Dallas's voice was excited and expansive.

Dallas motioned for Sara to follow him.

Nothing in the world could have prepared Sara for Dallas's newly decorated office. Shiny foil lightning bolts in every shade of the rainbow zigzagged across the room on a background of fuzzy electric blue wallpaper. The ceiling was painted a powder-puff blue with chunky white clouds that gradually darkened to represent a night sky with stars, moons, rainbows, and shooting stars.

Sara looked down at the floor, her jaw

dropping. White tile with polka dots the same colors as the lightning bolts raced across the office to blend into one giant red circle. A huge white desk with a glass top and a red, white, and blue chair sat inside the circle. The natural wood cabinets were now stark white, with smears of color going in every direction. Gold and platinum records, awards, certificates, and citations were aligned on one very large wall. The glistening gold frames seemed to be hanging from a braided red wire that ran horizontally and vertically across the wall.

"God! Is this great or what?" Dallas clapped his hands as he raced around the room to view it from all angles. "I told them I wanted my eyeballs to stand at attention. Man, they are at attention! This is really a wake-up room! What do you think, Sara?"

Sara blinked. "It's certainly different." She longed for sunglasses.

"I told them I wanted something different. They gave it to me. God, this is so great. Do you think it's a room that will give me inspiration? How could it not," he said answering himself. "Stay here, Sara. I have to pay the guys. We'll start dinner in a few minutes."

Sara sat down on the weird-looking chair

in the shape of the American flag. She closed her eyes and immediately felt better. She didn't open her eyes again until Dallas touched her shoulder. "I have the feeling you don't like this room."

"It's a bit . . . much for my taste, Dallas. I'm a pretty conservative person. The only thing that's important is that you like it. I don't know if they'll ever photograph it for *Architectural Digest.*"

"Are you kidding! Those people call me at least once a month. They're dying to get my house in their magazine."

It was Sara's turn to be amazed. She nodded. "I guess we should start dinner, huh?"

"Well, sure. While the turkey is cooking we can go down to the studio. I want to show you something first, though."

Five minutes later, Dallas opened his bedroom door with a flourish. "See this mess. Adam said I had to take it over. All this stuff was in the office. It was an Adam office. I wanted a Dallas office. Now, do you understand?"

"Dallas, what *is* this stuff?"

"I guess it's my life. My holdings. My records. All kinds of stuff. It might as well be in another language. I'm going to call Adam tomorrow and tell him he has to take it all back. Even if I could take care of this, it wouldn't leave me any time for my music. Every member of the band has stuff like this except Sandi. She hasn't been with the band long enough. I had to lend her money yesterday. Adam never would have given her a loan. He's too stingy, and I'm too generous. And we're brothers. Figure that one out. He told me not to trust anybody or they'd rob me blind."

"He told you the truth, Dallas. You have to be careful with the people you hire. You need to do background checks and don't *ever* let them handle your money. I had a lawyer once who tried to double bill me. You also have to pay careful attention to your credit-card charges, too. People make mistakes all the time. Today you just can't be careless. This all looks like a monster job. Did your brother take care of things by himself or does he have office help?"

"I don't know. Adam is the kind of person who can do anything. He sees everything through to the end. I get frustrated and quit if it doesn't go right. Adam never gives up. He's like me, he doesn't have a private life. The music, the business, the money, it takes over and *consumes* you. Sometimes I wish I was a janitor. There are days when I want to run away and never come back."

Sara laughed. "Sometimes I wish I was a schoolteacher. Let's open a bottle of wine and make a toast while I get the turkey ready. You can call your brother and wish him a happy Thanksgiving."

"I like you, Sara. I really do."

"I like you too, Dallas. I really do."

"Once we're married I'm going to hire security guards for you."

"Oh, no, Dallas. Don't do that. My patients won't like it."

"They'll chew you up and spit you out. They rip your clothes off. They follow you and stare at you while you're eating. They try to break into your house and your cars. Some women actually send me their underwear. I don't know if you can handle it. It won't go away, and it only gets worse."

"We can talk about that later. Let's get that wine and start the turkey."

"What shall we drink to, Sara?"

Sara's stomach lurched. "How about to a long and happy life?"

"I like that. To *our* long and happy life."

The knot in Sara's stomach doubled in

size. Maybe this was all a dream. On the other hand, maybe she was insane. As she sipped at her wine she argued with herself.

No one else is knocking on my door. Every relationship I've had has been a bust. Plus, I have strange feelings that I have to come to terms with. This man is going to make my life comfortable and luxurious. He won't make demands on me. I can have my own hospital. I can help people who otherwise wouldn't receive help. I can help save more lives. I won't have to answer to money-hungry bottom-line medical corporations manned by greedy doctors. I'm going to be forty years old soon. Men aren't interested in forty-year-old women. Men want young, dumb, and stupid women who they believe will make them feel young again. There's nothing wrong with what I'm going to do. I committed. I'm doing it. I can handle being Mrs. Dallas Lord. Sara Lord. Dr. Sara Lord. No, it should be Dr. Sara Killian. I'm not giving up my name for anyone. I was born with it and I'll die with it.

After Sara slid the turkey into the oven on the bottom rack, the two pumpkin pies on the top, Dallas said, "Did I ever show you my gymnasium?"

"No. I didn't know you had one."

"Come on, Dr. Killian, and feast your eyes on this room. It even has a sauna." Sara trotted after Dallas like a puppy.

"Wow! My sister works out regularly. She'd love this room."

"It's got everything. Sixty-inch television screen, stairmaster, treadmill, NordicTrack, rowing machine, state-of-the-art muscle-building equipment, stationary bike, and all that stuff over there that I haven't figured out yet. The sauna is behind the door, and there's a complete bathroom with Jacuzzi."

"I'm getting tired just looking at all this. Do you use it much?"

Dallas flushed. "I've never used it. I just wanted to have it. You know, in case I ever wanted to use it. Adam has a gym, too. He exercises religiously. He eats healthy food, too. He hardly ever eats red meat. He'll only have one drink at a time. Once in a while he smokes. He quit a long time ago, but sometimes he takes a cigarette. Especially when I get on his nerves. He's a really good cook. When the band first started up he used to cook for us so we could save money by not eating out. It was a job because there were so many of us. Even when times were lean we always had enough good food."

"Sometimes, Dallas, you make your brother sound like the devil and an angel at the same time. Did you ever sit down with him and tell him what you *really* feel? Brother to brother. Carly and I do it all the time. It helps to clear the air. I thought you were going to call him. Do you want to do it now?"

"Later. Let's go down to the studio. I want to play a couple of songs for you. Or, would you rather watch a movie?"

"Let's go to the studio. I'd love to hear you sing. I love Roy Orbison. I have all his tapes."

"I do too."

"Then let's go." Sara linked her arm with Dallas's. It felt right and it felt good.

"You should smile more often, Dr. Killian."

Sara laughed. "So should you, Mr. Lord."

"Sit right here, Sara. I'm going to sing you a song. It needs some backup, and you can do that once you've heard it. Are you ready?"

Sara sat cross-legged on a pile of thick cushions, her attention rapt as Dallas positioned his guitar. He closed his eyes. She knew he was in another world, a world of his own making. Tears blurred her vision as she listened to the words Dallas had created just for her.

A long time later, Dallas hunched his shoulders, his eyes wide-open. "Did you like it?"

"Like it! I loved it! It's beautiful. Does it have a name?"

"Of course. 'Sara's Song.' I love writing ballads. I think I got just the right mix. It's sad, it's haunting, and yet it's *alive*. It's just two verses. It's what I feel for you, Sara. I wrote it just for you. When I fine-tune it, we'll record it. Do you feel comfortable singing with me?"

"No!" Sara blurted. "I don't think I'm good enough to sing with Dallas Lord. Just because I sing with the choir doesn't mean I'm good enough to be professional."

"You worry too much. All this stuff is digital. I can make you sound better than Sandi and the other girls. Besides, this is just for you. Or us, if you prefer. No one is ever going to hear it but the two of us. That's what makes it special. I'll make two copies for you, the master and an extra. I wanted to do something special for you. It's all I know how to do, Sara. Do you really like it?"

"Dallas, I don't know what to say. It was so beautiful it brought tears to my eyes. What an incredible talent you have. I will treasure this song forever. I want to say something, but I don't know the words." Her voice turned suddenly shy. "I feel the same way, but I wouldn't have been able to express it like you did. I guess I am still stunned. Thank you, Dallas. I'll keep it safe forever and ever."

Dallas laughed. "Forever is a very long time, Sara. You have to keep the master copy safe. There are people out there who pirate our stuff. A Dallas Lord song goes for big bucks. Will you promise me that you won't play it for anyone? I want it to be ours. Maybe someday, when we're really old, we can decide if we want to release the song. Are you okay with that?"

"Sure. What if someone steals it? I've been known to lose things. I'm not saying I will, but what if?"

"You have the master. Once I give it to you, you are responsible for it. That's why it's called a gift." Dallas chuckled.

"I'll probably worry myself sick over it." Sara's heart felt like it was swelling inside her chest. The overwhelming urge to have him take her in his arms was back with her. She closed her eyes to ward off the light-headedness she was feeling.

"Don't tell anyone about it," Dallas said. "If you keep it a secret, no one will know you even have it."

"Did you tell anyone you were writing the song, Dallas?"

"Only Sandi. She won't tell anyone."

A chill ran up Sara's back. "I promise I'll keep it safe for us," she said.

"Of course you will. It's going to be my wedding present to you. It just needs a little fine-tuning. Do you want to hear the song I'm working on for Billy's memory? After I play it for you we can do 'Sara's Song' with you doing the backup. I have a copy of the words for you. This is great, isn't it, Sara?"

Sara shivered. "It really is great, Dallas. When are you going to call your brother?"

"You really want me to do that, don't you?"

"Only if you want to, and I think you do. I can go out to the kitchen while you make the call."

"All right, I'll do it now. You can stay."

Sara shook her head. "I'll baste the turkey. Are you going to tell him about the song?"

"No way!" Dallas's voice was vehement. "I'll buzz you on the intercom when I finish the call."

In the sterile-looking kitchen, Sara leaned over the kitchen sink. Is this what she went to school for, all those years? Was Dallas Lord her destiny? If her parents were alive, what would they say if they knew she was going to marry a rock star for material reasons? She wasn't going to think about the love and passion part right now. If she put all her own fears and worries aside, could she be happy knowing and believing she could make Dallas's life better and her own as well? Dallas needed her. *I need him, too. God, what will people say when they hear about this? The last time someone needed me was when Carly was fifteen. An eternity ago.*

She sighed. "Like Scarlett said, I'll think about this tomorrow."

Chapter Eight

Adam Lord tugged, wrestled, and finally—
using his booted foot—shoved the monster
Christmas tree through the gates leading to
the courtyard. He heaved a mighty sigh
when he became aware of seven curious
sets of eyes on him. "The real challenge,"
he muttered to the dogs, "is getting it into
the living room." The six pups yipped and
squeaked their excitement at these strange
goings-on. The mother dog, now named Izzie, barked as the pups scrambled in and
among the branches. Izzie continued to
bark, running back and forth to the gate and
then finally tugging on Adam's pant leg. She
backed up and ran back to the gate, her
barks more shrill and harsh-sounding.

"Okay, okay, I get it. I didn't padlock the
gate. You want to see me do it. You want to
hear the sound of the lock. That means your
pups are safe." The padlock snapped into
place, hitting the metal flange. "No one goes

in and no one goes out. The guys are safe, Izzie."

Adam eyed the huge fir tree and the pups crawling in the branches, Izzie hovering nearby. His very first Christmas tree. In his very own house. He felt happy, wonderful, and at peace with himself. It was the Christmas season, and he was going all out for the first time in his life. He'd even planned a small cocktail party—inviting the broker who'd sold him the house, two of his neighbors, a Wachovia Bank officer and his wife, his new veterinarian, and the florist who'd decorated his house with fragrant evergreen boughs, mistletoe, and poinsettias. He even had presents to put under the tree, all dog gifts ordered from the Delight Doggie Shoppe.

Ninety minutes later, Adam stood back to survey his handiwork. The sixteen-foot-high Douglas fir stood regally in the corner, its tip reaching the vaulted ceiling. He sucked in his breath as he bent to rescue two of the precocious pups guzzling water from the tree stand. He looked around. The house was definitely lived-in now. Everywhere he looked there were pee stains. Even though he'd cleaned and scrubbed, the stains were still there. Well, he had a bead on that, too, a dog trainer, supposedly the best in his field, was due to arrive shortly. The man had guaranteed tranquility by nightfall.

Fit and trim, light on his feet, Adam was no match for the six cavorting pups as they beelined for the low branches of the tree, tugging ferociously, snapping and snarling when the needles scratched their tiny faces. Izzie watched indulgently as Adam picked the pups up and carried them to the sink in the laundry room. He washed them with a citrus-smelling shampoo and wrapped them in fluffy yellow towels. He should have worn a raincoat.

The bath ordeal over, Adam headed for the second floor, all seven dogs trailing behind. Izzie was last, so she could boost the runt whose rump was too fat to make the steps. They watched his every move. The moment his Nikes thumped on the floor the pups were on top of them. As it was, his shoe-laces were little more than thin threads, the inner soles tattered. When he returned from the bathroom, fully dressed, one pup was asleep inside his sneaker, one was curled up on his wet jeans, two of them were tug-ging on his sock. He could see the holes from where he was standing. Pups three and four were tussling with each other as Izzie watched from her position on Adam's pillow.

Adam jumped out of the way when the doorbell shrilled to life. They were a mini herd as they galloped to the top of the steps, then tumbled down the rest of the way. He opened the door to admit a pudgy man wearing a Braves baseball cap with a whistle around his neck. The bedlam was silenced immediately when the whistle blew. Adam blinked. The trainer's voice was musical-sounding when he said, "Mr. Lord, it's 1:20. By 6:20 this evening, you will be able to hear yourself think. Show me where their beds are, get me a beer, and do yourself a favor and disappear until 6:15." Adam did as instructed and retired to the living room, where he closed the pocket doors before proceeding to string the lights on his Christmas tree. From time to time he smiled as he listened to the whistle in the kitchen.

No one in their right mind had seven dogs. No one in their right mind bought an all-terrain vehicle for $70,000 just for seven dogs. The Range Rover was his Christmas present to himself. The keys were on the mantel. He was still trying to make up his mind whether to wrap them or not.

The tree was finished at three o'clock. The dogs' presents—chewies, squeak toys, new leashes and collars—all wrapped by four. He looked around. It was definitely festive. He wished suddenly that someone was sitting next to him on the sofa. Someone to talk to. Someone to tell him the tree looked beautiful. He didn't stop to think, he reached for the phone to dial his brother's number.

"Dallas, it's Adam. Listen, I was wondering if you'd like to come to South Carolina and spend Christmas with me. Just the two of us. I put my tree up today and decorated it myself. Yeah, I know it's early, but it's my first time. I want to have plenty of time to enjoy it. I have these seven dogs. Yeah, yeah, seven. You're right, Dallas, I almost forgot you're leaving for Vegas. The dogs take up all my time. When you wind it up, come here instead of going back to LA. We can talk about *that mess* in your bedroom when you get here. Hell, yes, the house is already decorated. From top to bottom. I swear, Dallas, it looks just like those pictures we used to look at in Millie's catalogues. Do you remember how we used to promise each other we'd have houses like that someday? I have the house, but it doesn't feel right because you aren't here. What's there to think about, Dallas? Either you want to come or you don't. We need to talk, Dallas. And, each of us needs to listen to the other one. I'm glad you're getting married. No, of course I'm not angry that you want Al for your best man. It's your wedding. All I ever wanted, Dallas, was for you to be happy. Okay, then, it's settled. Call me when you're ready to leave Vegas. I'll pick you up at the airport. You want me to bring all seven of the dogs. Sure. I just call them One, Two, Three, Four, Five, and Six. The mother's name is Izzie. The runt is Six. You want me to call him Dallas? Sure. Dallas Six it is. You want me to do *what,* Dallas? Sure, sure, licorice, Jujubes, and a new comic book in an orange string bag. It's okay, Dallas. I knew where you were coming from back then. Have a safe flight. Dedicate your first number to Dallas Six. I'll see you next week. Dallas, I do love you. I just want you to know that. I guess I'm getting mushy in my old age. Maybe it's that my little brother is getting married. The rest of the stuff is all bullshit. Okay, Dallas." His voice was gruff and choked-sounding. To his ear, Dallas's voice sounded the same way. "Good-bye."

Adam smacked his hands together. "Ah, life is looking good." He looked at his watch. He had time to run to Harris Teeter to get the orange bag.

Later, he was all thumbs when he cut the orange, nylon mesh in the pattern of a Christmas stocking. Twice he got a lump in his throat when he remembered how Dallas had thrown the stocking at him when they were children. Well, that was then, this was now. He jammed the stocking full of Jujubes, and licorice, squeezing the Superman comic book down into the toe of the stocking. He attached a red velvet bow to the top of the stocking with Scotch tape before he hung it on the mantel next to the seven stockings for the dogs. He started to laugh when he stared at the seven red velvet stockings with their appliquéd designs at fifty bucks a pop. Dallas's homemade creation was six dollars tops, if you didn't count the cost of the red bow. And he had a dozen oranges to eat.

It was ten minutes of six when Adam popped a cola drink, his feet on the coffee table. It was dark out now, the lights on the tree winking in the dark room. The room looked so beautiful he felt himself start to choke up. It occurred to him suddenly that he hadn't heard the whistle for a long time. Five minutes to go. He slid the pocket doors open, tiptoeing quietly toward the kitchen. He peeked around the corner, clapping his hand over his mouth to keep from laughing. Mother and offspring were lined up in a neat row, their eyes expectant as they waited for their next order. When the whistle sounded two short blasts of sound, the line moved to the right. Seven more blasts followed. One by one the dogs ran to their tartan plaid beds. Five and Six mixed up the beds and were rewarded with one long piercing belt of sound. They immediately rectified the situation and were rewarded with a treat.

Tom Silk clapped his hands, his musical voice full of praise as he patted the dogs and tweaked their noses.

"I see it, but I don't believe it. They actually listened to you. Izzie listens, but the pups do as they please."

"That's because you let them do as they please. At this age they need to be confined. You've got the doggie door, so they can go in the garden at will to do their business.

You must praise them. It's your tone of voice more than what you say. The whistle is something they understand. You can't abuse it. You have to stop feeding them that crap you've been dishing out. Dry dog food full of nutrients is what they get from now on. Once they get used to the new food they won't be peeing and pooping every two minutes. You're keeping all of them?"

Adam looked at Izzie, who was watching and listening. "Of course." Izzie lay down with her head between her paws. The pups were sound asleep.

"I've taken the liberty of writing out some guidelines to make it easier for you. Each blast of the whistle means something. Repetition is how they learn. The pups are going to make a lot of mistakes in the beginning, so you need to be patient, and praise goes a long way if they're trying. Izzie picked it up right away. She'll help. Where did you get these dogs if you don't mind me asking? I would have thought you were a horse man."

"I have a ranch in Wyoming and yes, I like horses. I found Izzie and her pups in the garden. I think she got in when the man came to read the meter. I keep the garden gate locked now because she gets spooked if it's open. I think she's afraid I'll turn her out. I would never do that, but she doesn't know it yet."

"Oh, yes, she does. Dogs are more intuitive than humans in my opinion. She knows these little guys are a handful, that's why she helped out. She's still afraid you might sell them off or take them to the pound. She needs to be reassured. When she trusts you completely, you'll know it. No one will have to tell you. When that moment comes it will be unlike anything you ever experienced. Trust me."

"Okay. Listen, I'm having a small Christmas party next week. Would you like to come?"

"You mean with a date in dress-up duds without the whistle?"

Adam laughed. "Yeah."

"I'll be here. If you have any problems, call me even if it's the middle of the night. I can be here in fifteen minutes if there's an emergency. By the way, I'm a vet."

"I didn't know that. Did you give it up?"

"Nah. It gave me up. I can't put a dog to sleep. I just can't. I'm one of those guys who wants to take all the dogs home with me. This works. The animals like me and know

I like them. I'll see you next week. This is just a guess on my part, but I think those pups will sleep through the night. Leave some food and water out in case they wake up. Can I ask you something?"

"Sure."

"You look familiar. I know you aren't from around here. This is a crazy way-out question but are you any relationship to that rock star Dallas Lord?"

"He's my brother."

"My girlfriend is his biggest fan. She has every single album of his. You're the guy behind the scenes, huh?"

Adam shrugged. He wasn't going to get into that. "You could say that. Thanks for everything." He handed over a check.

"Remember now, your two favorite words from here on in are 'repetition' and 'patience.' "

"I'll remember."

Adam closed and locked the front door. He talked to Izzie as he made his dinner. "Let's me and you go into the living room and watch some television, Izzie. We can look at the tree, and I can tell you the story of my life. I think I know how you might feel. I was in a place like that myself for a long time. So was Dallas. You and I are going to bond, little lady. Big time."

At two in the morning, Adam got up from the couch and stretched, yawning wearily. He turned off the television set before he followed Izzie to the kitchen to check on the pups. Izzie whined, her eyes going from the pups to the whistle on the hearth. "Oh, oh. Our first problem." Adam dropped to his haunches as he stared at Numbers Five and Six curled together in Dallas Six's bed. "You know what I say, Izzie, the hell with it. No whistle. Let them sleep. You know that story I was telling you earlier about Dallas and me. We used to sleep together because Dallas was always scared. I was, too. This is okay." The spaniel licked at Adam's face, her eyes expectant.

Adam checked the locks on the door, turned the night-light low, filled the water and food bowls before he left the kitchen. In the doorway leading to the dining room he turned. "It's one of those either or decisions, Izzie. You can come upstairs or you can stay down here." Izzie's tail swished as she trotted from one tartan-covered bed to the other. Satisfied, she trotted after her new master and reached the top of the steps before he did.

"In my wildest dreams I never thought I'd be sleeping with a dog at the age of forty-two. I get the right side. I snore, and I'm all over the bed. I also sleep like I'm dead. You can ring a bell in my ear, and I won't wake up until seven o'clock. Just so you know."

The spaniel bounded onto the bed. Adam watched as she searched out a space that was comfortable to her. When she finally found it, she dragged the king-size pillow to the spot at the foot of the bed. She waited until she was satisfied that Adam was almost asleep before she woofed softly.

"Good night to you, too, Izzie."

Chapter Nine

Dallas stood on the tarmac, his eyes straining to see through the torrential rain. He knew the private sleek, silvery Gulfstream that would take him to Las Vegas was out there somewhere. He made a mental note to think about getting his eyes checked when he returned to LA. As he waited for the pilot he struggled to remember the last time LA had such a horrendous rainy season. He couldn't come up with a time or date. It was cold, too. He hated the cold. Sunshine and bright lights always made him feel good. He didn't like the dark either. Not many people knew he slept with the bathroom light on and two night-lights. He looked around. Where the hell was the damn pilot? With the money he was paying, the guy should have been waiting for him with a thermos of hot coffee since he'd waved off any idea of anything other than a one-man crew. He wanted to sleep through the flight and didn't want anyone fussing over him, asking for autographs, or making idle conversation. Most of all he didn't want to answer questions about the future of the Canyon River Band.

"Mr. Lord. I'm sorry I'm late. Some of the roads are flooding, and traffic was backed up for miles. Nasty day for flying, but I hear the sun is shining in Vegas. I have a favor to ask, Mr. Lord."

Dallas stared at the man. He hated the word favor. It always meant he had to do something he didn't want to do. Usually a favor meant something besides an autograph.

"Let's hear it."

The pilot spoke in a rush, trying to get the words out in one long stream without taking a breath for fear the favor wouldn't be granted. "I'd like to bring my brother Bruce along. He's got a . . . problem. I want to get him into a rehab clinic I heard about outside Las Vegas. He's in no shape to fly commercial, and driving him there would be risky. Right now he's so strung-out he doesn't even know what his name is. I've tried to do charters the past couple of years so I'd be home for him. It isn't working. This is my last shot. If it's a question of money, I'll pay you whatever you think is fair. You're the only passenger, so there are empty seats. I know it's a lot to ask."

"Have you always taken care of him?" Dallas asked.

"Yeah, and my ex-wife didn't like it. She booted him out six or seven times, and then I had to go out and find him. Our marriage was rocky at that point anyway. She divorced me and married a dentist. The pressure just started to build and build. There are days when I wish I could walk off into the sunset and not look back. I often wonder what it would be like to be, you know, totally free, with no worries and no fears. Think about it, a new name, a new identity, starting over somewhere with no one knowing who you are and not caring. No one to answer to. It's a dream is all it is. You can't hide from your responsibilities. He's my brother for God's sake. I can't just let him swing in the wind. Like I said, this is my last shot. He's only twenty-two. Nobody needs to know he's on this flight, if you know what I mean."

Dallas wasn't sure what that meant exactly, so he pretended he did. "Sure. That's what big brothers are for—helping little brothers."

The pilot sighed. "Sounds like you have a big brother."

"I do."

"Brought you a thermos of coffee and some Danish, Mr. Lord."

"Thanks, Don. Do you have any other family?"

"No, just me and my brother. Maybe some distant cousins, but I have no idea where they are or how many there are."

"It's just me and my brother, too. Where is your brother?"

"That's him over there, dancing in the rain. Today he thinks he's Fred Astaire. Last night he was climbing Mount Rushmore. You go ahead and get on board, Mr. Lord. I'll get him settled up front."

"I'll sit in the back. I appreciate the coffee and Danish. Is this storm going to be a problem on takeoff?"

"I've been in worse. I'm a good pilot, Mr. Lord. This plane is a beaut. I'll set you down smooth as silk. Thanks for understanding about my brother."

"It's okay, man. We all gotta do what we gotta do."

"Buckle up, it's going to be a bumpy ride most of the way."

Dallas watched as the pilot hustled and shoved his brother up the steps to the plane. He was a straggly-looking kid, unshaven, with limp, stringy hair. With Dallas's help Don managed to get him into his seat and buckled up. "I don't think anyone saw us, do you?" the pilot asked nervously.

Dallas wished his eyesight was better. "I don't think so. Are you sure he's going to be okay?"

"Hell, no. Take a good look at him. He's in La La Land."

"Maybe you should tie him in the seat or something."

"Jesus," was all the pilot could think of to say.

"We could knot some of the blankets together and tie them around the seat. I'll check on him from time to time. The flight isn't that long."

Dallas felt like crying and didn't know why. "I'll sit across from him until he falls asleep," he said when they finished tying the blankets around the back of the seat.

Twenty minutes later, the Gulfstream was airborne. Dallas tightened his seat belt, his eyes on the passenger across from him. Twenty more minutes went by before the pilot's brother settled into a sound sleep. Dallas untied the blankets before he went to his seat at the rear of the plane. He was asleep within five minutes. He slept so soundly he didn't feel the gut-wrenching turbulence, the sheer drop in altitude, or the pilot's panic-filled voice on the intercom. He was also oblivious to the swinging oxygen masks floating in the air. When one of them slapped him in the face he had the presence of mind to clamp it over his mouth. He was aware then of the dizzying descent of the aircraft. He barely had time to tuck his head between his knees before he felt the solid impact of hitting something. The next thing he knew he was staring at the sky and stars above. He was still strapped into his seat, but he could see the forward section of the plane off in the distance. He tried to grapple with the horror he was experiencing. Was he having a nightmare or was this the real thing? He looked around, aware that the tail section of the plane had ripped off from the main body. He panicked when he couldn't undo the seat belt.

"Think, Dallas," he mumbled. "There has

to be a way out of this. Where's that Swiss Army knife, the little one that Adam gave you a long time ago? You always carry it. Is it in your pocket? Get it, cut the belt. Get out of here. What's in the tail section? I don't know. Get out. Get out now. There's always a fire when a plane goes down."

He struggled to get his hands in his pants pocket, but the belt was too tight. He squirmed and jiggled until his index finger made contact with the small knife. He used up more panic-filled minutes trying to inch the knife from his pocket. Finally he was free of the seat restraint. He thanked God that he had untied the pilot's brother.

The moment Dallas's legs lost their rubbery feeling he started to run, shouting for the pilot whose name he couldn't remember. Thick, black, oily smoke raced toward him. He turned and ran to the east, aware for the first time of the deep sand under his feet. They were in the desert somewhere. Instinct forced him to drop to the ground just as a loud explosion and a huge ball of fire shot upward. The ground rumbled beneath his trembling body. He started to sob then, his fists pounding into the sand. He lay still for a long time, aware that he was safe and

Doesn't here she killed again.

there was nothing he could do for Don and his brother. He felt dizzy and disoriented when he finally struggled to his feet. He walked as close to the burning plane as he dared. No one could have survived the explosion. If he didn't know anything else, he knew that. He turned to walk away, heading back to the tail section of the plane. He burrowed in the deep sand and found his small travel bag, still lodged under the seat. His eyes filled with wonderment that his belongings were still intact. He slung the bag over his shoulder and set out on foot. He had no idea where he was or where he was going or why he wasn't waiting for rescue workers to find him. He concentrated on putting one foot down into the sand and then pulling it out. *They will not know about him since there are 2 on the plane*

Within an hour he was exhausted. The sun beat down on his bare head. He started to stagger then, a feeling of light-headedness coming over him. He crumpled and started to crawl. He wondered how long it would take before he blacked out totally. Was he going to die out here in the desert? At that precise moment he didn't know and he didn't care.

The sun was directly overhead when he

heard a voice that sounded far away. He stopped his crab-crawling and tried to look upward, but the sun blinded him. "Whatcha doing way out here, mister?" a cranky voice demanded. Dallas tried to answer, but his thick tongue and cracked lips wouldn't allow it. He pointed to his mouth.

The man smelled of many things, but Dallas didn't care. For one brief second he wondered if he was staring at God. "Lean on me, son, and I'll git you over to my truck. It got air-conditioning. Is this here your bag?" Dallas managed to nod. "You git yerself lost out here?" Dallas nodded again. It was easier than trying to explain.

"There be a motel down the road, 'bout eight miles or so. You want I should take you there?" Dallas's head bobbed a third time. "It ain't much, but it's clean. Cheap too. Eats is extra."

The blast of cold air rocked Dallas back in his seat. Nothing in the world had ever felt this good. Not his first concert, his first whopping paycheck, his first time at sex, nothing.

As the truck barreled over the hot, dry sand, Dallas wondered why he was still alive and the others were dead. He also wondered if this grizzled old man knew about the plane crash. He almost asked, then changed his mind.

"I seed a fire out there in the desert. I got to thinkin' maybe the government was settin' off one of them bombs. I was goin' to take a look-see. Then I seen you. Didja notice it, son?"

Dallas shook his head.

"You headed for Vegas? Or wuz you there and someone rolled you and that's how you ended up way out here?" It sounded as good an excuse as any to Dallas. He nodded again.

Dallas lost track of time as the old man rattled on about living in the desert and his trailer that was set back a piece from the motel. He was starting to doze off when his driver announced they had reached their destination. He was grateful for the older man's help in getting out of the car and into the small cabin next to the office. "You got enough money left to be paying for this cabin, son?"

Dallas fished in his pocket and withdrew two fifty-dollar bills. He handed both of them to the old man. "Keep one for yourself," he managed to croak.

The old man turned anxious when Dallas stumbled against the wall. "I'll turn on the shower for you, son, and pull down the bed. Maggie will bring you some drinkin' water and a bowl of ice. Doncha overdo it now. I'll sign you in. What's your name?"

"Name?"

"Gotta write it on the register."

"Jack."

"Jack what, son?"

"Piper." He wondered why he was lying. Later he would worry about it. "Is there a television?"

"Yes sirree. Maggie got herself one of them satellite dishes out to the back. I git it on my set, too. You need sleep more'n you need television. Water's just right. You scrub up good but be careful with your face and shoulders, they're right sunburned. Maggie will fetch you some stuff to put on it. I'll be leavin' you now, son. Thanks for the fifty bucks."

Dallas undressed and stepped into the shower. The water felt almost as good as the air-conditioner had felt earlier. As he was lathering up for the second time he heard movement outside the bathroom. "It's Maggie Deering, Mr. Piper. I'm leaving the water and ice on the dresser. Don't mind the smell of the ointment, it fades after a bit. It will take the heat out of the burn. I serve supper at six if you're hungry. Tonight we're having meat loaf. There's always plenty left, so you can eat anytime. Dinner's two dollars. I'm locking the door behind me, Mr. Piper."

Dallas waited until he heard the door close before he stepped from the shower. He didn't bother to dry himself off. Instead he applied the evil-smelling ointment to his face and shoulders before he padded to the bed and climbed in. In a half stupor he leaned over for the remote control and turned on the television set. A satellite dish meant he would be able to turn on CNN. He played with the buttons until he saw the bright CNN at the bottom of the screen. His jaw dropped and his eyebrows inched upward when he heard the field reporter announce his death. His eyes closed and then he was asleep, the television droning on.

Dallas woke eight hours later to total darkness. He blinked as he tried to focus on the television screen. He was freezing cold, and he had to go to the bathroom. He was also wide-awake. He turned on the shower again and stood under the hot water until he felt warm enough to crawl back into bed. His watch on the night table said it was one o'clock in the morning. The white Styrofoam box sitting next to the television drew his eye. He hopped off the bed to see what was in it. Meat loaf, roasted potatoes, emerald green peas, and bright orange carrots along with a generous chunk of corn bread with melted butter. A wedge of cherry pie sat on top of everything. The meal was cold, but Dallas wolfed it down in minutes. He was finishing the pie when the top-of-the-hour news came on. He watched, fascinated at the people milling around the crash site giving off sound bites. According to CNN he was dead, charred to a crisp along with the pilot. He looked around for a phone, but there was none. Maybe there was one in the office of the motel. At this hour of the night it was closed. What were Adam and Sara thinking? Were they mourning him, realizing how much they loved him now that he was gone? He wished he knew. Someone told him once that famous people became more famous after they died.

Dallas pulled the light coverlet up to his chin. It was comfortable now that he'd turned off the air-conditioning. The ointment was helping also. He felt a thousand percent better now. As he listened to the field reporters his thoughts took him back to the tarmac earlier yesterday when he talked to the pilot before takeoff. He understood now why the authorities thought he was dead. They didn't know the pilot's brother had been on the plane. The bodies were charred beyond recognition. Who would mourn them? No one. Don and Bruce had no family. Who would take care of the charred remains? The airline? The Pilots' Association? Was there such a thing? It occurred to him then to wonder what had happened to the plane to cause it to spiral to the ground. They were talking now about a black box that would have the answers. Did planes just fall apart in midair? How had the rear end of the plane been ripped off? Why had he survived and not the others? Was it supposed to mean something? He wished then that he was more religious. Divine intervention. Why? He needed to call Adam and Sara and tell them he was alive.

Walk away into the sunset with a new name and new identity. The pilot couldn't do that, but he could. *If he wanted to.* Maybe this was the reason he had survived the crash. Maybe he was meant to start a new life somewhere else. Was this divine intervention? He wasn't even sure what the words meant exactly. *Walk away into the sunset with a new name and new identity.* If he walked away, things would fall apart. He'd never see Adam or Sara again. He could do all the things he wanted to do but never had the time to do. For starters he could get himself a dog so he'd have a buddy. He could check into one of those special places and get himself evaluated. Sara said there was nothing wrong with him. With special help he could learn to function in Adam's world. He wondered if he had the guts to commit to such a thing. He could do it. *If he wanted to.* Maybe he should just check into a hospital and ask for "the works." He thought then about the mess he'd left on his bed back in the canyon house. If he got help, the day might come when he'd be able to sort through it and actually understand what it was all about. *If he wanted to.* Of course Adam would chew his ass out for doing something he considered reprehensible. But then, maybe Adam would be proud of him once he learned he could

function on his own in the world. He
squeezed his eyes shut as he tried to picture
the pride in Adam's face. He wouldn't have
to stay dead forever. At some point in time
he could resurface and concoct some kind
of story that would make things right. *If he
wanted to.*

Dallas punched at the pillow behind his
head. He needed to be clear in his mind who
he was going to be doing this for, if he decided to do it. Himself or Adam? "For me. I
want to be like everyone else," he mumbled.
As he watched the commentary on his life
unfold via CNN, Dallas let himself daydream
about walking up to Sara's front door with a
bouquet of yellow roses and ringing her bell.
He'd be dressed like Adam in a suit and tie
with a regulation haircut. He smiled to himself when he pictured her wide smile as she
threw her arms around him and kissed him
soundly on the lips. Sara deserved the best.
Maybe in time he could become the best. If
not the best, then maybe he could become
just a regular guy in Adam's shadow. If
things went right, he might even want to go
to college someday. It was never too late to
get an education.

The big question staring him in the face

was where was he to get the money to do all this? He had a wad of cash that he'd planned to gamble with in his duffel bag. It would last him a while, possibly a year if he was frugal. Back in the canyon he had money in a special safe he and Billy Sweet had built into the floor of his walk-in closet. Even Adam didn't know about the safe. There were two things in the safe, money and the harmonica Adam had given him. In the beginning he'd only planned to keep a few thousand in the safe for emergency money, but Billy had said, "Man, what's the point? You need to fill this sucker up in case things go bad." He'd taken his friend's advice and as near as he could remember he had close to a million dollars in tight, compact bundles. Having the money and getting to it were two different things at this point in time. As Adam always said, where there's a will there is a way. He didn't need to think about that now.

Dallas gulped at the bottle of warm cherry soda that Maggie had left with his dinner. He longed for a cold root beer. He grew tired of seeing himself on television, so he started flipping through the channels, but he always came back to CNN. So far he hadn't seen

Sara. He wondered why. He listened to the announcement concerning his brother. He snorted when he heard that he was going to make an announcement later in the day.

What to do. Should he do it? How to do it? *Make up your mind, Dallas. Either you're going to do it or you aren't. If you aren't, you need to find a pay phone and call the authorities or Adam and Sara.*

Dallas rolled over in bed. What was it Adam always said? When in doubt, do nothing. If it was good enough for Adam, it was good enough for him. He slept again, soundly, deeply, and restfully.

At eight o'clock, Maggie Deering rapped on Dallas's door. "Breakfast's in ten minutes if you're hungry."

Dallas hopped from the bed, stunned to see his clothes washed and folded. He put them on, sniffing as he did so. They smelled like a sunny day after a hard rain. The money from his trousers was on the dresser. He scooped it up. He walked gingerly over to the main cabin. He ached from head to toe, but his sunburn was definitely better. He was also very, very hungry.

"How are you feeling this morning, Jack?" Dallas looked over his shoulder for Jack until he remembered; *he* was Jack. "Much better, thank you. Thanks for washing my clothes and leaving me the food. It tasted so good I ate it all."

"Get your appetite ready because I serve up a hearty breakfast. My man, he liked a hearty meal on wakening. Steak, potatoes, saw mill gravy, and biscuits. You aren't getting that, though. I whipped up some pancakes, eggs, bacon, and sausage. I also have some homemade apple dumplings with real cream."

"I'll have some of everything," Dallas said. He drank his first cup of coffee in two gulps, the second in three gulps; the third he sipped as he ate. When he was finished, he said, "I don't think I ever ate this much at one time in my whole life."

Maggie preened. "Everybody says that who eats here," she said with no show of modesty. "I love cooking. We're having roast chicken tonight if you're staying on. Are you?" she asked bluntly.

Dallas surprised himself when he said, "I'll be staying for three or four days. I still feel kind of rubbery if you know what I mean."

"The desert sun can kill you. Good thing Moses found you when he did. He was fretting here all night worrying about you. He ate when the sun came up. Moses is a good man. An honest man. You can't hardly find men like him any more. My man, he was like that. Where you from, Jack?"

"I move around a lot. Mostly California." Obviously this kind lady wasn't into rock stars or rock music. "What's going on in the world?" he asked as he pointed to the television on the counter.

"Not much. A plane went down in the desert yesterday. Everyone on it was killed. Sad, real sad."

"How many people?" Dallas asked.

"Two. Some singer and the pilot. I didn't pay much attention. I don't like hearing stuff like that."

Dallas nodded. "Me too. How far is the nearest town?"

"Dumont must be ten, maybe twelve miles. Is that where you're headed? Moses said you were rolled." She clucked her tongue. "Did you win big?"

"Yeah. I got some left, though."

"They take your car?"

He hated lying, he really did. "Yeah. I have to get another one. Do you think Moses will take me into town?"

"Sure. He doesn't do anything all day but wander around. Once in a while he kills a rattlesnake."

"How does he live?"

"He is not a bum if that's what you're thinking. He has a ton of money socked in the bank over at Dumont. Used to own a big junkyard. There's money in junk. He's from the East somewhere. He came out here to the desert because of his lungs. He likes to watch game shows on television. Once in a while he goes into town and has some beers and plays a little poker. He likes the simple life. He isn't as old as he looks. The sun did that to him. Told you, the sun is a killer. Walk on back. He's sunning himself outside."

"How much do I owe you, Maggie?"

"Nothing. Moses gave me your fifty dollars and you still have a credit after the room rate is deducted. Most likely I will be owing you a refund when you leave. Will you be here for supper?"

"Yes, ma'am, I will."

Dallas walked around the back of the motel office. Maggie was right, the crusty old man was taking the sun, his weathered face peaceful. Dallas stared at him a moment longer than necessary.

"You committing me to memory, son?"

"In a way. You look contented. Peaceful. I don't think I ever felt that way in my whole life." He sat down on a wooden crate, his eyes puzzled.

"Howzat?"

"Decisions, responsibility, life. Sometimes it seems like it's going to choke the life out of me. Even when I take a day off I know that the next day will be the same. I just put off things and taking that one day off makes it worse. I heard from Maggie you had a junkyard back East."

"Mighty stressful, junk. Had to hire security to protect all that junk. Had to get guard dogs to watch the security people. Money started going out faster than it was comin' in. Decided to pack it in and come out here to the desert when my wife died. Didn't have no kids. I can breathe better here. How much did you lose when you got rolled, son?"

Dallas hated lying. He hesitated a moment too long. The old man's eyes snapped open. "You on the run, son?"

Was he? He hadn't decided yet. He nodded, his decision made. He met the watery gaze head-on. "I need to go to town to get some kind of vehicle. I'll have to pay cash. I don't have a driver's license. It could be a problem."

"Money can buy most anything, son. You want to jaw about this a little more or would you like me to mind my own business?"

Dallas thought about the question before he replied. "It will probably be better for you if you don't know too much. I want to get a haircut and some clothes."

"Maggie knows how to cut hair," Moses said. "Never did cotton to men with long hair. She does a professional job. It don't pay to call attention to yourself if you're . . . avoiding people. About that there driver's license. I think I might be able to get you one that will pass inspection. It will cost, though. I can buy you the vehicle and register it in your name. They know me in Dumont. Money talks. Guess you know that. Town ain't all that big. Nothing much goes on, so people have to spec-u-late. Might be a good idea for me to buy the clothes, too. Do you get my drift?"

"Do you think you could get me a cell phone?"

"Don't see why not. You pay in advance and leave a hefty deposit. Ain't got nothin' planned for today, so we might as well start out. You need to wear a cap and pile that hair on top of your head, son. I think I got a cap somewhere. Maggie can cut your hair when we get back. Folks over to Dumont don't understand a man wearing diamonds in their ears." Dallas removed the stud from his ear and stuffed it in his pocket. He might need to pawn the two-carat diamond earring at some point.

Moses came out of the trailer holding a baseball cap that was as worn and tattered as he was. "This here is my most prize possession. Joe DiMaggio hisself give it to me personally. I'm jest loaning it to you, son."

Dallas scooped up his long hair and piled it on top of his head before he jammed on the cap. "Put these on," Moses said, holding out a pair of wire-rim sunglasses. He squinted against the sun. "You don't look a-tall like that there singer now." He cackled with glee as he climbed behind the wheel of the ancient truck.

"How did you know?"

"Son, your face was plastered all over the news last night. No need to worry. I ain't never spilled a secret. When we get back it might be a good ideer to have that talk. I might be able to help you. They said only good things on the television about you. I'm not sayin' I want to know your business now. What I'm sayin' is you need to think through what I think yer plannin'. A secret's no good unless one other person knows it. You should know that, son."

"I didn't do anything wrong, Moses. Maybe what I'm planning on doing is wrong but . . ."

"We'll talk later. Maggie will make us some lemonade and we can jaw all day. I git real tired listenin' to her talk about them soap operas she watches all day long. She's a fine woman and a fine cook. She looks out for me. Everybody needs someone to look out for them even when they say they don't. You git my drift?"

"Yes."

"How come a big strappin' feller like you ain't got hisself married?"

"It's a long story, Moses. Real long."

The rest of the trip into Dumont was made in silence. Moses parked on a shady, tree-lined street. "You git out and walk around. Don't take that cap or them glasses off, you hear? I won't be but an hour or so. You kin see the whole town in that time. You git done seein' everything before I git back, you wait in the truck." Dallas nodded. "I'm gonna need some money, son."

Dallas reached into his back pocket. He handed over a fistful of money to the old codger. Moses spit on his finger and he flicked through the bills. "This should do it."

Ninety minutes later, Moses pulled the Chevy Blazer he was driving alongside the truck. A pile of packages were on the front seat. "You drive my truck, son. Just follow me. Here's your new license. It cost almost as much as the truck." He cackled at the deal he'd pulled off.

Dallas relaxed behind the wheel of the rickety, rusty truck. For the first time in his life he felt at peace with himself.

It was a little past noon when Moses gave his nod of approval to Dallas's haircut. "You look like one of them college professors now." Dallas grinned.

"He does, doesn't he?" Maggie said, admiring her handiwork.

Moses motioned for Dallas to go indoors while Maggie swept the outdoor patio. "I been thinking, son, about that talk we said we were goin' to have. I think maybe you might be lookin' for advice. I ain't got no book smarts, but I got common sense. Maggie now, she has both. Do you think you might want to include her in our little talk? I can vouch for Maggie. She'd die before she'd give out a secret. Think of us as your mam and pap for now. Let's check the news to see what's goin' on. You might want to rethink whatever it is that you're plannin' on doin'."

Dallas nodded. No one but this old man had ever called him son. He liked the way it sounded.

"What's fer dessert, Maggie?" Moses called.

"I was going to warm up the apple dumplings and put some ice cream on them unless you want hot fudge, Moses."

"I'll take both," Moses said smartly.

Not to be outdone, Dallas said just as smartly, "Me too."

Moses changed the channel to CNN. Dallas moved up closer to see his brother Adam lash out in anger at one of the reporters. "Did you hear him? I always wanted to do that. They get in your face and won't back off. Then if you do something or say the wrong thing, they hack you to bits." To Moses he said, "That's my brother Adam."

Moses thought he would have to be deaf, dumb, and blind to miss the pride in Dallas's voice when he said the words "my brother."

The screen door slammed behind Maggie as she leaned the broom in the corner. "Chicken pot pie for lunch. Set the table, Moses. Ice tea or coffee?"

"Guess she ain't makin' lemonade today. Fridge must be kickin' up agin. Looks to me like that oven is kickin' up, too."

"Stop complaining, Moses. So what if the pie is a little darker on one side. It tastes the same. If you want lemonade, I'll make lemonade."

"Coffee's fine," Dallas said, as he eyed the immaculate kitchen with the homey knickknacks and green plants on the windowsill, and then compared it to his sterile state-of-the-art kitchen in California. Sara would call this kitchen cozy, and he would have to agree with her. He liked the pudgy woman with the thick braid of hair and twinkling blue eyes. He put her age at somewhere in the middle sixties. She looked like one of the mothers or grandmothers he and

Adam used to look at so longingly in the catalogues Millie kept in the house. She wore an apron the way mothers did and she had a smudge of flour on one cheek. Probably from the pie dough. He barely knew her, but he liked her a lot. He knew in his gut she had no hidden agendas, just the way Moses had none. Instinct told him he could trust both of them with his life.

Thirty minutes later Maggie passed around the apple dumplings. "You're that fella on the news channel, aren't you?" Dallas stopped chewing to stare at her. He nodded, his face miserable. "I was in the back in the tail section. The plane exploded before I could get to it. There wasn't anything I could do. I don't know why I was spared and the others weren't."

Maggie leaned across the table. "We're going to let these dishes set for now. I think Moses and I need to pay attention to you, young man. God works in mysterious ways. Everyone knows that. You never question the Lord. I learned that when my man died. He has a reason for everything he does. Now, why do you want to be Jack Piper?"

"Told you she was smart," Moses cackled. "Let's have a cigarette to go with this dee-licious coffee."

"Don't try to butter me up. You know your limit's five, Moses. You're not supposed to be smoking at all. Well, how many?"

"Two," Moses lied.

"One, that's it."

"One's good," the old man said. It was a process they went through at least a dozen times a day. Left to his own devices, Moses would chain smoke. With Maggie guarding the cigarettes, he had no choice but to obey because it was for his own good.

"You go ahead now, son, and tell us everything from the git-go. We're goin' to sit here and listen and won't say a word till you're all done. Maybe we'll give you some advice and maybe we won't. You can trust us both. Ain't that right, Maggie?"

"Whatever you tell us will go no further," Maggie agreed.

Dallas talked until he grew hoarse. When he wound down he looked at Maggie and Moses expectantly. He didn't realize he was holding his breath until it exploded from his mouth like a gunshot.

"I was a schoolteacher for twenty years

before we moved out here to the desert. I can tell you where to go and what to do. Your Sara sounds like a very smart lady. It's obvious to me you feel inferior to her because of her education and her being a doctor. You love her, don't you? At the same time you're afraid to admit it. So you played it cool. Isn't that the way young people describe it today?" To Moses she said, "It's a way of saying something to save face in case something goes awry later on." Moses nodded sagely.

Maggie held up her hand. "You love your brother, and that's the way it should be. Moses and I know what it's like not to have children. Yet you resent him, and that's understandable given your circumstances. What happened to you, Dallas, happens to many children. You were allowed to slip through the cracks. It's unforgivable, but it's in the past. We can't get yesterday back. We have today and all the tomorrows yet to come. I know many people in the education field back in Los Angeles. If you want, I'll make some calls and set things up for you. I think you need to hear with your own ears from someone in the know that you are not retarded. And speaking of hearing, just how bad is your hearing?"

Dallas felt his jaw drop. "How did you know? I barely hear out of my left ear."

"I watch you read lips. If Moses or I say something to you when we're behind you, you don't hear us. Hearing aids are wonderful things. They've perfected them to the extent they're almost invisible. It can be fixed, Dallas. The television gave your age as thirty-eight. That probably means you should have reading glasses at the very least. Do you have trouble seeing?" Dallas nodded. "That can be fixed, too. Why did you wait so long?"

"I just gave up. Things were going from bad to worse with Adam. Then Billy died. I met Sara, and things started looking better, but I didn't know where to turn. I wanted to be . . . like Adam. For her. I didn't want to be Dallas Lord anymore. I wanted to be Joe Schmo. What I wanted was to be goddamn *normal.* Half my life is over. Do you have any idea how much I missed?"

"Of course I know. Unfortunately, you cannot unring the bell. Yesterday no longer matters. You *are* normal, Dallas Lord. You

have to believe that. Think of it like this—
you are going to go back to school with a
teacher who will give you one-on-one instruction. If that's really what you want. Are
you clear in your own mind about the con-
sequences of what will happen to your
brother, your estate, the band, all the things
that made up your old life?"

"My brother will take care of all that.
Everyone is financially set. Adam saw to
that. Sara has her profession. Sandi Sims is
the only one who concerns me. She has a
mean streak in her. She might try to manip-
ulate Adam, but he'll see right through her.
I worry that she might try to steal "Sara's
Song" from Sara. She's the only one who
wasn't provided for."

"Why?" Maggie asked bluntly.

"She was new to the band. I had . . . we
had . . . it didn't work for me. I knew she was
using me. It was easier to go along with certain things. I told you, I mentally closed up
shop. I'm not proud of it. It was what I had
to do at the time."

"Can you really give up all the fame, the
money, the notoriety, and adoration?"

"In a heartbeat." Dallas touched his chest.

"I have to find out what kind of person I am once the playing field is leveled. If I have to become Jack Piper to do it, then I'm Jack Piper. The only thing that bothers me is Adam and Sara. When someone like an artist dies, his pictures become more valuable. I saw a documentary on television, so I know how that works. I don't know if Sara will keep the song private. I don't think she would ever try to sell it for money. If what the documentary said was true, that particular song will be priceless in the music field. Sandi doesn't have any . . . ethics. I'll have to work on that."

"You'll be able to get lost in LA, Dallas, if you keep a low profile. If Moses or I can be of any help, all you have to do is call us. On your new cell phone." Dallas laughed.

"I know what I'm planning is wrong, but I'll never know what it's like to lead a normal life if I don't do it this way. I think I walked away from that plane crash for just this reason. I think God is giving me a second chance. I can't blow it this time."

Maggie nodded. "Your sunburn is healing nicely with the aloe. Why don't you and Moses take a walk so I can clean up here and get on with supper. It's all going to work out, honey. You call us anytime you feel down. We'll keep your secret."

Outside, Moses fired up a cigarette. "I snitched it when she wasn't lookin'." He was so proud of his sleight of hand Dallas didn't have the heart to criticize him. "Told you Maggie had smarts. You gonna go for them tests she talked about?"

"Yes. I'll get my ears and eyes checked, too. The whole ball of wax, Moses. But, the first thing I'm going to do when I leave here day after tomorrow is get a dog. My brother has seven. That's so hard for me to believe. He called one of them Dallas Six. Can you beat that?"

"A dog is a big responsibility. Sounds to me like you never took responsibility for anything but your music."

"Pretty damn sad, isn't it?"

Moses nodded. "Tomorrow I'll take you to the pound. Lots of animals there that are lookin' for a good home."

"Was there a reason why you didn't have kids, Moses?"

"It jest never happened."

"What about Maggie?"

"Couldn't carry a baby to term is the way she puts it. Wasn't meant to be I guess."

"I wanted a mom so bad when I was little. I used to cry myself to sleep. Adam did all he could, but he wanted a mom, too. More than a dad I think. Then when we started getting older we used to talk about what a father would do. You know, take us fishing, ground us when we did something wrong, go to ball games, and buy us hot dogs."

"You want a stand-in pap, I'll be glad to apply for the job," Moses said gruffly. "I know for a pure fact Maggie would love nothin' bettern standing in for your mam."

Dallas stared at the old man for a long minute, his eyes burning unbearably. When he couldn't stand it any longer he turned and ran to his cabin, where he howled his head off.

The old man knuckled his own eyes before he returned to the kitchen to talk to Maggie.

Dallas packed his duffel, straightened up his room, and hung up the wet towels before he headed over to Maggie's for his last breakfast. For one brief second he thought he was in the wrong place. He felt a lump swell in his throat when he saw the couple dressed in what he knew was their finest apparel. Moses wore a three-piece blue suit that smelled strongly of mothballs and had gone so far as to shave off his straggly beard, and it looked like Maggie had given him a fresh haircut. Her own hair was crimped, her face powdered, and she wore bright red lipstick. She wore a glorious flowered dress that rivaled an English garden.

"We wanted to give you a good send-off . . . Jack. We figured if we wuz goin' be your stand-in mam and pap, we needed to look like a bon-a-fide set of parents. We figure this makes it official."

"Living out here in the desert makes it easy to let yourself go," Maggie said. "It's hot and dry and there aren't that many customers anymore. At our age comfort seems to matter more than looks. Moses is right, though. We wanted you to be proud of us. We've never been parents before, and we aren't about to take this lightly. You can count on us no matter what. Okay, now it's time to eat. Put that cigarette out, Moses. You know the rules."

Dallas sat down, his eyes shining with delight.

"Now, son, what would you like for breakfast?" Maggie asked.

"Mam, I'd like whatever you're fixing for Pap."

"Don't that beat all, Maggie. He sounds just like me, don't he?"

"He sure does."

"I've only known you for three days, and I love you already," Dallas said.

Maggie yanked at the end of her apron to wipe at her eyes. Moses rubbed his eyes as he grinned from ear to ear.

Life is looking good, Dallas thought. *Real good.*

They gave him one last round of hugs and kisses, Dallas's eyes smarting with unshed tears.

"You're going to be fine, Dallas. You don't look anything like the real Dallas Lord," Maggie said. "Do you have the map Moses made for you?" Dallas nodded. "Promise you'll call us as soon as you find a place to live. We have some money, Dallas, in case yours runs out. Moses and I agreed to this, so all you have to do is ask. We can wire the money to you by Western Union."

"I'll be fine. I'm going to pick up my dog. He was a mess, and he smelled to high heaven from the pound. The groomer said I wouldn't recognize him when I picked him up. Big dog. Man's dog. He licked my hand. I think it's going to be okay. How do I say thank you?"

"Ain't no need for thanks, son. You jest do everything Maggie set out fer you. You got all them papers and phone numbers in your pocket, don't you?"

"I have everything. Well, I guess it's time to go."

"Guess so," Maggie said. "Will you call us on Christmas Day, Dallas?"

"You bet."

He was in the Blazer then, tears on his cheeks. He risked a glance in the rearview mirror. Moses had his arms around Maggie's shoulders as he patted her on the back.

He felt like they were his parents in every sense of the word.

When he reached Dumont, Dallas drove up and down the business street until he found an appliance store where he ordered a Sub-Zero freezer, a refrigerator, a six-burner Magic Chef with twin ovens and a double microwave oven, and a sixty-inch Mitsubishi color television set. He peeled off cash from his roll, seriously depleting his cash reserve. As an afterthought he asked where he could order a side of beef to go with the deep freeze.

"I can do that for you, sir. Would you like it delivered at the same time as these appliances?"

"Yes." More money changed hands.

"That will be thirty dollars for delivery." Dallas peeled a ten and a twenty from the wad of money in his hand.

"Where do you want this delivered, sir?"

Sir. His first true test. The young man in his thirties didn't recognize him. In fact, he hadn't given him a second look. So much for fame in the spotlight. Suddenly he felt wonderful. "Deliver it all to the Desert Inn Motel."

"Will you be keeping the sales slips, or should they go with the appliances?"

Dallas panicked. Adam would know exactly what to respond to the question. When in doubt ask questions. His shoulders squared. "I don't think I want them to know how much the appliances cost."

"Then how about if we just give them the

warranty cards and they can fill them out and return them."

Dallas sighed. "That's fine." He pocketed the receipts.

"Do you want a card to go with these? Are they early Christmas presents?"

Did he? Were they? "Sure."

"You can fill out the card," Dallas said not wanting the salesclerk to see what a struggle it was for him to write. "Just write . . . your son, Jack."

"Well, Jack, this is one zappo Christmas present. They must be pretty special people."

"They are. They really are."

"Nice doing business with you." Dallas nodded.

"We'll have everything out there and installed by four o'clock." Dallas nodded again.

Back in the Blazer, Dallas's heart took on an extra beat as he drove up and down streets till he reached a small private house set back from the road. The pristine white sign said it was the Classy Dog Groomers.

"Your dog is ready, Mr. Piper. He's very well behaved. Whoever owned him must have taken him to a groomer. He knew exactly what to do. He likes Lorna Doone cookies. You might want to pick up a box."

Dallas's face went blank. "Do you sell them?"

"You get them at the grocery store. I have two boxers you can have. You're going to need a leash and a collar. We sell those. I think red is good for a dog."

"Okay."

"He's a healthy dog, Mr. Piper. I took the liberty of calling the vet you had check him out. They say he's about four years old. If you wait here, I'll fetch him."

Dallas dropped to his haunches when the black dog was led out to the small office. The dog picked up his scent and bounded away from the groomer to throw himself at Dallas, knocking him over. He licked his face, his hair, and tried to hop on his lap. Dallas laughed, the sound ringing throughout the clinic.

"Did you give him a name yet?"

"His name is . . . Adam One."

"It's different. He looks to me to be mostly Lab. The vet agreed. In my opinion a Lab is the best dog there is. They're smart and they're loyal. As you can see, this dog is very loving. Both of you are very lucky to have found one another."

Still laughing as the dog tugged at the leg of his jeans, Dallas paid for the grooming, the leash, a water bowl, and the cookies.

"Okay, let's get you some lunch, Adam One. I threw out that bag of dog food the vet gave me. It looked like rabbit poop. We're gonna get some good stuff." The Lab pawed his arm to show his approval. He turned the Blazer and headed back to the main road, where he stopped at the first Burger King he came to. At the drive-in window he gave their order. "Six Whoppers, easy on the dressing and light on the lettuce. Throw on some bacon and double the cheese. I'd like two strawberry milk shakes and a large container of ice water."

They ate in the parking lot, devouring every crumb. When the dog sat up and stared at him, an expectant look on his face, Dallas bundled up the trash. "Okay, let's do it. Ten minutes. You go on the grass so I can scoop it up. Go!"

Thirty minutes later they were back on the road, the big dog's head resting on his right arm. Once or twice he woofed softly. Dallas rather thought it was to show his appreciation. He fondled Adam One's ears and talked to him all the way into LA. This was truly the first day of his brand-new life as Jack Piper, and he was loving every second of it.

"I earned this day, Adam One. I don't know if I deserve it, but I do know that I earned it," he whispered.

The Lab nuzzled his neck as he inched closer to his new master.

Chapter Ten

Each time the phone rang during the early-morning hours, Izzie snapped to attention. Twice she leaped from the bed to check on the pups. She also walked through the rooms, the phones ringing everywhere.

Promptly at seven o'clock, Adam's eyes snapped open. The phone rang twice while he was in the shower. He didn't hear it. In the kitchen he made coffee and poured juice; before he scanned his list of instructions Tom Silk had left him. Whistle in hand, he gave off three sharp blasts as he opened the kitchen door. "Everyone out, everyone does what they're supposed to do and then you eat. GO!" If they were bigger, he would have been trampled. Izzie nudged Dallas Six, who appeared to be lingering. The fat little pup waddled to the top step and peed a stream. Repetition and patience. Patience and repetition. Adam cleaned up the mess, washed his hands, and poured coffee. "Let's see what went on in the world while we slept, Izzie."

His back to the television screen, Adam listened as the *Today Show*'s hostess, Katie Couric, announced the latest-breaking news. Adam winced when he heard the words private airplane crash. He turned to see a picture of his brother Dallas flash on the screen. The phone rang almost immediately. His heart pounding in his chest, Adam barked into the phone. Sweat beaded on his brow as he listened to Al Cherensky's choked voice. What seemed like an eternity later, Adam said, "Thanks, Al. I'm on my way. Listen carefully. This is what you have to do. I'll have to charter a plane right away. I'll see all of you in LA. Take care of things, Al, until I get there. Don't fall apart on me now."

Don't think. Move. Don't think. Dallas can't be dead. Don't think. Move. Wind shear. Not Dallas. Never Dallas. Thank you, God, for giving me the good sense to call my brother last night. Don't think. You know what you have to do, so do it. Later you can grieve. You have the rest of your life to grieve. Don't think.

All Adam's years of training and discipline

kicked in. Phone in hand, he made calls at rapid-fire rate, dressing and packing as he did so. Two briefcases jammed to over-flowing were added to his pile of luggage.

In the kitchen he looked around, panic settling on his features. God, what should he do with the dogs? Tom Silk's number on the top of his instruction list stared up at him. He punched out the numbers. "Tom?"

"Mr. Lord. Jesus, I'm sorry. I just heard. What can I do for you?"

"You can come over here right now and go to California with me. I'll make it worth your while. I can't leave the dogs. I *won't* abandon them. I chartered a plane. We have thirty minutes to get them ready and get to the airport. Will you do it?"

"I'm on my way."

Adam's clenched fist shot through the television screen. Sparks showered upward. Blood spattered in all directions. Pain shot up his arm. The pain was nothing compared to the pain in his heart. Izzie growled, the pups scurrying about his feet. He knew he should blow the whistle, but he didn't have the strength. "It's what it is, gang. We're go-ing to deal with it the best way we know how." He bent down to pick up Dallas Six to cuddle next to his cheek. "He didn't even get to meet you. Son of a fucking bitch!" He set the pup down next to Izzie as he raced through the house, pulling plugs and closing the blinds. He checked the locks one last time. He took a long moment to stare at the Christmas tree and then the stockings hanging from the mantel. His eyes smarting with unshed tears, he removed the homemade stocking and carried it out to his luggage. He jammed it into his carry-on bag and didn't know why.

Tom Silk knocked on the kitchen door. "I got here as fast as I could. There's a whole gaggle of media out front. I pulled around the back. If we move fast, we should be able to outrun them. You take the bags, and I'll take the pups. Izzie will follow us. Jesus, a man could go to war with less than these dogs have. Move, move, I got it covered. I do this for a living, remember?"

The pups squealed and yelped as Tom spread everything out in the back of his rickety van. The whistle sounded every two seconds until the pups were so confused they lay down in their beds. Izzie hovered but calmed when Adam crooned to her from his seat in the front of the van.

"Show time!" Tom bellowed, as he peeled away from the curb, his worn tires squealing. "Oh, shit, they spotted us."

"I'll pay for the tickets," Adam said.

"What does worth my while mean, Mr. Lord?"

"It means name your price. In other words, money is no object."

"Ah. Listen, I'm . . ."

"I know. I'd rather we didn't talk about it. I'm strung real tight. I can't talk about my brother right now."

Tom settled his worn baseball cap more securely on his head. "So, how'd it go last night?"

Last night, if you discounted his stocking stuffing, was safe ground. "I guess you mean the dogs. The pups slept like you said they would. Six had an accident. He was the last to go through the doggie door and I guess he couldn't wait. Actually it wasn't the doggie door at all. I had the big door open and he couldn't do the step or get over the hump. It worked out. Izzie got a little upset. It's what it is. She slept with me, even used one of the pillows. Guess that means she trusts me just the way you said."

"Nah. That's little stuff. You'll know it

when it happens. Do you mind if I call you Adam? That mister stuff isn't what I'm all about. I hate all that formal crap. Man, you couldn't have gotten me at a better time. Business is really slow. No one wants to lay out money for dogs when the holidays are around the corner. Mitzi, she's my girlfriend, fiancée actually, anyway she wasn't real happy but she understood. Do you have a place in LA?"

"No. We'll be staying at my brother's house in Mandeville Canyon. It's all fenced in. Top-of-the-line security. I don't know how long this is going . . . what I mean is . . ."

"I know what you mean, Adam. My time is yours. Don't worry about the dogs. As long as they see you, and you spend some time with them, things will work out. This is the right thing you're doing. We're coming up to the airport turnoff. You'll have to direct me from here. I don't travel in the circles you do, and my knowledge of chartered private planes is nil. Do I do long-term or what?"

"You go out on the tarmac. Someone will drive the van back and park it. You can call your girlfriend from the plane and tell her where to pick it up. After they call us."

"What's it like to be rich?" There was no envy, only curiosity in Tom's voice.

"It has its own set of problems. I probably have more sleepless nights than you do. Did. Lately I've been sleeping rather well. That's just another way of saying it isn't what it's cracked up to be. I think I was happier when I was struggling. When you get to the top you think you're on Easy Street. You aren't. That's when the real devil kicks in and you have to kick, claw, and scratch to stay there. Once you slip it's all downhill, and you don't have the stamina to climb back up. It's a goddamn rat race is what it is. The faster you run, the bigger the rats."

"I'm sorry I asked. There's your plane. What now, coach?"

"I'm not an expert at this even though you might think I am. Stay with the dogs until I speak with someone. I'll take the bags out. You travel light I see."

"What you see is what you get. I told you, I'm not fancy. When you work with animals it's got to be wash-and-wear. Am I going to be an embarrassment?"

"Hell no. It's okay, Izzie, I'll be right back. You and the pups are coming, too, girl."

"I need some help here."

The flight crew stood on the stairs, their eyes on Tom Silk and the yipping, yowling puppies.

The pilot stepped forward. "John La Crosse, Mr. Lord. I'll be your pilot this morning. This is Michael Trainer my copilot. To my left are Tracy Blevins and Marie Landry. Nobody said anything about a bunch of dogs."

"With the money I'm paying for this flight nobody had better say a word about these dogs. Where I go, they go." He stretched the truth a bit when he said, "They're trained."

"They'll have to go in cargo."

Adam's eyes narrowed. "We're all going first-class. It's a long trip and I'm in a bit of a hurry, so let's cut the bullshit and get airborne. While you're doing whatever it is you have to do perhaps one of these nice ladies will get us some coffee, and not that coffee you run through those rusty pipes inside the galley. Now! Please have someone bring our baggage aboard."

"Who does that fucking guy think he is?" the copilot hissed to the stewardess.

"I'm the fuck who's paying you to fly me

to California, so let's do it. Now, get the hell out of my way so my dogs can get on this plane."

"He's Dallas Lord's brother. Show a little compassion. All you have to do is look at Mr. Lord to know he's a basket case. Once a jerk, always a jerk," the young stewardess sniffed.

"Jesus, now you tell me."

"A little kissing up goes a long way." The stewardess sniffed again.

The moment the plane was airborne, Adam moved to the back of the plane. "I have a lot of thinking to do, Tom. I'd appreciate it if you'd stay up front with the pups."

"Sure. Is there anything I can do?"

"If there was, I wouldn't hesitate to ask. I'm thankful you're here. I have a feeling those two hostesses are going to play with the pups all the way to LA. It's a long flight, so kick back. Don't forget to call your girlfriend. The stewardesses should know where your van is parked."

Adam leaned back in his seat. *Think business now. Forget for the moment that Dallas is your brother. Make a plan. Think in terms of damage control. Think, think, think. Dal-*

las's death is the biggest thing since Elvis's demise. Don't make the same mistakes Colonel Parker and Elvis's entourage made. Don't let this turn into a media circus. Think, plan. Plan and think. What's the best way to handle this? What would Dallas want?

Dallas would want the whole three-ring circus. The circus wasn't going to happen. He'd see to that. He needed to think about the band and what would be best for all of them. More important, he had to think about where to bury Dallas. They'd never discussed death, so it had to be his decision. Once, years ago, the guys had been talking about cremation, and Dallas had said, "What a way to go. You just go up in smoke and your ashes get carried all over the world."

Maybe he needed to think along those lines. How in the name of God was he going to burn his brother's already burned body till nothing was left but his ashes? How could he fit him into a box and then bury it six feet under the ground? How? How did other people do it? People did it because there were no other options. A mausoleum above ground might be a possibility. Dallas would still be locked in a box inside a concrete structure. Dallas, free spirit that he was, would hate it.

Adam switched his thought to financial matters. Dallas had a fifty-million-dollar life insurance policy with Lloyds of London with a million dollars going to each band member who had been part of the Canyon River Band for ten years. Nancy would get Billy Sweet's share. As executor and beneficiary of his brother's will and estate, Adam stood to inherit everything, right down to the insurance on the January Far East tour. The Asians had kicked up a fuss about the policy, but in the end they'd come around when he'd shown them it was standard fare where the Canyon River Band was concerned. So much money.

Adam squeezed his eyes shut. No amount of money could make up for the loss of his brother. He just had to do the right thing for everyone involved. He shuddered when he thought of what lay ahead of him.

Sara rolled over, snuggling into the softness of her nest. Normally she was a sound sleeper, waking a minute or so before her alarm went off. She hadn't set the alarm last night when she returned from Dallas's house. She cracked one eye to stare across the room at the closed window blind. It was still dark out. Rolling over a second time afforded her a look at the bright red digital numbers on the bedside clock: 5:30. The flashing light beneath the time said it was December 10.

Sara rolled over on her back and laced her hands behind her head. Even though she was awake, she didn't have to get up. She could stay in bed until noon if she wanted to. There was nothing on her agenda today except a trip to town to pick up her wedding suit. Carly's mint green outfit wouldn't be ready until tomorrow. Maybe she should wait until then and pick both up at the same time. But then what would she do with herself all day? She closed her eyes remembering Dallas's poignant good-bye at the gates. She looked at the clock again. His plane would be landing in Vegas any minute now. He'd called just after takeoff.

Damn, she might as well get up. If she didn't, she'd lie here and think about the possibility that she was making the biggest mistake of her life. Or she was making the one decision that would guarantee her a lifetime of happiness. On the other hand, if she got up and went downstairs, she'd have to face the worry in Carly's eyes. Hunger and the need for her caffeine fix won out. She could be out of the house by nine to finish up her Christmas shopping. Dallas had given her a roll of hundred-dollar bills that was so huge, so thick, that her purse wouldn't close. He'd asked her shyly to buy some presents for the guys in the band as well as his backup singers. He'd gone on to say when he got back they'd have a whiz-bang Christmas party on the twenty-first of December for the whole band. It was her job to get the tree and hire a florist to decorate the house. Then, he'd said, on the evening of the twenty-third, they were going to Charleston to spend Christmas with Adam. She didn't think it was a good idea, but Dallas had won her over, and she'd finally agreed. To say she was dreading the visit would be the understatement of the year.

Dressed in the ratty flannel robe that she'd had since her first year of college, Sara puttered around the kitchen mixing the batter for pancakes, frying bacon, and perking coffee. Breakfast was her favorite meal of the day; Carly's, too.

While the bacon drained, Sara turned on the seven-inch television set Carly kept on the counter to hear the early-morning weather reports. Carly was big on raincoats and umbrellas and liked to be prepared for all kinds of weather conditions. She, on the other hand, couldn't care less, but voices in the kitchen this early in the morning sounded comforting. To her it was like having a real family who talked about the day's upcoming events.

She didn't want to be an old maid. An old-maid professional. An old maid doctor. It was time for lights and sounds and people in her life. Nellie and Carly were both right. She needed a life. Dallas Lord was going to give her the kind of life people only dreamed about. Her heart skipped a beat and then another. Life was going to be so good.

Sara rubbed at the corner of her eye. *I wish I knew if Dallas loved me. He cares, I know that. But, I want to hear the words. I need to hear the words.*

Would he say them at some point? They could be wonderful companions for one another. Tina Turner was right, what did love have to do with anything anyway? She'd had love not once, not twice, but three times, and what did it get her? Heartache and misery, that's what. At least she knew where she stood with Dallas. Things would be in the open, and there would be no pretense. Life would be whatever she made of it. And that wasn't so bad.

"What are you doing up so early, Sara? You should be sleeping till noon these days," Carly said. "Ah, pancakes. My favorite. Are we having warm blueberry syrup and melted butter?" She snitched a slice of bacon and danced away as Sara was about to swat her hand with the spatula. "Oh, oh, listen. There's been another plane crash. Shhh, I want to hear." Carly turned the volume louder on the small television set.

"How many pancakes, Carly?"

"Shhh. I think you better turn off the griddle and come here, Sara."

"You listen for both of us. I hate seeing stuff like that. How many pancakes, Carly?"

"Sara, get over here!"

Sara wiped her hands on the towel she was holding. "All right! Is it someone we know? Oh, dear God!"

"You *can* handle this, Sara. Take deep breaths. That's good. Now, drink this," Carly said, her own face as white as her sister's.

Her hand when she handed over the glass of brandy was just as shaky as Sara's.

Shaken, Sara clutched the squat glass of apricot brandy, her knuckles whiter than snow. Coughing and sputtering, she gulped at the fiery liquid. "Maybe there is some kind of horrible mistake. Dallas called me from the plane. He was so excited about everything. How can he be . . . *dead?*"

Carly poured coffee. Her voice was quiet, hushed, when she said, "There is no mistake, Sara. The crash is on every single news channel. A reporter from CNN was in Vegas on vacation. They broke the story first. Think, Sara, should we be doing something? Do you think we should go up to his house? When Mom and Dad died you handled everything. I don't know what . . . maybe we should call Nellie. She's good with . . . you know, times like this."

Sara stared off into space. Her gaze seemed to be fixed on the clock over the refrigerator. "Get my purse, Carly, and bring the battery-operated recorder in the desk. I want to play something for you."

Carly returned to the kitchen within minutes. She watched as her sister fit the small cassette in the machine. She listened, her eyes filling with tears. When the machine shut off, she said, "Sara, that was so beautiful."

"Dallas told me I shouldn't play this for anyone. I think he meant . . . while he was . . . alive. It was supposed to be our song. You know, just for us alone. He even gave it a title, 'Sara's Song.' He said maybe when we were old he'd release it. It was supposed to be my wedding present."

Carly sat down opposite Sara. She leaned across the table. "I can't think of anything more beautiful or wonderful. Yesterday it was worth millions. Today . . . today it just became priceless."

Sara wiped at the tears on her cheeks with the napkin clutched in her hand. "What are you talking about?"

"I didn't mean to sound crass. What I meant was you have something in your hand that is priceless. You should probably put it in the vault. Playing it now will only make things worse. That's what you're going to do, right, play it over and over?"

"He can't be dead, Carly. Dallas was the most alive person I ever met. Being a doctor, I know how fragile life can be. He lived each day the way most people only dream of living. He was so excited because he and Adam had this really great conversation. We were . . . going to go to South Carolina to spend Christmas with him."

"What are you going to do about Dallas's brother?"

"Do?"

"Yes, do? He'll be flying in soon, you can bet on that. Are you going to go up there? You know, introduce yourself, ask if there is anything you can do?"

"No. I'd just be in the way. I really don't think I can handle any of that right now. It would just be a reminder of what might have been. We don't want our lives invaded. Maybe we should think about going somewhere for a little while. Something has been hanging over my head for a month now. Dallas . . . what he did . . . said was, he had this eerie feeling that Billy was always with him, waiting. He said 'waiting,' Carly. Like, you know, he had this premonition. He really spooked me. Most times I could jolt him out of it when it looked to me like he was becoming, for want of a better word, obsessed. I'm just so relieved that he made things right with his brother. For Adam's sake as much as his own."

Both women jerked upright in their chairs when the phone on the wall behind Sara shrilled to life. Neither made a move to answer it. Finally, Carly reached for the phone. She muttered a cautious, "Hello."

"It's Nellie," she whispered. Sara shook her head.

"She's devasted, Nellie. No, we're fine. Of course we'll call. I'll stay with her all day. I'll have Sara call you later."

Carly put down the phone and turned to her sister. "Don't make a liar out of me, Sara. Be sure to call Nellie later."

"Carly."

"Yes."

"I don't know . . . what I mean is, I'm not sure I was in love with Dallas. I loved him. Being in love is different than loving someone. He . . . I think he felt the same way. There were days when I was sure I was in love. Then there were days when I was sure I wasn't in love. Maybe I don't know what love means. God, I feel like someone wrenched out my guts. He said we didn't have to pretend with each other. He was going to build me a hospital. I let him convince me that life was going to be beautiful from here on in. He wasn't going to tour anymore.

Cutting records, doing a benefit every so often, was his way of cutting back. He said he'd be home for supper every night. We were going to get some pets and maybe think about adopting an older child. Not right away, though. He really loved this house. He wanted to know everything about us when we were growing up and where we all fit. Like where did we have the Christmas tree, where did we play our games, that kind of thing. He was so different. So sweet, so gentle, so very kind." Tears flooded Sara's eyes as she struggled with her emotions.

Carly stared helplessly at her sister. "I didn't know . . . I thought . . . Listen, Sara, I'm having some trouble with all this. Are you saying you were going to marry him for his money?"

"No. In a way. God, I don't know. He seemed to *need* me. I guess in my own way I needed him, too. I don't honestly know if I would have gone through with the wedding. I was blowing hot and cold, more cold than hot. I feel so . . . empty and . . . guilty. I'm alive and Dallas is dead. I wanted to . . . you know, go to bed. I really wanted to make love to him. He thought . . . felt . . . I don't know, some kind of special respect for me.

Old-fashioned. I thought it was sweet until my hormones kicked in. There was a point where I was really lusting after him and he . . . ignored it. He said when we were married we could live in bed. He was so old-fashioned where I was concerned. I do . . . did love him, Carly."

"Things happen for a reason. We had this discussion so many times. You were the one who always said things and events were preordained. Are you saying now that's wrong?"

"No. I can't believe he's gone. I just can't."

"Sara, don't fall apart on me. It's happened, and we'll deal with it together. I'm here for you the way you're always here for me. Let's shower and dress and be ready for whatever the day has in store for both of us. You go up first and I'll clean up the kitchen."

Sara nodded, her gaze fixed on the small-screen TV.

Sara was halfway up the steps when she turned around and went back to the kitchen for the tape and recorder. In the living room she stopped at the desk and withdrew the envelope full of tapes she'd made with Dallas the day before Thanksgiving. In her

room, she placed everything in the voluminous quilted shoulder bag she was never
without. She didn't know why, but she felt
less jittery and nervous knowing the tapes
were safely in her bag.

In the bathroom, Sara sat down on the
edge of the bathtub, dropping her head into
her hands. She tried to conjure up Dallas's
face behind her closed lids, but his counte-
nance refused to materialize. She cried then
because she didn't know what else to do.

Fresh from her shower, dressed, Sara
started to cry again. With nothing better to
do, she climbed into her bed to hug her pillow as she roll-called her life. Maybe she
wasn't supposed to be happy the way her
friends from school were happy, with their
families. Maybe she was meant to go
through life with only her career for fulfill-
ment. Or was it that she was one lousy
judge of character when it came to the men
in her life? Where was the man who would
make her pulses pound and her heart sing?
If Dallas could do it once, someone else
could do it again. She needed patience and
she had waited patiently and now Dallas
was gone. She would never, ever know if he
was the man she was destined to spend

the rest of her life with. She thought he was. Was she wrong? And then the biggest question of all: Would she have gone through with the wedding or would she have backed out at the eleventh hour? She simply didn't know.

"Sara, are you okay?" Carly called from the foot of the stairs.

Sara slid off the bed. "I'm okay." The clock told her she'd been asleep for several hours.

"Come on down. They're showing Dallas's brother. There is a film crew at Dallas's house. God, it looks like the world is camping outside his gates. His brother is going to make a statement. Hurry up, Sara."

Sara sighed. What could Adam Lord say that would interest her? Nothing.

Wearily she walked down to the family room where Carly had the large-screen TV tuned to CNN, the volume turned high. She accepted a cup of coffee from her sister before she sat down in her favorite chair to stare at the man responsible for Dallas's Canyon River Band's financial success.

"So that's what a Great White looks like," Carly murmured. "He's a hunk. That's a Savile Row suit, custom-made. I know that for a fact because Dr. Mitchell has one just like it. Fits him like a glove. Designer shades, a monogrammed shirt, hand-made shoes. He's a walking bank account. He doesn't look to me like he's grieving. Does he look like he's grieving to you, Sara?"

"People react to grief differently. You know that, Carly. The man has to be in total shock. I know I am. So are you for that matter."

"He looks pretty calm and cool to me. I don't think I like him." Carly's voice was stubborn, petulant-sounding.

"You don't know him, Carly. You shouldn't say something like that."

Sara stared at the man standing near the gates she'd driven through so many times. Overhead, helicopters hovered, men leaning out as far as they could with their cameras as they struggled to get the best shots while someone inside held on to them with ropes tied around their waists. The noise overhead was deafening.

And then Adam Lord took over the entire television screen. Sara felt herself flinch as she stared at the man who was Dallas's brother. She didn't realize her hands were clenched into tight fists until Adam took a step backward. His voice was cold and controlled when he said, "Push that mike in my face again, and it's your lunch." He stepped back, adjusted the polished sunglasses. "Please, I'm asking all of you to respect our grief and our privacy for now. I realize you all have a job to do, but I have a job to do, too. Dallas was my brother. For now, please, just give me some space."

The sun glared down on Adam's polished sunglasses. Sara wished she could see his eyes. A moment later he swung his lithe body into Dallas's Jeep, the one she'd driven so many times.

"Is it true, Mr. Lord, that Dallas was planning to get married? Tell us who she is. We'll find out one way or the other," a reporter shouted.

"My God, Sara, they know!" Carly said.

The Jeep roared up the driveway, the helicopter following.

Carly turned the television off.

"He didn't answer them. He doesn't know my name, or he's forgotten it. If no one knows my name, they can't hound us."

"Get real, Sara. This is Dallas Lord we're talking about here. That means there are big bucks involved in any pictures, any stories no matter how far-fetched. Big Al Cherensky knows about you. So does Dallas's ex-girlfriend. It's possible the whole band knows by now. Another thing, the guy Dallas hired to replace Billy Sweet met you. You are out of your league, Sara. Those rag magazines have money to burn. Dangle big money in front of anyone and eventually you'll get someone who will talk."

"I really think we should give some thought to going away for a little while. Me, especially. You're still going skiing with Hank, right?"

"We leave at the end of the week. Listen, Sara, I just had a horrible thought. Does Dallas's ex-girlfriend know about the song?"

A numb look on her face, Sara nodded.

"Remember what I said earlier about the song being valuable. If he finds out, Adam Lord is going to want it. When artists die their paintings suddenly become more valuable. Even when they're awful they are still valuable. This is the same kind of thing. Are there any other copies of the song that you know about?"

"There aren't any. I have the master copy and one other copy plus the sheet music. Dallas gave them to me. They are mine, and

I'm not selling them. Nor am I giving them back. Dallas and I agreed the song was just for us."

"Sara, that was then, this is now. The rules have changed. Hell, right now I don't think there are any rules. If I were you, I'd take the tape you played for me to the vault right now. If you have anything else of his you want to keep private, take it, too. I'm going with you. Just let me get my purse. I'm driving, too. You look too whacked-out to my eye. You need to get a grip on things."

Sara stared at her younger sister so long her eyes started to water. She was right of course. "If you're going upstairs, bring my bag down with you."

"Where's your safety deposit key?"

"In my wallet."

In the car, Sara put on her sunglasses. "I'm sure we're being melodramatic, Carly." The lack of conviction in her voice caused Carly to snort in disgust.

"They're going to find you, Sara. They'll dig back to Billy Sweet and go on from there. I'm sure of it. I think you are, too. What did you think about the brother?"

Sara chose her words carefully. "I think he was holding his grief in check. He was rigid. Right now he needs to get a handle on things and make solid decisions. From what Dallas told me, Adam is not a man who cares what anyone thinks or says. He's a law unto himself. I would hope he'll do what is best for everyone. This is just a hunch on my part, but I think Adam Lord puts himself last."

"Sara, what are you going to do about the funeral?"

"Nothing. It will be one of those A-list, short-list, invitation-only funerals. I can always go to the cemetery at a later date. Dallas would understand." Sara leaned closer to her sister. "Carly, I feel sad, numb, and I want to cry. On top of that I feel this overwhelming sense of . . . *guilt.* Why is that? Is it because it was him and not me? Because I'm still here and he's gone? Tell me the truth."

"Normal. Honest. When we leave the bank, let's stop at St. Margaret's and say a rosary and light a candle for Dallas."

"I would like that very much. Thanks, Carly, for being my sister."

"My pleasure. Now, look, don't act like you have something valuable when you go to the vault. Pretend you're putting insurance papers in the box. Don't take all day either. They clock you. Sooner or later someone is going to come nosing around. I watch *Diagnosis Murder* and *Murder, She Wrote.* That's how they do things."

The moment the safety deposit box slid back into the opening, Sara felt her shoulders lighten. "I'll keep it safe, Dallas. That's a promise, and I never break a promise," she whispered to herself as she made her way out to the car. "I miss you already. Sing for the angels, Dallas." Tears rolled down her cheeks again. She couldn't stop them, and she didn't care. She didn't care about anything.

Adam entered his brother's house through the kitchen door. The members of the Canyon River Band were sitting around the kitchen table drinking coffee. As one they asked if there was anything they could do. Adam shook his head.

Upstairs he walked up and down the hall, looking in the bedrooms for one he thought would be comfortable. He finally settled on a small room at the end of the hall. The room overlooked the tennis court and pool area. He pulled the drapes and turned on the lights. He could still hear the helicopters, but at least they wouldn't be able to pierce the heavy curtains with their telephoto lenses.

The first thing he did was unpack and change his clothes. The moment his room was tidy, he sat down on the edge of the bed, his briefcase in his lap. His hands trembling, he opened the leather case and extracted a framed picture of himself and Dallas taken the night of his brother's first concert. Dallas's arm was around his shoulder, and both of them hammed for the camera. It was one of his most treasured possessions, and he never traveled without it. The picture was always the first thing that came out of his bag when he was on the road. Hot tears pricked the inside of his lids. A tear slid down his cheek as his shoulders started to shake. His clenched fists beat at the mattress. "Why? Why Dallas?" he cried hoarsely.

And then all hell broke loose down below. He could hear shrill shouts, loud squeals, and sharp whistle blasts. He ran to the hall to see Izzie bounding up the steps, the fat pups streaking past her in their haste to get to him. He squatted at the top of the steps.

Izzie bowled him over, the pups circling him, yipping and yapping like a miniature band of Indians. Tom Silk's whistle might as well have been underwater. The band members stared in awe as Adam tussled with the dogs.

"Sorry, Adam. Izzie knew you were up here. I couldn't stop her. Right now this whistle is worth shit. Tomorrow it will be different. I guarantee it."

"It's okay, Tom. They need to get the feel and smell of the house. We're going to be here for a little while. Let them roam today." His voice choked up when he said, "Where's Dallas Six?"

"He's the one pooping in the corner. I'll take care of it. Go about your business, Adam. By dark they'll be in line. Give some thought to sleeping accommodations. By the way, there is some glitzy-looking chick in the kitchen who is looking for you. Said her name is Sandi Sims."

Adam nodded. Sandi could wait. He had other things to do right now. The pups leapfrogging ahead of him, Izzie in their wake, Tom Silk bringing up the rear, Adam searched out Dallas's bedroom. When he found it, he entered and closed the door behind him. He looked around the oversize room, surprise registering on his face at the mess in the middle of the bed. Other than the stacks of files and folders, the room had a spartan look to it. Pictures of the band at different concerts dotted the walls. On the night table next to the king-size bed was a large gold frame with a picture of him cut from a magazine. In the lower right-hand corner in Dallas's childish scrawl was written, My Brother Adam.

Adam bit down on his lower lip so hard he drew blood. A lump the size of a walnut formed in his throat.

To Adam's trained eye it looked like no one had ever used the room. For some reason he'd expected to see piles of junk and clothes littered about. Two rock and roll magazines that looked untouched and unread were on a table next to a chair that looked like it had just come off a showroom floor.

The room length walk-in closet held very little. He counted nine pairs of jeans, most worn and faded, some with holes in the knees, Dallas's trademark. Shirts hung on hooks, boots and sneakers and one pair of shiny dress shoes were lined up like soldiers. A tuxedo and dress suit hung at the far end of the rod in a cleaning bag. A duffel bag, battered and worn, was on the top shelf, a winter jacket and windbreaker stuffed inside it. Dallas's wardrobe. The lump in Adam's throat grew.

The dresser drawers were almost empty. One drawer held Fruit Of The Loom underwear, at least forty pairs. A second drawer was full of white cotton socks and two pairs of black dress socks. A third drawer held two dozen ironed tee shirts. The last drawer held four sweaters.

Clothes obviously were not a priority for his brother. But then he'd known that.

Adam stared at the files and folders. How overwhelming it must have been for Dallas. How threatening. He tried to remember where the office was. Down the hall and to the left.

Adam opened the door and immediately closed it. Now, this was a Dallas room. Cautiously, he opened it again and stepped inside. He snapped off a smart salute to the flaglike chair before he sat down in it. It swiveled. He took several moments to marvel at the blinding colors, at the electricity of the room. Yes, this was *definitely* a Dallas room. He couldn't help but wonder what Dallas had planned to do in here. He sniffed. Fresh paint and wallpaper paste. Even the floor had a new look to it. He wondered if he would ever know. Like the bedroom, the room had an unused feel. "I need a sense of you, Dallas. I need to feel you. Where in the hell did you live? If not in this room, if not in the bedroom, then where?"

The studio of course. He flew down the steps, his Nikes slapping at the stair treads as he galloped to the bottom of the steps and then down the long corridor to the studio with the red light over the door. This was Dallas's lair. This was the place where he spent his time when he was home. He probably ate in the room and slept on the floor. *Goddamn it, Dallas, how could you die? It wasn't your time.* His vision blurred. He swiped at his eyes with the back of his hand. "It should have been me, Dallas, not you." He sat down on a high stool, the one Dallas always posed on for the album covers. Hard driving sobs tore at him. He gave into his grief, the unreal sounds filling the room.

When he was emotionally and physically drained, Adam slid off the stool. He felt a hundred years old. "I don't know what to do,

Dallas. For the first time in my life I don't know what the fuck to do. I need some help here. I know you're up there watching me. I even bet Billy's got his arm around your shoulder. You're probably saying something like, 'Let's watch old Adam handle this.' Keep watching, guys, because I'm feeling my way."

Adam walked around, touching the equipment. A pile of sheet music was on the floor. He bent over to pick it up. Dallas's writing. Probably the last thing he'd worked on. He pressed the sheets to his chest. Dallas was never, ever, going to write another song, never race across the stage, never pick at his guitar. Dallas would never come into this room again. Ever.

Dallas was gone, but his music would live on forever. It was up to him to keep his brother's music alive. He could do it too. He had it in his power to rock Dallas's music and his memory into the twenty-first century. He would make the music world sit up and take notice. So what if his guts churned while he was doing it. Dallas would expect it, and he would do it for that reason.

Adam leafed through the pages in his hands. The beginning of a song in Billy's memory. Unfinished, of course. He rather thought the small blotches on the paper were Dallas's tears. How difficult this must have been for him. He scanned more pages. Different words, all for the Billy song. Maybe the band could do something with it. What was SS? More words, gentle words, pretty words. Words from the heart, but in snatches. What did they mean? For now it was a hodgepodge of nothing. He wished then he knew more about the music end of things, more about what went on in this room when the guys were together. In that respect he'd always been an outsider.

Time to go out to the kitchen and talk to the band. He hoped he would have the words when he faced them. What would they expect from him? Same old same old? Did they expect him to be cold and strictly business? Well, he might as well get to it and get it over with. In forty minutes he had to leave for the airport to claim Dallas's body. His stomach was full of knots when he walked into the kitchen.

Adam took the initiative. "Look, I don't think any of us want to talk this to death. It is what it is. We can't bring Dallas back. We have to go on. Dallas would like seeing all of you here in his kitchen drinking his coffee. I know he's up there writing a song about this as we speak. I've decided on cremation. Dallas wanted to be . . . what he wanted was to be scattered to the winds. He believed, and because he believed, I have to also believe, Dallas will become part of the whole world. I'll keep some of his . . . ashes and plan a memorial garden here in the canyon. I don't want to commercialize my brother's death, but I do want him to live on for all those young people who haven't tasted his music yet. To that end we'll all work together. If the world wants another Graceland, we'll give it to them. Not right away, though.

"Every rat in the world is going to come out of the woodwork. Stories are going to start circulating. I want each of you to give me your personal word that you won't say one word or give interviews to anyone. I'd like to see a show of hands. Good, I knew I could count on you guys. I'll arrange a memorial service at Good Shepherd for day after tomorrow. The service will be small and private. I don't know what to tell you about the tour other than to say it's off. I took out insurance, so no one is going to lose anything. Your salaries will continue for the next ninety days as specified by your individual contracts. I think it's safe to say your lives will not change financially. Dallas insisted early on that we carry megainsurance in case something like this ever happened. Is there anything you want to ask me?"

Big Al Cherensky stood up. "Did anyone call Sara?"

"Sara?" Adam said.

"The lady Dallas was going to marry. That Sara. You know all that, Adam. You're just in shock now. I'd do it, but I don't know where she lives. I'm sure she's heard the news, but it would be nice if one of us called her. You're the logical choice, Adam, since you're Dallas's brother. She left the hospital because her contract wasn't renewed," Al said.

"I told Dallas she was a quack," Sandi Sims said. "I just bet she wasn't experienced enough to save Billy's life. I told that to Dallas, too. He was having second thoughts about getting married. He told me so when he auditioned my friend to replace Billy. I want my song, too. It's mine."

"That's spite talking. What song are you talking about? The only song Dallas was working on was the one about Billy, and it wasn't going well. He couldn't get it right. You're just mad because Dallas broke it off with you. Admit it," Al said. "You're just jealous because he was going to marry Sara. Don't go saying bad things about her either. She's a real nice lady."

His head pounding, Adam listened to the verbal exchange. What the hell was going on here?

"I did the breaking off, jerk. I told Dallas I wasn't ready to get married. He was just stringing her along. She got him over a bad time when Billy died. He told me that, so don't go saying I'm making this up, Al."

Adam looked pointedly at Sandi Sims. "Maybe you should explain what you mean by *your* song."

"I can do better than that. I can sing some of the words to you. He was going to call it 'Sandi's Song.' "

Adam listened as she sang the opening lines of the song. The triumphant look on her face bothered him. Then he remembered Dallas's scribbles and the initials SS on some of the tattered sheet music. His voice was beyond cold when he said, "If it was your song, why didn't he give it to you? I didn't see anything in the studio, and he didn't tell me about it. Do any of you guys know anything?" The band members shook their heads.

"I just bet that . . . doctor took it and will try to claim it as hers. I'm staking my claim right now in front of all of you. It's up to you, Adam, to get it back. It was here a few weeks ago. If it's gone, then she stole it!" Sandi's face was so contorted in rage, Adam blanched.

"She's a doctor. She wouldn't steal. Doctors have ethics," Al said vehemently.

"Yeah, right. I'd like to know what you'd do or say if Dallas had written a song for you. I keep telling all of you, Dallas was having second thoughts about marrying her. When she sells that song, maybe you'll believe me then."

Al's voice was so chilly that Sandi moved to the end of the kitchen. "And your motives are pure, right?"

"What's mine is mine. Why don't we cut a deal here? We get the song back and record it. We split everything evenly. How's that for sharing?"

"That's enough. Dallas would have left something behind if there was such a song.

There was nothing in the studio but some scribbling. I need something more concrete to go on than your word, Sandi. I can't accuse a respectable doctor of stealing something Dallas might well have given to her. I am not about to let Dallas's estate become a legal battling ground."

"Yeah, well what are you going to do when she sells it and it goes to the top of the charts? It will, you know. She stole it right from under your nose. Dallas was . . . sometimes he didn't pay attention to things. He always did sheet music first, so it will be in his handwriting. How will you disprove that, Adam Lord? With the money she makes from selling the song, she could build a private hospital. That's probably her game."

"Shut up, Sandi, you don't know anything about Dr. Killian. Another thing, we only have your word that you did the dumping. Dallas told me personally he called it quits with you," Big Al said.

Adam rubbed his temples, hoping to lessen the pounding in his head. "This goes on hold for now. I have to leave for the airport. We'll conduct business after the services for Dallas. I don't want to hear another damn word about songs or love affairs. Is that clear? Split up, go to the cottages, and hang out there. We'll talk later."

"Mr. Lord, can I speak to you a moment?" Adam walked to the corner of the kitchen, the housekeeper following. "I just wanted to say how very sorry I am about your brother. Dallas, he told me to call him Dallas, never treated me like an employee. He was always kind and considerate. A lot of times he hired extra people to help me. He said he didn't want to overwork me. You probably don't know this, and he told me not to tell, but now . . . he helped put my boy through college. I don't want you to think I asked him or anything like that. One day he overheard me on the telephone with the college trying to arrange a payment plan. He just did it. He never said a word to me. Two days later the college called and said Josh's bill was paid in full by Mr. Lord. He got upset when I tried to thank him. Your brother did a lot of kind things no one knows about. Josh and his friends always had front-row seats for his concerts. I feel like part of my insides have been ripped out."

Tillie's shoulders started to shake as she fought the tears that were burning her eyes.

Adam took her in his arms and crooned soft words, his own eyes burning.

"It's okay, Mr. Lord, if you don't need me anymore. Don't be afraid to tell me. I won't have any problem getting a job. Dallas gave me a very generous Christmas bonus right after Thanksgiving. I'll be fine. I'll stay on as long as you need me. I just can't believe he's gone." This time the tears flowed unchecked. "He's never going to come into the kitchen again to ask me to make him a weenie with sauerkraut or try out his songs on me. I tried telling him hot dogs had too many nitrates in them, but he didn't care. He did love hot dogs. And marshmallows. He just loved junk food. Dallas knew how to cook. Did you know that, Mr. Lord?"

Adam's voice was gruff. "No, Tillie, I didn't know that."

"He told me how you used to cook for the band to save money. He was so very proud of you, Mr. Lord. He was forever telling Josh how smart you were and how you took care of everything for everyone. He made Josh swear he'd finish school and go on to get his master's. He said he would pay for it all. Dallas said to Josh the greatest gift he could give me would be to succeed in school the way you did. My boy is a certified public accountant and is thinking of opening his own office with a friend. I don't know who was more proud of him, your brother or me. He flew home from New York for Josh's graduation. At the reception afterward, Dallas entertained. It was the best. I know Josh will never forget that day. When I told him about . . . he got his old ten-speed out and took off. He didn't come back for seven hours. He was that upset."

Adam struggled for words that refused to move past his lips. He patted her shoulder as he tried to control his emotions.

"Enough of my prattling on like this. Now, tell me, what do you want me to do? Mr. Lord, will all these people be here for dinner?"

"Yes. Just do your best, Tillie. A buffet, anything really. Scrambled eggs will be fine. You better order enough food for the next few days. Can you handle it?"

'Yes, sir. Sir?"

"Yes."

"The doctor is a nice lady. Mr. Lord liked her very much. I only met her twice. Your brother was so worried the press would invade her privacy. He didn't want that to happen. I heard him singing the song to her. Then I heard them singing it together. It was a real pretty song. I wish I could remember the words, but I can't." She started to cry again.

Adam nodded. He found his voice. "Thanks for telling me, Tillie."

Adam walked outside, clenching his teeth so hard he thought his jaw would crack. Now he had to do the impossible. He had to claim his brother's body. How in the name of God was he going to be able to do that without falling apart?

Chapter Eleven

Sara huddled deep into the deck chair, a lap robe about her. It was unseasonably cool for this time of year. She shivered, but not from the cold, as she stared into the backyard, aware that it would grow dark soon. Like she cared. One day, one night. What difference did it make? Each day was the same as the one before it.

It had been a week since Dallas's memorial service. No one had contacted her, so she'd watched the service on television along with the world until she couldn't bear it a moment longer. They had cremated Dallas, but no one said what would be done with his ashes. Was it her place to tell someone he'd wanted his ashes dropped from an airplane so they would scatter, as Dallas had said, to the four corners of the world? Who would listen to her?

Christmas was short days away. That, too, would be just another day. Maybe she would spend Christmas with Nellie Pulaski and her cats. Then again, maybe she'd spend the day in bed. Nothing seemed to matter.

The door onto the deck opened. Carly was making pot roast. It smelled wonderful. Not that she would eat any. She no longer had to worry about the ten pounds she'd put on this past year. Her weight had dropped immediately on the news of Dallas's death. In ten days she'd lost thirteen pounds. A very unlucky number. Carly said she looked skeletal. "Sara, we're going to eat in ten minutes. I went up to the attic and brought down all the Christmas decorations. When we finish dinner, we're going to the market to pick up our tree. I picked one out the other day and put my name on it. I don't want to hear a word, Sara. I refuse to go away on a holiday and leave you here without a Christmas tree. We're doing the same thing we've been doing every year since Mom and Dad died. This year isn't going to be any different. When we're done with the tree and everything is tidy, I want to see you wrap my presents. *See*, Sara. I want to see you make the effort. Another thing, go upstairs and put some concealer under your eyes. You look ghastly." It was all said in one breathless rush of emotion.

"Yes, Mother. Is there anything else wrong with me?"

"A lot of things, Sara. You aren't making any kind of effort that I can see to get back on track. You can't wallow forever."

"It's only been a week since the service, Carly. What do you want me to do? I cleaned the house, washed the kitchen curtains. I did the grocery shopping. I carried in a ton of firewood and stacked it because you like a fire. I need this time to . . . think."

"About what? About marrying a man you weren't sure you were *in* love with or are you thinking about the private hospital you aren't going to get?"

"Yes to the first, no to the second. Every time I think about Dallas I get this sick feeling in the pit of my stomach. The day after Christmas I'm going to New York. I sent a lot of résumés to New York hospitals. I'll follow through while I'm there. See, I made a plan, and I'll stick to it. Do you want me to mash the potatoes before or after I go upstairs to put on some concealer?"

"After will be fine. Do you want corn or peas?"

"It doesn't matter. Okay, corn."

"Go!"

Carly babbled throughout dinner. Sara stirred and mashed at the food on her plate.

"You should be ashamed of yourself for wasting all that food. We don't even have a dog to give it to. Do you have any idea how many starving people there are in this world? Right now you don't care either, I can tell. It was a good dinner, Sara. You didn't even pretend to eat. If you get sick, I'm not taking care of you. Get your coat and let's go get the tree."

"Someone is ringing the bell. It's probably Nellie, so ask her to come along," Sara said, shrugging into her coat. "I'll be in the garage."

Carly stomped her way to the front door, her hands clenched into tight fists. She wished she could slap some sense into her sister. She yanked at the door, her eyes widening in surprise. *Be cool. Stay cool. Look blank.* "Yes?"

"Dr. Killian?"

"No."

"And you are?" Adam Lord said coolly.

"The person who lives here. And who might you be?"

"I'm Adam Lord." He handed over a business card. Carly looked at it. "So?"

"I'd like to speak with Dr. Killian."

"Why?"

"It's a private matter."

"My sister and I do not have *private* matters. Tell me what you want, and I'll see if she wants to speak with you."

Adam stared at the young woman in front of him. He was reminded of himself years ago when he acted as a buffer for Dallas. He switched his mind-set. "I want to talk to her about . . . Billy Sweet."

"You should go to Benton Memorial for that kind of information. My sister was one of many doctors who attended Mr. Sweet the day he died. I was the charge nurse. If there is nothing else, I have plans for this evening. Excuse me."

"I need to talk to Dr. Killian."

Carly felt a snarl working its way into her voice. Sara simply wasn't up to this. "Which part of what I just said don't you understand?"

"All of it. Fetch your sister."

"You are an arrogant bastard, aren't you?" Carly said as she slammed the door in Adam's face. The double-barrel lock shot home. A second later she was in the garage.

"Where's Nellie?" Sara asked.

"It wasn't Nellie. It was Adam Lord. I slammed the door in his face. He's just as arrogant as he looked on television. He demanded to see you, saying it was about Billy Sweet. He looked like he was lying. He literally demanded I fetch you. *Fetch you.* Those are his exact words. Listen. You can hear him ringing the doorbell. That means he's still out there. He's got balls."

"Maybe I should talk to him and get it over with."

"Absolutely not. The guy is a barracuda. You're too vulnerable now to deal with someone like him. He's the kind of guy who would chew you up and spit you out. He'll give up sooner or later."

"Does that mean we aren't going for the tree?"

"Well . . ."

"I know you mean well. I am not as vulnerable as you think. I'll talk to him, then we'll go for the tree. We knew he would show up eventually. I don't have anything to hide."

"What about the song? What if he asks about it?"

"The song is none of his business. I won't discuss it."

"That means you're going to lie."

"Yes, that means I will lie," Sara said matter-of-factly.

"Attagirl," Carly said, thumping her sister's back. "He's slick, Sara. Stay alert. Now, aren't you glad you put concealer under your eyes?"

"Open the door, Carly."

Carly opened the door. Sara stepped forward. "I'm Dr. Killian. My sister said you wanted to speak with me about Mr. Sweet. I'm terribly sorry, but I can't discuss Mr. Sweet with you, but I think you already know that. What is it you want, Mr. Lord?"

"I'd like to talk to you about my brother Dallas."

Carly suddenly squealed. "Someone is taking pictures. Look at all those people! I told you this would happen." For the second time in one night, Carly slammed the door in Adam Lord's face.

Both women raced up the steps to Sara's bedroom, where they ran to the window to view the commotion down below. "Those rag people know about you now, Sara. They're going to talk to the neighbors, the butcher, the cleaner, the dentist. They'll go through our trash. They're animals. They'll make a big thing out of the fact that your contract wasn't renewed. You'll never get a job now. Hospitals hate this kind of publicity. We'll have to close the house and move. We might even have to sell the house. We'll have to hide for the rest of our lives. We won't be able to work. Who's going to pay our bills?"

"We're not hiding from anyone," Sara said. "If any of those things happen, and we can't get jobs, then we'll be forced to sell the song. See, there's a solution to everything if you think things through. Now, do you want to go for the tree or not?"

Carly grinned at the sudden spark in her sister's eyes. "Damn tootin' I do. Let's go."

"Okay, now this is how we handle it. We make no comment. Let them take all the pictures they want. If we don't say anything, they can't quote us. When we get home, we'll pull the drapes, build a fire, and put up the tree. I was going to marry him, Carly. I figured it all out today. Do you know how I know? I picked up my wedding suit. I even picked up my shoes. I paid for them. The song has been bothering me. It was a gift. That means it's mine. We joked about it being a wedding gift. It wasn't. The private hospital was supposed to be my wedding present. I could give it back I suppose. But, if I did that, then my relationship with Dallas meant nothing. It meant something to me, Carly. It meant a lot. Dallas was a giver in every sense of the word. Writing and giving me that song was very important to him. I'm not giving it up. Does all this make you feel better?"

"Yes, yes, yes. Come on, let's go. I have this insane urge to smell balsam."

"Me too. I also have an urge for a hot roast beef sandwich."

The garage door slid up. Carly backed out the Jeep. The door slid down almost immediately. Within seconds, Carly had the Jeep in gear and was sailing down the driveway. She zipped around the corner going sixty miles an hour, the horde of reporters following.

The antique grandfather clock in the living room chimed twelve times. Sara stood back to view the tree. "Plug in the lights. Oh, my, it's beautiful, and it smells wonderful. I think this is the best tree so far. What do you think, Carly?"

"We say that every year. I think it's the biggest. I still can't believe we got it up ourselves. One of us has to remember to put water in the base every day. I want to wash up so you can make the hot roast beef sandwiches. Let's have hot chocolate, too. We'll eat in here with just the tree lights. It will be like old times, just you and me. I feel like a kid again. What'd you get me for Christmas?"

"Never mind. I'm not wrapping your presents tonight. I'm too tired."

"Yeah, me too. Those guys are still camping out there. It's midnight, for heaven's sake. How much do you want to bet they're out there when we wake up?"

Sara snorted. "That's a sucker bet. Do you want horseradish in the gravy?"

"Yep. Slice a tomato, too. Marshmallows in the cocoa. Ten minutes. I think I'll take a shower and see if I can get the pine needles out of my hair."

The phone rang just as Sara started to

ladle the gravy over the bread and meat. Her voice was cautious when she said hello.

"Dr. Killian, this is Adam Lord. I apologize for the late hour. I drove by your house several times during the past few hours, but the paparazzi are out in full force. I wanted to apologize for that. I had no intention of leading them to you."

"But you did. You can't make them go away. What is it that you want from me?"

"I want to know if you were going to marry my brother and if he wrote a song for you."

"Mr. Lord, I don't think that's any of your business. My personal life outside the hospital is my own. Right now I am between jobs, so my life is totally personal. I do want to express my condolences to you on Dallas's death. He was a wonderful person and I will miss him. It's late and I'm tired."

"I need to talk to you. I have questions that need answers. I can't wind up Dallas's business affairs if my hands are tied."

"I had nothing to do with Dallas's business affairs. I consider our relationship personal, and I don't care to discuss it with you or anyone else. If your hands are tied, they aren't tied because of me. I would appreciate it if you would get those people away from my house."

"I'm willing to pay you $5000 for the song."

"I assume you're joking."

"Okay, $10,000."

"Good night, Mr. Lord. Please don't call me again and do not stop by to chat. Let me get on with my life."

Sara broke the connection before she took the phone off the hook.

"Was that Nellie?"

Sara grimaced. "No, it was Adam Lord. He offered me five grand for the song and then raised it to ten. He wanted to know if I was planning to marry Dallas. I didn't admit to anything. Suddenly I feel like a different person. I don't know why, but I don't want him to know anything. Dallas took such great pains to keep it all private. I guess if I talk about it, I'll be letting him down. He trusted me."

"That's because you are a trustworthy person, Sara Killian. Let's put this on hold and enjoy our food and this glorious Christmas tree. Tomorrow is another day. It's also unemployment day. Did you ever, in your wildest dreams, think either one of us would be on the unemployment line? And there you sit with a multimillion-dollar song in your safety deposit box. Ironic isn't it?"

"It certainly is."

Long after the food was gone and the fire had died down, Carly spoke sleepily. "I don't think Hank is the one for me. I want rockets and flares when he kisses me. All I do is sweat. Maybe we should go to some third-world country and offer our services."

Sara wadded up her napkin and threw it at her sister. "It's time for bed, Carly. We'll do the dishes in the morning. Set the alarm and let's go upstairs."

"You're right of course. I have to admit something. He was a hunk."

"Who?"

"Who? Who do you think? Adam Lord. He's much better-looking in person than he is on television. He's so . . . chiseled. Hard, cold, and chiseled. Stiff, too. I bet he never smiles. How could two brothers be so totally different?"

"I don't know, and I don't care, and no, I don't think he's a hunk. I think he is one greedy, ambitious man. Ten thousand dollars for that song! He must think I'm stupid."

"He'll be back," Carly said as she opened

the door to her bedroom. "I guess I better take my phone off the hook, too, huh?"

Sara nodded.

"Night, Sara. I'm glad you're back among the living."

"Me too. Night, Carly. Remember to say your prayers."

"Yeah, yeah, yeah."

Sara smiled. It was her first real smile in weeks.

What happen to Dallas Cell Phone he had ???

Adam carried the pot of coffee he'd just brewed into Dallas's studio. Maybe here he could find some answers. Then again, maybe there was nothing to find. Was Al Cherensky telling the truth? If he had to bet the rent on Al or Sandi Sims, he'd have to pick Al. There was something about the backup singer that didn't ring true. Then there was Dr. Sara Killian and her mouthy sister. He knew in his gut there was a song, and he knew Dr. Killian knew he knew. Where was it? Did the good doctor have it? He looked up when he heard a soft knock on the door. "Come in."

Tom Silk poked his head in the door. "They're all settled. I hate to tell you this, but they're settled in your room. Izzie kept taking them out of their beds the minute I put them down. Those pups were getting dizzy from all the back-and-forth trips she was making. She wants you all together. I think for now it might be best, Adam. Izzie is scared, but then so are the pups. You're their constant. Do you know what I mean? They all sense your uneasiness, so I took the room next to yours in case they get frisky during the night."

"Want some coffee?"

"Does that mean you want some company?"

"Yeah. Yeah, I do. Are you a good listener?"

"Try me."

Tom Silk was the friend Adam never had time for, the brother he always wanted. They talked into the night with Adam doing most of the talking.

"Coffeepot's empty. My head feels the same way. Jesus, I can't remember when I talked this much. Any last-minute bottom-line summaries you want to give me, Tom."

"I don't understand something. If your brother gave the doctor the song, then he gave it to her. It's hers. What right do you guys have to take it back? If your brother hadn't died, you probably wouldn't even know about it until he or the doctor was ready to tell you, which could very well be never."

"You didn't know Dallas. He had no conception of money. None whatsoever. Knowing Dallas as I did, I know he never gave a thought to the value of the song. He would never think she'd sell it. If there really is a song, and I think there is, it's no penny-ante little ditty. We're talking a Dallas Lord song. We're also talking platinum here and megamillions to the owner. His estate is the owner."

"If you don't have it in hand, then you don't own it. Possession is nine points of the law. I understand your reasoning. Bud to bud here. The ten thou was an insult. I think you're selling the doctor short. If she were going to marry your brother, she's all torn up inside. She wasn't asked to the memorial service. No one has been in touch with her. How the hell do you think she feels? You gotta have some smarts in this world to be a doctor. She's probably strung as tight as you are right now. Let me be the first to tell you that pot of coffee didn't do you one bit of good. On top of all that, you led those ghouls out by the gate to her house. She's a target now. How's that going to look to a hospital or her patients? What you did was invade her life. In my opinion, and remember you asked for it, she had every right to tell you her personal life is none of your business."

"So you're saying I should give up on the song and just let her keep it? What if Sandi was telling the truth and it was her song? It's possible the doctor stole it. It's more than possible Sandi is lying. Dallas often . . . what he did was give things away for services. I could see him giving the doctor the song because she took care of Billy. If he wrote it for Sandi, he'd just change the name on it. Maybe he didn't even do that. Sandi knew the words. The doctor wouldn't even admit there was a song, but the housekeeper said she heard Dallas and the doctor singing the song. She could be confused about the words. Then again she could be on target. I've learned, Tom, when money is involved, there are no rules. For now I have to believe the song, if there is a song, belongs to Dallas's estate. Maybe she's holding out for big bucks. The hell with it. Let's go to bed. Tomorrow is another day."

"Just for the record, it's already tomorrow.

Give some thought to playing Mr. Nice Guy. My mother always said you catch more flies with sugar than vinegar."

Adam's voice was gruff when he said, "Dallas and I never had a mother."

"Hey, I'm sorry. If you want my advice, then do what you did when you found Izzie. Don't just think with your head. Use your heart, too. The doctor is a person, and as such she feels and hurts just like you do. Just the way Izzie did. She trusts you now. That's a plus in anyone's book. How much more money do people like you need? When is enough enough? I thought money was supposed to make people happy. I admit I've only been here a short while, but I never saw such a miserable bunch of people in my life. Aside from their grief is what I mean. I must be some kind of *schlump* because I can't wait to get up in the morning. Simple, honest living is the way to live. That's why I like animals so much. You can learn a hell of a lot from an animal if you're interested in listening and learning. I thought you were on the right road, Adam. Now this song business is taking you right back to where you were before Izzie came along."

Adam cringed. He shrugged because he

was tired of defending himself, his position, and everything else that went with it. "See you in the morning, Tom."

"Sleep tight."

"You bet."

In his bedroom, Izzie's tail swished before she jumped off the bed. She waited to be nuzzled before she nudged Adam along the row of small beds. All the pups were sleeping peacefully. Dallas Six had one of Adam's socks curled under his tiny head. Izzie bent down as if to take it out. "No, let him have it. Tomorrow we'll give him one of Dallas's socks for comfort. Guess that little guy is the runt, huh? Don't you worry, Iz, we're going to take good care of him. C'mon, let's hit the sack. It's been a hell of a day. Tomorrow we'll switch to Plan B as soon as I can decide what Plan B is." *How much money do people like you need? When is enough enough?*

Adam swung his legs over the side of the bed the moment the first early streaks of dawn crept into the room. As one, the pups leapt from their beds and beelined for the door, Adam and Izzie in hot pursuit. Dribbles and puddles dotted the steps as the pups' fat little bodies barreled through the open door.

While the coffee perked, Adam cleaned off the stairs before heading for the shower. He needed a plan. *How much money do people like you need? People like you. When is enough enough?* People like you meant himself. All night long he'd searched in his dreams for what Tom Silk called people like you. Before Izzie. After Izzie.

Did he dare go back to Dr. Killian's house. Did he dare call her again? Maybe Tom was right, and he needed to play Mr. Nice Guy. Well, hell, he was a nice guy. "Shit," he said succinctly as he wrapped a large fluffy blue towel around his middle.

The phone on the wall at the end of the vanity rang. In his opinion, bathroom phones were decadent. He picked it up and barked a gruff greeting.

"Jon James from the *Tattler,* Mr. Lord. Would you mind commenting on your brother's commitment to donate new wings to Benton Memorial Hospital?"

"No."

"Then would you mind commenting on Dr. Killian? Benton's administrator told me, and he didn't say it was a secret, that the doctor and your brother were planning on getting married."

"No."

"Would you care to comment on your visit to Dr. Killian's home last evening?"

"No."

"What are your feelings about Dr. Killian's contract not being renewed? Does it have anything to do with Billy Sweet's death?"

Adam ground his teeth together. *People like you.* "Print that statement and you and that rag you work for will be in court for the rest of your lives."

"Then it does have something to do with it."

Adam slammed the phone back in the cradle so hard it bounced off the wall. Now he had a second legitimate reason to visit Dr. Sara Killian's home. If nothing else but to warn her of what she was up against. He wished he could turn the clock back to when he was in South Carolina and his only worry was how to handle seven dogs.

Sara carried her coffee cup to the sink. "I'm looking forward to having breakfast out, Carly. I think it's my favorite meal of the day. I'm ready when you are. I checked all the doors and windows, and we'll set the alarm when we get into the garage. They're still out there, but there are only four of them."

"There goes the phone again," Carly grumbled.

"Let the machine take the messages. We should think about getting voice mail. Dallas had it. No extra gadgets, no wires, and no blinking red light. You have a code to get your messages. Dallas loved it," Sara said.

Carly took a last look around the kitchen before she pulled the cloth shade to the windowsill. "I just hate the idea that we have to hide out like this."

"It is what it is. There goes the phone again. Let's go. We are going to have a wonderful day. All the stores will be decorated. It's really brisk outside. We even have some money to spend. We need to give some thought to getting Nellie something really nice for Christmas."

"They're going to follow us, Sara."

"Let them. They'll be bored to tears. They might even give up."

"Anything is possible," Carly said. She revved the engine of the Jeep before she raced out of the garage and down the driveway. She gave two sharp blasts to her horn before her middle finger shot high in the air. "I had to do that, Sara, I really did."

Sara laughed as the brisk wind whipped

through her hair. "I know. I wanted to do it myself. Let's buy ourselves something really . . . decadent."

"Two decadent something-or-other gifts coming right up. They're following us, Sara."

"When we get to town, we'll lose them. This is our day, and we aren't going to give them one more minute of our attention. Drive, Carly."

Sandi Sims drove up and down the street three times before she decided to park her car on a side street. Her "cover," as she thought of it, was her neighbor's baby stroller. She yanked it and a pile of baby blankets out of the trunk. She strolled down the street the way the other young mothers on the block did. When she came to Sara's driveway, she turned the stroller and nonchalantly walked up the drive to the garage door. She withdrew a slender strip of wire from her pocket, slid it under the garage door, maneuvered it upward, and yanked the wire. The latch released, and the door slid upward.

Sandi pushed the stroller through and then crouched down to crawl under the door. She slammed it downward immediately. She waited ten long minutes to see if anyone was interested in her movements. Satisfied that no one was, she advanced to the alarm pad positioned next to the door leading into the kitchen. Duke Luchera, the band's drummer and electronics expert, had fallen for her story about her own alarm system. "Just come up with something that will deactivate my alarm in case I forget the code. I'm forever setting it off because I forget the sequence of numbers. The bells and whistles drive me out of my mind." She played with the little black box in her hand until the numbered sequence she was looking for appeared at the bottom of the keypad. She punched in the numbers. The armed red light turned to green. It was safe to enter the house. With the aid of her credit card, a skinny pick, and a steady hand she was able to open the door.

Sandi moved quickly then, ransacking the house as she looked everywhere for the cassette she knew Dallas had given Sara. An hour later her face contorted in rage when she realized the cassette and sheet music were not in the house. Maybe the good doctor carried them with her. Then again, maybe she had locked them up in some safety deposit box. She smirked when she looked around at the total destruction she'd caused. The blinking red light on the answering machine beckoned her. She pressed the message button and listened to twenty-two messages, six of them from Adam Lord. She erased all of them. The last thing she did before leaving the house was to tip over the magnificent Christmas tree.

In the garage Sandi stared at the Jaguar for a full minute before she climbed into the driver's seat. She popped the hood and climbed out. The complicated engine stared up at her. Well, she knew a thing or two about cars, engines, brake linings, and hot-wiring a car. She used up another ten minutes before she reset the alarm next to the kitchen door. That done, she fished in her pocket for the keys to her car at which point she gouged the driver's door as well as the passenger side door with the sharp end of her key. The jaguar hood ornament came off next. She tossed it in the stroller.

Ten minutes later she was in her car, heading home.

When she stopped for a red light, she used her car phone to call Dallas Lord's voice mail. She punched in his code and listened to Adam Lord's messages. None of them interested her. She saved the messages by pressing the star key. Adam would never know she had listened.

Loaded down with gaily wrapped packages, exquisite Christmas shopping bags and takeout Chinese, Sara and Carly parked the car in the garage, their shadows on the road shooting questions at them which they ignored.

Sara punched in her code and opened the kitchen door. Both women stared at the total destruction that greeted them. The floor and countertops were littered with flour, sugar, coffee, and broken dishes. The green plants from the windowsill had been thrown against the wall, some of the dirt still sticking to the rough plaster. The refrigerator door, the oven door and all the cabinet doors hung open. The pot roast and leftover gravy dribbled down the front of the refrigerator door.

They walked through the house in a daze, their arms still full of packages and Chinese food.

Carly sat down on what was left of one of the sofa cushions. "I told you this would happen. Those people are merciless. They want the song, Sara. The next thing that's going to happen is they are going to say you stole it. You had the motive and the opportunity. You were there almost every day since Billy's death. They're going to blame you, Sara. How are we ever going to clean this up?"

"Shhh, don't cry, Carly. We have insurance. I'll call the Disaster Master people. They come in with a whole crew and before you know it everything will be back to normal. Go find some forks. We'll eat here in the family room. We'll call the police after we eat. It's going to be okay, Carly. Trust me."

"Give them the damn song, Sara. What if they . . . try to do something to us? Isn't that what those kinds of people do?"

"I will not be intimidated. I absolutely will not. The song is safe. We're safe. We're going to file a police report. Now, go get the forks."

Sara bit into a crisp, crunchy egg roll. Carly stared at her pepper steak just as the doorbell rang. "Maybe they forgot to do something?" she quipped. "Where's Dad's gun?"

Sara stared at her sister. "It's on the mantel behind the vase. It's loaded, Carly. Be careful."

"Are you telling me you don't want me to shoot the son of a bitch?"

"I'm telling you to be careful. It might be Nellie. Look before you open the door."

"Are you just going to sit there and eat that egg roll?"

"I'm right behind you. You aren't the most graceful person on two legs. Don't, for God's sake, shoot your foot off."

"Who is it?" Carly shouted to be heard through the door.

"Adam Lord," came the response.

"Should I shoot through the door or wait till he gets inside."

"Wait till he gets inside. There is no point to making another mess."

Carly cocked the hammer before she opened the door.

"Come in, Mr. Lord, and yes, this sucker is loaded and the safety is off."

Sara took a bite of her egg roll. "She's a crack shot. Nervous but accurate. I hope you brought your cleaning equipment with you."

"God Almighty!" Adam squawked when he saw the destruction behind the two women.

Chapter Twelve

"If you don't want that pack of jackals out there to see this, you had better invite me in," Adam said as he craned his neck to see the devastation.

"Let him in, Carly," Sara said. The anger and bitterness she was feeling showed in her face. "I suppose you're going to tell me you don't know anything about this." She jerked her head to the side to indicate the destruction in the family room that could be seen from the foyer.

"That's exactly what I'm going to tell you. When did this happen? Who did it?"

Sara shrugged. "If I knew who did it, do you think I'd be standing here having this conversation with you? Right now you're my best suspect. We were out all day. Whoever it was had our alarm code. This is from your camp, Mr. Lord. Dallas had my code, no one else, so that brings suspicion right back to you. I intend to tell the police that, too. In other words, I don't believe you. We were just about to call the police when you rang the bell."

"I didn't do this nor did I have anything to do with it. I'd like to look around. Breaking and entering is not my specialty. It's illegal, and I'm an attorney. As such, I'm sworn to uphold the law. Is the rest of the house like this?"

"Every room," Carly said.

"I'm no detective, but I think it's safe to say someone thinks you have something they want."

There was a snap and crackle to Sara's voice when she said, "You're the only one who thinks we have something, and you offered to buy that something. That puts you at the top of my list, and that's exactly what I'm going to tell the police."

Adam made his rounds. He returned, his features hard to read. "This is total destruction. I feel partially responsible. What I mean by that is my coming here could have triggered this. I think Dallas would want me to take responsibility for what has happened here. His estate will pay all damages and it will save you filing an insurance form. Once you file a claim, your rates jump sky-high.

Do not take my offer as an admission of guilt. Assess the damage and call me."

"The damage is going to be high. Some of our stuff is irreplaceable. It belonged to my parents and grandparents. Heirlooms. This went beyond search and seize. This . . . is . . ."

"Vicious. Hateful. Spiteful. I can't see any reason to topple your Christmas tree."

"What do you want, Mr. Lord?" Sara said. The bite in her voice was hard to miss.

"I want the truth, and I want the song. If you really don't have it, and you aren't lying to me, you have nothing to fear. If I decide you do have it, I'll sue to get it. In the process your lives will become so unpleasant you will beg me to take it off your hands. Look, I don't want it for myself. I want Dallas to live on forever. If I can make that happen, I will. Undoubtedly, the song, if there is a song, is the last thing my brother wrote. Like your heirlooms, it's priceless. Let's cut a deal here and now. Sandi Sims is saying my brother wrote the song for her. She knows the words, and she's saying Dallas was going to back out of his marriage to you and marry her. That's something you'll have to deal with in court. I think you know Dallas was one of the most generous people in the world. Sandi is saying he felt sorry for you, and that's why he gave you the song. He did things like that because he didn't think it through. I'm not saying that's what happened. What I am saying is you are going to have to prove that the song belongs to you."

"I told you he would say that, Sara. People like you think you can do and say whatever you damn well please. Guess what, we're people, too. We're honest, hardworking people dedicated to healing the sick. I don't want to hear any more of your belches, Mr. Lord. Don't you people have enough money? How much more do you need? Do you need another house, another airplane? Get out of our house."

People like you. Something alien attacked Adam's stomach and throat. "Are you trying to profit from my brother's death?"

"No. I might ask you the same question, Mr. Lord," Sara said.

"Dallas was my brother. I have to safeguard his estate. I'm asking you nicely to give me the song. Name your price or take your chances in court. I warn you, it won't be nice. In the end both your careers will be destroyed. The world will see you as moneygrubbing hangers-on. The press and tabloids will slice you to ribbons."

Sara felt sick to her stomach. From the look on Carly's face, she, too, was feeling sick. Sara marshaled all her strength. "I think you should leave, Mr. Lord. Please don't come back here. In the morning I'm going to apply for a restraining order against you. If we have to, we'll get an unlisted telephone number. Before you leave, though, I'd like to ask you something. Does the fact that Dallas gave Sandi Sims a check for $100,000 have anything to do with this? Is his estate going to sue to recover that money? Where would a backup singer of modest means get that kind of money for repayment? *Now,* you can leave, *Mister Lord.*" She made his name sound obscene.

"I don't know anything about that. I haven't had a chance to go through all the financials yet. If Sandi owes the money, the estate will go after it. Sandi Sims knew the words to the song, Doctor."

"If she knows the words, then all you have to do is set them to music."

"Sandi said Dallas made a tape. She can't remember all the words. We have an airtight case, Doctor."

"File your papers, Mr. Lord. I'll take my chance in a court of law."

"For someone of your intelligence, Dr. Killian, that's a very stupid attitude. I'm prepared to give you fifty thousand dollars and top billing and by top billing I mean the whole nine yards. Dallas wrote the song for you because you were planning to marry, etc., etc. You can sell your story to every magazine and tabloid in the world when the song hits the top of the charts. You'll be so big in Europe and Asia you won't be able to count the money fast enough. You'll make millions, and you'll never have to work again. Either one of you, if you're a sharing family. From where I'm sitting that is not a shabby offer."

"This is not about money, *Mister Lord*. Why does everything always come down to money? Dallas said it was your middle name. My sister and I spent long years of schooling to be able to do what we do. We like to work. We do not need millions of dollars. It's people like you who need millions of dollars." She wasn't sure, but she thought she saw grudging respect in Adam Lord's eyes. And something else she couldn't name.

People like you. "A hundred thousand. That's my final offer. Please don't deprive Dallas's fans of his last work. I agree the money has nothing to do with it."

"That was my line, not yours. It always comes down to money in the end. Please leave, Mr. Lord," Sara said.

"Why are you being so damn stubborn, so damn greedy? What do you want? Name your price. Honest, hardworking people that you are, you must have some kind of agenda. The highest bidder gets it, is that it?"

Once again Carly flicked the safety catch off the gun. She brought it up to her chest level. I'll shoot on the count of three, and this bullet will get you about six inches below your belt. *OUT!"*

Seething with anger, his options played out, Adam left. These two women were definitely not prairie flowers. They had grit and backbones of steel.

"I was going to shoot him, Sara, I swear to God I was. In the foot," Carly said in a jittery voice.

"Gee, I thought you meant what you said. Put the gun away and make sure the safety is on. I wonder why the person who did this didn't take the gun. They always take guns. Put it away. Guns bother me. I'm going to call the police."

It was after midnight when the last police officer walked out the door. Sara slammed it as strobes flashed from the sidewalk. She'd asked the police not to comment to the gaggle of reporters outside, but she knew it was a futile request. Everyone, even police, wanted their fifteen minutes of fame.

"Those cops will probably get fifty grand each for describing our house and our personal stats. They'll pay off their mortgages, trade in the family car, go out to a fancy-dancy restaurant, and all because our house was burglarized. We'll continue to live in fear as Adam Lord gets ready to sue us. I ask you, Sara, where is the justice in all of this?"

"I don't know, Carly. Let's go to bed."

"In what? They cut up our mattresses. I feel like I've been violated. Just the thought of touching something makes my stomach heave. I'm scared, Sara. I really am."

Sara, her eyes misty, put her arms around Carly's shoulders. "Mom always told us there is nothing to fear but fear itself. We can handle this. We can, Carly."

"Yeah, well, Mom always used to tell us something else, too. She said when you fight for principle, you always lose. He said he could ruin our lives. Sara, were you paying attention?"

"Of course I was paying attention. He's trying to intimidate us. There is nothing he can do. He can't prove anything. The first thing a judge will say is 'Show me proof.' He has no proof. He's guessing there is a song. If Sandi Sims knew for sure, she'd have the words down pat and they'd have cut a tape by now or whatever it is you do when you're getting a song ready for market. They can do all kinds of things with that pricey electronic, state-of-the-art equipment they have. Another thing, we have impeccable credentials and don't you forget it for one minute. Think about it, Carly, he started out at five thousand and now he's up to one hundred thousand. They have zip. I have an idea. I've been kind of thinking about it all day. I can call Judge Iverson and tell him our problem. He was Dad's best friend, and he's known us since we were babies. He's also my godfather. He'll know what we should do. Are you comfortable with that, Carly? Tomorrow, just to be on the safe side, I'm going to buy an extra recorder and we'll make some extra copies of the tape while we're at the bank. I won't mess with the master copy, though. Dallas wrote on the label, so it's his handwriting. I almost forgot about that. He labeled it Master Copy in block letters and then he wrote, To Sara from Dallas, and he signed his name, Dallas Lord. That makes it mine Carly, and I'm keeping it."

"It sounds good. I called Hank and canceled the ski trip. He didn't seem to care one way or the other. I'm not leaving you alone while I go off to have a good time. I'd be sick with worry."

"I wish you hadn't done that, Carly. I'm okay. I've got my stride back. Whoever would have thought a simple little song with my name on it could cause all this furor? Me of all people."

"We need to get some sleep. Let's curl up by the tree with the afghans." Carly yawned. "Tomorrow is another day. Do you know what really," she grappled for just the right word, *"pisses* me off? The tree. All Mom's ornaments are broken and the lights are smashed. That was just so cruel. We've had them *forever,* Sara."

"I know. I know. Go to sleep, Carly," Sara said as she threw one of her mother's afghans over her sister. "It will be a brand-new day before you know it. We'll put the tree back up in the morning. Then we'll go to Target and get some new decorations. It's what it is, Carly. It happened, and we can't change it."

Sara curled up next to her sister. She thought about Adam Lord and the strange look in his eyes. What did it mean? As her body fought for sleep, she struggled to remember everything Dallas had ever told her about his brother. In a million years Dallas would never believe his brother capable of anything but expert management. He would say Adam would never jeopardize his career, Adam had ethics, and he was honorable and forthright. He'd then summarize everything by saying Adam was an up-front, in-your-face person, and either you liked him or you hated him, that no one, not him and he was his blood brother, knew the real Adam behind his shiny veneer. Sara sighed. It was all too much. Before she closed her eyes for the last time she found herself wondering if there was a woman in Adam's life and what she was like. There was nothing wrong with a little *fantasizing.* Was she tall, willowy, and blond? Did she wear designer clothes and scads of makeup and delicious perfume? Did she have a name? Probably something exotic sounding. Maybe Sabrina or Tatiana or Gennifer with a G. A second weary sigh escaped her. Moments later she was asleep.

Adam paced the upstairs hallway, trying to come to terms with what had transpired earlier. He thought about his house back in South Carolina with all the treasures he'd collected over the years. How would he feel if some thief broke in and destroyed all he held dear? "I'd damn well feel like those women felt." Nothing had been taken. That had to mean the person or persons doing the breaking and entering were looking for something. Something small. Something that could be hidden in a flour canister or in a cushion. A tape. Who? One of the band members? They'd all gone back to their respective homes. Sandi? A very serious possibility.

An hour later, his pacing took on a frantic

beat. Izzie skittered to his side whining softly. "It's okay, girl. Just a little problem to deal with. Somewhere, someplace, in this house, there must be some kind of proof to back up Sara or Sandi's story."

He was at the top of the steps. Izzie stretched out when Adam sat down on the top step. "She was a real person, Izzie. I didn't expect that. At first I thought she was going to be a gold digger. Then I thought maybe she was starstruck. Now I think she's exactly what she is, a credible doctor with a sister who is a nurse. Neither one seems to be the kind of person Dallas surrounded himself with. Back that up, Izzie. Dr. Killian is a doctor without a job. In the morning we're going to check that out. We're also going to do a check on Dallas's personal bank account."

Adam leaned back against the wall. He stroked the spaniel's big head. It was a long time since he'd fantasized about anyone. There was nothing wrong with *fantasizing* as long as it didn't get out of hand. "I kind of liked her. I really liked her eyes and the direct way she stared at me. She was pretty in a wholesome way. I bet she's a knockout when she's dressed up. I sensed loyalty in her, and I think she genuinely liked Dallas. The sister was pretty verbal, but she was protecting the doctor. I liked that. I used to do the same thing for Dallas. There is a bond there, and that's good. So far, neither one has admitted there is a song. That's different from lying. This whole thing is making me sick. I keep asking myself what Dallas would want me to do, and I don't have the answer. It's almost Christmas. Jesus, I was really looking forward to it. Maybe we'll get a tree tomorrow. Never mind maybe. We're going to get one. I have a . . . I have a stocking to hang up. Want to go for a walk, Izzie, before we turn in?" The spaniel was down the stairs woofing softly as she padded her way to the kitchen.

It was four o'clock in the morning when Adam finally climbed the steps to his bedroom. He slept fitfully until six-thirty, his dreams full of a woman in a white coat with a stethoscope around her neck, when Tom Silk poked his head in the door to take Izzie and the pups downstairs. He groaned. Another day. Another set of problems lurked below on the first floor. He was sure of it.

* * *

The Disaster Master crew arrived promptly at eight o'clock. Sara and Carly had jackets and purses in hand.

"We'll be done by three, ma'am," the crew's chief said smartly.

"We'll be back by then. Just in case we're running late, I'll leave the check on the kitchen counter. Just lock the door behind you."

In the garage with the light on, Sara noticed that the jaguar hood ornament was missing from her car. Her fist shot out, making contact with the hard plastic window of Carly's Jeep. "Now *that pisses* me off."

"You drive, Sara. I have a couple of calls to make."

Sara listened to her sister, her jaw dropping when she heard her ask, her voice dripping sweetness, what a previously unrecorded Dallas Lord song was worth. "I don't think it really matters who I am. Just give me a number. Well, why not? There is priceless and then there is priceless. How many zeros are you talking about? Oh, I see. You know what, I'll get back to you."

"I don't think that was a smart thing to do, Carly. How did you know whom to call?"

"I have some of Dallas's albums and a few of his tapes. I just called the company on the label."

"I guess you know your phone call will make the six o'clock news tonight."

"So what! I didn't give my name. It's very difficult to trace a cell-phone number. Even EMS has a hard time finding people who call in with a cell phone. I wasn't on the line more than three minutes. Maybe it will give Mr. Lord pause for thought. Where are we going, Sara?"

"To O'Brien's furniture store. I think if we explain what happened, they will deliver us some new beds and den furniture. Later on we can get the rest. So, how much did they tell you the song was worth?"

Carly's eyes glazed over. "He said it was the three front numbers that were important. To me it could mean a hundred million. That can't be right, can it, Sara? I remember reading somewhere that one of Michael Jackson's songs earned that much money, and he's still alive."

"I suppose anything is possible. No wonder Mr. Lord wants it so bad."

"Did you believe him when he said Dallas was going to call off the marriage?"

"No. Dallas couldn't wait to say I do. I think he was trying to one-up his brother. He's had this fear all his life that he was retarded."

"What?"

"You heard me. He isn't . . . wasn't. I'm not sure if Adam and the band knew he wasn't. Dallas truly believed they all thought he was retarded. He said it was simpler to just go along with it. The reason he thought it was simpler was because he believed it."

"My God, how awful."

"Yes, it was awful," Sara said quietly. "Can you imagine carrying something like that on your shoulders all your life?"

"Are you sure, Sara? Did you tell him he wasn't?"

"Carly, I'm a doctor. Of course I'm sure, and, yes, I told him. I wish you could have seen his face. I will never, ever, forget the joy I saw in that man's face. I will remember it until the day I die. At that precise moment Dallas became a different person. That's another reason why I know he wasn't going to cancel the wedding. I want to always remember him like he was that day, alive, vibrant, ready to take on the world and not hide behind his music. He literally came into his own. He said something kind of funny yet sad to me. He said, Now I can eyeball my brother and not look away. He made me cry. That was the night he gave me the master copy of the song."

"Then by God, we aren't giving it up! Let's get one of those spiffy satin couches. With a chair to match."

"Whatever you want. You better call the insurance company before we go into the store. Just ask for Joe Hamilton. The number's in the address book in my bag."

Carly yanked at the voluminous quilted bag that belonged to Sara. "What *do* you have in this bag, Sara?"

"My life."

Sara pulled into a parking space at O'Brien's Furniture Mart just as Carly broke the connection. "We have to get a copy of the police report and fax it to Joe. We also have to make a list of the damage. There is a $200 deductible. Maybe we should have taken Mr. Lord up on his offer to furnish the house."

"I don't want anything from him. I don't think you do either. We're going by the book here. When we start doing things *his* way, it's all over. Trust me on that. Now, let's go pick out that satin couch and chair."

Adam carried his breakfast coffee outside so he could watch his dogs romp with Tom Silk. He couldn't remember ever being this tired. He had slept less than three hours last night. Each time he closed his eyes all he could think about was Sara Killian's shocked, vulnerable face. Each time he closed his eyes he found his thoughts going to Dallas and why someone like Dr. Killian would be interested in him. He'd bet his life savings she wasn't a rock fan. Was she after Dallas's money and the glory of being married to a celebrity? He didn't think so.

What if there wasn't a song? What if he was spinning his wheels for nothing? No, there had to be a song. Would Dallas have hidden it? Would he have given it to someone to safeguard? To his knowledge the only person Dallas had ever trusted was Billy Sweet. Did Dr. Sara Killian have the song, and was she going to keep it until just the right moment, or would she announce she had it and get a bidder's war going? "The very least you could have done, Dallas, was to leave me a clue, something to go on," he muttered.

When Adam finished the coffee in his cup, he stomped into the house for a refill. What was really bothering him was that he'd found himself *attracted* to Sara Killian yesterday. When she'd calmed down, he'd seen a peculiar glint in her eye he couldn't identify. He'd felt rather buoyant after that.

"Anything in particular you want me to do today, Adam?" Tom called from the pool deck.

"I'm going out for a Christmas tree around noon if you want to come along. I have some things to take care of first that will take all morning."

"Jeez, that's my favorite thing to do. Take your time. I'll forge ahead with my training. Do you need any help decorating the tree? More to the point, do you have any decorations?"

Adam grinned at the wistful look on Tom's face. "Absolutely I need help. I'll call someone and order everything. Listen for the gate buzzer, okay?" The grin stayed with Adam as he tried to visualize the stunned surprise on the trainer's face when he presented him with a brand-new Dodge Ram van on Christmas morning. Dallas wasn't the only one who was generous.

Adam dived into the mess in Dallas's bedroom. It was after ten before he had all the files back in place in the office. He removed the contents of the desk to carry to his own room. The pile was small and consisted of Dallas's personal checkbook, which he never bothered to balance, loose bills, paid receipts for things he'd bought, scribbled notes, and a small jeweler's box. His eyes started to burn at the sterile, antiseptic life his brother led. Where were all the personal things that made up a person? Where was the junk everyone collected? His stomach became a hard-fisted knot. He wanted to cry for his brother. Hell, he *needed* to cry. He did cry then, hard, racking sobs that shook the bed on which he was sitting. He cried for the would-haves, the should-haves, and the could-haves.

Drained of all emotion, Adam's analytical and methodical mind took over. He found the entry in Dallas's checkbook for the money Dr. Killian had mentioned. He knew in his gut there was no signed promissory note anywhere. Sandi Sims would say the hundred thousand was a gift. If there was no way to dispute it, he would have to write it off.

Adam never had a problem doing two things at once. His left hand pawed through the scribbled notes as his right hand flipped through his file for the detective agency he'd called to run a check on Sandi Sims and Sara Killian. He punched out a set of numbers, his left hand still sifting through the notes. He identified himself when the detective's voice came over the wire. He listened, a frown building on his forehead.

"The doctor is just what she says she is. She has an impeccable reputation. While she was serving her residency, she turned in a colleague for tampering with the drug cabinet on her shift. She was involved in an intimate relationship with the doctor in question at that time. She's a good credit risk, has no driving violations, and her coworkers speak highly of her. Her bank balance is healthy but not robust. She makes her car payments on time and pays her utility bills when they're due. That's it. I'm going to fax you my file on Sandi Sims when we hang up. I came up with squat where Benton Memorial is concerned. No one there will talk. I tried everything. The guy you need to talk with is Harry Heinrick. They call him the Hawk. My bill is included with the fax. Merry Christmas, Mr. Lord."

"Same to you."

Adam stared out the window, his thoughts chaotic. The detective had read off his report on Sara Killian but was faxing Sandi Sims's report. Now, what did that mean?

In Dallas's attention-getting office, Adam picked the pages from the fax as soon as they slid to the base of the machine. He scanned them, his eyes narrowing. He carried the six-page report back to his bedroom. On the surface there was nothing to get excited about.

Sandi Sims is a professional name of one Mona Wilson. She waited tables, sang in supper clubs, sold used cars decked out in a string bikini, with outstanding sales. She'd attended college for one year, then dropped out, at which point she did the race-car circuit. Could not confirm race-car stint because it appears she used a name other than Mona Wilson or Sandi Sims. At that time, the woman in question had flame red hair. For the past few years she has been linked with a series of older men, most of them "sugar daddies." One of the daddies paid for some pricey dental work and breast implants. She owns two condos, one of which is rented for a hefty monthly income. She lives in the other. Very luxurious. Both condos are paid for. Her bank account for someone her age is better than robust. She drives a late model 560 SL, compliments of one of the more recent sugar daddies. The bottom line is she has credit cards out the kazoo and the bills are paid by someone other than herself.

A scribbled note in the margin of the report read:

I think the guy who pays the bills is some high muckety-muck attorney. He pays in cash. Bills run three to five grand a month. The only description I could get fits hundreds of people. Dead end in that respect.

Adam snorted. The report fit half the women in California. He tossed the pages on the bed and dialed Sandi's number from memory. She picked up on the third ring, her voice sleepy-sounding. "It's Adam, Sandi. Why didn't you tell me about the hundred thousand dollars Dallas lent you?"

"He didn't lend it to me. He gave it to me. He told me to do something nice for my parents for Christmas. He suggested a cruise with all the trimmings. Are you saying you want it back? I paid for the cruise and everything. It was a gift, Adam." All sleepiness was gone from her voice and was replaced with a nasally whine.

Adam took the aggressive approach. "That's not what it says in Dallas's checkbook. It says, 'loan to Sandi.' "

"I don't believe that! If that's true, then why didn't he have me sign something? It was a gift. You can't make me pay that back. I won't pay it back. Why are you being so ugly about this?"

"A hundred thousand dollars is a lot of money. That must have been some cruise. Where exactly did you send your parents? Around the world?"

"To the Caribbean. That's where they wanted to go. I had to buy new wardrobes for them and give them shopping money. It was Dallas's idea. He didn't say anything about giving back the balance. He also told me to buy myself something nice for Christmas. For heaven's sake, Adam, where is your Christmas spirit? Do you have any news on my song?"

Adam hung up on her in mid-sentence. She was lying about the hundred thousand. He felt it in his gut. If she lied about that, what else did she lie about?

The second call on Adam's list was to Benton Memorial Hospital, where he left a message for Harry Heinrick that was simple and to the point: I'll be in your office at one o'clock.

Adam flopped back on the bed. He wished he were back in South Carolina with the dogs in his own house. Christ, how he hated this black-and-white modern glass-and-chrome house of his brother's. He bolted from the bed in a rush. Pockets. He hadn't gone through any of Dallas's pockets. Even when he was a kid, Dallas jammed stuff in his pockets until he was bottom heavy. In his haste to get off the bed the small jeweler's box fell on the floor. His face flushed, he picked it up. Inside, nestled in black velvet, was a magnificent diamond engagement ring with a matching wedding band. He didn't have to be told the stones were flawless. He wondered if Dallas had help picking the rings out or if they were his own choice. He stuffed the box in the pocket of his jeans. The jeweler's box gave him a bona fide excuse to go to Sara Killian's house again.

There was a spring in his step as he made his way down the hall to his brother's bedroom. He admitted to himself that he was looking forward to seeing Sara Killian again. He couldn't wait to see her reaction to the rings in his pocket.

Adam drew a deep breath before he opened the door to Dallas's walk-in closet. He was immediately drawn to the jeans hanging on the hooks. He knew he was going to find something.

He rifled the pockets and found the usual junk: a wadded-up napkin with several bars of scribbled music, a pen that was out of ink, a tattered rabbit's foot minus the fur, a key he didn't recognize, twenty-seven pennies, and a small bottle of Bayer Aspirin. A second pair of jeans held a receipt from Burger King, two dollars in loose change, three matchbooks with scribbled words he couldn't make out, a second key, two packages of Trident chewing gum, a second bottle of Bayer Aspirin, and two crumpled dollar bills. The third pair of jeans had $335 dollars rolled into a wad with an elastic band around it, a key, an empty aspirin bottle, a stubby pencil, a pack of half-eaten Life Savers, and three pebbles.

Adam left everything in the pockets except the keys. They seemed identical. He matched them up, putting one on top of the other. All the grooves lined up. What did the keys unlock?

Whatever it was would have to wait. He had to get on his stick and head for town with his meeting with Harry Heinrick.

Chapter Thirteen

Sara opened the kitchen door to be greeted by total silence. A citrusy scent, not unpleasant, assailed her nostrils. The house sparkled. She looked around, marveling at the thoroughness of the cleaning crew as she meandered through the house. All the shredded furniture, mattresses, and debris had been carted off.

"Look. They even cleaned out the fireplace and laid logs. All we have to do is light up. Here comes the furniture," Carly called from the front window.

Two hours later, their new beds made, the furniture in place, the tree waited in the stand to be decorated.

"I don't think we bought enough lights. I love lots and lots of lights on the Christmas tree. I'll go to the drugstore and get more. I can pick up some Boston Chicken dinner," Carly offered.

"It's better than cooking," Sara said.

"I have to take your car. Mine is on fumes."

Sara groped in her black bag and tossed her sister a set of keys. "I'm going to take a quick shower, then I'll light the fire. We can pretend we're Camp Fire girls like we did when we were kids. You better get two strings of lights."

"Will do. I'll be back in thirty minutes."

Carly didn't return in thirty minutes or in sixty minutes. Sara went outside three different times to stare down the road. Each time she entered the house, she became more agitated. She paced in circles, then she cursed the newness that surrounded her. Everything was all wrong. Nothing felt right. When the doorbell shrilled, she almost jumped out of her skin. She ran to the door expecting to see Carly, her arms loaded with dinner and Christmas lights. The last person she expected to see was Nellie Pulaski.

The old nurse held up her hands in a gesture of reassurance. "Carly's okay, Sara, but there was an accident. A bad one. The air bag saved her life. EMS took her to Benton and Harry called me. The police were coming to tell you, but I said I would do it. She's going to be fine, Sara. As long as you know and believe that, everything else is okay. She does have a fractured shoulder."

Sara grappled for her bag among the day's purchases. "What happened?" She couldn't fall apart. She needed to stay in control. Nellie would never lie to her.

"The brakes failed on the curve, and Carly lost control. The roads are kind of slick this evening. It's been misting for several hours."

"That's impossible. I had the Jag serviced a month ago. Aside from some ugly scratches on the door and a broken hood ornament, the car was in perfect shape." Sara's voice turned hysterical when she said, "Nellie, there was nothing wrong with the goddamn brakes."

"Right now that isn't important. Carly needs to see you. As you well know, nurses and doctors make the worst patients. She's convinced she's going to be crippled or deformed. For life! They had to give her a sedative to calm her down. She really is okay, Sara. Your car is totaled, though. I think you need to tell me what's been going on, Sara. Everything."

Sara recited the entire story, from the day of her first visit to Dallas's estate to the trashing of her house and buying new furniture. "I'm telling you, Nellie, my brakes were fine. That was no accident." The hysteria was gone from her voice, replaced by a cold, angry tone.

"Are you saying someone tampered with your brakes?" Nellie demanded.

"If you were me, what would you think?"

Nellie muttered something indistinguishable.

They made the rest of the trip to the hospital in silence, each woman busy with her own thoughts.

"Be calm now, Sara. This is not life-threatening. Carly will be home by tomorrow evening. I'm staying with her throughout the evening. I already told the Hawk, and he said it was all right. Something is bothering that man. I never saw him so jittery. Guess the holiday contributions aren't coming in as fast as they should. He wanted to know what it would take for me to come back to work. I gave him the finger. Okay, here's the floor. Pinch your cheeks. You're too white. Carly will pick up on it."

"She's been fighting the sedative," the charge nurse said. "Don't stay too long, Sara. She needs to rest." Sara nodded.

"I'm sorry about the car, Sara. I know how

much you loved it. The brakes just gave out. Was anyone else hurt?" Carly's voice was so sleepy-sounding, so groggy, Sara could barely make out the words.

"No one else was injured. You're going to be fine, Carly. Nellie said you can come home by tomorrow evening."

"What did the doctor say?"

"Who cares what some doctor says? If Nellie said you can go home, then you can go home. Right now, though, you have to stop fighting the sedative and go to sleep. Nellie's going to stay." A murderous look in her eye, Sara brushed at Carly's damp curls plastered to her forehead.

The moment Carly drifted off to sleep, Nellie said, "I already checked the chart and spoke to Dr. Olsen. I know you're itching to be off to do something, so go to it. Everything here is under control."

"Can I borrow your truck, Nellie?"

"Sure. Take it easy now, Sara. Think things through and deal with this with your head and not with emotion."

Sara nodded. "It was supposed to be me in that car, Nellie. Not Carly. I'll be back after I . . . I have something to do."

"Sara, be careful. All of this . . . this . . .

that wasn't what I meant when I told you to get a life. These people, they're way out of your league."

Sara sucked in her breath. "If you were a betting woman, Nellie, who would you put your money on, Nellie, me, or *them*?"

"You, kiddo. Win, Place, and Show."

"Okay. I'll be back. If I end up in jail, will you bail me out?"

Nellie nodded, her eyes sparkling.

"Kick some ass, Sara," Carly mumbled from the bed.

Outside in the fresh air, Sara took great gulps of the misty night air to steady her nerves before she climbed into Nellie's ancient pickup truck. She drove slowly until she felt comfortable with the heavy-duty truck that was almost as old as its owner. Nellie loved this old truck. Right now Sara loved it, too. She made one stop at the house for her father's gun.

Sara was halfway out the door when she turned around and headed for the phone. She dialed Dallas's number from memory. A strange voice responded on the other end of the line. "This is Dr. Killian. I'd like to speak to Mr. Lord, please."

"This is Tom Silk, Doctor. Adam left about

fifteen minutes ago. He should be back in about forty-five minutes. Would you like to leave a message?"

"No." Sara broke the connection. She looked at her watch. Most people were in for the night by ten o'clock. Where would Adam Lord go at this time of night? To Benton Memorial to check on his handiwork? To the police station? If he went to either place, that would tip his hand. No, he probably went to talk to his accomplice. Lawyers who were sworn to uphold the law wouldn't dirty their hands with something as serious as this.

Sara crumpled then, sinking down into the depths of the new sofa. Somebody had tried to kill her. Somebody who didn't care if she lived or died. Didn't that person know how precious life was? Red-hot anger rivered through her. She didn't stop to think. She barreled through the door and out to Nellie's truck. She dumped the gun and the heavy black shoulder bag on the passenger side of the seat. Her first stop was the police station, where she demanded to see the investigating oficer in charge of Carly's accident.

At the end of her long tirade, she eyeballed Detective Luzak, and said, "I'm going to tell you something, and I don't want you to put it down to female hysteria. I've had this feeling for the past few days that someone is watching and following me. I want that to go on the record. This was no accident. I just had my car serviced a month ago, and new brake pads were installed at that time." She rummaged in the black bag till she found the service report from the Jaguar dealer and copy of the police report from yesterday. "These two incidents are related. The person who broke into my house tampered with my car. My sister could have been killed. What are you going to do about it, Officer?"

"I'm going to go to the lot where your car was towed. I'll check it out myself, Dr. Killian. I go off duty at eleven, and the lot is on my way home."

Somewhat mollified, Sara said, "The morning will be time enough."

"I'm off duty tomorrow. I'd just as soon do it this evening. I'll call you as soon as I know anything. If what you say is true, then I'll come back here and follow through. Be grateful the air bag saved your sister's life."

"I am grateful, Officer. You have no idea just how grateful I am. My sister is the only family I have in the world." The sob in her voice did not go unnoticed by the kindly detective.

"I'll call you the moment I know something, Dr. Killian."

Back in the ancient truck, Sara took a deep breath. Without thinking, she reached for one of the cigarettes Nellie always kept on the dashboard. Coughing and sputtering, her eyes watering, Sara puffed furiously on the menthol cigarette.

She needed a game plan. If she sat here long enough in the police parking lot, surely an idea would come to her. She continued to puff on her cigarette, her eyes smarting as the smoke billowed up around her head in the close confines of the truck cab. She did her best to relax, hoping some workable plan of action would come to mind.

Adam poured himself a cup of coffee and carried it to the table, the dogs swarming about his feet. He took the time to tussle with each one of them, Izzie watching from her position by the back door.

"You look done in, Adam," Tom Silk said as he sipped at his own coffee, one eye on the gate monitor above the kitchen door.

"It's been a long day. I had meetings with

this . . . idiot from Benton Memorial. I was at the courthouse for hours. It's never easy when someone dies, but when that someone is your brother *and* Dallas Lord, everything is compounded a hundred percent.

This place is like a prison fortress. There are no words to tell you how much I hate being here. I see Dallas everywhere. Sometimes I think I hear him. I get this eerie feeling that he's actually here in the house. Is that weird or what? Earlier today I swore I smelled his aftershave. Izzie was sniffing, too." Adam shivered to make his point.

"Are you going to go ahead with your plan to turn this place into another Graceland?"

Adam frowned. He bent over to pick up Dallas Six, who cuddled in the crook of his arm. "Your tone of voice tells me you don't approve of shrines."

"I imagine it would be a monumental undertaking. Who's going to oversee something of that magnitude? Do you just turn it over to someone and then walk away? This is just my opinion, but somehow I don't think your brother would want that. If he did, why would he lock himself away up here. Why would you want to tamper with something that had its place in the sun?"

Adam rubbed at his temples. "I guess I feel like I owe it to Dallas. So much happened in our lives that he couldn't deal with. I always wanted to do the *right* thing. I've come to realize doing the right thing sometimes wasn't right for Dallas if you know what I mean. One day I think Dallas would want a shrine, and the next day I *know* he wouldn't." He held out his coffee cup for a refill. Tom filled his cup and his own as well.

"Did you return Dr. Killian's call?"

Adam looked at his watch. "It's late. I'll call her in the morning." He stared across the table at Tom, who was peering at the monitor. Izzie growled. The six pups raced to her side, their plump little bodies wiggling with anticipation, their tails wagging furiously.

"I think you better take a look at this, Adam. Now, that's a kick-ass truck if I ever saw one. Were you expecting company? Man, that truck looks *solid.* That sucker even has a running board. I saw this old movie once where Rommel and his desert rats were mapping out strategy with a truck just like this one. It's just sitting there. Maybe it's someone casing the place. Do you want me to call the cops?"

Adam walked over to the door to get a better look at the monitor. "What the hell! That looks like . . . yeah, it does look like Dr. Killian."

"I think you're right. Should I release the gate?"

"She didn't ring the buzzer? Maybe she just wants to sit out there. Where do you suppose she got an ancient vehicle like that?"

"Maybe it belonged to her great-grandfather. I don't believe she just drove up here to stare at those gates and neither do you. Uh-oh, she's backing up. Oh, jeez, now she's going forward. No, no, she's backing up again. She's going farther down the drive."

"Shit! She's doing that to get up speed. She's going to ram the gates! Open the damn things! Quick!"

Tom was too late. Both men watched the shower of sparks that shot upward as Nellie Pulaski's ancient truck plowed down the gates and roared up the driveway.

"Son of a bitch!" Adam swore as he ripped opened the door, Izzie and the pups in hot pursuit. Tom Silk brought up the rear. Humans and dogs skidded to the side when the heavy-duty truck ground to a halt. A section of the gate that was attached to the side of the truck fell to the ground with a loud crashing sound.

Nine pairs of eyes watched as Sara Killian leapt from the truck, gun shaking in her wobbly hand. Izzie howled her displeasure. Sara cupped her right hand with her left hand to steady the gun. "Try and kill me will you, you sneaky bastard. Well guess, what! I'm alive and I'm standing here. I'm the one with the gun. You move even a muscle and it's all over. My sister could have been killed! She's in the hospital. Is that damn song worth my life or my sister's life? No, it is not. Fear and intimidation are not going to work on me, Mr. Lord."

"What are you talking about? Is that gun loaded?"

"You're damn right it's loaded. Watch this, you son of a bitch!" Without a moment's hesitation Sara fired off three shots, nipping Adam's bare toes. Tom Silk danced backward as Izzie and her pups ran for cover. "The next one will get you right between the legs. I've got two more clips so don't . . ." Sara grappled in her mind for a word Carly would use to make her point. "Don't *piss* me off. You know what, you're right. I do have the song. Guess what else, you bastard. You aren't getting it! All you people do is lie, cheat, and steal. What you did to my car is attempted murder. Don't even think about trying to tell me you didn't do anything. I damn well know you did. The only trouble is, my sister was driving my car. My baby sister. I've looked out for her all her life, and I have no intention of letting some lowlife shark like you change things. I will not tolerate it! Do you hear me?" A second round of shots filled the night air.

"I don't know what you're talking about." *She looked after her baby sister all her life just the way he'd looked after Dallas. That must mean something.*

"Oh, yeah, right. Like I'm really going to believe you. I don't. I'm reporting you to the police, and you can pull your dumb act on them and hope they believe your story, because I certainly don't. Now, I'm going to tell the whole world about that damn song. How do you like that, *Mister Lord?* Your big mistake was messing with my sister. I told you not to move. Do it again, and you'll be bleeding. I know just where to shoot you. I know just how much blood will pour out. I won't lift a finger to help you. In case you forgot, I'm a doctor."

"Listen to me. I didn't do anything to your car, nor did I do anything to your house. I did not have anyone do it for me. I'm truly sorry about your sister. I can account for my whereabouts the day of your break-in. Now, put that gun away before you shoot someone."

"Don't tell me what to do," Sara said. She wavered then, aware of how her legs were trembling and her hands were shaking. Out of the corner of her eye she saw the damage the gates had done to Nellie's truck. Another bill. Tears welled in her eyes, but the gun in her shaky hands remained at attention. Everything caught up with her then. A sob ripped out of her throat as her knees crumpled. Within seconds the dogs surrounded her, yipping and yapping as they tried to lick at her tears and cuddle into her arms. Izzie stood sentinel until she saw Tom Silk move to the side. Only then did she nuzzle her neck, forcing Sara to stroke her silky head.

"Who do these dogs belong to?" Sara gasped.

"Me," Adam said.

"*You!*" She made the single word sound like he was the devil from hell.

"Do you find that strange?" What he found really strange was that Izzie and the pups seemed to love her. Maybe it was a female thing. Suddenly he felt jealous. He snapped his fingers for Izzie to come to his side. The spaniel lifted her head, stared at him, but remained where she was.

"Of course I find it strange. Dogs are supposed to be shrewd judges of character. Call your dogs. I need to call the police." Sara stared at the gate panel and winced. "I'm not paying for that gate either. We'll call it square for what you did to my house."

Adam watched as Sara maneuvered until she was on her knees, the gun in her left hand. Tom reached out an arm to help her, but she waved him off with the gun. He backed away immediately.

"When are you going to get it through your head that I had nothing to do with your robbery? Stop playing Annie Oakley and let's go into the house and have some coffee and talk about this rationally."

"I'm calling the police. I want them to know where I am. Just in case. Coffee will be fine, *Mister Lord.* I'm partial to Irish Cream."

His hackles rising, Adam said, "We can handle that, can't we Tom?" *Just in case.* What the hell did that mean?

"Yeah. Yeah, we can handle that."

The gun steady in her hand, Sara said, "I'll go in last. I'd appreciate it if you'd quiet those dogs. This whole thing is giving me a headache." She felt like Gumby, Carly's favorite childhood toy, as she walked into Dallas's kitchen. She had one bad moment when she remembered how Dallas had tried to impress her with his spaghetti dinner. It all seemed like so long ago. She needed to sit down. The headache was fast becoming a reality.

Sara chose a seat behind the table that would allow her to watch the two men and the dogs. If Adam Lord was telling the truth, she had nothing to fear. If he was lying, she'd just made the biggest mistake of her life by coming indoors with these two men. They were bigger and stronger and could overpower her in seconds.

"How would you like your coffee, Doctor?" Tom asked, his eyes on the gun in Sara's lap.

"This isn't a social visit, gentlemen. Black. Strong and black." She wondered if she were losing her mind. What sane person would do what she'd just done and then sit down and have coffee with someone she felt was trying to kill her?

Tom backed toward the kitchen sink. Adam sat down across the table from Sara. Elbows on the table, he cupped his chin on top of his closed fists. If his gaze was uneasy, it was because of the gun in Sara's lap. He listened to the drip of the coffee going through the filter before he spoke. Sara held up her hand for silence as she rummaged in the black bag for her cell phone. First she called the hospital and spoke to Nellie. Satisfied that Carly was sleeping, she then called Detective Luzak. She listented, her eyes narrowing.

Adam watched in disbelief as Sara's arm came up to the table level. The gun was pointed dead center with his heart. Perspiration beaded on his brow as he heard Sara say, "Please, Detective Luzak, I want you to repeat what you just said to me to Mr. Lord. By the way, I'm sitting at his kitchen table. Yes, Dallas Lord's house in the canyon. I'll stop by in the morning to pick up your report for the insurance company. Just a second, and I'll put Mr. Lord on the phone."

Adam reached for the cell phone, his eyes never leaving the gun pointed at his chest. He listened, anger raging through him. He thanked the detective, ending the call before he snapped the phone shut. He slid it across the table. "I didn't do it, Dr. Killian. The only thing I am guilty of is trying to buy the song from you. If you had told me the truth from the begining, we wouldn't be sitting here now as adversaries."

"You could have had someone do it for you. People like you don't dirty their own hands. I don't trust you. The song is worth millions of dollars. People kill for a lot less." She gulped at the coffee. It was so hot her eyes started to water. It was the best coffee she'd ever tasted.

Adam leaned across the table. "I'm getting damn sick and tired of hearing you and your sister refer to me as quote 'people like you.' You make me sound like I sprouted from hell. I'm as normal as you are, as normal as Tom here. I am not an attempted killer nor do I know anyone who is."

Sara held out her cup for a refill. "Those are just words. Instead of worrying about a song that doesn't even belong to you, maybe you should be trying to find the person or persons who are trying to kill me and trying to frame you at the same time. If what you say is true, and I don't for one minute believe it is." She snorted, a very unlady like sound. Dallas Six hopped onto her lap and started to lick her face. Her face softened, and she smiled at the fat puppy, tweaking him behind her ears. "Your brother would have loved this little dog, Mr. Lord."

She's pretty, Adam thought. Strange feelings coursed through him. If his brother had been in love with her, he could understand why. The sudden urge to gather her close and whisper that things would be okay made him blink. He watched as she finished the coffee and held out her cup a third time. Was it his imagination or were her eyes getting glassy? He turned in time to see Tom pour Irish whiskey into the cup before he added the coffe. He mouthed the word, NO, but it was too late. Sara held out her hand for the coffee cup. Tom shrugged and handed it over.

"That coffee is going to keep you awake. Why don't I drive you, home, Doctor?"

"Drive me home! Not likely, *Mister Lord.*

Besides, we haven't finished our business. You were going to give me a list of places and people who can vouch for your whereabouts the past few days. Let's do that right now. Tomorrow I'll personally check it out." The gun moved imperceptibly but was still rock-steady. Dallas Six was asleep in her lap. Sara slurped from the coffee cup, then squinted, trying to bring Adam's face into focus. She couldn't remember ever being this tired. The events of the past few days had taken a terrible toll on her body. Nellie had said she looked like she'd been through a meat grinder. She had to go to the bathroom, too. How was she going to do that with a sleeping dog on her lap and a gun in her hand?

Adam slid the paper across the table. Sara pretended to study it, but the words ran together in one large blur. She folded it with her free hand before she jammed it into the black bag. "I'm going to leave now, gentlemen. Get your dog off my lap. On second thought, I'll put him down myself. Ohhh, whoops," Sara muttered as she struggled to remain upright, the gun in her left hand swerving all over the place.

"Is the safety on that gun?" Adam asked nervously.

"No, it is not," Sara said, enunciating each word slowly and carefully. "I'm a crack shot. So is my sister. Women need to protect themselves from people like you."

"That does it! Sit down, Dr. Killian, before you fall down. In case you haven't noticed, you are as drunk as the proverbial skunk. You are in no condition to drive anywhere."

"Drunk! Me! You must have me confused with Dr. Granger. I sip at wine. I never even finish my glass. So there. Why are you saying that?"

"Because we didn't have Irish Cream coffee and because Tom was trying to please you, he added Irish whiskey to your coffee. I think you had about four double belts. I apologize, and Tom apologizes. You can sleep it off in any one of the bedrooms."

"Oh, no. I hate this house. It's not . . . it's not . . . cozy. I like *cozy*. You got me drunk. Are you planning on having your way with me? I have a gun! See! I want to go home. I have to check on my sister. Nellie is going to need her truck. You really are a bastard. You aren't getting that song. Nobody is getting it. I'm going to burn it. What do you think of that? When I burn it, will you leave me and my sister alone?"

Adam's fist crashed down on the table. He totally ignored the gun in Sara's shaking hand as he grasped her by the shoulders. "One more time, Dr. Killian, I did not have anything to do with what's been happening to you. I think you are absolutely right, and you should burn the song. I'll be finishing up my business here in the next few days, at which point I will return to Charleston with Mr. Silk and the dogs. I'm going to sell this house and donate the money to a retired musicians' fund. I don't know if Dallas would approve of what I'm going to do or not. So you see, what you do or don't do with the song is up to you. For whatever it's worth you have my apology for intruding into you and your sister's life." The gun was in his hand the next second. "When you sober up I'll give this back to you."

"A likely story," Sara hissed. She threw her hands in the air. "Go ahead! Shoot me! See if I care! Well, what are you waiting for?"

Adam removed the clip from the gun. He stuck it in his trouser pocket before he marched over to the oversize black bag.

"Good God, it's a wonder you don't have a permanently dislocated shoulder. What in the hell is in there?"

"None of your business. My life. Carly's life. I carry it with me all the time so people like you can't . . . don't . . . My bag is none of your business."

Adam felt his eyes start to burn. "Sit down, Sara. Tell me about your bag. I used to have a briefcase I carried with me all the time. I still have it. Who are you, Dr. Sara Killian? I really want to know. Let's sit down here with the dogs and . . . talk."

"I thought you said I was drunk. Why would you want to talk to a drunk?"

"Let's just say you're pleasantly sloshed. Were you really going to shoot me?"

"Yes."

"I like honesty."

"Criminals and crooks always say that to throw the other person off guard. I like this dog. He loves me."

"Don't get attached. They're mine." His voice was too defensive-sounding even to his own ears when he said, "They love me, too. I feed them and take care of them just the way I took care of Dallas. Just the way you take care of your sister. You were going to tell me about Dr. Sara Killian."

Sara shrugged. "Carly and I grew up in a small town called Hastings in Pennsylvania. We lived in a brown shingle house on Bridge Street. We had a big backyard with lots and lots of plum trees. We had best friends the way kids do. My father never quite accepted that we were girls. He wanted a son so bad, he tried to turn us into boys. We weren't very good at it. We wanted to play with dolls and do girl things. We didn't want to go fishing and hunting and hike in the woods. It seems now that there was always friction in the house. Mom didn't like what he was doing to us. For some reason it didn't matter what she wanted or what we wanted. Carly was more malleable than me which is strange because she's really her own person. Later on I conformed. I don't know why. I guess children always seek parental approval no matter how old they are."

"I never had parents, so I wouldn't know," Adam said. "At least you grew up with a set of parents who loved you. Dallas and I only had each other."

"It wasn't all that wonderful. It wasn't like

Mom and Dad were pals. They were parents. Our friends were what made us want to get up in the morning. The McDermotts lived next door. They were a big family, lots of kids. There was Gene, Anna, Eleanor, Margie, Dootsie, Clarence, and Paul, and, of course, my best friend Barbara. Mary was Carly's best friend. I had a crush on Paul. They even had a dog named Cappy. He bit me once on the hip. Just jumped up and bit me. I howled my head off, and my dad gave me a swat because he said I must have done something. I didn't. I was just standing there, and the dog bit me for no reason. Barbara is married now and has a son who is a CPA. They live in Detroit. We write every so often. She has a family and a high-pressure job, so that doesn't leave much personal time. She's sentimental like me, and, like me, she's family oriented. They have family picnics and reunions. Someday I'm going to go to one of them. Barbara invites me. The only thing is Barb has the family and I don't. Their dad was the sheriff. I thought that was just great. I think when I was little I lived in fear that if I didn't do what my dad wanted, he would have Mr. Mc Dermott arrest me." Sara stopped talking long enough to take a deep breath. Her vision was clearing a little, and she didn't feel quite so nauseous.

"Was it a big town or was it little?"

"Very little. About twelve hundred people. Everyone knew everyone else. The telephones were party lines. Our phone was two short and one long ring. We could walk everywhere. There was a creek behind the house. We'd go wading and make little pools where the water was up to your knees. At night we'd play Red Light, Green Light. Carly and I cried for weeks when we moved to California. We both hated it. Now that I don't have a job, I might go back to Pennsylvania. I like small towns. I hate the politics of a big hospital. I might even set up private practice. It occurs to me, Mr. Lord, that you are soaking this all up like some big sponge. Are you going to use it against me in some way at some point?"

"No. I think you can call me Adam. I also think in your heart you know I am not guilty of the things you accused me of. If you were, you wouldn't be sitting here talking to me."

"I don't want to believe Dallas's brother would harm me. Who? I need to know who it is that's terrorizing me. Were you telling me the truth when you said you didn't care about the song?"

"I was telling you the truth. I care, but I don't care. It has to be your decision. There's something I want to tell you. I went to see Harry Heinrick at Benton Memorial Hospital. I want you to listen very carefully to what I'm going to tell you. You can verfiy this anytime you want."

A long time later, Sara stirred. If she had been truly drunk before, she was stone-cold sober now. "Dallas did that?"

"Yes, he did. I had a hard time with it. Mr. Heinrick said you were the best doctor ever to work at Benton. Dallas must have loved you very much to do something like that."

"Are you going to go through with what Dallas promised?"

"No. Heinrick understands the reasons why I won't honor Dallas's promise. I believe he's going to offer you your job back. Will you take it?"

"Not in this lifetime. I think I'm okay to drive now. I guess we should say good-bye. I want to make sure we understand something. I'm not paying for that gate and I'm not giving you the song."

"Understood."

Sara smiled.

"You should do that more often. You're very pretty when you smile."

"Dallas always said you were a handsome dude. I think he was right."

Adam threw back his head and laughed. "It would appear we have our own mutual admiration society here. Now, tell me, is there anything I can do to help you?"

"Find the person responsible. I think I'm sorry about the gun. I feel out of sorts, and I'm worried about my sister. Plus, I hate meandering down Memory Lane. Good-bye, Mr. . . . Adam."

Adam reached for Sara's outstretched hand. Suddenly he didn't want her to leave. He didn't want to accept the knowledge that he was never going to see her again. Something was happening here he didn't understand. Maybe it started happening when Dallas Six jumped into her lap. Maybe a lot of things.

Her hand was soft, the nails short and buffed. Good strong hands. Capable hands. He wondered how they would feel on his face and chest. Women always like to massage a man's chest. And back. Other places, too. He seemed to be having trouble with his breathing, so he took hard little puffs of air and coughed to cover what he was feeling. He was still holding her hand.

Maybe it wouldn't have happened if the pups hadn't barreled out of the house to beeline to the spot where they were standing. Later he told himself it was purely reflexive. Whatever it was, he pulled Sara to him, his lips found hers in a matter of seconds. The world as he knew it, changed in the time it took his heart to beat twice. And then the world exploded around him as his head threatened to rock right off his shoulders.

Unaware of the pain Adam was experiencing, Sara murmured, "I *liked* that. Do it again." Still, it wasn't the same as the time Dallas kissed her and her head almost blew off her neck.

"Before or after I die of the pain. Look! That little monster bit me and kept right on biting me. He must have thought I was hurting you."

"How sweet," Sara cooed. "I'm a doctor. I can fix this right up. My goodness, it does look nasty. You're going to need a tetanus shot after I dress the wounds."

"Wounds as in plural? Jesus, how many times did he bite me?"

"Looks like three marks. He's trying out his second teeth. You're a pretty good kisser. Dallas was good, too. Guess it runs in the family," she said brazenly.

Adam hopped around on one foot. "You didn't do so bad yourself. When I'm healed maybe we could do it again."

Sara reached in her bag and pulled out a small brown bottle and a syringe. "Stand still. This is going to sting."

"Do you always come prepared like this?"

"Aren't you glad I am so prepared? Now, drop your pants."

"Here? Out in the open like this. Tom can see from the window."

"Does he have something different than you have?"

"That's not the point."

"What is the point?" Sara said tapping the syringe. A spurt of liquid shot out of the needle.

"I hardly know you."

"That didn't stop you from kissing me. As my sister would say, we swapped spit. Drop them."

Adam inched his pants down midway on

his right buttock. Sara snatched the fabric and gave a yank. The needle shot home before Adam could bellow his outrage. "Nice buns." She stifled a giggle. Carly would be so proud of her.

Adam felt like a ring of fire curled around his neck. He didn't know where to look, so he picked up Dallas Six and cuddled him close to his cheek.

"I'll send you my bill."

"I have insurance," Adam said smartly.

"So do I. I hate those forms. I'll have to charge extra if you expect me to fill them out. Good night, Adam. I stand by my original statement. You're a pretty good kisser."

"Brazen hussy," Adam hissed.

"That's the nicest thing you've ever said to me."

"Let me know how your sister is."

"Okay. Change the dressing tomorrow morning and put more peroxide on the bites. Relax, you're going to live."

Adam watched until the monster truck's taillights were pinpoints of red light in the distance.

"I saw that. I saw that," Tom chortled from the open doorway. "You really sweeped, or is that swept, her off her feet? She comes in here, blows down your gate, almost shoots your toes off, and you end up kissing her and dropping your pants all in five minutes."

"Shut up!" Adam said as he stomped his way into the house.

Tom laughed. And laughed.

The dogs barked and howled.

Adam tripped over the doorstep, his face as red as his neck.

Chapter Fourteen

Sara tiptoed down the corridor to Carly's private room. Her gaze missed nothing in the quiet corridor hospital. The charge nurse and the floor nurse were filling out paperwork and sipping coffee. The charge nurse raised her eyes, spotted Sara, and nodded. Nellie, with a sixth sense that was unequaled and the eyes of a hawk, poked her head out the door, her finger to her lips in silence.

"You . . . ah, you look . . ."

"You can say it, Nellie. I look like . . . hell. This has been some night. Is Carly okay?"

"She's sleeping like a baby. I expect she'll milk this for all it's worth, but then so would I. Now, tell me what happened."

Sara sighed. "Everything and nothing. I think I banged up your truck a little, Nellie. I crashed through Dallas's gates. I'm surprised I wasn't electrocuted. I didn't even think about *that* till later. I'll pay for any damages. He didn't do it, Nellie. He's got all these dogs, and they just love him to death and he loves them. I was so sure. Then I wasn't sure. I shot at him and almost nipped his toes. I wanted him to know I meant business. You should have heard me swear. I felt like some deranged person. I'm going to send Carly to my Aunt Florence's house in Nevada, so she'll be safe. This is a lot to ask, Nellie, but will you go with her?"

"What a silly question. Of course I'll go with her. Will she want to go is the big question."

"She has to go. I'll make up some story about going to New York to interview. She won't want to be alone at the house with everything that's been going on. I'm not sure what the story is with her and Hank. They're on. They're off. Between the two of us, I think we can convince her."

"What else happened? I know there is more. I want to hear everything."

"They got me drunk. Maybe it was my own fault. When I calmed down, they said I needed coffee and I said I liked Irish Cream. I meant the flavored kind from Gloria Jean's. They didn't have any so Tom, and don't ask me who Tom is, added Irish whiskey to the coffee. I slurped it down like it was a milk shake. Three cups, Nellie. Adam said I was sloshed. I sobered up really quick. Shock will do that to a person. He kissed me. Nobody, Nellie, ever kissed me like that before. Except Dallas that one time," she said sadly. God, Nellie, listen to me."

"I am, and I like what I'm hearing. You're sure now he's not responsible for what's happening."

"I'm sure. My head, my heart, and my gut tell me I'm right. I saw his face when I told him about Carly. Among other things I spilled my guts about my childhood. I don't understand what happened to me tonight, Nellie. That person who did all those things was me but it wasn't me."

Nellie smiled. "That was the real Sara. This other Sara we all know who is so proper and aloof is a myth. She's not real. It's like you read a book and copied the character and said, 'This is who I'm going to be.' Your father is responsible for that, Sara. To this day you are still trying to be the person he wanted you to be in your professional as well as your personal life. That's wrong. Tonight you severed the tie. So, is he a good kisser? How do you think he'll be in bed? Do you think he'll be better than Dallas?"

"Nellie! I'll never know, will I?"

"You're dying to talk about this. So, let's get to it."

Sara giggled and realized she liked the sound. "The best. I think, and this is just my opinion, but I think he's going to be . . . magnificent in bed. He's sort of a thinker, slow and steady. People like that . . . you know. Underneath his facade I think he's a very caring person, but you wouldn't think so until you got to know him. I told him I wasn't paying for his gate and I wasn't giving him the song. He said it was okay with him. He's selling Dallas's house and donating the money to a retired musicians' fund or something like that. He's coming to terms with Dallas's death. He's also going to leave in a few days to go back to Charleston. Maybe it isn't meant to be, Nellie. Every time I look at him, I see Dallas. It breaks my heart. Why did he have to die, Nellie?"

"Ours is not to reason why. Make it happen, Sara. You only walk through this life once. Make that walk count."

"I won't chase him. He knows where I live. He has my phone number. This is stupid. It's rebound stuff, and in the end that never works. I don't want or need another affair."

"What if he's shy when it comes to women? What if he's afraid of you and what you can do to him professionally?"

"That's just too much to think about right now. I'm going home, Nellie. I'll get a few hours' sleep and come back. Perhaps we can have breakfast together. I'll call my aunt Florence and pack Carly's things. I want you both to leave right from the hospital. I don't want Carly going back to the house. We'll talk later, okay. Thanks, Nellie, for everything, but most of all for being my friend. I have a story to tell you about the Hawk when I get back."

"I have one to tell you, too. Go home, Sara, and get some sleep."

"I want to see Carly first. I'll just peek in the door."

"Thirty seconds, Sara. Carly needs her rest."

"I know. I need to see her, Nellie. I promise not to make a sound." Satisfied that her sister was indeed sleeping, Sara stayed an extra moment to stare at the cumbersome cast on her sister's shoulder. Carly would be fine once she adjusted to the discomfort.

*   *   *

The phone in the kitchen started to ring the moment she entered the house. She armed the security system before she grappled for the portable phone. Thinking it might be Nellie, she answered the phone, her eye on the clock.

The voice was stern, almost unrecognizable, but she would have known it any where. A smile tugged at the corners of Sara's lips as she listened. "Dr. Killian . . . Sara . . . I am not a complainer by nature, but don't you think you should have given me some pain pills?"

"You could take some aspirin and call me in the morning." She was flirting and enjoying every second.

"It is morning, Sara."

"So it is. A nice cup of hot tea relaxes a person. You could try it."

"What will that do for my rear end? I can't sit down, because there is a lump the size of a lemon on my rump."

"I see. Are we flirting with each other, Adam?"

"I am. How about you?"

Sara smiled at Adam's confession. "Yes, but I'm not very good at it."

"Neither am I. Why don't we cut right to the chase and have a real date. I call you up, you say yes, I bring flowers and ring your doorbell. I have to tell you I'm pretty rusty at the dating thing."

"I am, too. When do you think you'll call me?"

"Hang up, and I'll call you right back. You're going to say yes, right?"

"Yes, I'm going to say yes." Sara laughed aloud when the dial tone hummed in her ear. She replaced the phone in the cradle. It rang a second later. "Yes," she blurted.

"I didn't ask you yet. You're fouling me all up. Will you have dinner with me this evening, Dr. Killian? Someplace casual. No primping and no fussing."

"I will if you promise to stop calling me Dr. Killian." *She had a date. With a man who could make her head spin.*

"Do you want to hang up now?"

"Do you?"

"No. What should we talk about?"

"I guess the thing that's foremost on my mind, the person who is after me. Do you have any idea who it could be?" She almost blurted out she was sending Carly to her aunt Florence, but bit down her lip instead.

Nellie always said never tell everybody everything. It was probably very good advice.

"Do you have an alarm system?"

"Yes. It was on the day my house was broken into. I've locked all the dead bolts."

"Not many people have the smarts to disarm an alarm system. Be careful. I have a couple of ideas, plus a lot of suspicions I plan to follow up on today. I'll report any progress this evening. Is seven good for you?"

"Seven is fine. How's the pain?"

"I lied."

"I know."

Adam laughed. "I'll see you at seven."

"I'm looking forward to it."

"I am, too."

The smile stayed on Sara's face during her shower and while she turned down the bed. It went into hiding when she brushed her teeth, but surfaced again when she snuggled with her pillow. And then the tears flowed. "Oh, Dallas, I miss you. It should be you and not your brother who is going to take me to dinner. It's just a silly little dinner date. It doesn't mean anything. Really it doesn't." Seconds later she was sound asleep, her pillow soggy with her tears.

* * *

Sara knew there was a smile on her face when she woke even though her pillow was still damp. She didn't need a mirror to verify that today was going to be a wonderful day. Nellie would take Carly to Nevada where she would be safe. She was going to deliver the song Dallas wrote for her to Judge Iverson for safekeeping, so she could get on with her life. She hoped that life would include Adam Lord's friendship in some small way.

The clock on the nightstand said it was seven o'clock. She'd had little more than three hours of sleep, and yet she felt on top of the world. In less than an hour she showered, washed her hair, styled it, made coffee, changed the sheets on her bed—just in case—and packed Carly's bag. The undecorated Christmas tree gave her a bad moment. She decided she could fit decorating it into her schedule as long as she remembered to pick up several strings of lights. And a bottle of very good wine. Just in case. If she was in luck, she might be able to find a new outfit for her casual date with Adam. Then it would be back to the hospital to see that Nellie and Carly got off on their trip. After that she would return to the house, take a bubble bath, and wait for her date. Or, she could juggle things and visit the hospital first. One jam-packed day coming up. She knew she was going to love every single minute of the hustle and bustle she was creating for herself. Maybe she wouldn't have time to think about Dallas and what she was doing by dating his brother. It's just a silly little dinner date, she told herself over and over. The sheets and the wine didn't mean anything.

First things first. She had to go to the bank to get the tape and the sheet music. Did she need an appointment to see Judge Iverson? If she said it was an emergency, she was certain her father's old friend would somehow manage to fit her in for a brief appointment. If things went awry, she could always package up the tape with a letter and leave it with the judge's clerk. She knew she was doing the right thing by giving the judge the tapes for safekeeping. If anything happened to her or Carly, the judge would be the one to handle their affairs. Carly had convinced her not to leave the tapes in the safe deposit box, reminding her of the time she'd pretended to be Carly and even forged her signature to get her sister's passport out of the box at the last second before a trip to Europe. Judge Iverson was a sworn officer of the court and would keep the tape safe.

In the garage, Carly's keys in her hand, Sara remembered her sister saying her Jeep was out of gas. Damn. Was it literally out of gas or had Carly just said that? She fit the key into the ignition, her eye on the gas gauge. Take a chance or not? There was too much on her agenda today not to chance it. She made it to the gas station six blocks away just as the Jeep started to sputter and cough. She hopped out, pumped her own gas, paid the bill, and was back on the road heading for the bank within minutes.

Midway between the bank and the courthouse, the fine hairs on the back of Sara's neck started to prickle. She risked a glance into the rearview mirror. The same dark blue Taurus that had been behind her on the way to the bank was still with her. Was it a coincidence, or was it something else? At the last second she swerved hard right without turning on her blinker. The Taurus kept on going but picked her up a block away. She fumbled in her black bag. The gun was probably at the bottom of the bag. Adam Lord had taken out the clip and hadn't given it back. The extra clip was in her jacket back at the house. So was the Taser gun she usually carried with her late at night.

Her heart pounding, Sara executed another right, then a left, and headed back the way she'd come. Her next stop would be Benton Memorial so she could alert the security guard, who in turn would call the police. Now her whole day's schedule was screwed up.

The guard listened carefully as Sara rattled off her story. "Look, Mr. Phelps, I didn't see the person, the windshield was tinted, and the sun was glaring on the glass. All I know is the car was with me all morning. I'm not sure about this either, but I think there was a car behind the Ford that was tailing me. Whoever it was stayed with us. I realize it isn't in the parking lot right now, but when I leave here it will be following me. There was no license plate on the front of the car so I couldn't get a number. I know I don't work here anymore, Mr. Phelps, but I would appreciate it if you would help me. I don't think Mr. Heinrick will mind your donating a few minutes of your time. If you need me, I'll be on the fourth floor visiting my sister."

Carly was sitting up in bed, a scowl on her face. Nellie was wagging a no-nonsense finger under her nose. Intimidated, Carly nodded in agreement to whatever the old nurse was saying.

"You're looking good, Carly. How do you feel?"

"I've felt better. This damn thing itches. The food is terrible. Six weeks I have to wear this thing!"

"It could be worse, Carly. Be glad you're alive and well."

"I am glad. I'm also glad no one else was hurt. I'm not going, Sara. All Aunt Florence wants to do is play Old Maid and Monopoly. And she cheats. She's going to fuss and hover. You know I hate hovering. Why can't I stay with Nellie at her place? I can go to Hank's place. I still have a key. He won't mind."

"Listen to me, Carly. I want you as far away as possible. You love Aunt Florence. Nellie needs to get away, too. I'll feel better if I know you're safe. You aren't in any condition to . . . you know, put up a fight or run or . . . stuff like that. Adam and I are going to . . . work on this together."

"Adam, is it? So that's what is putting the

sparkle in your eye. Why'd you make up that story about running? All you had to say was you have this thing going, and I'll be in the way."

Sara blinked. "I didn't think you'd go for it." The sly wink Nellie shot in Sara's direction was all the proof Carly needed.

"I knew it! I saw the way that guy looked at you. I thought it would take him longer to come around. At first he seemed like a real tight-ass. He has defininte possibilities, and he's rich. I approve! I know you aren't over Dallas, so take it slow and easy."

"It's just a casual dinner date. He's leaving in a few days to go back to South Carolina. I'll probably never see him again. I'll be heading for New York soon."

"Planes, trains, buses, cars. Overnight mail, telephones, fax machines. Love notes via a fax has to be the greatest. Don't screw this up, Sara."

"Okay, Carly. Can I help you get dressed?"

"Nope. Nellie said I'm on my own. I feel top-heavy. Guess I'll get used to it. I was discharged thirty minutes ago. I take that to mean we're free to go."

"Guess so. Do you have everything, Nellie?"

"I went home to get everything right after you called. Steven is going to board my cat and dog. We're taking my Pontiac. The truck would be too jarring for Carly. I'm going to leave the key to the truck and my apartment with you, Sara. You never know if that Tinkertoy Carly drives is going to work or not. My truck is parked in my stall at the townhouse building; you can't miss it. If you prefer, I can drive it over to your house before we leave. Both of us can stay as long as you want us to, Sara. Take care of your business here and call to let us know how things are. Does the old lady really cheat?"

"Just the way you do, Nellie. Don't worry about the truck. If I need it, I know where to get it."

"Ah."

Carly came out of the bathroom. "Are you sure this is the right thing we're doing, Sara?"

"I'm sure. Have a good trip and don't take too many jaunts to the casinos."

"Did you go to see Judge Iverson yet?"

"I'm going to the courthouse when I leave

here. Nellie will fill you in on everything. Don't get that cast wet."

"Sara."

"Take care of yourself. You're the only sister I have."

"I will. Don't give Nellie a hard time. Promise."

"I promise. C'mon, Nellie, we're outta here. My sister has things to do and places to go. Translated that means she has to buy some new duds so she sparkles. Use that smoky eye shadow. It makes your eyes look mysterious."

"Go!"

Sara stood by the elevator as Carly settled herself into the wheelchair, a rule of the hospital. When the elevator door swished shut, she heaved a sigh of relief. She headed for the EXIT sign over the door and took the stairs to the emergency room.

"Any luck, Mr. Phelps?"

"No sign of a dark blue sedan or any other strange car, Dr. Killian." The security guard handed her a card. "Detective Nelson said to call him on your cell phone if you spot the car again. He said if you do call him, you're to keep driving and don't stop. They'll send a car to pick up whoever is following you."

"Thanks, Mr. Phelps. Have a nice holiday."

"You too, Dr. Killian. We miss you around here."

Sara smiled and waved, her gaze raking the parking lot. There was no sign of a dark blue sedan anywhere. Maybe it was all her overactive imagination.

Sara steered the Jeep into the traffic, one eye on the road and the other on the rearview mirror. As she parked the Jeep in the courthouse parking lot, she remembered the gun in her shoulder bag. The metal scanner in the courthouse would pick it up in a second. She stashed it under the seat, crossed her fingers, and said a prayer that it would still be there when she came out. She took several deep breaths before she felt steady enough to climb out of the car. Again, her gaze swept the parking area for any sign of the dark blue sedan. The eerie feeling that someone was watching her stayed with her as she crossed the parking lot to the building.

Aware now of everyone and everything, Sara scrutinized each person who came near her as she made her way to the seventh floor where Judge Iverson had his offices. She spent forty-five minutes being shuffled from room to room before a clerk escorted her to the judge's office.

Judge Ronald Iverson was a tall, handsome, robust man in his middle sixties. He worked out with a vengeance four days a week and a low-fat diet, coupled with his strenous exercise routine, allowed him to maintain his weight. If he touched up his hair with Grecian Formula, he was the only one who knew it. Sara was amazed at how well he was aging each time she saw him. A widower for six years, he was rumored to like very young women and never stayed long with any one of them because he believed variety was the spice of life. If memory served her right, he would retire at the end of next year. Then it was Palm Springs, golf, tennis, and long-legged beauties for the rest of his life.

"Sara Killian. Excuse me, Dr. Sara Killian. It's so good to see you. How's Carly? Sit down sweetie. I have ten minutes before I have to take the bench. Is anything wrong? Ah, don't tell me you got one too many traffic tickets," he joked, his pricey porcelain caps glistening in the lamplight. Sara wondered how he could stand being in a room without windows all day long.

"I wish it were that simple, Judge. I hope I can get this all out in ten minutes. Just let me blurt it out, and if there is anything you don't understand, I can fill you in later. I need you to keep something safe for me." Sara rattled on, the words shooting out of her mouth faster than bullets. "I don't know who it is, Judge. The only thing I know for certain is I am deathly afraid something is going to happen to Carly."

"Good Lord. I don't believe what I'm hearing. I'm having cocktails with the police commissioner this evening. I'll goose him a little. You know Carly has a level head on her shoulders. She outgrew that bubble-headed business years ago. You need to stop mothering her, Sara. Sha can take care of herself. Now let me be sure I have all of this straight. What I'm holding in my hand is the song Dallas Lord, the famous rock star, wrote for you. It's worth millions of dollars to the owner, who at the moment is you. Mr. Lord's brother wants to buy it from you for a paltry amount of money so the world can enjoy Dallas's last song. How am I doing so far?"

"You're doing fine, Judge."

"You want me to keep this safe for you until you know exactly what it is you want to do with the song. I can do that, Sara. I have a safe right here in my office. No one has the combination but my clerk and me. Is this the only copy you have and is this the only handwritten paper in your possession?"

A devil perched itself on Sara's shoulder. "The paper is a photocopy. I haven't been able to find the original. I guess it's in the pile of papers Dallas gave me to keep for him." Sara lied and didn't know why she was lying. "Yes, that's the only cassette," she lied again. "Dallas wrote the song just for me. It was supposed to be a wedding present."

"So this is what they call the master copy?"

"I guess so. Dallas just handed it to me. I don't know what the difference would be between a master and a copy. Perhaps the sound. You'll keep it for me then?"

"Of course. Do you ever plan to sell it, or are you going to give it back to the estate? Do you have some kind of a plan? Millions of dollars are at stake here, young woman. I can understand why some chicanery might be going on."

"I've had so many plans I don't know if I'm coming or going. Nothing seems to work. I'm afraid to stay in the house."

"Listen. I have an idea. I own a cabin in the

Alpine Forest, where I like to go when things pile up on me. There is plenty of food, water, and firewood. It's a snug cabin, and you and your sister will be very comfortable. I want you to go there and stay for a while until whatever has been happening around here blows over. It sounds to me like the brother is a greedy bastard. Your father would never forgive me if something happened to either one of you girls. I want you to take this key and go up there today. Here, I'll write out directions. I don't want to worry about you."

"I can't go today, Judge. I . . . we can go tomorrow. I . . . Carly and I can stay with friends this evening and leave in the morning when it gets light."

"I want you to call me the minute you start out. I'll alert the troopers to watch out for you. Give me your promise, young lady."

"I promise."

"Good girl. I hate to cut this visit so short, but they're waiting for me out there."

"I understand. Thank you. Carly and I really appreciate your help."

"Put your mind at rest and let me handle things. That's what friends are for."

Sara sighed. She wondered as she rode down in the elevator why she didn't feel any better than she had when she entered the courthouse.

Her dark glasses in place to ward off the bright December sunshine, Sara settled herself in the Jeep, but not before she surreptitiously removed her father's gun from under the seat. She started to feel better almost immediately. No one knew the gun wasn't loaded. Hating the feel of cold steel in her hand, Sara shoved it into the bottom of her black bag.

Ever alert, Sara carefully scanned her surroundings. Everything appeared normal, but she still had the feeling strange eyes were watching her. Was this the lull before the storm? As the Jeep moved along in the steady stream of traffic, Sara shifted her nervousness into a neutral zone as she listened to the ominous voice of the weather forecaster. Snow in the higher elevations. Rain down below. There was no sun in the forecast for the next three days. Sara lifted her polarized sunglasses to perch them on top of her head. She lowered them immediately when the sun bounced off her windshield, temporarily blinding her. It was a rare day when the weatherman hit it right.

A mile down the road, Sara found another

rarity, a parking place directly in front of a drugstore that said it was open twenty-four hours a day. Inside she purchased three boxes of mutlicolored lights and six peppermint candy canes for the Christmas tree.

Waiting for a break in traffic, Sara did a mental check on her list of things to do. She'd be home by noon. All she had to do now was find a casual outfit, pick up a bottle of wine, and grab some lunch before she headed home to decorate the tree and relax in a hot bubble bath.

In a small boutique, Sara settled for the first outfit she tried on, a colorful swirling skirt with a soft as silk off-white blouse. Her electric blue jacket would match the skirt perfectly. Casual but elegant. She spent more time choosing the wine than she had choosing her new outfit. At the last second she opted for fast food, going through the drive-through at Taco Bell. She munched on her wrapped sandwich as she made her way home. It was ten minutes to twelve when she entered the house. The first thing she did, after locking the door and turning on the alarm system, was to throw the gun clip and an extra one into the bottom of her bag. She stared at the Taser gun for a full two minutes before she tossed it into the already overloaded bag.

The tenseness in her shoulders seemed worse somehow. She continued to stare at the black bag, aware that something didn't feel right. Her eyes narrowing, she studied the contents before she withdrew the gun clip she'd had in her pocket. She picked up the heavy gun and jammed the clip inside. Things felt better. Almost.

Sara hooked the strands of lights together. Hundreds of tiny lights winked at her. Tears pricked at her eyelids. Some Christmas. *I miss you, Dallas. This was supposed to be our first Christmas together.* Damn, now her eyes were going to be red and puffy. She straightened her shoulders, blew her nose lustily, and continued to decorate the tree. Just as she hung the last ornament and stood back to view her handiwork, the phone rang. Her voice was harsh and crumbly-sounding when she said, "Hello." When there was no response she repeated her greeting twice. Her shoulders shaking, she slammed the phone back into the cradle. Someone checking on her? The phone rang three more times in the next half hour with the same results. Suddenly she felt violated, exposed, vulnerable.

The phone still in her hand, she dialed Dallas's number from memory. When there was no answer, Sara left a message for Adam on the answering machine. "Pick me up at 210 Coriander Street. It's a complex of town houses a half mile down the road from my house. It's 2:30. I'm leaving now because strange things have been happening here."

Sara raced upstairs to pack a small bag. Her new purchases in hand, she made two trips to the garage. She felt like crying again when she turned off the tree lights. Was life ever going to be the same? The joy and anticipation she'd felt earlier over her date with Adam was gone. What she felt now was fear, anxiety, and a total sense of loss.

When she drove away from the house, she knew she wouldn't return. And if she did, it would be to pack her things. She wasn't sure, but she rather thought Carly felt the same way.

This time when she left the house, she didn't bother setting the alarm. What was the point? There was also no point in looking back. She drove faster than usual in her hurry to get to Nellie's town house. When there was no parking space to be found, Sara parked in front of the manager's office to see what could be done. "If you're a friend of Nellie's, then I don't see any reason why I can't let you use the indoor garage. Here's the remote garage-door opener. Just bring it back after you park your car. Will Nellie be gone long?"

"Possibly a week or so. I appreciate this. Thank you, Mr. Owens."

"Anything for Nellie. She treats everyone in the complex and won't take a dime for her help. It's my pleasure, Dr. Killian."

The town house was spacious, two full bedrooms, each with its own bath, a formal dining room with a vaulted ceiling, and a step-down living room. The eat-in kitchen was colorful and homey, with green plants, shiny cooper, and checkered curtains. The furniture in the living room was old, comfortable, and well-worn. Baskets of cat and dog toys and a scratching post took up one full corner. A small artificial Chirstmas tree with presents underneath stood in the room's other corner. Sara turned on the tree lights as she peered at the name tags on the gifts piled under the tree. There was one for her and one for Carly and one for the Hawk. A long skinny box that had to be a fishing pole had the name Steven on it. Other small packages said Cosmo and Mandy. Nellie's cat and dog.

Back in the kitchen, Sara fixed herself a cup of tea. She was going to sit down and relax and pretend she didn't have a worry in the world. Then and only then was she going to take the bubble bath she had promised herself.

While she waited for the water to boil, Sara thought about her grand plans for the evening and the clean sheets she'd put on her new bed earlier in the day and the expensive bottle of wine she'd bought. Just in case. "Nobody gets it all," she muttered as she carried her tea back to the living room. A soap opera where the heroines were in constant peril was something she could deal with. Hell, maybe she could learn something.

"Please, God, make this all go away. Let me get my boring, sane life back. I promise to do whatever You want, be whatever You want. Just make this all go away."

Chapter Fifteen

Sandi Sims pawed through the mail that always arrived at the same time the *LA Times* arrived—late. Usually it was a good way to start the day—coffee, the mail, and the paper—if you were someone who started her day at two in the afternoon like she did. Today, though, she scowled when she saw the crackly white business letter whose return address said it was from Lord Enterprises. The catalogues, the resident mail, the utility bill, and the newspaper were tossed on the kitchen counter. It was only two o'clock in the afternoon and already she knew it was going to be a bad day. In many respects it could turn out to be the worst day of her life.

Stirring the sugar at the bottom of the cup, her eyes narrowed to slits, Sandi ripped at the crackly white envelope. Two green business checks dropped to the table. The letter was short, cold, and to the point. Adam Lord was retiring the Canyon River Band, effective immediately. A check for six months' severance pay and a check for a six-month premium for health insurance were enclosed. A reminder that a term life-insurance policy was paid in full until January 1 of the following year completed what Sandy referred to as a kiss-off.

Sandi reached across the kitchen table for her cigarettes and the portable phone. Smoke billowing upward, she dialed a number she had called a dozen times a day since Dallas Lord's death; Dallas's voice mail. It pleased her to tap into Dallas's voice mail. It was her way of staying on top of things. Adam received such interesting financial messages. So far, though, she hadn't learned a thing that would give her the edge where Sara Killian and the song were concerned. She punched in the code, pressed the appropriate buttons, and listened. She toyed with the two checks that totaled $25,000 as she listened to Adam Lord's messages. She scribbled notes on the back of the Lord Enterprises envelope.

Nothing was going right. By now she should have the song in her possession waiting for the highest bid to come through. She should be set for life. Instead she had a kiss-off letter and a measly twenty-five thousand dollars. If things didn't take a turn very soon, she would have to go back to pedaling her ass at two hundred bucks a night. Or—and she didn't even want to think about the or—she could downsize, move to one of those cramped garden apartments, sell the pricey sports car and the condos, and get one of those tacky Hondas half the residents of LA drove. If she was forced to go on the prowl again, she'd need a complete new wardrobe. The twenty-five grand would be gone in the blink of an eye. She didn't allow herself to think about the hundred thousand dollars she had conned out of Dallas. That was her emergency nest egg, never to be touched. She shuddered when she envisioned herself driving into a Burger King drive-through trying to hide behind dark glasses in the tacky Honda. Not in this or any other lifetime!

It was ten minutes past three when Sandi emerged from her bedroom dressed for the day in a canary yellow spandex dress with matching spike-heeled sandals. The Chanel bag with the tools of her trade—condoms, cell phone, a state-of-the-art mini–tool kit she'd extracted from a lowlife on the race-car circuit, magnet, and assorted miscellany—were at the bottom of the silk-lined bag. A small pouch of expensive cosmetics, her checkbook, keys, cigarettes, and gold lighter were transferred from her everyday Gucci shoulder bag.

At the last second she flipped over the newspaper to scan the headlines; she always wanted to know what the prominent people in LA were up to. A small article on page four caught her eye. Carlisle Killian, the sister of cardiologist Sara Killian, was injured in an accident that totaled Dr. Killian's Jaguar. Foul play is suspected.

"Right car, wrong sister," Sandi seethed. It was just her miserable luck that the wrong damn sister had the accident. As an afterthought she tapped into Dallas's voice mail a second time. She listened intently, scribbling furiously. The doctor was on the move! A smile stretched across her face when she broke the connection. She was back in business.

Sandi was locking the door when the phone rang. She reentered the apartment to pick up the phone on the fourth ring, a smile in her voice. She grimaced when she heard the voice on the other end. "I was just going out the door, love. Dinner? A surprise! I love surprises. Give me a little, teensy-weensy clue. You're right. It wouldn't be a surprise. The restaurant of my choice? Are we celebrating big or little? Big! I hate to ask this, lover, but what is in it for me? A life in the lap of luxury until I'm old and gray? In that case, I'm free all evening. A new outfit from the skin out! Are you serious? Of course I'm interested. Should I just have the store call you or send the bill directly? Do I have a limit? The sky! Goodness, it must be big! I know you're partial to red teddies with lots of strings and lace. I can come by around six for cocktails, or I can meet you at the restaurant. We haven't had an all-nighter for months. Are you sure you're up to it? Seven o'clock at the restaurant. I can't wait."

Sandi sat down on one of the kitchen chairs. Living the rest of her life in the lap of luxury. No more scrambling, no more hustling. A man Ronald Iverson's age couldn't live forever, no matter how often he played tennis and ate fat-free food.

In the bedroom, Sandi peeled off the spandex dress. The spike-heeled shoes flew across the room. Five minutes later she was dressed in bib overalls, Nikes, and a dark blue windbreaker. A Dodgers baseball cap covered her long blond hair. Her designer sunglasses were replaced with aviator glasses, the kind all the young studs in LA wore to make themselves look important.

Outside in the parking area, Sandi's gaze swept the line of cars parked under the long slate roof. She knew which cars had the keys in them, which cars had the keys under the mat, and which owners were sleeping. More than once she had helped herself to a vehicle with no one the wiser. She was always careful to replace the gas and adjust the odometer. Today the pickings were exceptionally good. She had her choice of a hunter green BMW, a white Audi, or a slate gray Range Rover. Two of the owners had rolled in a little after six, which meant they would sleep till around seven before they were ready to party again. The owner of the Range Rover was in Arizona on location. If she chose the Audi or the BMW, she had a little over four hours to use the vehicle. If, on the other hand, she chose the Rover, she could drive it for weeks with no one the wiser. She opted for the Range Rover because she'd borrowed it before and liked the way it handled. Just yesterday she'd borrowed a dark blue Taurus to follow Sara Killian. She looked around the parking lot, but the Taurus was gone.

Sandi tossed a brown canvas Gap bag onto the backseat. The Chanel bag would have clashed with her outfit. She adjusted the seat, helped herself to one of the owner's cigarettes before she backed out of the parking space. She knew for a fact Jim Laker had had the car serviced before he left, and there was a full tank of gas. An outdoor adventurer, Laker had a ton of camping equipment in the back, all of it stacked neatly. He went off for weeks to cleanse his body and live off the land. In her opinion, Jim Laker was a nutcase, but he had a healthy trust fund, something she found hard to ignore.

Sandi was almost out of the parking area when a FedEx driver flagged her down. She stopped, her eyes wary. She crossed her fingers that the driver didn't know Jim Laker. Obviously her disguise wasn't the best. She waited for the driver to make his way to the Rover, an overnight letter in hand. "Sign here, Miss Sims. Nice vehicle."

"Thanks. I like it." She scrawled her signature as she tried to read the messy handwriting on the air bill. Frank Ryan. A squiggle of fear worked its way into her stomach. Why would Frank Ryan be writing to her? A quick glance into the rearview mirror told her she wasn't holding up traffic. She ripped at the tab, noticing that her hand was shaking. At a dead stop, Sandi shifted into park and took her hands off the wheel. She was so nervous she needed both hands to hold the single sheet of note paper. It was a short note on lined tablet paper, sloppily written. Her stomach heaved when she read the message.

"Someone has been asking questions about you. A fax came into the office with your picture. I told them I didn't know you. It's a good thing you told me your real name or I would have spilled the beans. Call me. There is more."

The brief note was signed, Frank.

Her breathing ragged, Sandi backed up the Rover, then maneuvered the truck back into its original parking space. Her heart pounding, she whipped out her cell phone to dial the number on the note. Frank himself answered the phone.

"I got your letter. What is going on?"

"There was some private dick asking questions about you a few days ago. He wanted to know everything the guys knew about you. I gotta tell you, kid, I was the only one who recognized you. You're lookin' good these days. Most of the old guys are gone. You know how this business is. Besides, no one wants to get tangled up in someone else's misery. Everyone on the track is allergic to cops of any kind, especially private dicks. Are you in some kind of trouble, kid?"

"Not that I know of. I was singing with the Canyon River Band when Dallas Lord died. At the moment I'm out of a job. Dallas wrote one last song that was never recorded. His brother is trying to find it."

"And you don't know a thing about it right, kiddo."

"Actually, Frank, I do know a thing or two about it. Dallas wrote the song for me when we were . . . together. Things went awry and he got himself mixed up with some doctor who took care of Billy Sweet when he died. I think she either stole it or in a weak moment Dallas gave it to her because he was angry with me for breaking things off. The brother, who is a real buttoned-up guy, is like a wet hornet. If I had that song, I'd be sitting pretty right now. The breaks just never seem to come my way. How are things at the track?"

"Same old same old. If that guy comes back or more faxes come in, how do you want me to handle it?"

"Don't tell them anything, Frank. I don't want some suit screwing up any job offers that come my way."

"That was a terrible thing about the singer. Stay in touch, Sandi."

"You too, Frank. Thanks for sending the letter. I guess I need to start paying attention to what is going on around me."

"If you ever find that song and sell it, spread the wealth. I'm getting too old for all this shit."

"Count on it. Can we keep this just between us, Frank?"

"Sure, kid. Why else do you think I called you?"

"Thanks again, Frank, and Merry Christmas."

"Same to you, kid."

Sandi wiped the sweat beading on her forehead with her sleeve. She counted to twenty-five before her breathing returned to normal. So Adam Lord wasn't as dumb as she thought he was. Who else but Adam would hire a private detective to check into her background? Did he suspect she was behind Sara Killian's break-in? She hadn't left any clues, and she knew how to cover her tail. She slammed her clenched fist into the armrest. "I want that goddamn song!"

The sky opened up the moment Sandi steered the Rover into traffic, making it almost impossible to see. She took the first turnoff she came to, electing to find her way via side streets so she wouldn't risk having an accident. By the time she swerved into Nellie Pulaski's complex it was so dark and gloomy she had trouble seeing the building numbers. She drove through the parking area three times looking for the Jeep Sara Killian had been driving the day before. On her fourth go-round she realized the doctor might have gone out or stashed the Jeep somewhere else. Well, there was only one way to find out. She circled the lot again looking for an out-of-the-way space where the Rover would be safe and not noticed.

Sandi parked the Rover carefully before she climbed over the backseat. Somewhere in the back there was probably a rain slicker. If she went out in this deluge, she'd be soaked in seconds. She rummaged until she found a yellow-lined brown poncho and struggled into it, making mental notes as to how the things had been packed by Laker. At the last second she picked up a black ski mask and stuffed it inside her windbreaker.

Sloshing through the rain, Sandi searched out Nellie's building. She had no trouble opening the door that led to a small lobby and a bank of mailboxes. The building seemed exceptionally quiet. Buildings like this usually had thin walls, through which stereos and televisions could be heard. Maybe this was a senior building where elderly people lived. It would certainly account for the lack of bicycles and baby carriages that were usually parked in the lobby. Nevertheless, didn't seniors have hearing problems? Televisions and stereos would be louder. There were also no cooking odors of any kind. She wondered if it meant anything. Another few minutes were used up as she tried to assess the situation. She decided none of it was important. The time was four-thirty.

Her ear to Nellie's door, Sandi spent a

good five minutes listening to total silence beyond the doors. She squinted, trying to see through the small magnified peephole in the middle of the door. With nothing directly in her line of vision, Sandi withdrew the small pick in her tool kit. She fit it into the cheap lock. Within seconds the dull brass knob turned in her hand. She squinted again as she looked through the peephole. Nothing had changed. There was no sign of Sara Killian or the person named Nellie.

Sandi pushed back the hood of the poncho and pulled on the ski mask. She let herself into the apartment, closing the door quietly behind her. She looked around, seeing everything at once. She'd seen similar layouts when she'd been apartment hunting. The bedrooms and bathrooms were off to the left, the dining room and kitchen to the right. Tiptoeing across the carpeted living room, she followed the sound of soft music and what sounded like running water. She grew light-headed when she recognized the Dallas Lord song. She waited quietly in the small hallway until the water was turned off. The soft splash and muttered, "Ooooh," had to mean the doctor was taking a bath and the water was hotter than expected. Perfect.

She couldn't be more vulnerable than when she was naked.

Again, Sandi waited until she was certain Sara was immersed completely in the water before she crossed the bedroom to where a large black bag rested on the bed. The same black bag the doctor was never without. Her eyes were murderous when she dumped the contents on the bed and found no sign of the cassette. She stuffed the gun and the clip into the pocket of her poncho. The Taser went into the pocket of her windbreaker. She stared at the two rings of keys, pocketed the one with the most keys because she recognized the safety deposit key. The second key ring must belong to the owner of the apartment. She left it on the bed. The wallet with Sara's credit cards and driver's license went into the hip pocket of her overalls. Where was the damn tape? Blind with rage, she fished out the gun clip, stared at it a second, and then slid it home. The heaviness of the gun surprised her.

The song ended and was replaced with a second one of her favorites. She listened, mouthing the words she'd sung so many times. She shook her head to clear it when she noticed the small vanity area outside the bathroom. It was supposed to be a plus to tenants because bathrooms steamed up; vanities outside the bathroom were the in thing these days. She had one herself. However, it wasn't the vanity but what was on it that interested her. A blow-dryer with what looked like a very long cord was plugged into the wall. *If* she wanted to, she could pitch it into the tub from where she was standing. It would take just a second to kick the partially open door to the side and toss the blow dryer. Surprise would be on her side. The doctor wouldn't have a chance.

Sandi adjusted the ski mask so that her eyes were barely visible. With the blow-dryer in one hand, the loaded and cocked gun in the other, she kicked open the door. She almost laughed then when Sara covered her breasts. "Stupid bitch," she hissed under her breath. A heartbeat later, she saw fear and recognition cross Sara's features and settle in her eyes.

Her bare breasts were no longer important. Sara grasped the edge of the tub and threw herself over the side and onto the floor just as the blow-dryer hit the water. She floundered for a moment before she whipped the towel at Sandi's legs. The singer danced backwards, losing her stance. She recovered and pointed the gun at Sara's head. Her voice was a venomous low-pitched growl when she said. "Where is it?"

Sara knew exactly what the person towering over her meant. There was no point in pretending she didn't. "I don't have it. I gave it to Judge Ronald Iverson to keep for me. You'll never get your hands on it. Who are you? How did you find me? Where's Adam? He's the only one who knew I was here. Go ahead, kill me. They'll catch you and for what? A stupid song! Is it worth going to jail for the rest of your life? I'm going to give the song back to Adam. You can tell him that for me. I don't want anything from you crazy people. If you're going to kill me, do it now or get out of here." With what dignity she could muster, Sara reached for the towel she'd whipped at Sandi and wrapped it around her naked body. She watched in stupefied amazement as the intruder backed away, past the vanity and across the bathroom. Too weak in the knees to follow, Sara sat down on the edge of the vanity stool. She needed to turn off the power or call the maintenance people to do it. When she heard the sound of the door closing, she rolled onto the floor, sobbing hysterically.

Sara continued to lie on the floor, her closed fists pummeling the tile. If she hadn't moved when she did, she would be dead. She needed to get up and dressed and get out of here before the intruder returned. Why had he or she left? Surely it wasn't her less-than-perfect oratory. No, it must have been when she said she was giving the song back to Adam or when she said he was the only one who knew where she was.

Sara tottered to the bedroom. She wanted to cry all over again when she saw the contents of the black bag spread all over the bed. Other hands had touched the things she held most precious in her life. The ugly hands of a person filled with hate and greed. As she piled the things back in her bag, she realized the intruder had kept her father's gun and the extra clip. The Taser as well as her wallet and keys were also gone. She had no money, no credit cards. What was she supposed to do now? Damn, why hadn't she listened to Judge Iverson when he told her to go to Alpine Forest. If she had done what he wanted, she'd be safe now in his cabin. Oh, no, she had to hang around for her date with the biggest piece of scum walking the earth.

Would Adam Lord show up at seven to finish her off? Would he continue to play the game? Of course he would. He was a pro. Tears rolling down her cheeks at her own stupidity, Sara rummaged in Nellie's closet for a warm set of clothes. Everything was sizes too big, but she didn't care. She had to get out of here and she had to get out now, but she needed money. She had to get gas and have the oil checked before she headed out. Surely Nellie kept some cash in the house. Was she the sugar-bowl type or would she hide it somewhere more secure? It took her fifteen full minutes before she found the old nurse's secret three-hundred-dollar stash in the back of her Betty Crocker Cookbook. Sara took it all, wadding it into a roll to stuff into the lined corduroy trousers she was wearing.

Sara took a last look around the apartment. She had absolutely no idea where the electric panel was, and she had no time to look for it. She'd call Nellie when she was safe in the cabin and explain what happened. As long as no one entered the apartment, things should be fine. Carly would know about things like that because she constantly watched crime shows.

Leave the lights on? Don't leave the lights on? Did it matter? No, it did not. Adam Lord, snake that he was, would know she was onto him the minute his ally reported back to him. She was delirious if she thought he would show up at all.

Outside in the rainy night, Sara felt such fear she could barely stand erect to lock the apartment door. She pressed her forehead against the cold feel of the wood to ward off the light-headedness that was threatening to overpower her. *Get a grip, Sara. You're alive. You have transportation and you have money. You're going to a snug harbor where you'll be safe. Tomorrow you can call Judge Iverson and have him contact Adam and give back the song. Move! Move now!*

Sara obeyed her own warning and ran to Nellie's truck. Rain sluiced down, soaking her already wet head. She barely felt it. *Don't think about anything but getting on the highway. Go, go, go!* Her mind shrieked.

Visibility was so terrible, Sara started to shake all over again as the oversize windshield wipers furiously attacked the windshield. She knew how to drive in the rain, why didn't other people? The traffic was stop and go, red taillights blinking for miles in front of her. The worst time of day to be on the road.

How could she have been so wrong about Adam Lord? Wrong wasn't quite the right word. Stupid was more like it. Stupid and blind. She felt herself start to shrivel inside. As she crawled along in traffic, her thoughts were chaotic. Less than an hour ago she'd stared at her own death with wide-open eyes. Carly was the athletic one in the family. Where had the insight come from to flop out of the tub the way she had? Total, all-consuming fear had given her the adrenaline surge she needed to survive. She had to call someone to tell them what happened. Who? Detective Luzak? Judge Iverson? Was the cell phone still in the black bag? She couldn't remember seeing it. Had the intruder taken it? When traffic stopped again, Sara rummaged in the bag. The cell phone wasn't there. She was on her own now, cut off from everyone. When would someone start to miss her? Would Detective Luzak stop by the house? Would Judge Iverson check up on her when he didn't hear from her? Would Adam Lord try to pick up her trail? And the intruder, what was he or she doing right now? Were they somewhere behind her in the miles of traffic? How would she know and what could she do if they were behind her? The stark reality of her situation slammed her in the face.

All her life she'd been a bookish person, sedentary, dedicated to her profession. She didn't do any of the athletic things Carly did. Everything she'd learned when she was a Camp Fire girl was long forgotten. Not so with Carly. She knew about the woods, which berries were safe to eat, which bugs were full of protein. She could build a fire by rubbing two sticks together. Carly knew how to survive and had the merit badges to prove it. All Sara'd ever got for her years in the organization was a badge for perfect attendance. What a sad commentary on her life.

The will to survive and her wits would get her through this. She had to believe in herself, or she didn't have a chance.

Sandi Sims parked in the Range Rover's assigned spot. She calmly exited the vehicle, walked around to the back to repack the neat cargo hold. The courtesy light's overhead bulb cast a dim bluish light to the yellow-and-brown poncho as she dried it off with the sleeve of her windbreaker before she folded it neatly the way it had been. Satisfied that Jim Laker would never know she'd borrowed the car, she climbed back into the driver's seat, turned the key, adjusted the seat to the way it had been before she drove it out of the lot. She'd pumped exactly one and a half gallons of gas into the tank just minutes ago. She toyed with the idea of adjusting the odometer. Would Jim notice the nine-mile difference? Not likely. She replaced the key under the mat, locked the door by pressing the button at the base of the window but left the door to the cargo hold open. It made a loud clicking sound that was jarring to her for some reason.

Inside her apartment, Sandi shed her clothes as she pressed buttons on the cell phone. She cut off the call before it could be completed. She needed to think. The shower was always a good place to contemplate life. Ronald Iverson had what she wanted. That's what the big surprise was. Two new outfits wasn't going to cut it. Neither was a fancy dinner and a night in bed with the old guy. An hour ago she'd been prepared to commit murder to get the tape when all the while her old lover had that very same tape in his possession. If Sara Killian hadn't flopped out of the tub when she did, she'd be a murderer. Did California have the death penalty? For the life of her she couldn't remember. The judge would know. Life in prison for attempted murder wasn't something she wanted to think about. Sara hadn't recognized her. Just to be on the safe side she was going to dump the clothes she'd had on. When people were in fear of their life, they had extra sharp perceptions. The doctor might remember her pant legs, her sneakers, something.

Naked, Sandi sat on the edge of the tub. Had it been a mistake to let Sara Killian live? The shock she'd experienced when she heard the doctor say she'd given the tape to Judge Iverson was the reason. Not to mention her greed. She should have followed through. She cursed her greed and sloppiness.

Sandi dressed in a dove gray pantsuit. This evening was not going to be as the judge had planned. There would be no grand dinner in a fancy restaurant, no marathon sex until she had what she wanted.

Would Iverson take the tape and sheet music home with him so she could verify it? She decided it was unlikely. The judge wouldn't trust her any more than she trusted him. There was too much money involved and the stakes were too high.

Before she left the apartment, Sandi gulped down two fingers of Wild Turkey bourbon, the judge's favorite liquor. Her eyes smarting, she grabbed the trash bags that held her clothes. She'd find different Dumpsters on the way and drop the bags separately, just in case some wise cop put two and two together. While she waited at a traffic light, she dialed the judge's private home number. The moment she heard his voice she went into her spiel. "Something came up, Ronnie. I'm on my way to your house. I'll blow the horn when I get to the gates. Be outside waiting for me. Please be on time. We'll talk about it when I see you." Did she just make another mistake by calling the judge on her cell phone? She felt like a nest of hornets were buzzing around inside her head. The dashboard clock said it was 6:45. Adam Lord would be on his way to pick up Sara. She realized she'd made another mistake by taking the doctor's gun.

If she'd left it, the good doctor probably would have put a bullet right through old Adam's heart. It was all starting to look messy. Messes could be cleaned up.

Sandi pulled into the driveway of Judge Iverson's Brentwood home and gave two light taps to the horn. The gate moved soundlessly as the judge walked through the opening. He wasn't carrying anything. The tape was small; it could be in his pocket. She had to remember the judge didn't know she knew what his big secret was.

Was she operating on Plan B or Plan C? She simply couldn't remember.

"Climb in, honey. Buckle up. Sorry about the change in plans, but something came up. I need to talk to you in private, where there are no prying eyes. I thought we'd go to that small Italian restaurant with the busy parking lot."

"I thought you hated Italian food. Where did you get this car?"

"It belongs to a friend of mine because the windshield wipers aren't working very well on mine. I do hate Italian food. I didn't say we were going to eat. I said we were going to the parking lot."

"You have certainly had your share of

problems with that foreign car. It seems like every time I see you you are driving a friend's car. I told you to buy American."

"I know you did, sweetie. This is just fine, and there are a million just like it on the road. No one will recognize either one of us. I know how you worry about things like that. With the way the rain is coming down, we're better off in a car like this. And how was your day, sweetie?"

Chapter Sixteen

He had a hard-on just watching her turn the wheel. The scent of her perfume, the animal nearness of her, forced the judge to roll down the window. He smelled his own aftershave when the rain pelted his face. She had given it to him some time ago, and he always used it sparingly so it would last. Sometimes when he was sitting on the bench listening to presented evidence he'd get a wiff of himself and a particular memory would surface. Then he'd have to call a recess for ten minutes so he could close his eyes and get it off in the privacy of his chambers. Plain and simple, he was addicted to Sandi Sims. He knew it, and so did she. Why else would he be sitting in a restaurant parking lot in a steamed-up car, with a hard-on that was down right painful?

The urge to move closer, to grope for her, to drag her head to his lap was so strong he gritted his teeth. Sandi Sims didn't like spontaneous moves. She liked to be in control, choreographing, arranging, seducing. She liked playing little-girl and big-daddy games. At times it made his skin crawl, but the emplosion of passion at the end of the game made the sick routine bearable. He grew light-headed when he thought about the outcome of the evening once he told her about his surprise.

He waited expectantly now that the engine and defroster were silent. She turned, a worried look on her face. "I think I might be in a little trouble, lover. Wait, hear me out. I know about your surprise. I wish you had told me sooner. I'm going to tell you everything. You're an attorney as well as a judge, so whatever I say to you is privileged and confidential. Don't interrupt me until I'm finished. Several hours ago I tried to kill Sara Killian. She'd be dead if she wasn't so agile. She just flopped out of the tub a second before the blow-dryer hit the bathwater."

The judge listened in horror, his mind racing as he recalled headlines of colleagues brought down by women like Sandi Sims. He thought about his wife Myrna and her long illness and how much he missed her.

His children would never understand his relationship with someone like Sandi Sims. He could feel his stomach start to heave at what he was hearing. The cold, stinging rain was like an ice cloth to his feverish face. He made no move to roll the window up. He should be at his daughter Cissie's house helping the children decorate the twelve-foot Christmas tree.

He could get out of this. He really could. All he had to do was open the car door and get out. The restaurant would call him a cab. Until now the only thing he was guilty of was having sex with a woman young enough to be his daughter. There was no statute on the books that said a judge couldn't have sex with a young woman who knew her way around the world. He hadn't said aloud that he had the tape Sara gave him. He might be guilty in his thoughts and his intentions, but that was all he was guilty of. The hard mound inside his trousers was softer than jelly now. He had to do something, say something to make this all go away. In his gut he knew it wouldn't go away. Stall. He had to stall for time.

"Ronnie? Sweet love, say something." Another time, another place, her purring voice would have had him climbing the walls. A time or two he'd thought he'd been peeled off the ceiling. "You have the tape. Sara told me so herself. I think it's wonderful that you called me as soon as you realized what you had in your possession. Think about it, lover. We can travel the world. The money will roll in forever. You won't have to go back to the bench ever again. Just think what you can do for your kids with your share. You said Cissie was having a hard time making ends meet even with your help. Children need so much. You're going to want your grandchildren to have the best possible education. Now you can buy your grandson that Cherokee he's been wanting so badly. You can pay for his insurance. Neither one of us will ever have to balance a checkbook again. We'll be together, just you and me, twenty-four hours a day. Forever and ever."

The judge finally found his voice. "Attempted murder is not something to take lightly. Sara is not a fool. She'll put two and two together, and she'll come up with four. She came to me because she trusted me. I cannot betray that trust. In my wildest dreams I never thought you capable of such a wicked thing. How could you, Sandi?"

"Listen to yourself, Ronnie. How could I? You were considering keeping the song for personal gain. That gain included me. People kill for a few lousy dollars. The end result is the same. Someone gets richer and someone gets poorer. Sara is alive. I didn't kill her, so I am not a murderer. Look at it this way. Dallas Lord is dead. All his assests go to his brother Adam Lord, who is incredibly wealthy in his own right. He could live ten lifetimes and never touch his principal. This song will just add another couple of lifetimes to his list. Dallas meant the song for me. Sara came along at the wrong time and stole what was rightfully mine. Do you care to dispute that, lover?"

"It doesn't change the fact that you tried to kill Sara Killian, a woman dedicated to saving lives. Don't mix apples and oranges. I want you to stop it, Sandi. I will not be an accessory to murder. I might be many things, but a murderer I am not."

"Does that mean you want out? Are you saying you're willing to give it all up? All we have to do is go up to Alpine Forest and make sure Sara has an accident. I know you sent her there. You see, lover, I know you so well. You probably told her to go there and lie low until this all blows over. You wanted time to talk to me, to plan on a way to get away with it so that no trail ever led back to you. I'll do it. You won't have to get your hands dirty. You weren't listening to me, lover. Sara didn't recognize me. She thinks I was one of Adam Lord's hired thugs. She's blaming all of this on him. I covered my ass, Ronnie. Are you saying you're having second thoughts?"

"As well as third and fourth thoughts. This is out of my league, Sandi. Yes, for a few minutes my greed and passion got in the way. I regret that now."

"Where is she, Ronnie?"

"Now, Sandi, how would I know where she is?"

"I'm one step ahead of you, lover. I know you told her to go to your cabin in Alpine Forest. All I have to do is look at your face to know its true. You sent her to the same cabin you took me to. Do you remember all those wonderful weekends we spent there and how happy we were? It can be that way again, lover. Just you and me and all that lovely money."

"There has to be a better way. I will not be a party to taking a life."

"Just for fun, what kind of scenario did you come up with? Were you going to say someone broke into your safe? In the courthouse, for God's sake. That's just too funny for words. Or, were you going to take the tape home and say someone broke into the house and ransacked it? Then what were you going to do? Were you planning on heading for some banana republic where you would be safe? What? I need to know, lover. If you have a better plan than mine, I want to hear it."

"I didn't get that far in my thinking. I hate to admit my thoughts didn't go beyond wanting to tell you I had the song. There is something else, too. All day today I had the feeling someone was watching me. Maybe the brother hired a private detective to spy on you and that led him to me. Don't you see, this is getting out of hand."

Sandi's face grew thoughtful. "It's funny you should say that. I've had that feeling a lot lately. I hear steps following me, I turn, and no one is there. I think it's Adam Lord or that guy he brought with him. It's just a feeling. Chalk it up to guilt on both our parts. So, lover, what is our bottom line here? Think before you answer and give some thought to what it would be like to *have it all* the way the Adam Lords of this world have it all. We need to come to a decision. If we're going to go to Alpine Forest, we have to dress warmly. We'll need a four-wheel-drive vehicle. I can borrow one, so that's no problem. You come with me while I get a change of clothes and I'll drive us to Brentwood so you can change your clothes."

"If I don't agree?"

"Then you're a fool."

"Then I guess I'm a fool. If anything happens to Sara Killian, I'll have to tell the authorities what I know."

"I wouldn't do that if I were you. What I told you was privileged and confidential. You cannot betray my trust. Give me the tape, lover. I know you have it in your pocket. You've been clutching at it all evening."

"I can't do that, Sandi. Don't do something you'll regret for the rest of your life." He saw the gun in her hand, saw how rock-steady it was. He thought about his dead wife Myrna and his daughter Cissie at home decorating the tree with the kids. Young Jack would have to wait another year or so for the Cherokee. Maybe he could find a used one that looked good. Then he thought about his son Mitch. His plane, if it was on time, would land at LAX in a few hours. Home for Christmas. Betsy would arrive in the morning with her newest boyfriend, the one she said was finally "it." The one she was dying for him to meet.

"Give it to me, Ronnie. I won't ask again."

He wanted to see Cissie, the grandkids, Mitch, Betsy and the "it," so he handed Sandi the tape. "What are you going to do, Sandi?"

"Are we still on privilege and confidentiality?"

"Unfortunately, yes," he lied, going along with her ignorance in hopes of surviving the nightmare.

"Then I'm going to take care of business. This is your last chance. Want to come along?"

He opened the door and stepped out of the car. He wanted to meet "it" more than anything in his life, wanted to go on the hunt for a used Cherokee. Tomorrow he wanted to go to the cemetery, the cemetery he hadn't gone to for years to beg Myrna's forgiveness. Like a granite tombstone was really going to give him absolution. He took another step backward and then another. He knew what she was going to do before she did it. He felt the pain before the bullet struck him on the side of the head. And then he felt nothing.

"I gave you every chance in the book, lover. Because you were so kind to me during our time together, I'm going to send your grandson a brand-new Jeep Cherokee. A bright red one. Anonymously. I'll even send Cissie a generous check, anonymously. By the way, I didn't buy any outfits today," Sandi shouted before she rolled up the window.

It was amazing, Sandi thought as she drove out of the parking lot, that not one person came out of the restaurant to investigate the shot. The hard-driving rain and the sporadic thunderbolts probably accounted for the lack of interest on the part of the restaurant's customers. No vehicles had even entered the lot. A very slow night by all indications. She blew on the barrel of the gun the way she'd seen the actors do in the movies.

She had things to do and places to go. But first she had to return the vehicle she was driving and borrow Jim's Rover again. It was gassed and ready to go. If her luck held, she could be in Alpine Forest by midnight. The Rover, according to the commercials, could take her anywhere, despite the weather and terrain. Sara would be asleep. It was all so perfect it was almost scary.

Adam drove out of the canyon, an eerie feeling between his shoulder blades. He could count, on one hand, the number of times during the course of his life when he was forced to look over his shoulder, and four of those times were when he was a kid. For days now he had suspected he was being watched and followed. Every time he stopped short or turned around, no one looked suspicious, but he couldn't shake the feeling. Even Tom had commented that he thought someone was lurking beyond the perimeters of the estate because Izzie and the pups constantly sniffed at the fencing. The dogs weren't eating normally either, something else that was starting to worry him.

The rain was vicious tonight. A perfect evening to stay home and watch an old movie on television. With popcorn. Maybe Sara would be of the same opinion. Hell, his feet were already soaking wet on the run from the house to the garage. He'd probably catch a goddamn cold and be sick when it was time to fly back to Charleston. His stomach started to knot up at the thought of leaving.

Adam craned his neck to see the street signs, but with the wind and rain, visibility was almost zero. He needed radar. He looked at the panel of the car with all the red and green buttons. It wouldn't have surprised him in the least to see a digital message start to flash across the instrument panel. Obviously such a thing hadn't been invented for cars, or Dallas would have owned it. "I miss you, Dallas. I'm doing my best. It probably isn't good enough by your standards, but I'm trying. Wherever you are, I hope you can hear me. I wish so many things. I guess you did, too. Yet, neither one of us made those wishes come true. All I have to go on now are my own instincts, and those instincts tell me the course I've elected to take is the right one. If I'm on the wrong track, you need to give me some kind of sign. I always thought that hereafter stuff was bunk. Now I'm not so sure. I wish we had talked about things like that. I can't help but wonder what you would think of me taking Dr. Killian out to dinner. I still feel a little uncomfortable about it. Some kind of sign about that would be nice, too. Dallas, there is something I don't understand. Why in the name of God, didn't you have some backup? In your business backup is the name of the game. I've been flying blind since I got here. I keep telling myself you did leave a clue somewhere. Sandi Sims almost had me believing her. It's one big mess, Dallas. Someone is trying to kill Sara. Somebody wants the song very badly. Guess you didn't think that far ahead since you didn't know your days were . . . What I mean is no one expects to die. Billy Sweet is the perfect example. For some reason people always think they're going to live forever. It was Billy's time to go, but it wasn't your time, Dallas. I don't know how I know that, but I do."

Feeling sheepish, Adam lit a cigarette. He

rolled down the window a little, ignoring the rain as it shot through the opening in swift, stinging pellets. He lowered the window more to try to read the upcoming street sign. Good, he was in Sara's neighborhood now. All he had to do was go two more blocks, make a right on the road that would take him to the complex to which Sara had fled. He wondered what the strange things were that she'd mentioned when she left the message. Whatever it was, it must have scared her to make her bolt. Aside from last night's irrational behavior, he thought Sara Killian was a levelheaded woman. He corrected the thought. Dr. Killian was an intelligent, level-headed woman. She wouldn't get spooked for no reason. Doctors couldn't afford to panic. From what he'd seen and observed, they usually had nerves of steel to go with their bedside manners. Whatever the strange thing was, it must have been serious to make someone like Sara leave every-thing behind.

The car in front of Adam slowed, allowing him to see the rain-swept sign swaying in the wind—Oxford Garden. Now all he had to do was find the ancient truck and a park-ing space. He used up twenty minutes looking for the truck and Sara's sister's Jeep. A bolt of lightning, rare at this time of year, ripped across the sky illuminating the buildings signs with arrows pointing in all directions.

Adam hopped from the car and raced to the building. He hoped there was a clothes dryer in there. He had no idea what he could do for his waterlogged deck shoes. He rang the bell once, twice, and then a third time. When there was no response, he turned the door handle. It opened easily to his touch. From the doorway, the fine hairs on his arm prickling, Adam called out. "Sara, it's Adam! Is it okay to come in?" When there was still no answer, he moved cautiously, his heart taking on an extra beat. He kept calling Sara's name he walked through the living room across to the dining room and then to the small hallway that led to the bedrooms. Obviously his earlier assessment of Sara had been wrong. It was clear she had panicked a second time and was no longer in the apartment. Clothes were everywhere, the closet doors pushed to the side. There was no sign of the heavy black bag Sara always carried with her, confirmation that she was gone.

The bright lights over the vanity were on, but the bathroom was dark. He pushed at the door to shed light from the hallway as he called Sara's name again. He sucked in his breath with a hard swallow when he saw the filled tub and the cord from the blow-dryer that led to the tub. "Son of a bitch!" Stepping backward to the vanity area, he pulled the plug. He moved then, faster than he'd ever moved in his life to try to find the circuit breaker box. He ran his finger down the hard black panel until he found the square he wanted. He shoved it back into place before he raced back to the bathroom. For one brief moment he thought his head was going to rocket right off his shoulders at the sight of the blow-dryer in the water. The floor was soaking wet, a wet towel in the open doorway. What he surmised were Sara's clothes were on the floor in a heap next to the bed. This certainly explained the absence of what Tom called the kick-ass truck. Afraid for her life, Sara had run yet again. Where was the sister? Where was the owner of the apartment? The little he knew about Sara led him to believe she had arranged for them to go somewhere else, somewhere she thought they would be safe.

She was willing to take the hit for whatever was going to happen. Now she was on the run. Where would she go? Was anyone helping her? Was she out there in this weird storm, just driving aimlessly, or did she have a destination in mind? He had to admit he didn't know. What he did know was that Sara Killian was in mortal danger.

His deck shoes sloshing on the carpet, Adam looked around for a phone. When he saw it, he sat down on the edge of the bed, and he dialed the number at the house in the canyon. While he waited for Tom to pick up the phone, he cataloged the things on the bed. Aware of the scent of gardenias, he picked up a frothy slip and sniffed. He noticed the tags on the garments laid out across the pillow. Even with so much on her mind, Sara had managed to find the time to buy a new outfit for their date. His eyes started to burn as he looked at what he surmised was debris from the bottom of a purse or bag. A half stick of chewing gum still in the wrapper, a tattered roll of mints, little bits of foil, and what looked like tobacco granules. Either someone had cleaned out her bag or Sara had done it herself. "Tom, it's me. Has Sara called? All right, listen to me.

I want you to settle the dogs, leave plenty of food and water for them, and drive down here. Bring my briefcase, some money, and my gun. It's in the top dresser drawer. There is an envelope with cash in the freezer. Dallas always hid cash there under the ice-cube trays. I guess it rubbed off on me. We'll talk when you get here?"

Adam looked at the clock before he walked back the bathroom to stick his hand in the tub water. It was still warm, which meant Sara hadn't been gone that long. An hour, possibly a little longer. He didn't even want to think about how Sara got out of the tub in time. The water on the floor had to mean she had leapt out, splashing and dripping in the nick of time. His heart started to pound in his chest at the thought.

His eyes wild, Adam looked around. *All of this for a fucking song.*

At eighteen minutes past seven the doorbell rang. Adam opened it to admit Tom Silk. "I think I got everything," Tom said. "Do you have any towels?"

Adam was busy shuffling through the papers in his briefcase. He jerked his head in the direction of the bathroom.

"Yow!"

"Yeah, yow. Someone tried to kill Sara Killian. She must have the reflexes of a cat to have gotten out of that tub in time. She's on the run, and we have to find her before that whacko finds her."

Toweling his hair, Tom said, "My money is on that skinny singer. You said yourself the band was all present and accounted for yesterday. They're all home with their families for the holidays. The singer is single, with only sugar daddies for company. Do you think it's a good idea if I call around to see if I can locate her? I brought her file with me. She has parents here in California."

"Good idea, but don't alarm the parents. Make up some excuse about delivering a Christmas present or something. Were the dogs okay?"

"Of course. Izzie did something kind of strange this morning. You were still asleep. She had just come down the staircase off the kitchen when she stopped in her tracks, looked around, then beelined to the staircase in the foyer. I don't think her feet touched those front steps. She whined, but she didn't bark. She ran up and down the hall, sniffing and whining. I bet you have yourself a nest of mice somewhere."

"Thanks for sharing that, Tom. Listen, I feel that time is of the essence. Whoever is after Sara could be following her as we speak. We have to find her."

"In the city of Los Angeles? Get real, Adam. There is no way. The weather is still as bad as it was when you came down from the canyon. I'll make my calls from the kitchen so we don't get in each other's way."

"The detective agency is closed for the holidays, so I'm going to try to locate someone from that racetrack where Sandi used to hang out. We don't have much else to go on except that short list of names of Sara's friends the detective provided. I'm going to work on that first. I rather think Dr. Killian is a private person who has little time for friends and socializing. Cross your fingers that we come up with something."

"Good luck," Tom muttered as he made his way to the kitchen.

Adam stared at the six names on the investigative report. He mentally erased Nellie Pulaski's name and moved on to Harriet Willowby whose answering machine said she was in New York for the holidays. Janice Baker's husband said she had delivered a seven-pound baby earlier in the day and wasn't available. Nor did he know where Dr. Killian could be reached. The third name was Jack Drake. His answering machine said he was in Hong Kong until January 18. The fifth name was Sara's CPA. Screaming kids and a shrill wife could be heard in the background when the accountant came on the line to say he hadn't seen or heard from Sara since before Thanksgiving. "We have an appointment to do her taxes January 10." The sixth and last name on the list was Judge Ronald Iverson. The report said the judge was a family friend. Family friends were the kind of people Sara might rely on. It was worth the try. He dialed the number and waited while the phone rang nine times before being picked up. The voice was older-sounding, but cheerful. Adam went into his spiel.

"The judge was here earlier but he went out. Then he came back to take something out of the safe. Sometime's he's forgetful. Someone was waiting outside for him. I saw the headlights. He did say he probably wouldn't be back until tomorrow."

"This is very important, ma'am. Did the judge say where he was going?"

"No. Even if he did, I wouldn't be at liberty to discuss that with you."

"Can you tell me this? Has Dr. Sara Killian been to see the judge? I'm afraid something might have happened to her. She's missing. I thought she might have gone to the judge if she thought she was in some sort of trouble."

"Sara! Sara would never get into trouble. She's too levelheaded. Somebody was here ealier. The judge met them out by the gate and left. Let me look in his appointment book. I'll just be a minute." Adam tapped his fingers on the end table. He felt his heart start to pound in his chest. "Mr. Lord, is it?"

"Yes. Adam Lord."

"Sara met with the judge earlier this morning at the courthouse. He entered it in his logbook. He always brings it home at night and makes notes. He didn't make any entries tonight that I can see. What kind of trouble is Sara in?"

"She's missing, ma'am. We don't know where she might have gone. Can you think of anything? I was hoping she went to the judge for help."

"The judge has a cabin in Alpine Forest, way way up there in the mountains. I suppose it's possible he took her up there if what you say is true. He watched over Sara and her sister because he was such good friends with their father."

"Is there a phone in the cabin?"

"Mercy no. It's very rustic. I go up once a year to clear away the cobwebs and do a general cleaning. There's no central heat. The cabin is winterized but you have to be a hardy individual to stay there at this time of year. I heard on the radio that heavy snow in the higher elevations was predicted for today as well as the next few days."

"Can you tell me how to get there, ma'am?" Adam carefully wrote down the directions. "Ma'am?" It was a long shot and a wild one at that. His brain whirled as he tried to figure how best to phrase his next question. "Did Sara ever bring Sandi Sims to the house?"

The housekeeper's voice was indignant when she said, "That young woman is no friend of Sara or her sister, Mr. Lord. She's a pest. She used to call here sometimes seven or eight times a day. The judge took an interest in her, and he watches her probation schedule as a personal favor to one of his lawyer friends."

Adam's fist shot in the air. "Well, thank you very much. If the judge returns this evening, will you tell him I called. I'd like to leave my phone number as well as my cell-phone number." He repeated the numbers twice to make sure the housekeeper copied them down accurately.

"Bingo, Tom! Did you get anything?"

"Sandi's parents say they haven't seen her in a couple of months. They said she calls every Sunday afternoon. She gave them tickets for a trip to New York after the new year because the mother likes Broadway shows. They said she lives in a very pricey condo in Santa Monica. The father worries about how she pays the mortgage. They sounded like normal parents. What did you get?"

Adam told him. "Do you agree that maybe, just maybe, the judge is one of Sandi's sugar daddies?"

"I'd bet the rent. How about you?"

"Yeah. Yeah, I would, too. Do you think the judge took Sara up to his cabin, or do we think Sara went alone? Would she have given the judge the tape to keep for her. What other reason would she have for going to the courthouse this morning?"

"Maybe she went there to drop off a Christmas present. People do that, Adam. The judge is supposed to be a family friend. It's obvious Sara trusts him."

"True. But and this is a big 'but' . . . Sara probably doesn't know the judge knows Sandi Sims. It's a damn triangle is what it is. I don't know anyone in this town I can call to get a fix on the judge. You're as much of a stranger as I am. Wait a minute, I do know someone. Call Benton Memorial and ask for Harry Heinrick. He probably isn't there at this time of night, so try and weasel his home phone number if you can from the operator. I'll call the CPA back to see if he knows anything."

The CPA's line was busy. A moment later, Tom chortled. "Got it!"

Adam dialed the number. He didn't realize he was holding his breath until he heard the Hawk's voice on the other end of the line. He identified himself. "I need some help, Mr. Heinrick, and I need it right away. I'm willing to reconsider my decision in regard to the hospital. I think Sara might be in grave danger. No, no, I'm not blaming you or the hospital. I need information. Since you live in the area, I thought you might know or might have heard . . . I need to know what kind of a judge Ronald Iverson is. Not so much in court but in his private life. Do you know? Is there any way you can find out?"

"I don't know the man at all. However, Dr. Granger, one of our doctors, plays golf with him on a regular basis. He's on duty tonight. I could call him for you. Are you serious about reconsidering our earlier talk?"

"Yes. Dallas made a commitment to you, but he did it for all the wrong reasons. You accepted that commitment for the same wrong reasons. As I said, I'm giving it serious thought. I want you to understand, I'm not making a promise. I would appreciate it, Mr. Heinrick, if you would call Dr. Granger and get right back to me. Call me on my cell phone. Do you have a pencil?"

Ten minutes later, Adam's fist shot into the air a second time. "All this Dr. Granger knows is Iverson was really hung-up over some singer. He said he was like a lovesick teenager. Before the singer he was a love-'em-and-leave-'em kind of guy. Singer, Tom. It has to be Sandi Sims. Who else could it be? Heinrich said Granger told him she was blond and shapely. Iverson said her legs went all the way up to her neck. Said they were better than Tina Turner's legs. It might be a stretch, but it's all we have to go on."

"So what's our next move?"

"Either we head back to the house for some warm clothing, or we rummage here for whatever is at hand. The housekeeper said the higher elevations were due for snow. If we're getting this kind of rain down here, it's safe to say it's snowing pretty hard higher up. On second thought, Dallas didn't have any heavy-duty clothing with the exception of a jacket. Look around and see what you can find. That goes for socks and boots."

"Adam?"

"Yeah."

"Is the judge the good guy or the bad guy?"

"I don't know, Tom. I don't think Sara knows either."

"Do you think it was the judge who tossed the blow-dryer into the tub?"

"I don't know that either. I suppose it's possible if Sandi told him about the song. If he didn't know about the song, he would have no reason to stalk Sara. My money is on Sandi. While you're looking for the clothes, I'll see about a flashlight and some food."

"We're going to look for Dr. Killian?"

"Unless you have a better idea. We have to try, Tom. At least I do. If you don't want to come along, it's okay."

"Hey, count me in. I liked the lady. I just hate the cold weather. Let's hope the owner of this apartment has some long johns."

Adam's voice was grim. "I'll put that on my list of things to hope for."

Chapter Seventeen

Numb with cold, Sara banged on the truck's heat vent with her clenched fist. Her reward was a continuing blast of frigid air. She wanted to cry her frustration at the icy air roaring through the vents even when she turned the heater to the Off position. She was accustomed to an instant blast of warm air in her luxury Jaguar when the occasion warranted, not this rinky-dink heater that spewed cold air no matter what. Obviously Nellie didn't feel a need to have her heater checked for the short ride to the hospital from her apartment. To make matters worse, the windshield wipers were sluggish, their old blades caked with ice and snow.

Sara had only a vague idea of where she was beyond the fact that she was on Route 5 heading north. Careful to stay what she thought of as two car lengths behind the vehicle in front of her, Sara focused on the red taillights in the swirling snow. Somewhere along the way she'd lost track of time. If she were in the operating room, she would know to the split second how much time she had used up and how much time was left until it was time to suture her patient. This was a nightmare. She wasn't even sure now at what point the light snow had intensified to this blinding, swirling blizzard that was making her blood run cold. She was driving blind and she knew it, but as long as she could see the taillights of the car in front of her she felt a small measure of comfort. She couldn't help but wonder if the driver of the car behind her was feeling the way she was. Eventually she was going to have to pull over to the side of the road to chop at the ice on the wiper blades. How far to the right did she dare pull over? How much shoulder was there? What if the driver behind her slammed into her? Would she dare get out? Well, she had to, but definitely not on the driver's side of the car. Gingerly, she pulled over and stopped. There was no middle console in the truck so she slid over to the passenger side and got out that way. The only problem was she had no tool to chop at the ice. She longed for hot coffee and warm, dry gloves. Mittens actually, the kind her mother used to knit for her when they lived in Pennsylvania and she played in the snow. When they got wet there was always a dry pair waiting and they were always bright red, with white tassels at the wrist.

The gusty wind and snow slammed her against the side of the truck. Head down, her arm snaked out to grasp the broad ridge around the windshield where she grappled with the oversize blades. The ice and snow were at least an inch thick, impossible to break off. A sob caught in her throat. She lifted the blade and whacked it down on the windshield. Ice flew in all directions. Slipping and sliding, she inched her way around the hood of the truck to do the same thing to the driver's blade. She had to bang it three times before she heard the chunks of ice skitter across the frozen snow on the hood of the truck.

Back in the driver's seat, Sara inched her way onto the road. The red taillights behind her stayed with her as she tried to catch up to the pinpoints of red light ahead of her. Had the driver behind her stopped when she did? Was someone following her? Such a ridiculous thought. No one knew she was coming up here. Even the judge didn't know because she hadn't called to tell him she was coming. The person behind her was probably an ordinary citizen trying to get home to his family. The thought didn't make her feel any better.

What seemed like a long time later Sara almost fainted when she saw the neon lights on the side of the road. The car in front of her inched to the left; she followed suit as did the car behind her. She wanted to cry her relief, but knew the tears would freeze on her eyelashes and probably break off. God in heaven, would her eyeballs ever feel the same? And then she was inside the steamy, warm Mexican restaurant. She asked for the ladies' room where she ran her frozen hands under the faucet. She didn't think she'd ever be warm again. What she needed now was a gallon of hot coffee and some piping hot soup.

The restaurant seemed to be full. The chatter was of the storm and road conditions. Taking a high stool in what she surmised as the smoking area, Sara rummaged in her bag for one of the stale cigarettes she'd been carrying around with her for months. When she cupped her hands around the big heavy mug of coffee, she noticed that two of her fingernails were broken. Her hands were tingling, as were her feet. It didn't matter. She was starting to feel warm. She had no idea how she looked, and she didn't care. Nellie's clothing, while several sizes too big, was warm. She smoked the stale cigarettes, vowing never to buy another pack, while she drank cup after cup of coffee. When she felt warm enough and relaxed, she started to look around. The restaurant was small but crowded. When one table cleared, it filled almost immediately. No one seemed to be paying any attention to her. A blast of arctic air swept through the restaurant when a four-man work crew entered. Sara scrutinized them carefully. They belonged. She was sure of it. They didn't even look in her direction. She looked around again but didn't recognize anyone. The driver of the car behind her was faceless and nameless. If he was still in the restaurant, she couldn't pick him out. She finished her bowl of bean soup and the two buttery tortillas. She promptly ordered a second bowl of soup because she had no idea when she'd eat again. She finished the soup, asked for one last refill on the coffee, and ordered coffee and a container of soup to go.

Her bladder protesting all the liquid she'd consumed, Sara headed for the bathroom, which smelled strongly of Pine-Sol. She admired the hand-knitted mittens on the young girl ahead of her in line. "I'll give you twenty-five dollars for them," she blurted.

The girl giggled, and said, "Sold!"

"Can you tell me how to get to Alpine Forest from here?"

"You mean that gated community?"

"Yes, that's the one."

"You have to have a pass to get in there. Do you have one?"

"Yes," Sara lied. Nellie's truck was the only pass she needed. She was, after all, a pro at knocking down gates. She copied down the directions.

"We're going that way if you want to follow us," the young girl said. "We'll blow the horn when you're supposed to turn off. Are you sure you want to pay me twenty-five bucks for these mittens?"

"I'm sure. My wipers keep freezing and the leather gloves I had on were useless. My mother used to knit mittens like yours, but they were red."

The girl laughed. "My mother's favorite color is yellow. I have eleven yellow sweaters and four pairs of yellow mittens." Sara smiled. Was she ever that young? She could remember when Carly was the same age as the young girl, but couldn't remember herself at that age. She shivered and wondered what it meant if anything.

"We'll wait for you by the door."

"I won't be long," Sara said.

Outside it seemed like the storm was worse. Sara pulled the drawstring on the parka hood tighter. The mittens felt warm and toasty.

"Now, *that's* a truck!" the young girl's companion said.

"It certainly is. It doesn't have a heater, or if it does, it doesn't work. I drove all the way from LA without heat."

"Jeez," the girl said. "This is my friend Buck. I'm Gina."

"Do you want me to take a look at the heater for you?"

"If you wouldn't mind."

"We'll sit in our truck, honey," Gina said. "Make it work for this nice lady."

Twenty minutes later the young man returned. "There is a little heat coming out. Not much. I think you'll be okay till you get to Alpine Forest. I cleaned off your wiper blades. Stay close behind us and when I blow the horn two sharp blasts you turn left. The roads are really bad, and you don't have chains. You need chains up here when it snows. If you had a set, I'd put them on for you."

"Thank you so much. Can I pay you?"

"Absolutely not!" Gina said. "You already gave me twenty-five dollars."

"Drive in first gear," Buck said as he climbed into his own Dodge Ram.

"Okay. Thanks." These young people were so fearless. The storm was a lark to them while she, on the other hand, was scared witless.

The young couple waved happily as they headed out of the parking lot, Sara right behind them. "I was never that young. I know I wasn't. I wasn't happy like they are either," she muttered.

Visibility was nil. Even though she was literally riding the Ram's bumper, she could barely see the taillights ahead of her. She risked a quick look in the side mirror. Twin headlights were behind her. It didn't have to mean anything.

It seemed like an eternity later when she heard the two sharp blasts of the horn. She tapped her own lightly before she flicked her turn signal. She drove slowly toward the dim yellow light at the guard's station. There was no guard, and the gate was up. That was good. She wouldn't have to lie and make up excuses. Now, all she had to do was follow the arrows the judge had made on his map. His was the only cabin that didn't belong to the gated community. He'd explained that he had owned his land and the cabin since the late fifites, and he'd refused to sell out to the developer. The way he'd put it was, "I ignore them, and they ignore me."

The moment she drove past the last street, Sara knew she was in trouble. There were no tire tracks to follow, no taillights to be seen. The judge had said to drive in a straight line and she would eventually come to a huge double tree at the end of his drive-way. The oversize mailbox was cemented inside a brick pillar. The judge had said she'd have to be blind to miss it, and sure enough, when she climbed from the truck for the third time to scrape the ice from the wipers, she was in front of the mailbox. God must be watching over her. She climbed back into the truck and turned onto what she hoped was the driveway. A half mile down the road she glimpsed the dark shape of the cabin. She sobbed her relief as she grabbed the coffee and the soup in her mittened hands. This is so stupid, stupid sooo stupid.

The key. Where was the key? Had the intruder taken it? No, she'd put it in the envelope with her birth certificate. Her hands fumbled through the papers and envelopes at the bottom of the bag. A mighty sigh escaped her when she felt the key through the envelope. Seconds later she was inside the cabin, which was as dark and cold as it was outside.

The fire was laid; all she had to do was light a match. Thank God the kindling and the logs were dry. Sparks showered upward, lighting up the huge room. Oil lamps were everywhere. She lit them all. While she waited for the logs to blaze, Sara prowled the cabin, dragging quilts and blankets to the hearth, where she spread them out. The kitchen had a potbellied stove, the logs waiting for her to strike a match. She remembered to open the damper before the fire took hold. She thanked God for the indoor bathroom. Obviously the judge had a septic tank somewhere outside. The giant wood-box that went all the way to the ceiling was loaded with clean dry logs. The cabinets in the kitchen were full of canned beans, canned spaghetti, tuna, and Spam. If need be, she could stay here for weeks and not starve.

The big question, though, was she safe here in this cabin? She saw the baseball bat in the corner by the door. Did the judge bring his grandson Jack up here? She decided it was as good a weapon as any, so she picked it up and carried it over to her make-shift bed to slide it under the down comforter. She heard a noise then. Her heart pounded in fear as she tried to decide if it was one of the logs splitting in the fire or someone outside. She looked around at the undraped windows that left her feeling vulnerable and exposed. Anyone outside could see every move she made. If there was someone out there with a gun—her gun—they could shoot her through the window. She knew now that she had made a mistake coming here. She was truly trapped.

She moved to the darker corners of the

kitchen. One by one she turned out the oil lamps. Now she could see the blinding whiteness beyond the windows. She moved quietly from one window to the next to see if there were any footprints to be seen. The pristine white snow was untouched. Outside the wind howled and shrieked. Inside, shadows that looked like obscene monsters danced on the walls of the cabin. The fear stayed with her.

She ran to the door, then, when she heard the same strange noise a second time. It sounded as if someone was on the roof. Was there an attic or crawl space in the cabin? Stupid, stupid, stupid. If there was space above the ceiling, the only entry would be from the inside via a pull-down ladder or a trapdoor. With a fire roaring up the chimney, no one would even think of coming down the way Santa did. There had to be a foot of snow on the roof, making footsteps soundless. An animal looking for warmth? The thought was so ridiculous, Sara grimaced. She felt like the sitting duck she was.

Sara eyed the only door in the cabin. It was sturdy and stout, like Nellie's truck. She knew little about architecture but the cabin looked like it was overbuilt. The beams and heavy black bolts and flanges were awesome, as if some warrior lived here who was securing his fortress. She had no idea what kind of wood the door and the cabin were made of. Not pine. Pine was a soft wood. Oak she thought. The heavy-duty bolts on the door pleased her. One was vertical and one was horizontal. The uncovered windows were another story. Multipaned, the wood in between the squares would shatter if someone threw something against them or tried to throw his body through the window. She asked herself what Carly would do in this situation. She'd probably rack her brain, trying to recall a movie where she'd seen the same scenario acted out and resolved in ninety minutes.

Sara paced, staying close to the wall and away from the windows. She took a deep breath. She would never be able to go to sleep until she was sure there were no threatening forces outside. The way she saw it, she had two choices. She could either sit and suck her thumb, or she could go outside and investigate. She maneuvered her way to the kitchen, opening cabinets and drawers in search of a flashlight. She finally found one in the bottom drawer. It was large with a shoulder strap, the kind that took a big square battery. Holding it down toward the floor, she turned the button. Weak yellow light lit up the corner. She hunched down to remove the battery and fit in a new one. Bright golden light filled the corner.

Sara retraced her steps to the door. Once she opened the door she was fair game for anyone out there stalking her. She debated a full five minutes. She was bone tired and her body still had a chill that the fire hadn't erased. This was one of those now-or-never times in a person's life. Her heart skipped a beat when she undid the heavy locks. She yanked at the door, the force of the wind and snow driving her and the door backward. With her back to the outside, Sara pulled at the door to close it. She had to use both hands to close it tight, the flashlight banging against her leg as it dangled from the strap she'd looped around her neck. She felt the heat leave her body as she tried to plow through the drifting snow. The light, angled downward, showed that her previous footprints had been obliterated. She didn't realize she was holding her breath until it exploded from her mouth in a loud *swoosh*.

Obviously, she told herself, she was paranoid. It was probably the firewood creating the strange noises she'd heard. Still, the nervous feeling stayed with her. She knew she wouldn't rest until she'd checked the area surrounding the cabin. Her steps were tortured, her weary, tired body protesting each one as she strained to see through the swirling snow. There were no footprints to be seen until she came to the area by the kitchen window. The snow under the window overhang was shallow, the ground showing through in the area closest to the foundation. Large, deep footprints. She gasped in horror as she ran, slipping and sliding back to the front of the house. At the door she hesitated. Where was the person who made the footprints? Did he go into the house? If she opened the door would that person grab and kill her?

Sara looked around wildly. In her panic, she'd destroyed the footprints she'd made when she first came outside. It was impossible to tell now if there were any prints other than her own. Suddenly her knees gave out on her and she was in a snowdrift. Fine, stinging snow whipped across her face. *Look in the window, look in the window,* her mind shrieked. Where was the baseball bat? Did she take it out of the covers? Did she lean it up against the door when she went out? Yes, yes, yes. She pulled herself up to the windowsill. The fire blazed, casting the room in jumping shadows. Was one of those shadows a real-live flesh-and-blood person? The black bag holding her life sat next to the makeshift bed. Where were the keys to the truck? Were they in the black bag or were they in her jacket pocket? She pulled off one of the yellow mittens to grope inside the pocket of her jacket. Her cold fingers closed around the key. *Thank you, God.*

She needed the bat. How best to get it? If there was only some way to lock the door from the outside so the person inside couldn't get out. The force of the wind would blow the door inward, slamming it against the wall where the bat rested. Trying to get the bat from behind the door would give the intruder time to drag her into the room and then it would all be over. No, it was best to go to the truck and drive away. "Please, God, help me," she prayed as she struggled through the snow to Nellie's truck.

Dear God, she hadn't locked the truck. What if someone was waiting inside? Did she dare take a chance and get in the truck? The only other option was to take off on foot and try to head back to the gated community. If the tire tracks hadn't filled over, she could follow them. If new snow filled the tracks, she was on her own. "Please, God, help me."

How long would the person inside the house wait for her to return? Any minute now they'd be coming out to check on her.

Try for the truck or go it on foot? Petrified, Sara struck out in what she thought was the way she'd come. Coming toward her was a looming figure that to her mind looked as big and as frightening as Big Foot. She was going to die out here in this godforsaken place, and her body wouldn't be found till the spring thaw. She swung the flashlight upward.

She wasn't really out here in a snowstorm. She was safe at home and this was just one really bad nightmare. She knew it was a nightmare because the figure staring at her in the glow of the flashlight was dead. She would wake any minute now. Any second.

"Dallas?"

Chapter Eighteen

"Pull over, Adam, before you kill us both. You aren't used to driving in snow and I am. As a matter of fact, I don't think you're used to driving at all. Limos and chauffeurs are more your style. I understand that you feel the need to be doing something, but this ain't it, big guy," Tom Silk said.

"You're right. It's been years since I drove in snow, and at that it was a mere dusting swirling across the road. I've missed out on a lot of things. It's all yours, Tom. I have to warn you, for the past hour visibility has been nil. I've been following the guy's tail-lights in front of me."

They drove in silence, each man busy with his own thoughts. What seemed like a long time later, Tom said, "Listen, we're all over the damn road. We're playing with our lives here, Adam. Are you sure you want to continue?"

Adam's voice was grim. "Yes, I'm sure. Sara's life is in danger. Pull over so I can scrape the windows for you."

Hunched over the wheel, his eyes glued to the swirling snow beyond the windshield, Tom muttered under his breath. Adam ignored him as he struggled to see through the cascade of snow falling all about them.

"Where the hell are the goddamn work crews is what I want to know?" Tom cursed when the Rover fishtailed and then righted itself. "Try for the weather report or the news. I think we should have called the police or the sheriff up there instead of trying to make it in this storm. This isn't good, Adam. If Dr. Killian left earlier in the day, she probably made it before the weather got bad. We're chasing ghosts. We don't even know for certain she's up here."

"I know, Tom. Ah, here we go. News on the hour. Oh-myyyy-God!"

"Is that the judge . . . ?"

"That's the one. Shhh. He's in critical condition, but he's alive. I guess that answers our earlier questions. He is definitely not in on this venture. According to the police, no one saw or heard anything. Of course you have to look at the flip side of that particular coin, which means he could have been in on it and then chickened out."

"I'm going to pull over; our wipers are so frozen they aren't moving. I can't see a damn thing. Get out on your side and see what you can do."

His teeth chattering, Adam climbed back in the truck. His efforts to clear the blades had been feeble at best. "The only time I ever saw snow like this was in the movies. Do you really think Sara got up here before the weather turned bad?"

"I don't know, Adam. It's been snowing for hours. There must be eight or ten inches, maybe more out there, and it's drifting badly. We've been driving for more than two hours, and I haven't the faintest clue as to where the hell we are. As far as I can see, it's a crapshoot if we've even gone fifty miles."

"We have to keep going, but I am going to call the sheriff's office. I should have called him from the apartment before we started out. If anything happens to Sara, it's going to be my fault. I should have been on top of the Sandi situation days ago. I just couldn't comprehend that someone would kill for a song. One tiny little part of me says

Sandi *could* be telling the truth. Dallas could have written the song for her just the way she said he did. Then one or the other of them broke it off. Billy died and Sara Killian came into his life. I know Dallas. He *could* have changed the name of the song and given it to Sara. Dallas did a lot of strange things. He always meant well, but sometimes situations backfired on him. Sandi wants the big score and Easy Street for the rest of her life. Sara wants the song for sentimental reasons and doesn't care about the money." He was babbling, but he didn't care.

"What about you, Adam? What do you want?"

"I just want to get to where the hell we're going. I can't stand not knowing if she's safe or not. I want whatever Dallas wanted. The only problem is I don't know what Dallas wanted. I don't think we'll ever know. I don't believe Sara is the outdoor type, Tom. Can she survive this? Sandi, on the other hand, is as fit as they come. The big question is, is she in front of us or behind us?"

Tom snorted. "Give the doctor some credit, Adam. She got out of that tub in time. Dr. Killian has a brain. So does the singer, but she's eaten up with greed. The doctor is fighting for her life, which makes me believe she's a survivor. She probably has more brains than the two of us put together. Try the sheriff again. You need to get out and clear the wipers again, too. Jesus Christ, Adam, this is fucking suicide. Is that a truck in that drift? Be careful, Adam."

"The line is busy. They probably have a hundred accidents they're working on. Even if I get through to the sheriff, do you think they'll make Sara a priority? We have no concrete facts to back up our story. What if they do try to find her, and it turns out to be a wild-goose chase? They could have been helping someone else instead of chasing down a cockamamie story." Ten minutes later he climbed back into the truck. "There's no one in the cab of the truck. The person must be on foot."

They crawled along for another ninety minutes before Adam shouted, "Look, Adam, civilization! Lots of lights means a truck stop or gas station. We need gas and coffee. Maybe you can get through to the sheriff from here. Hold on."

Adam reached for what Dallas always called the Jesus Christ strap at the top of the door. The truck skidded, spinning around in a complete circle. "I knew that was going to happen. We've been driving on ice for some time. No vehicle, and I don't care how they tout it, is good on ice. It's not just snowing now. It's sleeting."

The restaurant was almost empty. Six pairs of eyes scrutinized the two men when the door slammed shut behind them. Adam stared them down as he stomped his way to a table, shaking the snow from Nellie's fuzzy orange jacket. Tom yanked at his bright pink knitted cap and stuffed it in his pocket.

Adam flagged down a waiter. "Coffee. Can I use your phone to call the sheriff?"

"Won't do you any good. We've been listening to the scanner all evening. There's a five-car pileup on 220 and a killer accident on 58. Everyone is out there helping. If you can't go any farther, you're welcome to stay here. There's a gas station a quarter of the mile down the road." Adam nodded curtly when the waiter smirked at his oversize tangerine-colored sweater that matched the fuzzy jacket.

"Get directions while I hit the men's room," Tom said.

Adam scanned the menu. "What do you

have that we can eat on the road," he asked as he finished copying down the directions.

"We're about out of everything. How does a fried bean sandwich sound?"

"Awful. I'll take two and two large containers of coffee."

When the waiter brought their food to go and refilled their coffee cups, Adam described Sara and asked the waiter if she'd been in the restaurant earlier. "She's a doctor," he added, hoping Sara's title would jog his memory.

"She was driving a big old ugly truck," Tom volunteered.

"Yeah, she was in here. She left with Gina and Buck. They were gonna show her the way to Alpine Forest. I heard them talking."

Adam then described Sandi Sims. "Was she in here tonight?"

" 'Bout an hour and a half ago. She took a coffee and soup to go—and a Hershey bar. Seems like you're all going to the same place. Going home for Christmas, huh?"

Adam sucked in his breath at the news. His gut instinct was right. "Seems that way, doesn't it?" He tossed some bills on the table.

Adam and Tom used up fifteen minutes

clearing the ice from the front and back windshields. They both cursed, making up words as they went along. "Let's get this show on the road, Tom. Stop for gas and some deicer if they have it. We don't have that much farther to go. Be careful, Tom."

Tom inched the truck onto the main road. It took him thirty minutes to drive the quarter mile to the gas station. Twice he had to roll down his window to make sure he was still on the road. They used up more precious time going five miles an hour to the turnoff to Alpine Forest. "Where do we go from here, Adam?"

Adam pulled out the housekeeper's directions. "Three rights, four lefts, and then another right. Follow that road till you come to a stone pillar with a mailbox. There's a huge double tree next to it. It's on the right-hand side of the road."

"I hope you have x-ray eyes because I can't see a thing. I don't even know if I'm on the damn road. Merry Christmas, Adam."

"The same to you, Tom. If I didn't tell you this before, I want to tell you now. You know, just in case. I've had thousands of people in my life, acquaintances mostly, but I never had the time to make a real friend. What you've done goes beyond friendship. I just want you to know I appreciate your friendship and everything you've done for me and the dogs. According to Dallas, I was never verbal enough."

"You're an okay guy, Adam, when you let your guard down. I think your brother knew that. He probably wanted it to be like when you were kids. Big brother, little brother, that kind of thing. I'm sure he understood that life and business sometimes get in the way of good intentions."

"Jesus, I miss him. I wish I could turn the clock back. I wish I could call him up and say, 'Hey, Dallas, let's take the dogs and go fishing. We'll make our own poles and use peanut butter for bait.' I can't do that, not ever, and I want to do it so badly I hurt. I hung up his Christmas stocking, didn't I, Tom?"

"Yeah. I saw you do it."

"Too much too little too late. Hey, there's the tree. I think I see the mailbox. Stop. I want to get out to look at the tracks. Two sets, Tom. One set is almost filled in, but you can still see them. The trees serve as an umbrella, and the snow isn't as deep. Three sets total. What the hell does that mean? Three different sets at three different times. You can tell by how much snow is in the tracks. Who is the third person?"

Tom's voice was grim. "Let's find out."

Sara's heart thundered in her chest. For one brief second she thought she was going to pass out. "Dallas? You're supposed to be dead. Is this a dream?" Blind anger roared through her. "You're alive!" she screeched. "You let me and the whole world think you were dead! That's despicable! You are a son of a bitch! What are you doing here? You want the song back, right? Everyone wants that damn song. Get away from me. Do you hear me, get away from me."

"It's me, Sara. I'll explain everything later. We have to get out of here. Hold on to my arm so we don't get separated."

"Don't tell me what to do. You can't possibly have any explanation I want to hear. Do you have any idea how many tears I shed for you? How could you do that to all of us? It's Sandi Sims, isn't it?"

"Yes. Sara, I don't want the song. I'll explain later. You need to trust me. All the way, Sara. I will not let anything happen to you. We need to go faster and don't talk.

Voices carry on the wind. She's like a mountain goat, and she's dressed for this weather. We aren't. Move, move. Go as fast as you can. I know a little bit about this area. Sandi brought me up here a few times. She said the cabin belonged to an uncle. I believed her at the time."

Sara stopped and tugged on Dallas's arm. He was alive. Standing here in deep snow, talking to her. Her anger disappeared as suddenly as it had come. He was alive. "Let her see you, Dallas. If she sees you, then it's all over. You can tell the authorities the truth."

"She'll kill us both. You have to trust me. Now move and no more talking. I mean it."

"I have Nellie's truck. That relic can get us out of here."

"Sara, pay attention to me. We have to go on foot. Sandi took the distributor cap out of the truck and tossed it. I came up here in a rented Honda. The wiper blades broke off when I hit that Mexican restaurant. In case you haven't noticed, it's sleeting. Everything is freezing. For God's sake, will you just listen and follow me."

"God, Dallas, why didn't you call the police?"

"I did. They thought I was a nutcase. You have to stop talking and move, Sara. If we can make it to the community of houses, we'll be okay. It's a long way to go, but we can do it. Hold on to me and *move!* If you don't listen to me, I'm going to slug you and drag you. Goddamn it, move!"

Sara's mind whirled. How could all of this be happening? "I need to know one thing and then I'll do everything you say. Is your brother in on this scheme with Sandi?"

"No."

"Okay, let's go."

Out from under the overhang of pungent pines, the wind was sharper than her father's old straight razor. Sleet whipped her across her face, forcing her to let go of Dallas's arm so that she could try to shield her head. When she reached out for his arm, it was nowhere to be found. Did she dare call his name? No. As Dallas said, voices carried on the wind. Her eyes half-closed, arms straight out in front of her, Sara trudged forward. Six steps into the crusty frozen snow that was almost to mid-thigh, and she was exhausted. She was going to die out here in this frozen place and all because of a song. When some nameless faceless person found her, would they try to remove the ice from her eyelashes and eyebrows? Would that person try to break off the ice? Would she look like a hairless wonder when they laid her out in the mortuary? She'd never been vain. Where were these thoughts coming from now?

Don't think about how tired you are. Dallas is alive. Don't think about anything except putting one foot in front of the other. Think about a safe house in the Alpine development and how good it's going to feel when a stranger opens their door to you. Think about spring and warm breezes and how pretty the first tulips and daffodils are going to look when they bloom. When you're done thinking about the flowers think about what you felt when you saw Dallas. She wondered if her brain would freeze inside her head. She should know the answer, she was a doctor for God's sake. She was saved from exploring the possibilities in her mind when she found herself facedown on the crusty snow. She felt a warm stickiness on her cheek. Thank God her eyes were closed. If she could only go to sleep. Just for a little while. She crawled forward because she knew it was the wise thing to do. The alternative didn't bear thinking about. How long could she keep this up? Where was Dallas? More important, where was Sandi Sims? *Behind you, behind you,* her mind shrieked as she struggled to her feet. "I can't do this," she whimpered.

Wind and sleet rushed at her, driving her backward until she toppled into a snowdrift under a giant pine tree whose limbs were heavily loaded with snow. It took every ounce of energy in her body to crawl out of the snowdrift, to get on her feet. She cried then. She wanted to pray to God. She wanted to promise all kinds of things if He would just let her walk away safely from this nightmare. She'd always hated people who made promises like that because they were frightened of the unknown. Hadn't she done just that a while ago? She couldn't remember. Would God remember? One thing she did know for certain was that her eyeballs weren't frozen. Yet.

Sara struggled on. Time lost all meaning as she concentrated on putting one foot in front of the other. More often than not she was on the ground, crab-walking. At some point she must have decided that crab-walking was faster than slogging through the crusty, crunchy snow. This is unbelievable, nuts

Where was she? Was she on the road leading to the community of houses or was she just bumbling around blind? The latter, she decided. She stumbled, tried to right herself, but failed. Once again she felt the warm stickiness on her cheeks. She started to cry when she thought her teeth were frozen to her lips.

She was sitting like a fat Buddha in the snow, sleet and snow slashing at her like some evil monster. She realized at that moment she couldn't feel her feet or her hands. She also realized she wasn't thinking clearly. What part of the body was the last to give out? She must not be a very good doctor. Any doctor worth his salt would know the answer. God how stupid is all this

The sound she heard behind her forced her to her feet. Dallas or Sandi Sims? Her adrenaline pumping, Sara surged ahead, her lungs protesting each step she took. The sounds she'd heard minutes ago were louder now, someone thrashing through the icy snow. *Damn it, Sara, move. Faster.* Her heartbeat speeded up. That was strange.

Her heart should be barely beating. Fear. Fear did strange things to a person, She knew what little body heat she had left was fast leaving her body. She was so groggy, so tired and sleepy, she could barely remember what her name was. "I-am-Dr.-Sara-Killian." Over and over she repeated her name. If she were going to die out here in the snow, she wanted her name to be on her lips. *DIE! You only die when all hope is gone. You were never one to give in, Sara. You were never a quitter. So what if you didn't win medals. You persevered, and you prevailed. You have to prevail now.* She stumbled and fell again, but this time she couldn't force her numb legs to obey the command to get up. Breathing like a tired racehorse, Sara crawled forward. The sounds behind her seemed to be getting closer. It was then she heard voices. *Adam? Tom Silk? Where are you, Dallas?* She had no intention of opening her mouth, much less shouting to give away her position, but she did it anyway. "Help!"

The sounds were closer. The voices farther away. She cried out again. This time her plea was louder, more forceful. She was slipping into that state where nothing mattered. She knew she was giving up. It didn't matter anymore. Nothing mattered.

"Sara! Sara, are you all right?"

"Of course I'm not all right. I'm dying. Can't you see that? I'm a doctor, and there's nothing I can do to save myself. My eyelashes are going to break off. It takes forever to grow eyelashes. My face is all cut up. Dallas told me to hold his arm, and I lost him. I tried to do what he said. I didn't call out until now. She's out there. I heard her. She's been following me. Dallas got lost. You have to find him. Maybe she got to him first. I don't know how I lost him.' "

"It's all right, Sara. We're going to take you to the cabin as soon as we figure out where it is."

"Don't ask me. I've been out here for hours. She was in the house. I had a small head start. I have to go to sleep."

"No! Listen to me, Sara. Forget that stuff about Dallas and pay attention. Tom is going to take one of your arms and I'll take the other. We'll be dragging you most of the way. It's the best we can do. The snow is too deep for us to carry you. Do you understand what I'm saying?"

"I'm not stupid, Mr. Lord. Sandi has my

gun. It was my father's. She'll kill all of us unless Dallas stops her. She tried to kill me this afternoon. How did you know where to find me?"

"It's a long story. Sandi shot Judge Iverson. We heard it on the news. We think the judge gave Sandi the tape you gave him to safeguard. We're assuming you gave him the tape. Are we right about that?"

"I only gave him a copy. The master copy is still in my safe deposit box. You have to find Dallas." Later she would think about what Adam had just said. Much later, when she was warm and more alive.

Adam's shoulders slumped. "It's not much farther. I can see a faint light from the cabin, and I can smell the woodsmoke. You're going to be okay, Sara."

Sara sighed. "Damn it, stop humoring me. Dallas said it was all a long story, too. He's out there with Sandi Sims. I told you we got separated. She has a gun. He doesn't have any kind of weapon, and he isn't dressed warmly enough. Damn it, don't you care?"

"Of course I care. Right now my first priority is to get you to the cabin. We're going to let Sandi come to us."

The cabin door opened and Sara felt herself propelled forward. The blast of intense heat from the fireplace slammed into her. She would have fallen if Tom hadn't grabbed her. She was alive and safe. For the moment. God hadn't forsaken her. She was glad now that she hadn't made any bargains with the Supreme Being. She turned around to find both men staring at her. She knew exactly what they were thinking and she couldn't blame them.

"I have to get out of these clothes. Parts of them are frozen to my body. I'd appreciate it if you'd put some more logs on the fire." Adam nodded.

Her body tingling from head to toe, Sara shed her wet clothes in the dark bedroom. She discovered a supply of winter clothing in one of the dresser drawers. An oversize woolly robe hung on the back of the bathroom door.

Still tingling all over, Sara marched out to the main room of the cabin wearing the judge's thermal underwear, battery-operated socks, and the thick robe. She sat down on the hearth, her hands outstretched to the fire. "We're sitting ducks in here."

"I know," Adam said. "As much as you

want to sit by the fire, you're going to have to move across the room." Sara obeyed. The storm outside continued to rage. "How long can she stay out there?"

"I don't know. I guess it depends on how prepared she was. I would imagine the cold will be getting to her by now. At some point she's got to seek some kind of relief. For all we know she might have gone to her car to warm up. The drive from the road to the cabin isn't all that far. God only knows where she parked. The only vehicle Tom and I saw was yours. We left our truck on the road. With trees on both sides she can't pass our truck. Of course I have no idea where the road we came in on leads. However, she might know. It's entirely possible she heard us when we found you. If she was smart, she would have split right then. Are you feeling better now?"

"Do you mean am I more with it? Dallas is out there. He's alive, Adam. I touched him. I talked to him. He's been following me for days. You said yourself you felt like someone was watching you. It was Dallas. Why won't you believe me? We didn't talk much because there was no time, and voices carry on the wind. He said he tried calling the police to tell them what was going on, but they thought he was a nutcase."

"Look, Sara, I know you believe you saw Dallas, but Dallas is dead. No matter how much you or I want to believe, and Jesus, I want to believe, you cannot bring someone back from the dead. I understand what you've been through and if thinking you saw Dallas kept you alive out there, then I'm all for it."

"Goddamn it, don't patronize me, Adam. Dallas is alive. I don't know who died in that crash, but it wasn't Dallas. I am not hallucinating. I have my wits about me. The person who took my hand and talked to me was a flesh-and-blood person. After the initial shock, I felt safe. He's been watching over all of us. Over you, too, Adam. It isn't his fault he was always one step behind Sandi. You didn't catch on to her either. You can apologize to me later when he shows up."

Sara crouched in the corner, her legs drawn up to her chin. She fingered her eyelashes and eyebrows. They seemed to be intact. She felt like crying all over again.

Adam and Tom leaned against the wall, then Adam slid to his haunches. The gun was steady in Adam's hand. He wondered if he had the guts to shoot a woman.

Tom's voice was a harsh whisper. "She could be anywhere, Adam. She could shoot through any one of those windows. She'll never try for the door. I don't think we have a snowball's chance in hell of getting out of this. She can't let us live. You know that. She knows we know what she did. Sara was her target in the beginning, but it's a new ball game now. And she doesn't know the judge is still alive."

"We don't know that for a fact, Tom. At some point she had to go back to her car to get warm. If nothing else, she'd check the weather station. This is just a guess on my part, but I think if she knew the judge was alive, she'd give it up and get the hell out of here. She thinks she has the original of the song. What she thinks she's doing is tying up loose ends. Kill Sara, kill the judge, and no one knows she was the one pulling the trigger. We suspected, but we didn't know for certain. We still can't prove a thing. Police go by facts and hard evidence. We have squat."

"So we just sit here and wait?"

"We just sit here and wait."

"I'd like something hot to drink," Sara said.

"This isn't a hotel, Doctor. We can't risk showing ourselves by crossing the room."

"You're right. It was a stupid thing to say," Sara said.

"Almost as stupid as saying Adam's brother is alive," Tom Silk muttered under his breath.

"I heard that," Sara challenged. A devil perched itself on her shoulder. "May I take this time to tell you both how lovely you look?" She focused on Adam. "Burnt orange or are they calling it tangerine this year? You should wear it more often. The color brings out the amber in your eyes." To Tom she said, "I had you down for a navy blue guy. Pale pink? With matching mittens?"

"That's enough," Adam said harshly. "This is no time for such nonsense. We had to use what was at hand. I left a check in the kitchen for your friend, listing the items we took. It's too quiet. We've been here about twenty-five minutes. If Sandi is going to make a move, it should be soon."

Tom slid to the floor, his legs stretched out in front of him. "My guess would be a fire. There's only one door to this place. She'll pop us as we run out. She can't let any of us live. She thinks she killed once, so what do three more killings matter?"

"Four. Dallas is out there."

Adam rubbed at his throbbing temples. "Why in the hell would someone build a cabin like this and only put in one door? There must be a building code of some kind."

"There's a window in the kitchen," Tom volunteered. "She can't watch the front and the back at the same time. I say we douse the fire and let the house grow dark. Let's make her fight for our bodies."

"Are you saying it's better to freeze to death than be shot?" Sara demanded.

"If you have another opinion, I'd like to hear it," Tom said.

"Watch my lips. My opinion is Dallas will come through for us. We have to sit and wait it out."

"Is it Christmas," Adam asked of no one in particular.

"If it was Christmas Eve a few hours ago, then it must be Christmas. A time of miracles. We could sure use one about now."

"Dallas is our miracle. I can't understand why you won't believe me." Sara sighed as she watched the dancing shadows on the walls. "I need to warn you, Adam, this is a different Dallas. Be prepared."

"Okay."

"You're humoring me again."

"People simply do not rise from the dead. I really don't want to talk about my brother. Let his soul rest in peace."

"He's not dead, Adam."

"He's dead. Now let's drop it."

"Would you care to make a wager?"

"What kind of wager?" Adam's voice sounded suspicious.

"You told me you promised Dallas Six to Dallas. If I'm right, I get the pup. I'll leave the explanations up to you. In my opinion, there's nothing worse than breaking a promise."

Adam stared at Sara in the dim light. Was it possible? Could Dallas really be alive? His head started to pound. Miracles happened to other people, not people like him and Dallas. It was Christmas. Christmas for as long as he could remember was a time of miracles. Make the bet or not? What if by some chance she was right. "I can't part with any of the dogs, especially Dallas Six."

"That's what I thought." Sara huddled

deeper into the woolly robe. "He's out there. Waiting and watching."

"Don't you think it's about time for him to make a move?" Tom asked.

"When the time is right. It's starting to get cold in here. I told you, he's not the old Dallas who does things on whims. Don't ask me how I know this. I just do."

"Did you hear that?" Adam whispered. He was on his feet in the blink of an eye.

"Yeah." A second later Tom was on his feet.

Sara huddled deeper into the corner.

Chapter Nineteen

He stalked her, carefully stepping into the tracks she had made. If she heard him, she gave no sign. He was careful to stay far enough behind her so that she didn't have the advantage over him. It was amazing that he could see her at all in the swirling snow. She stopped as though she were listening to something. He stopped, too, straining to hear whatever she thought she was hearing. The wind howled and shrieked as the icy snow buffeted upward in giant swirls. He thought for a second that he'd lost her when the snow obliterated her form, then he relaxed, knowing all he had to do was follow her steps in the snow. She was moving again, this time more purposefully. He waited a moment, and then called out to her. He cupped his hands around his mouth to be sure the sound carried ahead of him. "Sandi, it's me, Dallas. Wait up." She must have heard him because she stopped again. He remained where he was, statue still. He called out again. "I can't let you hurt Sara, Sandi. Give it up and go back now before something happens to one of us."

"Shut the hell up, Adam. Don't think you can scare me. I have a gun so be warned. The song is mine. Dallas wrote it for me."

"I wrote it for Sara. Who are they going to believe, you or me? I'll drag you through every court in the land. You can't get away from me, Sandi."

"Come and get me you stupid jerk."

"I warned you, Sandi. I gave you a chance. It's over now."

"It's over when I say it's over and not before."

The silence in the room was shattered by an eerie shriek, so high-pitched in intensity that Sara clapped her hands over her ears.

"What the hell was that?" Tom shouted.

"It sounded like a wild animal," Adam said.

A moment later the door to the cabin was kicked open. Sara struggled to her feet, gasping at the sight of Dallas with Sandi

Sims slung over his shoulder. Relief left her so faint she had to clutch at the door for support.

"Are you okay, Sara?"

"I'm fine, Dallas. You must be frozen. I'll get you some dry clothes." She was aware of Adam's stunned surprise and Tom Silk's gaping mouth. *So much for my hallucinations,* she thought.

"I'm okay, but can we build up the fire? I need something to tie up Sandi."

Adam stood in a trance, his eyes never leaving his brother's face.

Tom staggered out to the kitchen to hand over two red plaid dish towels. They all watched as Dallas pushed Sandi onto one of the kitchen chairs. He tied her hands behind her back, interlacing the towels with the spokes on the back of the chair. The singer's booted foot swung up and out. Dallas danced away as the chair toppled over. "Stay that way. This floor is cold, and it's going to get colder."

Obscenities filled the cabin as hatred spewed from Sandi's eyes.

"Adam, Jesus, it's good to see you. You must be Tom." Dallas snapped his fingers in front of Adam's face. "Did you hang up my stocking?"

Adam's voice was a croak of disbelief. "Dallas. Dallas, is it really you? Talk about your Christmas miracle. Yeah, yeah, I hung it up. I filled it, too. How . . . what . . . ?"

"I don't think I've ever known you to be at a loss for words, Adam. It's kind of nice. I hate to think what would have happened to the three of you if I hadn't shown up."

"I was thinking the same thing. Come here, little brother."

Tears filled Sara's eyes as she watched the two brothers hug each other. How sad that it took a tragedy to bring two people back together. When she was old and gray, she could talk about the time she personally witnessed a Christmas miracle.

Tom nudged Sara to move closer to the kitchen area where Sandi Sims sprawled in the upended chair. Sandi continued to curse, her voice venomous and vitriolic. Sara stared down at her. What would Carly do or say at this particular moment? Whatever Carly would do or say didn't matter anymore. What mattered was what Sara Killian thought or said. "I hope the authorities fry that jiggly ass of yours."

Tom said, "Hear, hear!"

"Judge Iverson is still alive. They operated on him earlier. You screwed up, Sandi. Attempted murder not once but twice is going to get you some real downtime. You'll be fifty or sixty when you get out of jail. Think about all that greasy food and starch you'll be forced to eat. Your face will be one big zit. No designer duds in the big house. No makeup. No hairstylists. You'll learn to love Lava soap, bedbugs, and coarse sheets. Those acrylic nails will be the first thing to go. Degenerates and lowlife scum will be your best friends when they aren't stabbing you in the back."

Sandi Sims stared at Sara with clinical interest. "It will never happen."

A chill ran up Sara's spine. The singer sounded so sure, so positive. "I'll make sure it happens. If necessary, I'll dedicate my life to that end."

"What will you use for evidence?" Sandi's voice was nonchalant as though she were discussing the possibility of rain.

"Let me worry about the evidence. I don't even know why I'm bothering to talk to you."

"I don't know either," Sandi snapped.

Tom poked Sara and jerked his head in the direction across the room where Adam and Dallas were huddled, talking quietly and intensely. "For two bright, brilliant people, it's amazing how they screwed up their lives. It looks to me like things are back on track. Adam told me the thing he wanted the most was to call up Dallas and ask him to go fishing the way they did when they were kids. Homemade fishing poles with peanut butter for bait. They'll probably take all seven dogs with them."

Sara smiled. "I bet they ask you to go along."

"Do you think so?" The frown lines between Tom's eyes disappeared.

"Yes, I do. I think you're going to be a good friend to both Dallas and Adam. I wonder what they're talking about."

"I think they're talking about everything they always wanted to say but never did. Everything they thought about over the years. They have a lifetime of words to make up for. The actions will come later. I wish I knew if it really were Christmas or not."

"I don't know, Tom. I've felt like I've been

in a time warp for days now. It seems to me it is. The only thing missing is Santa coming down the chimney."

"Give me a break!" Sandi Sims growled from her position on the floor.

"I wouldn't give you the time of day if you were in a dark room," Tom shot back.

"Neither would I," Sara said smartly. "I have to get Dallas some dry clothes. Keep your eye on our . . . Christmas guest."

Sara returned with a pile of clothing. "The bathroom is to the right. You need to get out of those clothes quickly, Dallas."

Sara sat down on the hearth, the heat from the fire toasting her back. "It's wonderful, isn't it? Your own Christmas miracle. I hope the two of you don't screw it up this time around. It's rare that anyone gets a second chance at anything. Do you have any idea of just how lucky you are?"

"Yes, Sara, I do," Adam said.

"Did he tell you how . . . what . . . ? Where has he been?"

"He said he would tell us everything when he was dry and warm. It must be a long story. You were right. He's not the same person anymore. I can't put my finger on what it is exactly."

"I think I know."

"You know?"

"I said I *think* I know. Dallas has always considered himself . . . for want of a better word, retarded. He is not retarded, he is dyslexic. I tested him one evening. I wish . . . I wish you could have been there to see the joy, the relief in his face. I swear to God, he changed right in front of my eyes. All of a sudden he seemed taller, his shoulders went back, then straightened up. That vague look in his eyes was gone. Don't say anything to him about what I just said. I'm sure he'll tell you himself at some point in time."

"Dyslexia? Jesus, and we all thought . . ."

"I know. You didn't have to voice what you thought. He knew what all of you were thinking. Can you imagine carrying that around with you all your life?"

"My God!" Adam's shoulders slumped. "I don't know what to do."

"That's good. That you don't know what to do I mean. Dallas knows. It's his turn now. My advice, for whatever it's worth, is to go with the flow. Don't look back. The past is gone. You can't change anything. Tomorrow isn't here yet. You have today to start a new life. All the sweet tomorrows are yet to come for both of you. Now that's a song title if I ever heard one."

Dallas crossed the room to sit down next to Adam, his gaze speculative.

Adam clapped his brother on the back. "Sara and I were just talking about how wonderful this all is. I like the word 'miracle.' Now, tell us what happened. Don't leave anything out."

"There really isn't all that much to tell. I flew to Vegas on a chartered flight. It was just me and the pilot. At the last minute his brother came on board. Don, the pilot, asked me if I minded if Bruce hitched a ride with us. I said no. I slept the whole way. I woke up when the plane broke up and hit the ground. I know it's unbelievable, but it's what happened. The main body of plane exploded into a ball of fire. I couldn't get close enough to check. Trust me when I tell you there was no way anyone could have survived that explosion. You could feel the heat a mile away. I didn't know what to do so I walked away in a daze. I just walked and walked. It was all I could do to remember my name. It was like that time I fell out of the tree. I walked for miles and miles. Then I fell asleep by some trees and bushes. I woke up with some guy standing over me. He smelled, and he had a straggly beard. I thought I was dead, and he was God. He had this beat-up old truck and he took me to a road stop with a motel in the desert. I hung out for a couple of days to come to terms with things.

"I had a wad of cash on me. You know me, I was going to hit the tables when I got to Vegas. I rented an apartment and a car. I didn't have any concrete plans at that moment. I bought some clothes, got a haircut, took out the earring and pawned it. I went to the pound and got myself a dog and bought him a pricey collar. I was set to begin a new life. I think I thought I could start over somewhere and just be an ordinary person. It was great walking down the street just looking in windows, stopping for a hot dog and not having people screaming and mauling me. I'm on a program at the university.

"For a while everything was mixed up. I finally realized I couldn't start a new life until the old one was ended. I thought I could just fade away and start over some place. My money was dwindling. I went up to the house to take some out of the safe. Your dogs knew I was there. The big one let me pet her. Guess she smelled my dog on me. Adam, do you know how good that sounds? Me saying, my dog. My landlady is watching him for me. I stuck around and listened to what was going on. That's when I started following Sara. I was always one step behind. I almost had Sandi when she came out of your garage, but she got away from me. I went to her old apartment, but she doesn't live there anymore. It got to the point where I didn't know who the hell I should be following. I decided to stick with Sara. The rain, the highway, the cops fouled me up so I didn't get to that nurse's apartment till after Sara bolted.

"I pulled over to the side of the road and tried to figure out where Sara would go to be safe. I knew she'd go to see Judge Iverson. Once, a long time ago, Sandi referred to her political friend Ronnie. Iverson's name is Ronald. Sara had told me the judge was a friend of her father's, so I put two and two together. I thought the old guy was playing both ends against the middle. I was right. It was stupid, dumb luck that I hit it and came up here. I didn't know if I was behind Sara or behind Sandi. I know now that I was behind Sandi. I saw her lift the hood of that old truck and toss something in the snow. I'm assuming it was the distributor cap. I was stumbling around in the snow, debating if I should let Sara know I was there, when I saw a figure move inside the house. I couldn't tell who it was. Then I saw Sara outside with the flashlight so I knew that it had to be Sandi in the house. I tried to lead Sara away, but she let go of my hand and I lost her. I turned back to go after Sandi. But she'd left the house. The three of us were stumbling around in blind circles.

"I don't know how much later I heard you two, and then I heard Sara call out. I knew the three of you would be okay, so I concentrated on Sandi and I stalked her. Just the way we used to stalk Billy Sweet when we were playing in the woods. I remembered all that stuff you taught me, Adam. Then I threw in a little scary stuff and started to call out to her. I spooked her. She panicked and I got a hammerlock on her. Here she is. God, I'm hungry. Is it Christmas? If it is, I have to make a phone call."

Adam laughed. "None of us seem to know. This is your show, kid. By the way, do you have a new name?"

Dallas grinned. "Yeah, Jack Piper." This

last was said in a hoarse whisper so it
wouldn't carry to the kitchen area. "I haven't
told you the best news, Adam. Are you
ready?"

Adam smiled at the joy in his brother's
face. He felt his whole body swell with love
for this person he was just starting to know.
"I'm ready."

"I got us a mom and dad. A real set of
parents. They look like parents, too. Maggie
wears an apron and she puts on powder and
curls her hair. She smells like food all the
time. She hugs you till you squeal. Her eyes
twinkle, and she can cook like an angel. She
used to be a schoolteacher. She runs a motel in the desert. Our pap now is something
else. His name is Moses and he's the one
who found me in the desert. He sneaks cigarettes from Maggie. He used to own a junkyard, but he lives in a trailer now. They
offered to give me money, Adam. They figured out who I was from seeing all the plane
coverage on CNN. I told them we'd call on
Christmas. They want you to be their kid,
too." Dallas's voice turned shy and uneasy.
"They're my Christmas present to you,
Adam."

"Parents? Are you kidding me?"

"I wouldn't kid about something so important, Adam. They look better than those pictures in Millie's old catalogues."

"Parents?" was all Adam could think of to say. "A mother and a father?"

"Yeah. They like to fuss over you. It feels real good. They care about everything. Neither one had any kids. What do you think?"

"I think we should invite them for Christmas is what I think. We can send a plane for them. Will they come?"

"You bet they'll come. Whip out that cell phone of yours and start making calls. You need to think about presents, too. What do you give a mom and dad, Adam?"

"I don't know, Dallas. We never had this problem before. Something special." Both men homed in on Tom Silk who was listening to the conversation, his eyes wide in wonderment.

"A cruise would be nice for the four of you. I always got my dad a tie and a book for my mom."

"A cruise sounds good," Dallas said.

"Then let's do it."

"Okay. Do you like my present, Adam," Dallas asked shyly.

"Kid, it's the best. The best. Parents, huh?"

"Yep."

Adam laughed. Dallas clapped him on the back as he, too, burst into laughter.

Thirty minutes later, all the details taken care of, Adam said, "Okay, Jack. I assume you plan on staying dead for the time being. What do you suggest we do?"

"Are you asking my opinion, Adam?"

"Yes, Jack, I am."

Dallas grinned. "I think the three of you should take Miz Sims to the nearest police station. Let Sara sign her complaint. Then I say we charter a plane and head for that house of yours in South Carolina so we can wait for our mom and dad. I'd like that, Adam."

"Me too, Jack. We could go fishing if you want. I know where there's a great river. The catfish are as long as your arm. If we catch any, we throw them back. Is that understood?"

Dallas threw back his head and laughed. "Understood. Listen, Jack Piper is going to need some money and some credit cards. Will you take care of it, Adam?"

"For you, Jack, anything. The big question

now is, how are we going to get out of here?"

"Try that cell phone of yours. I have to pick up my dog. My landlady is probably sick of him by now. He howls when I'm gone too long."

Adam punched out numbers. "What'd you name him?"

Dallas guffawed again. "Adam One."

"Turn about is fair play." He called the sheriff's office. "It'll be a couple of hours before they can get to us," he said when he broke the connection. "I think we can all live with that."

"I can't go with you, Adam. I'm going out to see if I can find the distributor cap to Sara's truck. I'll meet you at the Mexican restaurant."

"You'll never find it, Dallas. Take your own truck. It's gassed and ready to go. If the storm lets up, you'll be able to drive. We bought some deicer. It's on the front seat. The heater works fine. We'll make arrangements to have Sara's truck towed to LA when the weather clears. We'll have someone from the sheriff's office drive us to the restaurant, then we'll head for the canyon to pick up my dogs and then you can pick up yours and we'll be on our way to South Carolina. I have a tree and everything. It might be dead by now but I have a tree and a mantel. Just like the pictures we used to look at in the catalogues. The picture will be complete now with a set of parents. You're invited, Sara."

"Thanks but no thanks. I will take a ride to the airport, though. Do you think I can get a flight to Vegas? I'd like to spend what's left of Christmas with my sister and Nellie." *Don't look at Dallas. Be cool. Tomorrow is another day. Just be happy for him and his brother. They both deserve this time. Be happy for them. Happy, happy, happy. You don't matter, Sara. Accept it. Let them be happy.*

"We'll charter you a plane. Our new parents can take the same flight back to Charleston. Is that okay with you, Jack?"

"Absolutely."

"Then I accept your offer," Sara said. Damn, he didn't sound like he cared one way or the other what she did.

"Sara, I'm sorry about Benton Memorial. I'd like the chance to make it up to you," Dallas said.

"That's not necessary . . . Jack. I more or less decided to head East and see how I like the Big Apple. But first I'm going back home. I'm going to rent a house and walk around and then do absolutely nothing for as long as I feel like it. I'm going to look up all my old friends, especially Barbara McDermott De Mera. I need to find out exactly who Sara Killian is once and for all. Maybe she can tell me. I need to do what you did, Dallas." There, she'd told him exactly what and where she'd be. The next move was up to him.

"Will we ever see you again?" There was a catch in Adam's voice that did not go unnoticed by Dallas.

Sara shrugged because she didn't trust herself to speak.

"So who is buried, or cremated, in your . . . you know?" Tom asked.

"Don's brother. They didn't have any family. Don took care of Bruce the way Adam took care of me. They were orphans, too. I sent money anonymously to pay for the funerals from my wad of cash. When things are back to normal, I'll initiate a search for any distant cousins or relatives and do the right thing. Call the hospital, Adam, and see what the judge's condition is. Find out if it's Christmas."

"He's stable. His family is with him. Today is Christmas Eve. We were two days ahead of ourselves. I wonder how that happened."

"I guess it was meant to be this way."

"Yeah, guess so," Adam said.

"I'm going to get dressed," Sara said.

"It's cold out there so bundle up," Dallas said.

"Yeah, it's real cold out there," Adam said.

"Freezing cold," Tom volunteered.

Tears burned Sara's eyes as she shed the warm woolly robe. The tears dripped down her cheeks as she pulled on a gray wool sweater and heavy corduroy trousers. It was over. She could give Dallas back his song and move on to her new life, whatever that new life would turn out to be. She choked back a sob. What was wrong with her? The aftermath of shock. She sat down on the bed, her shoulders shaking. She had her life back. Dallas Lord was alive and well. The brothers were united and would lead long, happy lives. "What about me?" she whimpered. "Merry Christmas, Sara Killian."

*   *   *

Sara stood on the tarmac staring at the private jet that would fly her to Las Vegas. She had to turn around and say good-bye to the three men behind her. Childishly she crossed her fingers that she wouldn't cry and make a fool of herself. Good-byes were never easy for anyone. She turned then, her eyes shining with tears. "Merry Christmas!" A second later she bounded up the steps. In the doorway she turned again, and shouted, "I'll send the tape back when I get home."

Sara buckled her seat belt. Moments later the private jet taxied down the runway. She was airborne within minutes. She howled her misery to the empty cabin. She was still crying when the jet set down on the runway, her eyes red and puffy. Inside the terminal, she stepped into Nellie and Carly's waiting arms. She cried harder, her whole body shaking with the force of her sobs. "Merry Christmas," she blubbered.

Tom tried to make his voice sound cheerful. "You guys are like a couple of sad sacks," he said. "Would you mind telling me why that is? Dallas is back among the living.

We're all here safe and sound. The judge is improving. Sandi's in the lockup, and you two guys are going home to spend Christmas together with a new set of parents."

"We're tired," Adam said.

"Exhausted," Dallas said.

"Bullshit!" Tom Silk said.

"What the hell is that supposed to mean?" Adam demanded.

"Whatever you want it to mean," Tom said smoothly as he herded the dogs up the steps to the jet that would take them all to Charleston.

"You should have gone after her, Dallas."

"I was going to say the same thing to you, Adam."

"I asked her to dinner. Just once. Just dinner, Dallas."

"I don't have a problem with that. Sara's her own person. I screwed up with that business at Benton. I don't know what ever possessed me to do something like that."

"We all make mistakes. Recognizing those wrongs and correcting them is what it's all about. Are you in love with Sara?"

Dallas evaded the question to pose one of his own. "I saw you looking at her back in the cabin. Are you in love with her?"

"She was someone I thought I'd like to get to know better, but to answer your question, no, I am not in love with her. However, if you tell me you have no interest in the doctor, then I would like to take her to dinner at some point in time." His voice was sly-sounding, but Dallas missed the tone because he was busy looking around the cabin of the plane.

"I don't think it matters one way or the other. Sara has her life mapped out. She has things to do and places to go. Those things and places don't include me or you either for that matter, Adam."

"I can tell you how to get to that small town in Pennsylvania where she's going. The one she grew up in. You fly into Pittsburgh and drive the rest of the way. That's if you're interested."

Dallas's voice turned testy. "I don't recall saying I was interested. You, on the other hand, said you would like to take her to dinner. At some point in time. You could just as easily take that same plane you mentioned and rent your own damn car. That's if you're interested."

"Hey, hey, it's Christmas Eve. This is no time for fighting over a woman who obviously isn't interested in either one of you," Tom said.

Dallas slumped down into his seat. Adam did the same thing. Tom Silk smirked to himself.

"Adam?"

"Yeah."

"I'm not retarded. Not even mildly. I'm not slow either. You know, slow-witted."

"I know that, Dallas."

"Then why didn't you tell me so. Why did you let me believe I was."

"Dallas, look at me. I did tell you. You refused to believe me. How in the name of God could you be retarded and do what you do . . . did? When you got an idea into your head, I couldn't shake it loose. No one could. You have to take responsibility for that yourself."

"Billy . . ."

"Dallas, sometimes Billy was an asshole. Yeah, we knew him from the time we were kids, and he was our friend, but that doesn't make what he did right. I tried to tell you about that, too, but you didn't want to listen to me because you thought I was jealous of your friendship. Each of us, in our own way, was swimming upstream. All of that is behind us now. It's in the past, and we can't unring the bell. From this day forward we're starting over, and we're on a wide-open road. I'm up for anything that helps us along that road."

"Me too, Adam. How long do you think I can get by being Jack Piper?"

"As long as you want." Adam burst out laughing at the look on his brother's face. Dallas leaned across the seat. "I know you didn't expect me to say that. God, Dallas, I'm so glad you're alive."

"Did you collect on my insurance? Merry Christmas, Adam."

"Yeah. I'm going to have to work on that one. This is going to be the best Christmas we ever had. The best."

Tom Silk shivered at the shadows in both men's eyes. He shivered again when he watched the brothers stare at the speck in the sky—a plane like the one that had taken Sara Killian out of their lives.

Chapter Twenty

Adam poured ice tea from the frosty pitcher. Dallas shifted his papers and books to the side of the table before he accepted his glass.

"You seem restless, Dallas. Is anything wrong?"

"I feel like a criminal even though you paid back the insurance company and the tour insurance. I don't even want to know how you managed that. It was nice of you to take half the hit. I appreciate it. I don't owe anybody anything, monetarily. My life is more or less on track. Tomorrow is the Fourth of July. Summer is here. I don't think there are any more fish in Lake Moultrie for either of us to catch. Where do we . . . I go from here, Adam?"

"Where do you want to go, Dallas? The roads outside this walled garden lead everywhere. The choice is yours. If you want to go back to being Dallas Lord again, I can work out something the media and your fans will buy. It has to be what you want, Dallas. This is just my opinion, but I don't think you like being Jack Piper, ordinary citizen. Is it Sandi's trial that is looming on the horizon or is it seeing Sara at the trial that's bothering you?"

"Let's face it, Adam, Sandi has been telling everyone I'm alive from the moment they arrested her. If I take back my identity now, it will make you, Tom, and Sara liars before the whole world. No one is sure if the judge will come through or not. His family took him off somewhere, and no one even knows where he is. If he's a no-show, that leaves the three of you. I can't do that to you. I've been thinking about asking you to call a news conference so I can admit to the whole thing. A lie is a lie, Adam. There was probably a time when that wouldn't have bothered me. It bothers me now, though. I could go on *60 Minutes* or *20/20* and tell it like it is. This has nothing to do with the Canyon River Band, the money, performing, or any of that. I was born Dallas Lord and I want to die as Dallas Lord. I want to be Dallas Lord for whatever happens in between, too. I'm not in a big hurry, but I am thinking about it. What do you think, Adam?"

"I think I'm very proud of you, little brother. Whatever you decide, I'm with you. Is anything else bothering you?"

"That's pretty much it."

"Dallas, the tape Sara sent back to you is still on the foyer table. Are you *ever* going to open it?" Dallas shrugged. "I know where she is. You could call her."

"Why?"

"If I have to tell you why, there is no point to this discussion."

"I thought you . . ."

"Dallas, Dr. Sara Killian is a fine person. I asked her out to dinner. I ask a lot of people out to dinner. The two of us put her through a ton of misery. I'll grant you she's tough, but she's fragile, too. She looked so . . . sad when she got on that plane. I know she was crying. Tom saw it, too. For some reason I don't think she was crying because that sorry ordeal was over. I think it had something to do with you. I'm the first to admit I know nothing about women. This is just a guess on my part, but I think you know even less."

Dallas snorted. The pencil in his hand snapped in two. Adam's eyebrows shot upward. "How would you like some spaghetti for supper? I make really good spaghetti."

"Fine." Making spaghetti meant the discussion was over. "Do you mind if I invite a friend?"

"Great. Male or female?"

"Does it matter?"

"Of course it matters. Spaghetti sauce splatters. Women don't like their clothes peppered with little red dots. They dress accordingly."

"I didn't know that. Female. Alice Mitchell. She teaches at the College of Charleston."

Dallas's sigh could be heard clear across the room. Adam smiled to himself.

"Hey, guys, take a look at this," Tom Silk said breathlessly. "Second page, top right. Sandi Sims skipped out on her bail. She's on the run."

Adam threw the paper down in disgust. Dallas rolled his eyes. "I'm surprised she waited this long. They'll never catch her. Guess there isn't going to be a trial."

"Somebody should call Sara and tell her," Adam said.

"Somebody should," Dallas said nonchalantly. "Do you want basil and cilantro or just basil in the sauce?"

"Surprise me," Adam said.

"Surprises are good," Dallas said, and chuckled.

Sara reached for the cup of tea at her elbow. She looked around. The screened porch was spartan, with only a small plastic table and a folding aluminum lawn chair. It looked as temporary as it felt.

It was hard to believe it was the end of July. Thirty more days until Sandi Sims's trial. The upcoming trial had been hanging over her head like a giant black cloud. Sandi's lawyer was saying it was all circumstantial. She shrugged off the black thoughts as she stared through the screen into the flower-bordered backyard. The days had been warm and sunny, the nights cool and uneventful. Somehow she'd managed to while away seven months by doing nothing. She'd read all the latest books, planted a few tomato plants whose leaves were yellow and whose tomatoes only as big as green peas. She'd taken long walks, watched the soap operas, talk shows, and game shows until she couldn't stand it any longer. The thirteen-inch television set that came with the rental house hadn't been turned on in weeks.

"Sara?"

"Carly. What time is it?"

"Time for us to be heading out of this burg. Tell me again that you aren't angry with Hank and me for getting married."

"I'm not angry. I wish you had told me though. I didn't get to give you something blue or a wedding gift."

"Just make sure you give us a smashing gift on our first anniversary. I don't like it here, Sara. There is nothing to do and no place to go. All you do is watch those shitty tomato plants that are dying on the vine. You do know that you aren't going to get any tomatoes, don't you?"

"Of course I know that. Three more days, and I'll be out of here myself. It really is true. You can't go home again."

"You got yourself a plum job in New York. You should be very proud of yourself. Two hospitals fighting over you isn't shabby. Is it really what you want, Sara?"

"For now."

"That sounds so . . . I don't know, temporary."

"I only signed the contract for a year. Where's Hank?"

"Putting our stuff in the car. What are you going to do today?"

"Take a long walk. I might go all the way to St. Boniface. Then maybe I'll go up the hill behind our old house. I like to sit at the top and look down at the town."

Carly dropped to her knees. "The answers you're looking for aren't in this town, Sara. They're all locked up inside of you. You have the key. All you have to do is open the lock. By the way, have you heard from Dallas or Adam?"

"No, and I didn't expect to hear from them. Besides, Carly, this little town is at the end of the earth. They could never find me here in the Allegheny Mountains. Dallas and Adam are getting on with their lives just the way I am. Nellie calls every couple of days. She's working at the vet's office, and she loves it. She told me Adam donated the money for the new wings at Benton. I'm glad about that."

"I hate to leave you, Sara. You look positively miserable."

"That's your imagination. I'll grant you I

am not dewy-eyed the way you are, but I am very contented." *LIAR.*

"We'll write, Sara. Promise you will, too. A telephone call will be nice, too, once you get located. I'll let you know as soon as we get a nibble on the house. We are doing the right thing, aren't we? When and if we sell, we can pack it up together. I left all the utilities except the phone turned on."

Sara sighed. "If you want to change your mind, it's okay with me. You and Hank can live in it."

"If we sell it, that means we're homeless. You'll be living in some apartment in New York just waiting to get mugged and Hank and I will be in some shitty apartment somewhere trying to save money to build our own house. You can't put roots down in an apartment. The Killian girls will be homeless and rootless."

Sara sighed again. "I hear Hank calling you. That man does get impatient."

"Oh, but I can change that in a heartbeat." Carly's voice was trilling. Sara found herself wincing at her sister's blatant sexual innuendo.

"I'm coming, I'm coming," Carly called.

"Listen, Sara, do you know what I would do if I were you? I'd call the Lord brothers to say hello. You know, before you move on to New York. You'll see them at the trial, but maybe you need to, you know, break the ice a little."

"You aren't me and thanks but no thanks. Those two men are not part of my life. When are you going to understand that? My God, they didn't even send a note to thank me for returning the song."

"The same time you understand it. Men aren't letter writers the way women are. I repeat, you look miserable. Give yourself a break. Do something you always wanted to do. Do it for yourself, Sara. Throw caution to the winds and go all out. It's such a wonderful feeling. If I had to liken it to something, I'd say the feeling is akin to flying." As she pranced out of the way, Carly offered her parting shot. "In the years to come, I'd hate to have to refer to you as my old maid sister."

Old maid sister.

"Come on, Sara, walk me to the car. Whose house did you say this was?"

"Dr. Peters, the dentist. Mom used to take us to him when we lived here. I went to school with Jim Peters. We used to call him Putts. Do you remember him?"

"Vaguely."

"He's a sports writer in Buffalo, New York. One of the neighbors told me that. Nobody remembered me, Carly."

"You said it yourself, Sara, you can't go home again. There are no answers here."

"I know that now. Have a safe trip. I'll write as soon as I get settled. I'll send mail to the house, so you'll have to pick it up. Bye, Hank, drive carefully."

Sara stood on the sidewalk and watched the car until it turned off Spangler Street and headed down toward the main street. Her eyes felt hot and gritty.

Homeless and rootless. Old maid sister. Shoulders slumping, Sara headed back into the house and the back porch, where she finished her cold coffee. The tomatoes hadn't grown at all, and there was a new yellow leaf on the biggest plant. So what, she thought. So what.

"Hank, pull over. I have to go into the drugstore. It might take me a while to find what I want, so here are some Jujubes to keep you busy. Study the map so you don't get us lost. Don't blow the horn for me to hurry up either. This is a sedate little town, and people don't do things like that."

Inside the drugstore, Carly looked around for a phone booth. She asked the pharmacist to give her five dollars' worth of change. She dialed the long-distance information operator, jotting down the number after the operator repeated it twice. Again she asked for the operator and placed a person-to-person call to either Adam Lord or Jack Piper. Adam answered.

"This is Carly Killian, Adam. Is it okay to call you Adam? Is . . . Jack there with you? He is. Good, put him on an extension. Is that you, Jack? Listen up. I'm in this little town in Pennsylvania called Hastings. Population around eleven hundred or so. I'm on my way back to California, but I thought I'd give you a call before I hit the interstate. My sister is miserable. She's leaving in three days for New York, where she has this wonderful opportunity to aid humanity and save lives and all that good stuff, but her heart isn't in it, and when your heart isn't in something, it doesn't work. She found out the hard way that you can't go home again. Whichever one of you two guys is in love with her better get on the stick before it's too late. If I'm wrong and neither one of you loves Sara, then I apologize for taking up your time. I've always heard silence is golden. Okay, I don't have anything else to say. You two guys have a good day, you hear?"

Carly dusted her hands dramatically. "This is the last time I'll interfere in your life, Sara. You're on your own now." To the pharmacist she said, "I'll take two bags of Skittles and one bag of Gummi Bears."

In the car Carly kicked off her shoes as she opened her bag of Skittles.

"You called them didn't you?"

"Yep."

"What did they say?"

"Nothing. Nada. Zip. I left them speechless. Want some Skittles? They don't stick in your teeth like the Gummi Bears."

"Which one is your money on?"

"That I don't know. I should know that, Hank. Why don't I?"

Hank looked across the seat at his brand-new wife. Which one do you think Sara is pining for?"

"Dallas. Jack or whatever name he's going by. Then again, maybe it's Adam. She was excited at the dinner date they had planned. She even bought a new dress. I want to go home, Hank. I think we should think about having a baby real soon."

"How soon?"

"We could start tonight. If it's a girl, I want to call her Sara. Is that okay with you?"

"Which part? The tonight part or the name part?"

"Both."

"I'm okay with it. Are you sure, Carly?"

"Yes. I want my own family. Yours and mine. I want us to live in a small town, one that's a little bigger than this one. I want a real community, so we can get involved in everything our kids do. I want to belong to something and someone. I think Sara is finally coming around to the same kind of thinking. We have to stop eating all this junk, too. We need to set good examples."

"You are something else, Carly."

"Sara's going to be fine. I feel it. We can get on with our lives now. We'll just finish this batch of candy and won't buy any more. Do you want some more Skittles or Gummi Bears?"

"How about a Whopper, fries, and two Cokes?"

"Ah."

* * *

Sara slid her legs over the side of the bed. The Queen Mother of all headaches hammered inside her skull. It must have been the bottle of wine she drank last night while she watched mindless television shows. She frowned. She couldn't remember going to bed, much less what time she went up the steps. She also couldn't remember the game plan she had for today.

The plan came to her as she stood under the shower. How could she have forgotten? She was going to tidy up the Peters's house and leave for New York. In her brand-new Jaguar, thanks to the insurance company. It would take her an hour to pack her three bags, empty out the refrigerator, drop off the key with the rental agent, and be on her way to her new life.

Sara started to cry. She wasn't sure if it was because of the hangover headache, Carly's marriage, or the fact that neither Lord brother had bothered to call her to thank her for sending back the master copy of "Sara's Song" six months ago. Courtesy alone demanded some kind of acknowledgment. Surely they knew Carly would have forwarded the note or letter. *Don't make ex-*

cuses for them, Sara, she admonished herself. *Anything that came before today is yesterday's news and no longer important.*

Sara blew her drippy nose and gulped down four aspirins. Hours later, when she piled the last suitcase in the trunk, her headache was still fighting a war inside her head. She headed for town to pick up her mail and return the key to the rental office. Everything in the box was addressed to Occupant or Resident except a letter bearing the name Ronald Iverson. It had been forwarded by the Los Angeles post office. Not Judge Ronald Iverson, but Ronald Iverson, as in private citizen. What did that mean?

The engine idling, Sara read the short note in the parking lot. Apologies, apologies. Sandi Sims had skipped bail and couldn't be found. The trial was postponed indefinitely. The bottom line brought a grimace to Sara's face. There is no fool like an old fool. Sara crumpled up the letter and tossed it over her shoulder.

Sara fished in the black bag for her copy of "Sara's Song." She popped it into the state-of-the-art player. She listened to it all the way down Route 36 and then she continued to listen as she cruised on 220. By the time she reached Interstate 80, she knew the words by heart. She popped it out and listened to Roy Orbison all the way to New York.

So what if she was three days early. It would give her time to sightsee and do some shopping. She could cry in New York City just as well as she could cry in Hastings, Pennsylvania.

Chapter Twenty-One

He was dressed casually in creased khakis and a white dress shirt with the sleeves rolled to the elbows. He was tanned, clean-shaven with a fresh haircut. When he removed the aviator glasses inside the post office, customers turned to look at him. One young girl gasped and squealed. "Did anyone ever tell you you look like Dallas Lord?"

Dallas smiled. "All the time."

"Excuse me, can you tell me where Dr. Killian lives? I understand she's been staying here for some time."

"She was, but she left several days ago. She didn't leave a forwarding address if that's your next question."

"Do you have any idea where she might have gone?"

"You could ask the Realtor. The office is across the street next to the drugstore."

Dallas thanked her, all eyes still on him as

he exited the post office. He stopped a moment at the car to give his dog a biscuit. "I'll be right back." The dog woofed softly before he settled himself more comfortably on the passenger side of the car to gnaw at his biscuit.

Twenty minutes later, Dallas was back inside the car. He picked up the cell phone to call his brother. "I missed her by a couple of days, Adam. The way I see it I have two choices. I can go to New York and try to find her. Or, I can do what we talked about before I left."

"It's your call, Dallas."

"Then let's do it!"

"Dallas, are you sure? I mean are you *really* sure?"

"Call the guys. Set it up with them for right after Thanksgiving. We'll go public in December. We'll use the studio in the canyon house since it hasn't been sold. Are you okay with this, Adam?"

"I'm real good with it. For whatever my opinion is worth, I think you're doing the right thing."

"Okay, set it up. I'm on my way."

"Dallas, she would be real easy to find in

New York. A few calls to the different hospitals. I don't think it would take you more than a few hours to track her down."

"I think this way is best. I don't blame her one bit for being pissed off. If I were in her place, I would be, too. So would you. One of us should have called her."

"What's that *we* stuff, Dallas? You're the one who is in love with her."

"I'm not sure how she feels. She sent the song back. If it meant anything to her, she would have kept it. I'm worse than you when it comes to relationships. How's it going with Alice?"

"Good. She loves dogs. Not necessarily, Dallas. Sara is an honest person. You're alive, and she was giving you back your property. You told me yourself you didn't say one word to her about getting married. You were going to get married. That was your plan, wasn't it?"

"Back then it was. This is a different time and a different place. Jesus, Adam, I came back from the dead. That's pretty hard to deal with. As for Alice, you're halfway there. I'll see you in a few days—maybe a little longer. I'm going to sightsee some on my way. It will give me time to do some thinking. Did any of my reports come back? How did I do on the tests?"

"You aced them all. I can't tell you how proud of you I am. Drive carefully, Dallas. Enjoy the trip."

"Okay."

Ninety minutes later, Dallas pulled his car to the side of the road. If he took the eastbound entrance to I-80 it would take him to New York. If he took it west and then south, he would be heading back to Charleston in a roundabout kind of way. "Look at it this way, Adam One. I don't think Sara is the kind of woman who could live with someone named Jack Piper. By the same token, I don't know if she can live with someone named Dallas Lord either. I screwed up with that Heinrick guy. We made that one right, but there's all this other stuff to deal with. First I was dead, then I wasn't dead. That's enough to screw anyone up. So what if I saved her life? Maybe she doesn't know about that old Chinese saying." When there was no response from the dog, Dallas headed toward the entrance that would take him west and then south.

Jack Piper a.k.a. Dallas Lord had a performance to prepare for. The most important performance of his life.

Sara leaned over the patient's bed. She hated the sight of the tubes and the terminal sound of the respirator. But more than anything she hated the hopeless look in the children's eyes as they stood at the foot of their father's hospital bed. Grown children like herself. She thought she knew what they were thinking. Just yesterday she'd heard the oldest son say, "They can put a man on the moon, but they can't save Pop because his insurance ran out. What the hell kind of hospital is this anyway? What kind of people tell you to think about pulling the plug to save money? What are we going to do without him? Now if we had a barrel of money, you know they would have done something. Oh, no, we're just working stiffs getting by with our limited medical insurance. Pop is only sixty-one years old. That's too young to die."

And it was too young to die. The son was right. If the family had had better health insurance, more would have been done for the man. The thought made her physically ill. She wanted to say something to his children, but it was obvious they didn't want even to be around her. She belonged to the hospital, and as such they lumped her with all the other callous doctors they'd been forced to deal with. She made a note on the chart at the foot of the bed.

In the hall she leaned up against the wall as she squeezed her eyes shut before she headed for the lounge and her coat. She needed to think. The three doctors in the room looked up from their respective newspapers. "We need the bed, Killian. When in the goddamn hell are they going to give the okay to pull the plug?"

Sara ignored the young doctor as she filled her coffee cup. When she didn't rise to his challenge he got up to stand next to her, his face just inches away.

"He could hang on for another two weeks. Maybe a month. His insurance ran out. We need the bed, but they can't put him out because that loudmouth son of his threatened to go to the newspapers and the evening news. The media loves minority stories. You're their doctor. Get them to agree. He's brain-dead, for Christ's sake."

Sara moved to the far end of the room.

Out of the corner of her eye she noticed the other two doctors staring at her, uncomfortable looks on their faces. They gave up all pretense of reading their papers.

"Dr. Killian, I'm allowing for the fact that you're relatively new around here. This is how we do things. I have a kidney transplant patient coming in, and there's no fucking bed. A paying patient. Let the old man go already. They've been saying those rosaries for a month. The damn beads should be worn-out by now. You can hear them wailing all the way down the hall. It gives me and everyone else in this hospital the creeps. Get it through your head, you aren't doing him a favor by keeping him alive."

"I know all about your transplant patient. He's the one with all that bright green money we've been hearing about. The one who *paid* for the kidney donor. You listen to me now. I didn't spend half my life going to school to end up taking a life or telling a patient's family their father's life isn't worth anything. The man will die when he's ready to die, and I don't want to hear a word about his bill. For your information, it's been paid in full." Sara was about to say "by me," but clamped her lips shut. "That man in room

812 has worked all his life to take care of his family. His family is doing the only thing they can do, be there for him. Now that Mr. Ortega is at the end of his life he deserves whatever we can do for him. Don't even think about asking me again to talk to his family about disconnecting anything. If the Ortega family decides to go public, I will stand alongside them. I'm going to tell them everything I know about your kidney patient and those two . . . pretend doctors sitting behind you. All of you make me sick. You make me ashamed of being a doctor. Do you know what else? I'm ashamed of this hospital. I took an oath as you three did. To do no harm. I've done that. I will continue to do that. Now, get the hell out of my way."

"Dr. Killian, wait."

Sara turned to see the elder Ortega son. "Please, can I talk to you."

"Of course. Is something wrong?"

"My father's bill has been paid. There's even a cash credit. Do you know anything about it, Dr. Killian?"

"Does it matter?"

"Yes. Doctor, it matters. My family does not take charity. My father taught us to work for everything we have."

"Did someone tell you it was charity? Couldn't it be a gift?"

"People do not give thousands of dollars to families like mine. That much I do know. You paid it, didn't you, Dr. Killian?"

"Yes. Please, I want you to understand something. Your father is my patient, and I want him to live as much as you do."

"We are being selfish. We aren't ready to let him go."

"The quality of his life is gone, Mr. Ortega. Machines are keeping him alive. I do understand your feelings."

"If you remove the respirator, how long will he live?"

"Hours. A day. Possibly a little longer. I don't know, Mr. Ortega. Talk to your sister and brother and ask them and yourself, would your father want this? Then and only then, make your decision."

"What would you do, Doctor."

"I truly don't know. I tend to think I would ask for everything to be disconnected. It's no way to live, and it's no way to die. That's only my opinion. Your father deserves to die with dignity. Is there anything else I can help you with, Mr. Ortega?"

"On behalf of my family, we want to thank

you. Someday we will repay you. I don't know when or how, but it will happen."

Sara nodded. "I'm going to check on our father, then I'm going to lunch. I'll be back within the hour."

It was cold out. Freezing actually. Sara didn't think she'd ever get used to the weather here in the East. It was only the first week in December, but the weatherman said it would snow before the day was over, which meant she would have to take a taxi home or fight the rush-hour travelers on the hateful subway.

Sara walked toward the subway, her body shrinking into her heavy wool coat. She realized she hated the most famous city in the world. She hated the tall buildings, the hustle and bustle as people pulled and shoved, but most of all she hated the subway system. She hated the high rent she was forced to pay and the exorbitant fee to garage the car she was afraid to drive here in the city. She even hated the old crumbling hospital that was in need of a major overhaul. She hated the politics of the hospital, and, yes, she hated some of her colleagues. It was the same old garbage, just a different can. True she was making more money, but it was going out so fast she barely had a chance to count it. Maybe if there was a Nellie Pulaski somewhere in the vicinity, she might be able to tolerate this new life she'd made for herself.

She hated it all with a passion. She ground her teeth together in anger.

"Coming here was the biggest mistake of my life," she muttered into the wool scarf that covered her mouth. She was frozen, and she still had two blocks to go. She wanted to cry so badly she bit down on her lower lip. The salty taste of her own blood brought her up short. "So, make it right, Sara. Okay, I will!" She turned around in the middle of the street as people cursed and shoved her. For the first time in her life she gave a bearded man the finger and shoved back. My God, she was turning into a New Yorker!

Sara stopped in a deli, gobbled a quick lunch, and returned to the hospital. The time was ten minutes to two. At three-thirty, just as she was going off duty, she heard her name over the intercom. She ran, knowing the page was for Manuel Ortega's room, but she was too late. She stared at the flat line running across the monitor.

"He never wanted to be a burden," the oldest son said.

"The angels called him. I heard them," the sister said as she crossed herself.

"Papa opened his eyes and saw us. He knew we were here," the youngest son said.

Sara choked back her own tears. "Is there anything I can do for you?"

"No, Doctor."

Sara watched as a nurse disconnected the tubes and respirator, then pulled the sheet up to cover Mr. Ortega's face. She felt drained as she walked down the hall behind the Ortega family. The only thing left for her to do was to sign Manuel Ortega's death certificate. She said a prayer of thanks that the family had been spared the trauma of making a decision she knew they could never accept.

Just another day in a big New York City hospital.

Sara hailed a cab, climbed in to settle into the steamy warmth of the car. The driver, who said he was from Nigeria, asked her to repeat her address four times. "What are you doing driving a cab if you can't speak the language and can't read the signs?" Sara asked irritably.

The driver pulled to the curb and said, very plainly, "Get out!"

"What?"

"Get out my cab."

"I will not!"

"Then I dump you out!"

"Try it!" Sara shot back. "Now take me to the address I gave you, and you better hope you got it right."

Mercifully, the ride was short. Sara was careful to give the man only a 10 percent tip, which he sneered at. "Stupid female."

"Arrogant bastard," Sara retaliated.

Inside her apartment, her body shaking with frustration, Sara shed her three layers of clothing. The phone was in her hand in a second. She called the hospital and said she wouldn't be in tomorrow. She broke the connection before she was asked for an excuse.

"I hate this apartment. I absolutely detest hearing the elevator going up and down all night long. I can't sleep. I hate the dirty streets and the filthy grocery stores. I hate what I do. I hate it that other people forced me into a profession I can no longer tolerate. I hate me. Me. I hate who I am."

Sara sat down in the middle of the floor

and cried. "That's why nothing ever worked for me. That's why I couldn't commit to anyone. Especially Dallas. I saw in him the same problems I refused to acknowledge in myself. I denied everything my whole life. "No more!"

She was a whirlwind then, throwing her clothing into large green garbage bags that she dragged to the front door. Her pictures and framed diplomas went into a box any old way. So what if the glass broke. "Ask me if I care," she muttered.

Satisfied that all her belongings were in the bags, Sara picked up the phone to call the management company that leased her the apartment. "I'm vacating the apartment in ten minutes. The rent is paid until January first. I'll give you the address where you can return my security deposit. Make all the inspections you want. I won't be here. I'll leave the key on the kitchen table. This is not negotiable. So sue me. The lease was for six months, not a year. I had the option to renew in January. I'm choosing not to renew."

Her next call was to the hospital administrator. "I'm sorry, Mr. Darwin. This is the way it is. I understand everything you're saying. Yes, I'm breaking my contract. No, I will not reconsider. I've decided that medicine is not my forte. My career is no longer important to me. Actually, Mr. Darwin, I don't like your hospital. I don't like the way your people slough off the patients and make light of accidents. I don't like the high rate of malpractice suits that are filed against your staff. What? Then sue me, but you'll have to get in line."

Sara's clenched fist shot in the air. "My God, I did it! I finally did it! I burned all my bridges! I really can't go back." Carly was right. Sara felt like she could flap her arms and take wing. Carly had also said to soar with the eagles one had to be free. Sara had one more call to make before she called the telephone company to disconnect her phone. The phone in Charleston, South Carolina, rang twenty times with no answer. She frowned when the answering machine didn't turn on. She tried the number a second time with the same results. The story of her life. Too much, too little, too late. The frown between her brows disappeared when she realized she could take the scenic route and stop in Charleston. She was no longer on someone else's time clock. She was now a bona fide free spirit. Sara Killian, free spirit. She liked the way it sounded. She liked it a lot.

Two days later, Sara arrived in Charleston. She parked her Jaguar in a lot and set out on foot after she asked for directions to the Battery. The temperature was cool— probably, she surmised, somewhere in the low fifties—with the wind blowing off the water the way it was. It certainly beat the intense cold in New York. As tired as she was, her step was brisk and determined as she looked at the house numbers. Adam Lord's number was on the high gate to a walled-off courtyard. A bell on a long chain hung to the side. She gave it a hard yank. The sound carried far and wide. She rang it three more times with no response. Did she dare open the gate? Of course she dared. She was a free spirit. Free spirits could do whatever they pleased, whenever they pleased. She pressed down on the black iron handle, but the gate didn't move. Using her foot and her shoulder, she shoved the door. It opened slightly, giving off just enough room for her to get through. The heavy-duty springs attached to the top and the bottom forced it shut immediately. She stared in awe at the giant oak tree in the middle of the cobbled courtyard and the pruned camellia bushes laden with luscious blooms that were so heavy the branches almost touched the ground. Emerald green moss grew between the cobblestones. Instinctively she knew she wasn't supposed to walk on it. From somewhere she heard a trickle of water. A fountain or a fish pond? A fountain with a cherub holding another cherub nestled between thick fronds of fern the same shade as the moss at her feet. Two lonely-looking empty dog dishes sat next to the door that led into the kitchen. Benches with colorful cushions that matched the colors of the camellias beckoned. In the corner of one of them she saw a pack of cigarettes, lighter stuck in the cellophane wrapper. She sat down and helped herself to one of the cigarettes. A yellow ceramic ashtray in the shape of a frog was at her feet. She counted seven brown filters.

This, Sara decided, must be the most perfect garden spot in the world. Beyond the gates was the world, but that world was held at bay by the huge gates on their fortified hinges. She noticed the heavy iron chain dangling from a hook on the inside of the gate. Attached to the gate was the biggest padlock she'd ever seen in her life. Obviously when Adam was home with the dogs the gate was padlocked.

She hated to leave, but she needed a hotel room and sleep. Tomorrow was another day. Should she leave a note? What would a free spirit do? This must be one of those if you feel like it, do it, if you don't feel like it, don't do it questions. She felt like it. The only thing she had to write on was one of her New York checks. She voided out the front and wrote "I stopped by to say hello. Hope you and Jack are well. Regards to all the four-legged creatures." She signed it Sara Killian. The note went under the yellow frog ashtray which she placed on the wrought-iron table.

Three days later, Sara was back in her house in Los Angeles. She had one bad moment when she saw the large For Sale sign on the front lawn and the lockbox on her door handle.

Sara dragged her garbage bags upstairs and tossed them into the spare room. She adjusted the thermostat for warmth, then headed for the shower. Wrapped in a tired old flannel robe from the back of the closet, she rummaged for her New York cell phone, aware that even though she was calling locally, she would be charged as if the call were made in New York. She didn't care. Free spirits didn't care about such things.

"Nellie? It's Sara. I'm home. I mean I'm here at the house. I quit my job. I broke my contract and my lease. Everyone is going to sue me. What do you think of that?"

"Are you all right, Sara?"

"Never better. I'm a free spirit since a few days ago. I drove all the way from New York. I even stopped in Charleston to see Adam and you know who, but they were gone. I left a note. Free spirits do things like that." Then she burst into tears.

"Hang up, Sara. I'll be there in twenty minutes. Just stay put. Did you hear me, Sara?"

"Okay, Nellie. Can you bring some food?"

"Is Chinese okay?"

Sara sniffed. "Chinese is good."

"Then it's thirty minutes. Sit tight."

Sara used up the time making coffee and setting the table. Thank God Carly hadn't gotten carried away and packed up the household items. The fact that the power and water were still on made her wonder if

Carly had a sixth sense that she would return.

As good as her word, Nellie appeared at the front door in a little over thirty minutes. Sara fell into her arms. She started to wail again. "What's wrong with me, Nellie? Do you think I'm having a nervous breakdown?"

"I don't think any such thing. I think you're in love and are too damn stupid to acknowledge the fact. Now, let me take off my coat. By the way, how do you like this outfit? It's one of many your very kind friend paid for. I do miss that old orange sweater, though. He left me so much money I got my apartment painted, bought a new carpet and some new toys for my cat and dog. I still have money left. How'd he look in that sweater?"

Sara smiled, remembering her startled reaction when Adam peeled off the burnt orange jacket. "Really shitful." Nellie burst out laughing.

Nellie ladled out the food while Sara poured coffee. "You really need to broaden your palate, Sara. Chow mein is so blah. There hasn't been a thing in the papers lately about the judge, the trial, or that singer that jumped bail. I read the paper from cover to cover as you know. My job is unexciting but very rewarding in case you're interested. I hope Carly is happy. Just how long is an extended honeymoon?"

"I guess until their money runs out. They're somewhere in Illinois now, working to replenish their funds. She's happy, so that's all that matters."

"I suppose so. It must be wonderful to be young. I can't seem to remember life ever being wonderful. All I can remember is hard work, struggling to make ends meet, and more hard work. Maybe I'm just a cranky, jaded old woman."

"I don't think any such thing. You are a wonderful, warm, caring human being whom I love dearly. I don't know what I would have done without you, Nellie. I missed you so much while I was in New York. You know what, I knew it wasn't going to work when I accepted the job. I must have been out of my mind."

"You really quit?"

"Yep. Told them what I thought. Broke my lease, too. I sent the song back in January, Nellie. They didn't even bother to thank me. God, I can't do anything right. Were my expectations too high? Am I stupid? Do I swear some invisible sign that says I don't matter. Damn it, I do matter. I have feelings. I hurt and bleed just like everyone else."

"Is that a fact?" Nellie bit into an egg roll. "Look at me, Sara, and listen. In all the years I've known you, I've never seen any real emotion in you except when Carly had her accident. You're robotic. You do everything by the book. If I knew where that damn book was that you go by, I'd rip it to shreds. It's like someone programmed you. You keep everything locked inside you. Let's take Dallas Lord and talk about him. You liked him. I saw something in your eyes when you mentioned his name. However, he wasn't from that staid, straitlaced world of yours. He was a rock star. People would talk. People would point their finger at you if you were seen with him. You couldn't risk damaging that precious reputation of yours. You've never taken a chance or a gamble on anything in your life. You've let your life slip by. I know it eats at you that you aren't married with a family. It's your own fault, Sara. I can say this because I'm your friend and I care about you." She took a deep breath and went on.

"You're one of the best doctors I've ever seen and believe me, I've seen plenty. You're good at what you do, but you lack compassion and heart. You're afraid to get involved with a patient. The Ortega family was a first for you. You have never, Sara, for as long as I've known you, treated the whole patient. You treat the ailment. You would have to get involved if you treated the whole patient, and you couldn't risk that. Tell me I'm wrong, Sara. Tell me to mind my own business."

"You aren't wrong, and I would never tell you to mind your own business. When you're right, you're right. I never wanted to be a doctor. That's what my father wanted. I think my mother wanted it, too, but she wasn't as verbal as my father. I had to work twice as hard as everyone else to compensate for not being born a boy. I did everything he wanted. I literally gave that man my life. I didn't want to disappoint him. I worked my ass off. I gave up everything to do something I . . . I don't hate it, I just don't like it. Medicine is not for me. I need someone to explain to me how I can be good at something I don't even like. I'm just like Dallas, and I didn't want to be like him. I understood him, but I closed my eyes to my own failings. What the hell kind of person does that make me, Nellie?"

"It makes you a human being. Just think, you could have gone through the rest of your life being a robot and not knowing what life is all about. Somebody must think you deserve a second chance because that's what you have now. How you handle it is up to you."

"I bet my father is spinning in his grave right now."

"Stop playing with that chow mein and eat it. We both know it is impossible to spin in one's grave. In case we missed something, too damn bad. Let him spin. That man almost ruined your life. Just who the hell are you in love with, Dallas or the brother? The Sara I know is not a serendipity kind of person, so it's obvious to me you need some kind of plan, some kind of direction. Since Carly isn't here I'm electing myself."

"Plans never work out. Carly said we were homeless, rootless and that I was an old maid. She said that, Nellie, back in July. It's so true it's scary."

"If I were your fairy godmother and I appeared and said I'd give you three wishes, what would they be? What do you want more than anything in this world? Close your eyes and pretend you're talking to Carly. This has been so long in coming it's making me crazy. If you aren't going to eat that chow mein, push it over here. Contrary to belief, I can do two things at once. In this case, I can eat and listen. Let it rip, Sara."

Sara's voice was little more than a whisper when she started to talk. As she became comfortable with her thoughts and feelings, her voice grew stronger. "I want it all. I want everything I missed, everything I gave up. I want to be a kid for a little while. I want to know what it feels like to be a teenager without sixty pounds of books on my back. I want to dance and flirt. I want pretty clothes that swish and fuss about my knees and ankles. I want to wear perfume that makes people turn around to see who is wearing it. I want to fall in love and have that person fall in love with me. I want us to do all the things I never got to do. I want him to care if I don't feel well. I want him to make a mess in the kitchen when I'm sick in bed and he has to make me food. I want to do the same thing for him. A dog and a cat to make us a family. I want us to fight and kiss and make up. I want all of that. I want to be loved, so I can love back. I want someone to call my own. I want to be able to say, 'This is my husband.' I want his face to be the last thing I see when I close my eyes at night and the first thing I see when I open my eyes in the morning. I want to hear him tell me my cooking is wonderful or that it stinks. I want to see what I feel for him reflected in his eyes because he feels the same thing. Then and only then I want to get a space that is truly my own, maybe a garage or the basement, and I want to make pottery. I want to create and design something that says Sara Killian made this. I don't care if it's good or bad. I'll get better and improve with practice in time, but if I don't, that's okay, too." Sara stopped long enough to take a deep breath.

"You're doing real good, Sara. Listen to this, my fortune cookie says I am going to come into a windfall. Yours says—are you ready?" Sara nodded. "Yours says, 'In order to soar with the eagles, you have to be free.' "

Sara laughed. "You made that up, Nellie. What does it really say?"

"It says, 'A wise man never counts his change.' I have no idea what that means. It sounds pretty stupid if you ask me. I always count my change."

Sara smiled. "I do, too. So, are you going to grant my three wishes?'

"I don't have to grant them. Don't you know anything, Sara? Fairy godmothers only grant the impossible. Everything you mentioned is something you can do yourself. In fact, you are the only one who can do them. When you want something you have to go after it. If you don't, you get left at the gate. Now, what's our game plan?"

"I don't have one."

"Get one."

"Nellie, it isn't that easy. No one knows Dallas is alive but us. I don't even know where he is. The answering machine doesn't come on in Charleston. They're away. They could be anywhere."

"Criminals always return to the scene of the crime. Carly told me that."

"They aren't criminals, Nellie. What crime are you talking about?"

"Dallas's secret identity. No one would ever look for him at his own house. You told me it was for sale, and I saw it listed for five million dollars. Not too many people buy that kind of house. I bet he's holed up there. The brother, too, and all those dogs. It's the perfect place if you stop to think about it. We could drive up there. Or, you could drive up there just so you know, see if there are any lights on. Then you can come home and stew and fret while you think up a plan that won't be too obvious."

"Let's do it! I'll get dressed. How's the truck running?"

"Like a top."

Sara laughed all the way to her bedroom. She returned to the kitchen, grabbed her jacket, and they were off.

An hour later, Sara said, "I feel like a sneak. Carly used to do this when she was in high school. She'd make me drive past some boy's house sometimes eight or nine times just hoping he'd be outside. Do you feel like a sneak, Nellie?"

"Not at all. Are we just going to sit here by the gate with the lights off, or are we going to get out and walk around?"

"I can see lights. Someone is here unless the lights are on timers. If we go any farther, the dogs will start to bark. We didn't come up here to go in, Nellie."

"That's right. We just came up here to spy."

"Right. I'm going to call the house and see if anyone answers. That will tell us everything we need to know. I'll dial the number and you ask for some fictitious person. They don't know your voice. Just say it's a wrong number."

Nellie rolled her eyes but did as instructed. "A man answered, and I could hear other men in the background. I didn't hear the dogs, though. My goodness, you are twitchy tonight. You do love him, don't you? I need a name, Sara."

Sara took a deep breath. "I'm in love with Dallas Lord."

Nellie clapped her hands. "That wasn't so hard, was it?"

"No. The hard part is what if he isn't in love with me? He said he wasn't. I said I wasn't either, but I was lying to myself. I almost had myself convinced I didn't love him. Do you think he was doing the same thing?"

Nellie didn't know what she thought. "I'm sure of it."

"You are so full of it, Nellie, but thanks for saying that. God, I feel giddy."

"Then we better get you home before you do something that isn't in your game plan."

"Tomorrow is another day. I have a lot of tomorrows on my horizon, Nellie."

"Yes, you do, Sara."

"Let's go home, Nellie. I love this truck and you're right, it does run like a top. What would you say, Nellie, if I told you I wanted to get out of this truck right now and dance down this canyon road?"

"I'd say do it. I'll pick you up at the bottom."

"I'm going to do it. I am doing it. I really am. First I'm Mata Hari, then I'm Ginger Rogers, and God alone knows what I'll be when I get home."

"Try a woman in love," Nellie called over her shoulder.

"A woman in love is good," Sara shot back.

Adam watched his brother through the kitchen window, his heart swelling with pride. The change in Dallas was so overwhelming he was having a hard time dealing with what he now called the new Dallas. His brother was assertive, opinionated and he was no longer shy and withdrawn. If anything, he was in his face from morning to night, saying over and over, "I feel like I've been reborn." The rocker clothes and stringy hair were gone. The earring and the heavy gold chain he used to wear constantly had never been replaced. He wore Brooks Brothers loafers with tassels, creased trousers, and crisply ironed shirts. On any given day he could have passed for a relaxed Wall Street broker. The dog he'd rescued from the pound was healthy and fit and was always at his side. What Adam was seeing was a wonderful picture, something he never thought he'd see in his lifetime. If Dallas could just get his act together where Sara Killian was concerned, the picture would be complete.

Adam leafed through the mail. Release forms for Dallas to sign. In just a few days Dallas would rise from the dead and go in front of the cameras on prime time to tell his story. At the end of the live interview, the program would go to the prerecorded segment of the Canyon River Band playing "Sara's Song." It was going to be Dallas's swan song before he announced his retirement.

"How's it going, Dallas?" Adam asked, the screen door banging behind him.

"Not bad. Did anything important come in the mail?"

"Just the release forms and the water bill. You have to sign them now, so I can FedEx them back to the station. You're sure you're okay with this?"

"Adam, I can't live a lie. That's not who I am or what I'm about these days. I can make a life for myself doing whatever I want to do. I'm not saying I'll never record or write music again. I burned out three years ago. I don't know how or why I kept on going. Sometimes it's just time to hang it all up. This is my time. Hell, I might even go to college one of these days." He scrawled his signature in six different places. Adam scooped up the papers and slid them into the return envelope.

"I'm going to take these to town. I want to make sure they get out today. Can I get you anything while I'm there?"

"No. I made up my mind about something, Adam. After the broadcast, if I don't hear from Sara, I'm going to my ranch in Montana. I'm going to put down some roots and go on from there. I know where I want to go now, and I think I know how to get there. You found your niche in Charleston. Mine is in Big Sky country. Lots of space, fresh air, and peace. I want to hear the silence and the birds in the morning. Half my hearing is gone, so I need to hear these things now. The doctor called with the results of my physical. Aside from my hearing loss, which I knew about, I'm in good shape. I did have to get glasses, both for distance and up close. What do you think?" he asked, sliding on the wire-rimmed glasses. "They're bifocals," he said proudly.

Adam laughed. "You look more like a professor than a professor does. They make you look . . . bookish."

"I like that word. Bookish, huh?"

"Uh-huh. Dallas, about Sara. Have you tried to locate her? I told you before, she won't be hard to find."

"That's what you think. She quit her job at that New York hospital. She walked out on her lease at her apartment. I hired a private dick. She didn't leave a forwarding address."

"Jesus, Dallas, go to the sister or that old nurse. They'll know where she is."

"I can't find the sister. I left a message this morning on the nurse's answering machine. She hasn't called back."

"This came in the mail today. My cleaning lady sent it on with some other unimportant stuff. Sara made the first move, Dallas. It's your turn now." Adam watched as his brother's face turned white. He also noticed the way his hand trembled when he held the voided check. "Well, what are you going to do?"

"Why didn't you give it to me right away, Adam?"

"I don't know. I think I had this cockamamie idea that I could go out and find her and drag her back here. Then I realized that I was doing what I always did where you're concerned. I don't want to make any more mistakes."

"It's okay. I understand. I need to think about this a little. Hey, if you're in town pick up my suit, okay?"

"Suit?"

"Yeah, you know, suit. White shirt, tie, the whole works. Threads. Here's the ticket." Dallas rummaged among the papers on the kitchen table. "It's paid for."

"You're wearing a suit for the interview?"

"And my glasses and my new hearing aid."

Adam clapped his brother on the back. "Way to go, Dallas."

"Bookish, huh?"

"Yeah."

Adam could hear his brother laughing all the way to the garage. The sound felt so good and so right.

Sara dressed for the occasion; lunch with Nellie. This was her first real outing, as Nellie called it, since returning to Los Angeles two days ago. "Sara Killian, you look positively . . . *flirty.*" She wondered if there was such a word. Well, there is now. A giggle escaped through her lips. The sound pleased her. So did the skinny minidress. High-necked, long-sleeved, and *short.* The smoky panty hose made her legs look sexy, as did the shoes that were nothing more than a few straps glued to a sole and a thin heel. A white bolero jacket and envelope purse completed her outfit. Today the voluminous black bag was being left behind because it was empty. She might even throw it away at some point. Her shoulders felt physically and mentally lighter.

Sara gave her reflection one last glance. Earlier she'd gotten her hair cut and highlighted. She'd spent a whole hour on her makeup and had agonized for fifteen minutes over which perfume to spritz on herself for her first foray into the outside world she'd shut out for so long.

Nellie smiled her approval when Sara entered the restaurant. "I like your metamorphosis. I think it calls for a large carafe of wine that we will consume in its entirety. Is that okay with you?"

"Absolutely."

"Every man in this restaurant is looking at you."

Sara smiled. "I know."

Nellie laughed as she opened her menu. "I think we should order something absolutely decadent to go with the wine."

"You choose, Nellie, but not too decadent. It took me a whole year to lose fifteen pounds, and I don't want to put it back on. One pound, and this dress is history."

"How about a crabmeat salad?"

"That sounds good. Oh, God, Nellie, there's Adam Lord. My heart is beating so fast I can't breathe. What if he comes over here?"

"That's the guy who wore my sweater. You're right, orange isn't his color. So what if he comes over. Don't you want to know about Dallas?"

"Of course I want to know, but I don't want him to know I want to know. Look where they put him. He's going to be looking straight at me all during lunch. I don't think he recognizes me."

Nellie's voice was dry and droll when she said, "*I* didn't recognize you."

"He's staring at me. I don't think he knows it's me. God, I feel giddy. What should I do?" she asked out of the corner of her mouth.

"Smile. Wave. You know, do that thing with one finger. Invite him over. I should thank him for that very generous check."

Sara took a deep breath. She lifted her index finger and wiggled it. She managed to work at a sickly smile at the same time. He mouthed her name. Sara nodded. He was off his seat and standing at their table before she could blink.

In a jittery-sounding voice, Sara introduced him to Nellie, who invited him to join them for lunch. He accepted. Nellie kicked her ankle under the table.

"It's been a long time. Almost a year. How are you?"

"Good. I'm here on business. I'll be leaving on Monday."

"How is, ah . . . how is Jack?"

"Jack's good. Real good. Fit. He's taking life real serious these days. He keeps busy. Fit. Did I say that? He exercises a lot. You know, to keep fit."

"Is he here in LA?"

"Here in LA? Well, yes, as a matter of fact he is. Business. There's always business to take care of. How about you? My cleaning lady forwarded your note. I'm sorry we missed you."

"I was . . . ah . . . passing through. Actually, it was out of my way, but I had all the time in the world. I just thought . . . it would be nice. You did get the song, didn't you?"

"Yes. It was nice of you to return it. Did you go back to that little town?"

"Yes. I stayed for seven months. I could never live there again. You can't go home again."

"I've heard that. Did you go to New York?"

"That didn't work either. I'm here now."

"At loose ends?"

"Yes and no. I have . . . plans."

"I see. Will you be here long? If you are, why don't you come up to the house. I'm sure Jack would like to see you. He would really love to see you. He's ah . . . making changes in his life. What that means is he's going public. You might want to tune in on Tuesday evening. Eight o'clock."

"That's very interesting. What made him decide to do it?"

Adam closed the menu. "Look, this is all bullshit."

"Well, good for you, Mr. Lord," Nellie piped up. "I was just going to say the same thing. Let's cut to the chase here. My friend has been waiting for your brother to make a move in her direction. As you can see, this is not the same old Sara Killian we all used to know. Now, why is your brother dragging his feet? It's obvious to me the two of them could use some help."

Adam grinned. "He's been waiting for Sara to make a move. He's not the same old Dallas either. I'm not sure I like these new improved models. He's in love with you, Sara. He thought because of his . . . problem, you could never be interested in someone like him. You being a doctor and all."

"My friend here thought the same thing

but in reverse," Nellie chirped. "My friend has disavowed medicine as her life's work. She's going into the pottery business. What's your brother got up his sleeve?"

"He said he was going to Montana. He's thinking of going to college. I think you should say something, Sara."

"Listen, Adam, I can handle my own affairs. I don't think Dallas will appreciate your . . . interfering." She was so light-headed she was seeing two of him. Maybe it was the glass of wine she'd gulped.

"We sat in your driveway the other night. For an hour," Nellie chirped again.

"Nellie, for God's sake!"

"Sara, you are forty years old. Mr. Lord Jr. is almost forty years old. You two need to get it together. You can't play mind games with one another, and you need to stop acting like teenagers. You told me you were in love with him. Mr. Lord says his brother is in love with you. What is our problem here?"

"Nellie, don't say any more. She's getting on in years, Adam, don't pay attention to anything she says. He should have stopped me before I got on that plane you chartered for me. Did he do that? No, he did not. I wasn't that hard to find. A thank-you note for the song would have been nice. Did I get that? No, I did not. I rest my case." She downed the second glass of wine in two gulps.

Adam looked at Nellie. Nellie looked at Adam. "I think I'm going to skip lunch," Adam said. "Thanks for inviting me to join you. Make sure you tune in on Tuesday. Dallas will be leaving for Montana right after the broadcast. They're doing it live from Dallas's house. That's in case you have the urge to sit in the driveway again."

"You're enjoying this, aren't you?" Sara snapped.

Adam leaned across the table. "No, Sara, I'm not. It just seems very foolish to me that the two of you wasted so much time and are in danger of losing one another all over again. I've watched Dallas this past year. He has worked so hard, accomplished so much. He's ready to go prime time to bare his soul. He's not doing it for himself or for me. We made our peace. He's doing it for you, Sara. Then he's going to wait just long enough to see what you do. An hour, two at the most, and then he's gone. You think about that for the next few days. Have a nice lunch, ladies, on me." He tossed some bills on the table before he walked away.

"If you cry, Sara, all that gunk on your face is going to run, and you'll look like a ghoul. The man is right. More wine?"

Sara held out her glass. She felt miserable and wondered if she looked the same way. In between bites of the tasty crabmeat salad, she talked about Dallas. "I can't believe he's going public. Why would he do that with his whole life ahead of him? He could rock into the twenty-first century. Look at Mick Jagger. He's going to be prancing around until his legs give out. Performers like Dallas and Mick never retire. Dallas is thinking about going to college. That blew my mind." Her monologue continued until she wound down with, "Prime-time television means the world is going to see and hear everything. Everyone will be passing judgment. Forget damage control."

Nellie placed her knife and fork across her dinner plate. She leaned across the table, her gaze locked on Sara. "I guess he isn't the wishy-washy person you thought he was. He's taking responsibility for what he did, and he's going to let the chips fall where they fall. You were always afraid to do that, Sara. I'd say Dallas has guts. Did you see how proud his brother looked? People are very forgiving of their idols. Time will make everything okay. You're on the same road, Sara. I hope you aren't judging or condemning."

"No. I just don't understand how he can walk away from all that . . . what's the word I'm looking for? Stardom? Adulation? Money? Probably all of the above."

"Didn't you just do the same thing? God in heaven, Sara, you're a doctor. You're giving up all those years of sacrifice and schooling. You're going to ride into the sunset and what was it you said you were going to do? Make pottery? What's the difference? I wonder what the odds would be in Vegas of two people like you and Dallas doing something like this and then getting together again? One in a million, two million? The big question is, what are you going to do now?"

"Do?"

"Yes. What are you going to do? Adam said Dallas wasn't going to hang around after the broadcast. You talk a good game, but are you going to follow through? For some reason I don't think you're going to get up to bat again if you flub this up."

Sara gulped at the rest of her wine. Had she had three glasses or four? "You know, Nellie, a girl likes to hear the words first-hand. Just because Adam said what he said doesn't mean it's so. For all I know, he just wants to be rid of him."

"That's a crock, and you know it. What are you going to do?"

"I'm going home. I think I'll take a taxi. Neither one of us should be driving. Whoa, that wine was strong," Sara said when she stood up. She tugged at the skinny dress and almost lost her balance.

A voice behind her said, "Sara, is that you? Nellie, it's nice to see you again. How's life in the private sector?"

"Dr. Granger. Drinking your lunch again," Nellie snapped as the tipsy doctor ogled Sara.

"Your colleague looks like she had a little too much herself."

"Stuff it," Nellie snapped again.

Sara tried to focus on the handsome doctor who was now standing in front of her. "Brian, I am going to report you to the hospital. You're drunk. Do you know how I know you're drunk? You look like I feel. The only difference is I'm going home. In a taxi because I'm not fit to drive. You're going back to the hospital to take care of patients. I can do what I said. Nellie is my witness. I resigned from the medical profession. I'm going to be making pottery from now on. I'm also going to call the police and tell them you're going to be driving that Mercedes-Benz while under the influence. They might even give me a reward for turning you in. You're a disgrace to the medical profession."

"You do that. You just go ahead and do that," Brian Granger blustered.

"Don't think I won't. Where's my cell phone, Nellie? Damn, I think it's still on the bed with my black bag. Maybe it's in the bag. Maybe I lost it. Oh, who cares. I'll call when I get home."

"People are staring, Sara," Nellie hissed. "Everyone who is anyone eats here. There's a man with a camera pointing at us."

"Where?" Sara demanded. "Does he have a good shot of us?"

"The best," Nellie retorted.

Sara pulled her arm back and let go with

a rock-hard punch that almost dislocated her shoulder. Brian Granger fell to the floor.

"He's out cold, Sara. This will make the six o'clock news and the late edition," Nellie gasped. "I've wanted to do that for the last ten years. Thank you, Sara."

"It was my pleasure. Did they get my good side."

"Front and back. By back I mean that skimpy dress that hiked up all the way to your bra strap."

Sara dusted her hands. "No kidding. Should I make a comment? You know, so they get the story straight?"

"Why the hell not," Nellie muttered. "On second thought, let's quit while we're ahead." She yanked Sara's arm to drag her out of the restaurant.

Outside the well-known eatery, Sara tugged at the skimpy dress. To the parking attendant she said, "Get us a cab, please."

"Certainly, Dr. Killian."

"I'm not a doctor anymore, young man. I quit."

"She retired," Nellie said as she pushed Sara into the backseat of the cab.

"Spell your last name," the reporter who snapped their picture called out.

"Why should I? No. Nellie, tell him how to spell Brian Granger's name."

"Burn rubber, driver," Nellie barked.

"I'm probably going to get sick," Sara said.

"Not in my cab you aren't," the driver said.

"Can I get sick if I promise to give you a Dallas Lord original song?"

"No!"

"Shit!" Sara said.

Nellie buried her face in her plump shoulder to stifle her laughter.

Sara slept through the six o'clock news. Not so the Lord brothers and Tom Silk, who were dining on beef stew and crusty French bread when the evening anchor, his voice full of laughter, announced the day's lighter moment at a well-known eatery.

Adam's jaw dropped. Dallas pushed his glasses tighter on the bridge of his nose. Tom Silk said, "Holy shit!"

"That's Sara," Dallas said.

"So it is," Adam drawled.

"I never would have thought the doctor was a brawler," Tom said.

"That's Sara," Dallas said again.

"Good legs. Snazzy dress, what there is of it," Tom said.

"Which just goes to show you should never judge a book by its cover," Adam said as he bit into a chunk of bread.

"That's a cliché. You need to be more original, Adam. Sara's here in LA. No wonder I couldn't find her. Did I hear that guy right when he said she was going to make pottery?" Dallas asked.

"I heard that," Adam guffawed.

"How do you not want to be a doctor anymore?"

"How do you not want to be a rock star anymore? I guess if you want to know the answer to that question, you'll have to ask Sara?"

"It's not the same thing," Dallas said.

"The hell it isn't. What makes her any different from you? You're alike in so many ways. That's probably what drew you together in the first place. This is really good stew," Adam said as he filled his plate for the third time.

"It's the horseradish," Tom said.

"I'm going down there," Dallas said.

"You have our blessing," Tom and Adam said in unison.

*   *   *

Dallas was back in ninety minutes. "She's not there. The house was dark, and there are new locks on the doors. I tried to pick the lock, but I couldn't. There's a For Sale sign in the yard and a lockbox on the door. I looked through the garage window, and there was no car in the garage."

"Maybe she's with her sister or the nurse," Adam volunteered.

"I checked the nurse's apartment. No one was there either. I have no idea where the sister is. Where the hell could she be?"

"Maybe she's at her pottery shop," Tom said. Dallas shot him a withering look.

"Let it rest, Dallas. She'll see the broadcast and call or come up. Trust me. I know a *little* bit about women."

Dallas spent the next two and a half days pacing and rehearsing what he was going to say during his live interview. Sara spent the time reading about pottery at the local library.

On Tuesday evening, Sara settled herself on the sofa, Nellie at her side. The remote was in her shaky hand. A pot of strong black coffee sat on the coffee table.

"It's amazing that this has been kept secret. Everything in this town is up for grabs."

"It's on! It's on!" Nellie cried. "God in heaven, is that Dallas Lord."

"Oh, Nellie, look at him. He looks . . . he looks . . ."

"Just like his brother."

"He's wearing glasses. Nellie is that a hearing aid?"

"Yes."

"Oh, God, that explains so many things. I must be the stupidest person walking this earth. I'm a doctor, why didn't I pick up on his hearing and his eyesight? I used to think he was *spacey*. He probably didn't hear half the things I said to him. If his eyesight is bad, then he probably wasn't being spacey at all."

"What ever came before doesn't matter. Be quiet and listen to what he's saying. I thought you said he was . . . *ditsy*. That person on the screen is no *ditz*."

"No, he isn't." Tears dripped down Sara's cheeks. "I'm outta here, Nellie."

"Aren't you going to see the end?"

"I don't need to see the end. I'll make my own ending. I gotta go before people start swarming up there. Are you going to wish me luck?"

"Honey, you don't need any luck. It's all yours, just reach out. Go on, go!"

"Do I look okay?"

"You look fine. Go! Take my truck. I parked behind you. No sense in wasting time moving cars. Will you go already! If you floor that baby, you can get her up to eighty," Nellie shouted. "Take care of it, it's your wedding present."

Nellie was wrong. The old truck was doing eighty-five when a siren blasted the night air. Sara gritted her teeth as she pulled over to the side of the road. "I'm a doctor, Officer. I'm going to . . . an emergency. It's life and death. Please, I have to go."

"Follow me, Doctor," the cop said.

Lights flashing, siren wailing, Sara sailed up the canyon road behind the police cruiser. "I'll probably get ten years for this," she muttered.

Inside Dallas's mansion, Adam frowned at the sound of the police siren.

"Jesus, are they here already to arrest me? Listen, Adam, I have to get out of here."

"Look at the monitor, Dallas, and tell me what you see."

The color left Dallas's face. "C'mon, you

guys, clear out. The show's over. Get this film crew out of here, Adam."

"I love a happy ending," Tom said.

"It's the only way to go. Hey, we've got the best seat in the house. She's getting out of the truck. He's almost there. They're looking at one another. Come on, Dallas, move!"

"What are they waiting for?" Tom demanded.

"They're drinking in the sight of each other."

"Huh?"

"It sounded good, didn't it." Adam said.

"Yeah. Yeah, it did."

"Shhh," Adam said putting his finger to his lips.

"Gee, I wish there was sound."

"No you don't. Turn off the cameras, Tom."

Outside, Sara could only stare at the man coming toward her. Her feet felt rooted to the concrete.

"Are we going to get married or not?" Dallas asked.

"Are you asking?" Sara whispered.

"I'm asking."

"Then I'm answering, and I'm saying yes. I'm not a doctor anymore, Dallas. What I mean is, I'll always be a doctor, but I'm not going to practice medicine any longer. You really spooked me when you said you were going to build me a private hospital and all that stuff. I felt like you put a chain around my neck."

"I thought it was what you wanted. I'm not going to be a musician anymore either. I might want to perform someday, but that's way far into the future."

Dallas advanced a step. Sara advanced a step and then she was in his arms and then time stood still but only after the world exploded around them.

"We need to talk, Sara. We need to make decisions. Right now both of us are free. We don't have jobs, and that's by our choice. I'd like it if you'd tell me what it is you want, and then I'll tell you what I want. We have to agree and work at this together because we're going to be spending the rest of our lives together. I don't want either one of us to have regrets later on. Both of us have had enough of that. Let's sit over here on the grass and talk."

"I love you. I never said that out loud to anyone in my life. My heart feels like it's going to jump out of my chest. I fell in love with

you the night you walked into the hospital,"
Sara said.

"I waited all my life for someone like you,
Sara. It seems like I always loved you. I
can't put a time or place to it. If you absolutely need a time and a place, then it was
when I saw you guzzling one bottle of root
beer after the other. You didn't even burp.
That's the amazing thing. I love you, Sara
Killian, and I will always love you. You are
the wind beneath my wings."

"Oh, Dallas, that's the nicest thing anyone
has ever said to me. What are we going to
do? We need to do *something.* We can't just
coast. Promise you won't laugh if I tell you
what I really want to do. If it isn't feasible, I
can fall back and regroup. I want to make
pottery. I want to make something with my
hands. I want to sign my name to it. I want
someone out there to say, somebody
named Sara Killian made this. I don't know
why that's so important to me but it is. It's a
real stretch going from being a doctor to being a potter. It's not just that I want to do it.
I *need* to do it, Dallas. I also need to know
you won't think less of me if I do it."

"Sara, I want what you want. I want us to
be happy. Life is too damn short to be doing

something that makes you unhappy. Can you make pottery in Montana? Will it be too cold? We can get an extra furnace. What's the first thing you're going to make?"

"A bowl for your dog with his name on it. I have to start out small. Now, tell me about you. What will you be doing while I'm making pottery?"

"Will you laugh if I tell you what I want to do?"

"I would never laugh at you, Dallas. Tell me."

"When I get better at this writing business, I'm going to go to college. And . . . are you ready for the *and?*" Sara nodded. "I'm going to write a book. I only touched on it tonight during the interview. I want it to be my words, so that means I have to do it myself. I think I can do it. I want everyone to know what it was like for me, and I want them to know what Adam did for me. I don't want any secrets in my life."

"That's the most wonderful thing I've ever heard. I'll be there every step of the way to offer encouragement."

"I know I can do it. Do you really think you can live in Montana? It gets real cold there. It's Big Sky country. You can sell your pottery at the state fair. You might even win a prize. I saw something in your eyes once that I couldn't understand. I'm seeing it now. We had a very strange relationship. What is it I'm seeing in your eyes?"

"The same thing I see in yours. We were both stupid, Dallas. Oh, it feels so good to make decisions and to know both of us agree with each other."

"How would you like to fly to Vegas and get married in one of those drive-through chapels?"

Sara laughed. "I'd love it."

"I saw you on the news. You looked pretty good. What happened to the guy?"

"They fired him. Are you going to kiss me or not?"

"Damn right I'm going to kiss you. Get in the truck. I'd kill to own this truck. Do you have any idea how great this would be on the ranch?"

"You won't have to kill for it. Nellie's giving it to me for a wedding present. Are you going to kiss me now."

"I am going to kiss you now, Sara Killian. Then I'm going to sit here in this truck and sing you a song. Your song. We recorded 'Sara's Song,' and the boys loved it. All the proceeds are going to a foundation Adam set up for people with learning disabilities. It will be number one on the charts before you can blink."

"Are we going to be happy, Dallas, forever and ever?"

"Damn right we are. Now, pucker up."

A very long time later, Sara said, "I really *liked* that. Do it again, and don't stop till I tell you to stop."

He did, and he didn't.

Dallas tossed the last of his suitcases into the back of Nellie's truck. He felt his throat start to close when he saw his brother walk toward the truck. "Guess this is good-bye for now, Adam."

Adam's voice was gruff and hoarse when he clapped his brother on the back. He cleared his throat. "We agreed, Dallas, I come to Montana for your Fourth of July fireworks and you come to Charleston for Christmas. Easter is up for grabs and so is any other holiday on the calendar. I'm going to miss you."

"Yeah, me too. When I graduate, you're coming, right?"

"Nothing in this world could keep me

away, Dallas. Are you sure you want to get married in one of those drive-through chapels?"

"Yeah. We want the memory. Adam One here is going to be our witness. Anything goes in Vegas. I like it that your family is giving us a send-off. Seven dogs!"

Dallas dropped to his haunches to scratch first one dog and then the other behind the ears. When he came to Dallas Six he raised his eyes to stare at his brother. He knew if he asked for the pup, Adam would hand him over. "Give him a little extra love, Adam. For me. Where's Tom?"

"He went into the house to get your wedding present. Be happy," he whispered in Sara's ear.

"You, too, Adam. Thanks for everything. We'll write and call. Oh, oh, what's this?"

"A small token of our love and admiration. Her name is Rosie. Adam One already loves her. He spent the night curled up next to her. She's a Yorkie. A teacup. She won't weight more than four pounds full-grown."

"I don't know what to say," Sara said.

"You don't have to say anything. Just love her, she'll do the rest."

They were in the truck heading down the

driveway when Dallas backed up till he was within shouting distance of his brother. "Hey, Adam, I forgot to tell you that Adam One had his way with Izzie yesterday. We'll be back in nine weeks since we get the pick of the litter."

"Oh, God!" Tom Silk groaned.

"Didn't anyone ever tell you not to sweat the small stuff, Tom?"

"Be happy!" Adam shouted, his voice, full of laughter, ricocheting down the canyon.

"We will," Dallas shouted in return.